Demonica Underworld Compilation

Also from Larissa Ione

~ DEMONICA/LORDS OF DELIVERANCE SERIES ~
Pleasure Unbound (Book 1)
Desire Unchained (Book 2)
Passion Unleashed (Book 3)
Ecstasy Unveiled (Book 4)
Eternity Embraced ebook (Book 4.5) (NOVELLA)
Sin Undone August (Book 5)
Eternal Rider (Book 6)
Supernatural Anthology (Book 6.5) (NOVELLA)
Immortal Rider (Book 7)
Lethal Rider (Book 8)
Rogue Rider (Book 9)
REAVER (Book 10)
AZAGOTH (Book 10.5)
REVENANT (Book 11)
HADES (Book 11.5)
Base Instincts (Book 11.6)

~ MOONBOUND CLAN VAMPIRES SERIES ~
Bound By Night (book 1)
Chained By Night (book 2)
Blood Red Kiss Anthology (book 2.5)

Demonica Underworld Compilation

3 Stories by

By Larissa Ione

1001 Dark Nights

EVIL EYE
CONCEPTS

Demonica Underworld Compilation
3 Stories by
Larissa Ione
ISBN: 978-1-945920-65-3
1001 Dark Nights

Published by Evil Eye Concepts, Incorporated

Sign up for the 1001 Dark Nights Newsletter
and be entered to win a Tiffany Key necklace.

There's a contest every month!

Go to www.1001DarkNights.com to subscribe.

As a bonus, all subscribers will receive a free
1001 Dark Nights story
The First Night
by Lexi Blake & M.J. Rose

Table of Contents

Also by Larissa Ione	5
Foreword	12
Glossary	11
Azagoth	17
Hades	169
Z	311
Discover 1001 Dark Nights Collection Four	436
Discover 1001 Dark Nights Collection One	438
Discover 1001 Dark Nights Collection Two	439
Discover 1001 Dark Nights Collection Three	440
About Larissa Ione	442
Discover More Larissa Ione	443
Special Thanks	444

One Thousand and One Dark Nights

Once upon a time, in the future…

I was a student fascinated with stories and learning. I studied philosophy, poetry, history, the occult, and the art and science of love and magic. I had a vast library at my father's home and collected thousands of volumes of fantastic tales.

I learned all about ancient races and bygone times. About myths and legends and dreams of all people through the millennium. And the more I read the stronger my imagination grew until I discovered that I was able to travel into the stories... to actually become part of them.

I wish I could say that I listened to my teacher and respected my gift, as I ought to have. If I had, I would not be telling you this tale now.
But I was foolhardy and confused, showing off with bravery.

One afternoon, curious about the myth of the Arabian Nights, I traveled back to ancient Persia to see for myself if it was true that every day Shahryar (Persian: شهرىار, "king") married a new virgin, and then sent yesterday's wife to be beheaded. It was written and I had read, that by the time he met Scheherazade, the vizier's daughter, he'd killed one thousand women.

Something went wrong with my efforts. I arrived in the midst of the story and somehow exchanged places with Scheherazade – a phenomena that had never occurred before and that still to this day, I cannot explain.

Now I am trapped in that ancient past. I have taken on Scheherazade's life and the only way I can protect myself and stay alive is to do what she did to protect herself and stay alive.

Every night the King calls for me and listens as I spin tales. And when the evening ends and dawn breaks, I stop at a point that leaves him breathless and yearning for more. And so the King spares my life for one more day, so that he might hear the rest of my dark tale.

As soon as I finish a story... I begin a new one... like the one that you, dear reader, have before you now.

GLOSSARY

The Aegis—Society of human warriors dedicated to protecting the world from evil. Recent dissension among its ranks reduced its numbers and sent The Aegis in a new direction.

Daemani—Any being, but usually of demonic or angelic origin, who attracts the souls of the dead. Some *daemani* can block the souls from entering their bodies, while others are helpless to resist. Few *daemani* can release the souls without being in the proximity of another *daemani* or without help from a spell, a mystical item, or another being who possesses inherent or learned extraction abilities.

Emim—The wingless offspring of two fallen angels. *Emim* possess a variety of fallen angel powers, although the powers are generally weaker and more limited in scope.

Fallen Angel—Believed to be evil by most humans, fallen angels can be grouped into two categories: True Fallen and Unfallen. Unfallen angels have been cast from Heaven and are earthbound, living a life in which they are neither truly good nor truly evil. In this state, they can, rarely, earn their way back into Heaven. Or they can choose to enter Sheoul, the demon realm, in order to complete their fall and become True Fallens, taking their places as demons at Satan's side.

Harrowgate—Vertical portals, invisible to humans, which demons use to travel between locations on Earth and Sheoul. A very few beings can summon their own personal Harrowgates.

Inner Sanctum—A realm within Sheoul-gra that consists of 5 Rings, each containing the souls of demons categorized by their level of evil as defined by the Ufelskala. The Inner Sanctum is run by the fallen angel Hades and his staff of wardens, all fallen angels. Access to the Inner Sanctum is strictly limited, as the demons contained inside can take advantage of any outside object or living person in order to escape.

Memitim—Earthbound angels assigned to protect important humans called Primori. Memitim remain earthbound until they complete their duties, at which time they Ascend, earning their wings and entry into Heaven. See: Primori

Radiant—The most powerful class of Heavenly angel in existence, save Metatron. Unlike other angels, Radiants can wield unlimited power in all realms and can travel freely through Sheoul, with very few exceptions. The designation is awarded to only one angel at a time. Two can never exist simultaneously, and they cannot be destroyed except by God or Satan. The fallen angel equivalent is called a Shadow Angel. See: Shadow Angel

Shadow Angel—The most powerful class of fallen angel in existence, save Satan and Lucifer. Unlike other fallen angels, Shadow Angels can wield unlimited power in all realms, and they possess the ability to gain entrance into Heaven. The designation is awarded to only one angel at a time, and they can never exist without their equivalent, a Radiant. Shadow Angels cannot be destroyed except by God or Satan. The Heavenly angel equivalent is called a Radiant. See: Radiant.

Sheoul—Demon realm. Located on its own plane deep in the bowels of the Earth, accessible to most only by Harrowgates and hellmouths.

Sheoul-gra—A holding tank for demon souls. A realm that exists independently of Sheoul, it is overseen by Azagoth, also known as the Grim Reaper. Within Sheoul-gra is the Inner Sanctum, where demon souls go to be kept in torturous limbo until they can be reborn.

Sheoulic—Universal demon language spoken by all, although many species also speak their own language.

Ufelskala—A scoring system for demons, based on their degree of evil. All supernatural creatures and evil humans can be categorized into the five Tiers, with the Fifth Tier comprising of the worst of the wicked.

Azagoth

Acknowledgments from the Author

I very much want to extend a special thanks to Liz Berry and M.J. Rose for inviting me to be part of this amazing project. I've been dying to write Azagoth's story for a long time, and I can't thank Liz and M.J. enough.

I also want to send huge, squishy hugs to Liz, M.J., Lara Adrian, Lorelei James, Lexi Blake, Shayla Black, Cherise Sinclair, and Julie Kenner for their amazing support during a very hard time (the bracelet is gorgeous, ladies!) You touched me more than I can say!

On a similar note, hugs and thanks to Jillian Stein and the ladies of the Book Obsessed Chicks club. You are all so special, and I love you!

Chapter One

You can be a king or a street sweeper, but everybody dances with the Grim Reaper.
-- Robert Alton Harris

"There's very little that frightens me more than the Grim Reaper when he's horny."

From his desk chair, Azagoth snarled at the fallen angel standing in his office doorway. "I'm not horny." He frowned. "Okay, maybe a little." Or a lot. For six months he'd refused to bed the females Heaven had sent his way, but those halo-pushers didn't give up, because apparently, there was another angel outside waiting to get some hot Grim Reaper action. "But I'm not backing down. I'm sick of being used to create Heaven's little army of hybrid angels."

That was true enough, but there was far more to it than being tired of being used like a prize stallion. Satan himself had threatened Azagoth with an ultimatum, and while Azagoth and his realm were untouchable, his children were not. And no one fucked with his children. Not even the Prince of Darkness.

"My lord," Zhubaal said cautiously, "your deal with Heaven—"

"Deal?" Azagoth snorted as he reached across his desk for the expensive-ass bottle of Black Tot rum that Limos, one of the Four Horsemen of the Apocalypse, had brought him earlier. "It wasn't a *deal.* I volunteered to fall from grace to run this horror show of a demon graveyard. *They* changed the rules. *After* I gave up my life."

Yep, just a few decades after he'd been expelled from Heaven in order to create Sheoul-gra, a unique realm designed specifically as a holding tank for demon souls, Heaven changed the game. The archangels suddenly decided they needed a special class of angel to watch over anyone living in the human realm who was important to the fate of the world, and they insisted that Azagoth should father those angels.

And he had. For thousands of years he'd taken the angels they sent into his bed and created lots and lots of earthbound, hybrid angel children known as Memitim. But now he was done. Aside from Satan's threat hanging over his head, Azagoth was tired of screwing females who looked down their noses at him or who just laid there like sacrifices until he was done.

Oh, sure, there were the curious ones who at least made an attempt to participate, and there were the lusty few who figured they'd enjoy doing a bad boy. But for the most part, he might as well have been banging blow-up dolls.

Yeah, it was awesome.

Archangels were asshats.

"But sir, you need to do something. You're...testy."

Testy? Zhubaal hadn't seen testy yet. *Testy* had gotten Azagoth's last assistant disintegrated.

"Send the female back, and have her tell her superiors that...no, wait. Send her in." Kicking his booted feet up on the desk, he broke the seal on the alcohol bottle with a vicious twist. "I'll give her my message personally."

"As you wish."

Zhubaal gave a deep bow and left, returning within seconds with a tall, stately brunette in white and ruby robes, and Azagoth groaned. This wasn't an angel who had come for a roll in the hay. Mariella was a Heavenly messenger who swept in the way she always did, as if she owned the place, her head held high, her long strides sure and brisk.

"Azagoth," she said, all snooty and shit, "it's time to stop whatever game you're playing and get back to work."

He raked his gaze over her in a blatant show of sizing her up for sex. She wouldn't lower herself to screw him, but he got a measure of amusement out of screwing with *her*.

"So you're volunteering to spread your legs for me?"

She cringed at his crudeness as he knew she would. Most angels were *so* uptight. "I'm a liaison, not a bedmate. I'm here to convince you to stop being a fool."

"Ah." Keeping his gaze on the angel, he put the bottle to his lips and took a deep, long pull, savoring the sweet burn of the liquid pouring down his throat. He drank until Mariella's pinched, judgmental expression threatened to make her skin crack, and with exaggerated relish, he smacked his lips and wiped his mouth with the back of his hand. "Well, here's the deal. I'm not doing your bidding anymore."

"Yes, you are."

Carefully placing the bottle on a pad of paper, he pushed to his feet and moved around to the front of the desk, noting how she managed to keep that pinchy expression even as her copper eyes assessed him from head to toe. She liked his black slacks and turtleneck...and the way she went taut said she despised the fact that she liked anything about him. Man, he loved messing with angels' heads.

"Or?"

"Or," she said, her tone pitching low with gloom and doom, "we replace you."

He barked out a laugh. "Good. Replace me. I've been stuck in this realm for thousands of years, dealing with nothing but demons, evil humans, and the angels Heaven sends for me to service. Someone else can have this shitty job."

"I don't think you understand," she said silkily. "*Replace* is a nice word for destroy."

Azagoth's pulse kicked up a notch. It was fun when someone threatened him. *Game on.* "And I don't think *you* understand. You can't destroy me. I've put safeguards in place."

Her eyes narrowed into slits. "What kinds of safeguards?"

He gave a dramatic pause, partly to irritate the angel, and partly because he totally got off on dragging out the win. Finally, he steepled his fingers together like a cheesy cartoon villain and said, "The kind that will release all demon souls from Sheoul-gra upon my death."

She gasped in outrage. Because sure, it was okay for her to threaten him, but turnabout was clearly *not* fair play. "And Hades allowed this?"

Hades, who ran Sheoul-gra's Inner Sanctum where demon souls were kept, had little say in what Azagoth did, but they'd long ago hammered out a working relationship that gave the fallen angel independent authority over the Inner Sanctum. Azagoth could overrule him if needed, but in general, he left Hades alone.

"Actually," Azagoth said as he casually propped his hip on the desk, "it was Hades who suggested it."

"That blue-haired bastard."

He'd give her that one. Hades was a world-class dick. Azagoth liked that in a fallen angel. "Now," he said, "you get to listen to my demands."

"Which are?" she said through gritted teeth.

"I want a female."

She shot him an exasperated look. "What do you think we've been sending you? You keep turning them down."

"I don't want a female to fuck," he said, still being as raunchy as possible. It drove angels nuts, and sure enough, her lips puckered as if she'd sucked a lemon. "I want one to keep."

Outrage mottled her perfect, ivory skin. "You want an angel to *keep*? As what? A pet?"

"As a mate."

"Oh, that's precious." She laughed, and the blood that usually ran cold in his veins started to steam. "You want a mate? *You?* Why?"

Because I'm lonely. That was only part of it, but it was a big part. He could have simply told Heaven to stop sending him females because Satan had threatened to start killing Memitim if even one more was born, but he didn't want to spend the rest of eternity alone. He'd seen one of his daughters, Idess, willingly sacrifice so much for the male she loved, and she'd risked her life on more than one occasion to make sure other couples were happy. The depths to which people felt love had stunned him, and deep inside, it had sparked a desire to have that for himself.

That was assuming he *could* love. He hadn't felt anything but anger and amusement in thousands of years, and even those emotions rarely reached a level beyond what he'd consider mild.

"My reasons are my own," he said. "Send me a female to keep."

"I'm sure this female you want will be so happy to be constantly pregnant," she drawled.

"Oh, did I give you the impression that I'd keep making Memitim angels for you?" He pushed off the desk and moved toward her, enjoying the way her eyes sparked with anger and superiority even as she inched backward. "Well, newsflash, you Heavenly puke; no children that come of the union with my mate will ever be handed over to you."

She flared her cinnamon wings in annoyance, but he kept his own wings tucked away. When he took his out, it usually meant he was on the verge of killing.

He wasn't there yet, but he had no doubt this angel could push him to it.

Not that it took much.

"I'll inform my bosses, but don't expect an answer you'll like."

Even now, after he'd made clear that he held all the cards—or the souls, as it were—she continued to think she had the better hand. Amusing. *Mildly* amusing, of course.

"You're still not getting it, are you? I'll get what I want. There's no other choice." He halted in front of her, so close she was forced to look up at him. "And tell them that the next angel they send better be prepared to stay, because I'm keeping her."

"How nice," she said snottily. "Are you going to keep her in chains? Rape her if she refuses to bed you?"

Suddenly, his hand was clamped around her throat, almost of its own volition. Angels did that to him, made his body parts act independently of his brain. He felt her reach for her angelic ability to strike at him, but this was his realm, and here *he* controlled the use of power.

"Send someone willing." He bared his fangs, giving the angel an up-close-and-personal look at one of the things that made them so very different despite their angelic origins. "I'm warning you. Because the next angel who steps through that doorway won't be leaving. Ever."

Chapter Two

Lilliana scurried through the pristine white halls of the massive Archangel Complex, her heart beating like a hummingbird's. She'd only been here once, several hundred years ago, and it had merely been to deliver a message from her superiors in the Time Travel Operations Department.

This time, she was here because she'd been summoned, and that could only be bad news. Her direct supervisor, an angel humans would describe as nerdy and shy, had warned her that after her latest screw-up, she might earn more than just a suspension from TTO.

She broke out in a sweat at the thought. Her work was her life. The only connection she had with her dead mother. If the archangels took that away from her...she shuddered. Sure, she'd committed a grievous offense, but there had been extenuating circumstances. She'd been kidnapped, held captive, and forced to do things she hadn't wanted to do. Her nerdy supervisor understood...but he didn't think the head honchos would. Besides, rules were rules, and Heaven's tolerance for rule breakers was notoriously nonexistent.

Stomach churning, she entered the garishly maroon and gold offices of Raphael. *The* Raphael. She might vomit on his robes.

A petite, flaxen-haired female looked up from her crystal

tablet, a device that was the human equivalent of an electronic tablet device...if human tablets had advanced by about ten billion years. She gave Lilliana a bored once-over, pausing to wrinkle her nose at Lilliana's unfashionably loose brown hair. Lilliana could change it with a mere thought, maybe piling it on top of her head like a giant ostrich egg the way the other female wore it, but she'd never cared about current fashion. She did, however, care about looking stupid.

"To your left." Egghead went back to tapping on her tablet.

Lilliana turned down the hall, which ended inside a room with walls that seemed to be made of white smoke. A marble fountain, an extinct palm tree, bronze statues...the room was filled with the most eclectic mix of objects from different time periods.

An angel appeared before her from out of nowhere, and although she'd never seen Raphael before, she knew him instantly. He stood a full foot above her five foot eleven inches, and his golden hair fell in a shiny curtain around broad shoulders draped by a lush, purple velvet mantle. Jewel-encrusted rings circled every finger, and a gold sun-shaped pendant hung halfway down his chest, standing out starkly against his snowy white suit.

If she had to describe the style of his outfit, she'd go with royal-retro-pimp.

"You're late." His deep, dark voice rumbled through her, jangling her already unsteady nerves. "Late to a meeting with an archangel."

She was most certainly *not* late, but it didn't seem like a good idea to argue. "Ah...I got lost—"

He cut her off with a savage sweep of his bejeweled hand. "Your excuses don't interest me. I have a proposition for you."

Wow. What everyone said about archangels was true.

They were giant douchebags. With terrible fashion sense and taste in decor.

"What kind of proposition?"

"I understand that you're curious about the underworld."

Her pulse picked up a notch. Most angels nursed a deep hatred for anything related to demons and their realm, Sheoul, and one never knew how much trouble you could get into by being too inquisitive. Plus, too much curiosity threw up a red flag for those who watched for signs of potential defection to Satan's camp.

"I wouldn't say I'm overly curious," she said, choosing her words carefully, "but I do find it interesting that many ancient human structures are replicated in Sheoul and vice versa, and I'd love to study the links between them."

"What if I said I could give you that opportunity?"

She cocked an eyebrow. "I'd say...what's the catch?"

"The catch is a big one." He gave an ominous pause she suspected was calculated to make her lungs seize. It worked. "You'll have to take a mate."

What little air she had in her lungs whooshed out in a rush. "A mate?" she choked out. "Why?"

"Because this particular male wants a mate, and we need him, so he gets what he wants."

In other words, this particular male, clearly a standup guy, was using blackmail to get what he wanted. She licked her dry lips, buying herself time to speak without sounding as if she'd run a marathon. "And what about what I want?"

The archangel regarded her with disdain, as if what she wanted was of no consequence. "How about we go over all of the terms of this deal before you decide what you want."

"Of course," she said tightly. She had a feeling the terms were going to be pretty one-sided, and that side wouldn't be hers. "Who is he?"

"Azagoth, collector of souls."

Her heart stopped. Just quit beating. "The Forgotten One? The Grim Reaper?" Holy shit. He had to be kidding. "Is this some kind of joke?"

"I have no sense of humor."

She'd heard that about Raphael. About most of the archangels, actually. "But you want me to *mate* Azagoth?"

Raphael inclined his head in an impatient, curt nod, as if this wasn't something to get all worked up about. How could he be so calm?

Because it's not his *head on the chopping block, that's how.*

The ex-angel, sometimes known by those in Heaven as The Forgotten One, was occasionally spoken about with respect, but most often, contempt. He'd been a hero in Heaven, the person who first identified Satan as a rotten apple who was planning a coup against his angelic brethren. Because of Azagoth, Satan had been stripped of his wings and cast out of Heaven to create his own realm known as Sheoul, where he'd set up shop breeding evil minions.

Too late Heaven realized they should have put Satan down when they had the chance, because centuries later, his demonic creations began to die, and with nowhere to go, their disembodied souls wreaked havoc on the Earth. Azagoth volunteered to create Sheoul-gra, a holding tank for the souls, but *why* he volunteered was the topic of hot debates and wild conspiracy theories.

The only thing anyone agreed on was that he'd been corrupted by evil and was one of the most dangerous and powerful beings outside of Heaven. Fortunately, he was contained inside his own realm...but his reach extended far beyond it, and that had always been a concern for The Powers That Be in Heaven.

Raphael let her stew in her thoughts for a moment before adding, "And full disclosure; you can never leave his realm once you get there."

Her jaw dropped. Closed. Dropped again. Unable to leave Sheoul-gra? She'd be trapped. Imprisoned, just like she'd been when she was kidnapped by a crazy angel bent on getting revenge on an archangel, a situation that had gotten her into this mess in the first place.

Finally, she managed a squeaky, "Never?"

"Not...in the traditional sense." Raphael produced a cup of nectar from out of thin air and held it out to her, but she refused. She doubted her stomach could hold anything down right now. Plus, refusing something offered by an archangel gave her a sinful feeling of satisfaction. "But according to my intel, he possesses a *chronoglass*."

Surprise flew through her. "I thought we had the only two in existence."

"Apparently not."

"So he can time travel?"

Raphael shook his head. "He wasn't born with the ability. We believe he uses it to view current events in the human and demon realms."

What a waste. Angels with the ability to time travel could do so only under limited circumstances and with the assistance of a handful of very rare objects. *Chronoglasses* were the most versatile and powerful of all the time travel objects, and Azagoth's would be invaluable to Heaven.

"Wait...you said he can view the events of the demon realm too? How?"

"His *chronoglass*, unlike ours, is double-sided. One side allows a view of the human realm, and the other shows the demon realm." Raphael sipped the nectar she'd refused. "With his *chronoglass*, you can escape his realm once per day for an hour. But you will be restricted to the past, and as always, contact with anyone you know is not permitted, and so is any manipulation of events that could change history." He angled his body closer, putting on the pressure without saying a word. "So. What say you?"

I say you're insane. "As, ah...generous...as this offer is, I'm going to have to refuse. I have a job here."

He casually took a drink of the nectar, and she got the feeling that he was stringing a noose. "Do you."

She swallowed. Which wasn't easy, given the invisible rope tightening inexorably around her neck. "Excuse me?"

"Did you think we could let your recent transgressions slide?" He waved his hand, and one of the smoky walls became solid ivory.

Against the white backdrop, in perfect, high-def 3-D, a movie started up. A movie that showed her, three months ago, as she traveled through time to various locations to gather objects.

An angel named Reaver had asked for some special gifts for his five-thousand-year-old children, items from their childhoods. It was against the rules to bring objects back from the past, but he'd pulled her butt out of trouble once, and she'd owed him.

But holy crap, had she paid for what she'd done. Fifty years of time travel with supervision only, plus a hundred years of listening in on human prayers, sorting them, and presenting the most urgent ones to the Prayer Fulfillment Department.

So. Freaking. Boring. Humans could pray for really selfish, stupid stuff.

The movie jumped ahead, and she watched herself handing the items to Reaver. "I've already been punished for that."

"And clearly, you didn't learn your lesson," he snapped, suddenly and inexplicably irritated. "Because not a month later, you broke one of the most important time travel laws and caused an imbalance in Heaven that we're still trying to correct."

"I had no choice! If you'd just listen—"

"Silence!" He hadn't raised his voice, but the echo of his command circled the room a dozen times before fading away. "You say you had no choice, so now I'm giving you one. You can go through the dissection trials to have your ability removed. You will then be assigned to menial labor for the rest of your existence, or you can mate Azagoth and be able to time travel once a day. Which is it?"

She shook with a combination of rage that the circumstances of her crime were being disregarded, and terror that both punishments were not only horrible, but permanent. Losing her freedom was her greatest nightmare, and now she was facing it in a lose/lose situation.

"I need time to think about it." Even her voice trembled.

"I'm not giving you time," he said. "But I'm in a generous mood, so I'll tell you what. Go now to Sheoul-gra, and you'll have thirty Earth days to change your mind. At the end of the thirty days, the realm's exit will be sealed to you, and you will never again be allowed to leave except for an hour a day when you use the *chronoglass*."

Her belly twisted, and again, she was glad she'd refused the nectar. "Will I lose my wings?"

"No. You'll be like Azagoth...a fallen angel, but...not. He is like his realm; unique."

This could not be happening. She searched Raphael's handsome face for any kind of sign that despite his claim of having no sense of humor this was just a big joke, but the archangel's expression was all business.

"What about the Memitim? Will you still be sending angels to him to...breed with?"

She could hardly get the last part out. Azagoth was the father of all Memitim, and she seriously doubted Heaven would just let him stop producing little baby Reapers. Or maybe he wouldn't want to stop. Maybe he was like her father, donating baby batter for the greater good and not giving a shit about his offspring.

"He won't be creating any more Memitim. We're reversing their sterility and changing Memitim from a class of angel to an ability any angel can be born with."

How easy it all sounded. She wondered how the Memitim felt about the fact that their inability to reproduce was by design and could have been reversed at any time.

She closed her eyes and considered her options, crappy as they were.

The removal of an angel's time travel ability was brutal. Agonizing. And in some instances, fatal. Even if one survived, the process and the loss were traumatic, and the angel was never the same. Lilliana had encountered two angels who had undergone the process, and their empty eyes haunted her to this day.

As if having her ability taken away wasn't bad enough, she'd then be stuck doing menial tasks for the rest of her life...but on the bright side, maybe she'd be so lobotomized from the time-travelectomy that she wouldn't care.

And didn't that sound like a wonderful life?

Her other choice was to become the mate of a depraved angel, a male who was the keeper of demon souls. A male who had volunteered to be booted from Heaven...or, if the rumors were true, he'd not so much "volunteered" as *been* volunteered.

Sort of like what was happening to her right now.

Except that after she mated the Grim Freaking Reaper, she'd be stuck in his realm, which, by all accounts, was a shadowy, dreary place that resembled Athens—if Athens was drenched in darkness, overrun by creepy demon things, and had been decorated via an unholy alliance between Guillermo del Toro and Anne Rice.

Really, though, there was a clear winner here. Between the choices of suck and suckier, suck won out.

Opening her eyes, she gave in to the inevitable. "I'll go to Sheoul-gra," she muttered. At least she had thirty days to change her mind once she got there.

"I'm happy to hear that. You leave immediately." Clapping his hand on her shoulder, he leaned in, his voice dropping to a conspiratorial murmur. "Now, if one were to somehow get out of Azagoth's realm with his *chronoglass* within that thirty days, one's past transgressions might be forgiven. Especially if one were also to destroy the spying stone we believe he's using to spy on us."

She nearly tripped over her own feet. He was giving her a way out of this crappy deal?

Raphael stepped back and finished his nectar. "Oh," he said, as he tossed the empty cup to the floor and strode toward the exit, "and good luck. Azagoth is an asshole."

Chapter Three

Lilliana's skin crawled as she took in the massive palace before her. True to her intel and research, the building, and all those surrounding it, were fashioned after ancient Greek structures. Great pillars rose up from the ground to support walls that went on forever. But unlike the bone-white framework that typified Greek construction, everything here was blackened, as if polluted by centuries of smoke buildup. She wondered what would happen if she scraped her fingernail down a wall.

Everything here felt...wrong. Even the air buzzed with a low-level sinister energy, as if she were standing next to a leaking, demonic nuclear power plant. Instinctively, she reached for her angelic power, but it was as if she struck a barrier. She could feel her power inside her, but it was trapped somehow, and no matter how hard she tried, she couldn't reach it.

Raphael had warned her that her powers would be all but useless here, but she'd hoped that somehow he was wrong.

Not so much.

Shuddering, she inhaled the air that stank of decay and filth, and climbed the seemingly endless steps to a landing that was as sprawling as a football field. The doors before her, large enough to allow a pair of elephants inside, opened up as if by magic.

No one was standing at the threshold to greet her. She hadn't been sure what to expect, but silence and a warehouse-sized room filled with gruesome artwork and fountains that ran with blood wasn't it.

Lilliana walked inside, her pristine white gown dragging on the polished obsidian floor. She hated the stupid dress, but it was what Raphael had insisted she wear, as if she were some sort of child bride being offered up to a sleazeball who'd paid for her.

Which probably wasn't far from the truth.

At the far side of the room, a lone figure appeared through another set of double doors. Male. Tall. Blond. Handsome. Evil.

Fallen angel.

He gestured for her to approach, and although she'd been conditioned since birth to despise fallen angels, she obeyed. What choice did she have, after all?

"I am Zhubaal," he said, when she was a few yards away.

Up close, he was obscenely good-looking in his black leather pants and wife-beater that revealed a massive, muscular upper body, but the malevolence in his gaze made her shiver. Relief that he wasn't Azagoth was tempered with fear that her soon-to-be mate would be hideous...or that his eyes would be filled with something much worse than cruelty.

"I'm Lilliana," she replied as steadily as she could, but she cursed the slight tremor in her voice.

"I know." Zhubaal smiled, and if she'd thought his gaze was fiendish, his smile was a hundred times worse. This was not a male she'd want to piss off. "Tell me, do you feel like a sacrificial lamb?"

Fallen angels were assholes. "I was given more of a choice than any lamb."

He snorted and started down a long, twisty hallway. "Keep telling yourself that."

She amended her last thought. Fallen angels were *major* assholes.

They arrived at an arched doorway that seemed to be carved out of a solid piece of bone. A slab of thick wood studded with iron squeaked open at Zhubaal's shove.

Warm orange light spilled from the opening, illuminating a room that was chilly despite flames that stretched a full six feet in height inside the fireplace on the far wall. In front of the fire, there was a claw-footed oak desk scattered with papers, pens, and tiny jade animals.

And standing next to the monstrosity was an impossibly beautiful dark-haired male with eyes the color of vibrant emeralds. His expression could have been carved from a solid block of ice, and the blade-sharp lines of his jaw and cheekbones only emphasized the hardness of his appearance. The fang tips glinting between his full lips were the icing on the *oh-shit-what-did-I-get-into* cake.

"Hello." His deep voice turned her marrow to pudding even as a wave of heat licked her skin. "I'm Azagoth."

Dear...God. He was both magnificent and frightening. "I'm Lilliana," she said, somehow keeping her tone even, her words sure.

He strode toward her, his black slacks defining long legs, his European-style leather shoes tapping against the ebony floor, his rich gray dress shirt rolled at the sleeves to reveal powerfully muscled forearms. Lilliana resided in Heaven, where all male angels were perfect specimens of masculinity, but something about Azagoth made every last one of them seem average. Hell, even Raphael, with his jewels and furs, couldn't touch Azagoth's simple elegance and raw sexuality.

Or his deadliness.

He halted a couple of feet away. "Why are you here?"

She blinked, not understanding the question. Surely he understood the deal that had been struck between him and the archangels.

"Ah...I'm here for you."

He looked at her as if she were completely daft. "I know. But why *you*?"

"I don't know why," she answered honestly. This was a punishment, yes, but the archangels could have chosen anyone to toss up as a sacrifice, so why her specifically? She'd wondered, but in the end it didn't matter, she supposed.

Azagoth's remarkable eyes narrowed. "Then why did you agree to mate me?"

She wasn't sure she was ready to tell him. She could think of little more humiliating or insulting than trying to explain that being here was the least distasteful of two horrific options. "First, why don't you tell me why you wanted this?"

If she'd thought his gaze was cold before, now it glazed over with ice. "Obviously, I desire a mate."

"But why?"

He smiled, but it was as frostbitten as his eyes. "How old are you?" he asked, ignoring her question.

"I'm coming up on my four hundred and thirty-sixth birthday."

He made a sound of disgust. "So pathetically young." His gaze took a long, appraising tour of her body, and she bristled. "And you're wearing white. Your idea? Or did the archangels send you to me looking like a virgin ready for the volcano?"

He'd hit *that* nail on the head. "It wasn't my idea."

"But *are* you a virgin?" he asked, and wow, he had balls, didn't he. No, she wasn't a virgin—at least, not in one sense of the word, but the hell if she was going to give him the satisfaction of an answer. When she remained silent, he cursed. "You are, aren't you?"

"You say it like you might ask if I'm a cockroach. The sneer was a nice touch."

"A *virgin* cockroach." His mouth twitched in amusement. What a strange sense of humor. He returned to his desk and pulled a parcel out of a drawer. Lush gold silk surrounded the package, which was tied with a red satin bow. He handed it to her. "You will wear this."

She had no idea what was inside the package, but she'd had it with his attitude. "I have my own clothes, but thank you."

"Your shipment from Heaven is being delayed," he said, and she had a sneaky suspicion he had something to do with that. "So no, you don't have clothes. You will wear what I give you."

Okay, then. The question now wasn't whether or not she needed the full thirty days to decide if she was staying. The question was how long it would be before she could get out of here. At this rate, she'd be out the door in an hour. Screw the *chronoglass*. Dissection was looking better and better.

"Tell you what," she snapped. "I'll wear whatever is in this package if you start using the words 'please' and 'thank you.' And if you stop being a dick."

One dark eyebrow shot up. "The innocent little angel has teeth," he mused. "I like it."

She clenched said teeth. "Good. Now maybe you can show me to my room?"

"*Our* room," he said with way too much relish. "From this day on, we share a bed. We share *everything*."

* * * *

Azagoth wasn't sure what to think of the striking angel who had shown up on his doorstep, but he *was* sure she wasn't here of her own volition. He'd bet his pearly-white fangs that she'd been forced into mating him, and he'd bet the deal had been couched inside a "choice."

You can do what we "suggest," or your life will be a living hell.

The words, spoken to him by the archangel Gabriel, rang in his ears as if it were yesterday. Yeah, what the archangels called a "choice" was more like a prod with a lightning bolt in the direction they wanted you to go.

As he waited for Lilliana's reaction to his announcement, he gave her a good once-over. Okay, maybe a twice-over, because damn, she was *fine.*

Unlike most of the angels who came to him, Lilliana was in no way petite or delicate. She looked like the type of female who could hold her own against him in physical combat, and then melt into a puddle of ecstasy when the battle was over and he was between her legs. He admired that in a female.

Of course, there was a lot to admire about her.

Long, sable lashes framed eyes the color of the purest amber, and sturdy, angular features defined her ageless face. This angel was tall, solidly built, with only the slightest of curves in all the right places and muscles that gave her an Amazonian warrior aura. Her chestnut hair flowed over slender but powerful shoulders, and he wondered if it was as silky as it looked.

"The same bed, huh?"

Her question was rhetorical, so he crossed his arms over his chest and waited for a genuine reaction from her. In reality, he'd had another room prepared for her, but he wanted to see how she handled him. He wasn't easy to deal with, and any female who fell apart within minutes of meeting him wasn't going to last.

Despite what he'd said to Mariella yesterday, he wouldn't force anyone to stay. He was a cold, heartless bastard, but even he didn't want to spend eternity with someone who couldn't hold their own against him. He could deal with hatred, but he couldn't deal with fear.

A crying, cowering female in his bed just didn't do it for him. On the other hand, angry sex could be fucking hot as shit.

So which way would Lilliana go? Fight or flight? Hate or fear? The stubborn glint in her eyes told him that meek acceptance wouldn't be an option. Good. He didn't want a doormat for a mate, either.

She lifted her chin and looked down her nose at him in that infuriating way most angels did. As if he was so beneath them, what with his own realm, servants, and more influence than most archangels could claim.

"I was hoping we'd have time to get to know each other," she said crisply, "but I'll deal. Touch me without my consent, however, and you'll lose an arm."

So, fight over flight. And probably a touch of hate. He liked her spirit. She needed to work on her threats, however.

"Never threaten someone with losing a limb when you can go gorier. Try this next time: *Touch me without my consent and I'll gut you with my teeth and then strangle you with your own intestines.*" He imagined her saying that, and his pants grew uncomfortably tight. "See how much better that sounds?"

She glared. "If you'll give me paper and a pen, I'll take notes."

He was starting to like this chick.

"I'm assuming the angels have sealed the portal behind you so you can't leave unless I expel you?" At her clipped nod, he waved for her to follow him. "Come on. I'll show you to our room." He led her to the grand double doors at the rear of his office, and with a mere thought, they whispered open.

Lilliana stood in the doorway, gaping at his bedroom-slash-playroom. "Oh. My. Gaudy," she breathed. "Please tell me I can redecorate."

Zhubaal had warned him that females didn't appreciate man-cave decor. Or torture-room decor. Turned out he was right. "Sure. But nothing nautical. Or American Southwest."

She didn't miss a beat. "I was thinking more along the lines of screw-you minimalist. First thing that goes is the spanking bench."

Damn, he was liking her more and more. Too bad he'd have to break her little haloed heart.

"No furniture goes until you've tried it first. But the rest...meh." He gestured to the walls covered in rich tapestries, priceless artwork by famous human and demon painters, and giant mirrors framed in pure gold. "The color scheme was popular a thousand years ago. It's time for an update, I suppose."

She sniffed haughtily, which was *such* an angel thing to do, and stalked inside. And wow, nice ass. Perfectly packaged in the satin dress, it was a little less full than he liked, but there was still plenty of padding in that heart-shaped bottom. He could picture her bent over the spanking bench as he gripped her hips and thrust against her, her skin flushed with ecstasy and pink from sensual lashes.

"The bed can stay," she announced.

Of course it could. It was big enough to sleep six, which meant she could put a lot of space between them. She could try, anyway.

"The bathroom is through the doorway to your right," he said. "The hallway straight ahead leads to a kitchen, dining room, and TV room. I get pretty much every TV station in the world."

She frowned. "How?"

"Same way Heaven gets it. Demon technicians can warp and tune any manmade signal into something usable down here." He gestured to a huge oak cabinet. "The wardrobe on the left is yours. There are clothes already inside. I'll leave you to it."

She turned to him, that ridiculous gown sweeping across the floor. "Where are you going?"

"I have a job to do. Places to go, people to kill, and those demon souls don't admit themselves into Sheoul-gra, you know." He started toward the door. "Join me after you change, and I'll show you around your new home."

"Wait." She started after him, but as he swung back around to her, she checked up like she'd hit a wall, as if realizing that being alone would be better than being with him. "What about my powers?"

"What about them?"

"I have none." She hugged herself, no doubt feeling naked and exposed without them. "How am I supposed to defend myself in this place?"

"There's nothing here that can harm you. Except me." He glanced at his watch. He probably had time to usher in a few souls, show Lillian around, and check in with his *griminions* before his next appointment arrived. Looking up again, he caught her gaze. "But I can't think of any reason I should harm you...can you?"

She gave a forced smile. "Of course not."

"Good. Let's keep it that way." He headed toward the door again, pausing at the threshold to say softly, "I'm not a cruel person, Lilliana. But I'm not a forgiving one, either. Betray me and you'll see exactly how unforgiving I can be. There are no second chances."

He left her alone, closing the door behind him.

Chapter Four

Lilliana waited until Azagoth shut the door to stick out her tongue at him.

"Join me after you change," she mimicked. "I'll show you around your new home. Betray me and you'll see exactly how unforgiving I can be."

Yeah, real mature. But the guy was infuriating. And obnoxious. And handsome. She couldn't forget handsome. The image of him standing next to his desk lingered in her mind, the way he'd been so casual, and yet, there was a coiled intensity about him, as if he could snap her neck with one hand while chugging rum from the bottle on his desk with the other.

Why in the hell did she find that sexy? She was an angel, for Heaven's sake. She was supposed to be sweet and pure, and...that was a load of crap.

Angels were, in truth, ruthless warriors who fought for the side of good, often with stunning brutality. They fought dirty and didn't always follow the rules. Then there were the politics—many angels had their own agendas, and those agendas often didn't mesh with what was best for either the Earthly realm or the Heavenly one.

So, okay, she wasn't sweet and pure, but she probably shouldn't think Azagoth's lethal aura was sexy.

Tossing the package he'd given her onto the black satin bedspread, she looked around the room, and this time, she didn't bother to hide her shock. When she and Azagoth had first entered, she'd schooled her expression into calm nonchalance, but inside she had been hyperventilating.

She'd seen a lot in her centuries of life—demons and humans were extremely creative when it came to sex—but she'd never thought she'd be expected to participate in anything kinky. Heck, her ex, Hutriel, a high-ranking member of the angelic Eradicator Force who hunted the illegal offspring of angels and fallen angels, had despised the kind of messy sex humans and demons enjoyed so much. Angel intimacy, especially among the hardcore conservative old guard, was polite and clean, more of a merging of souls than bodies. Hutriel had *definitely* been old guard. He would have hated Azagoth's lair.

She wrinkled her nose at the huge wood and padded leather St. Andrew's Cross in the corner. It was much nicer than the one some sex toy salesman tried to get her to "try" when she'd walked past his store while hunting a demon once. And Azagoth's leather-wrapped restraints were a far cry from the sales guy's metal handcuffs.

Oh, but not to fear, Azagoth also had handcuffs hanging from a wooden rack next to the spanking bench. All sorts of restraints, whips, paddles, gags, and items she couldn't identify kept those cuffs company, and she shivered.

And yet...curiosity, and maybe a *screw-you* aimed in Hutriel's direction, nudged her over to the rack, and she found herself running her fingers over the surprisingly supple leather strands on the floggers and testing the fabric of the blindfolds. What would it feel like to be blindfolded and bound, completely at the mercy of someone like Azagoth?

Again she shivered, but this time, it was accompanied by desire curling in her gut and spiraling outward until even her skin flushed with pleasant tingles. Maybe she should be appalled by Azagoth's collection and her reaction to it, but she'd always been adventurous and eager to try new things. With the right male, she'd give this stuff a go.

But Azagoth wasn't the right male. So far, he'd proved to be an arrogant prick, and in any case, as soon as she found his *chronoglass*, she was out of here.

She moved over to the huge oak wardrobe and held her breath as she opened it. To her relief, there was nothing too weird hanging on the rack or sitting neatly on the shelves. But black wasn't her color, and leather wasn't her material. She was definitely a slacks and blouse kind of gal, so the midnight satin corset and metal-studded leather miniskirt got shoved to the back of the stack.

She finally chose a pair of plain black leggings, a maroon long-sleeved, fitted crop top with a turtleneck collar, and knee-high boots with four sets of buckles down the shaft. She checked herself out in the mirror, was surprised that the outfit wasn't completely horrible and actually flattered her athletic figure.

She'd always compensated for her lack of feminine features and curves by wearing her hair loose and long, and her clothes were always on the conservative, lacier side. But somehow, these form-fitting garments enhanced her femininity even more than the flowing, delicate gown she'd been forced to wear. Huh.

Sinking down on the massive bed, she opened the package Azagoth had given her. Inside was a simple but elegant Tiffany key pendant on a delicate silver chain. It was beautiful, but why would he want her to wear it?

She wasn't going to. Already she realized she had very little power down here, and one thing Azagoth wasn't going to take away was her ability to choose. Very carefully, she put away the chain and left the box on the mattress.

The mattress she was going to have to share with Azagoth.

Unbidden, an image of him naked and lying next to her as that deep voice whispered raw, naughty things, made her skin flush and her breasts tingle. Was that what the angels sent here for him to service felt like when they were standing in this room?

The thought was enough to knock her halo back on straight. There would be no sex, because she was leaving.

Taking a deep, bracing breath, she opened the door to Azagoth's office. The wall directly across from her had opened up, revealing a green-glowing cross-sectioned tunnel. A parade of demons shuffled through from left to right, each one escorted by a three-foot tall *griminion* shrouded completely in black. As she entered the room, the parade stopped, and Azagoth swung around. His expression remained neutral, but she swore his eyes darkened as he raked her with his gaze.

"Better," he rumbled.

"Flattery isn't your strong suit, is it?"

"And taking direction isn't yours."

So he'd noticed the missing necklace. Tough shit. She ignored him and glanced over at the tunnel. "What's going on?"

"These are souls of dead demons and evil humans. My *griminions* are escorting them into the lower Sheoul-gra levels known as the Inner Sanctum."

"Where Hades lives?"

He inclined his head. "Hades keeps them contained and suitably miserable until they're reincarnated."

She eyed the demon souls, which appeared to be as solid as they had been when they were alive. "I'm assuming demon souls are like those of humans? Non-corporeal while on Earth and in Sheoul, but solid in Sheoul-gra and Heaven?"

"It's exactly the same. Human and demon souls appear as ghosts on the Earthly plane, but are fully realized in Heaven and Sheoul-gra."

If only humans understood that their bodies on Earth were shadowy versions of what they would become after they died and returned to the Heavenly plane where they'd been created. They'd be much happier, not worrying so much about defiling themselves or even injuring their bodies. Their short human lives were but a thin thread in the fabric of their true existences, a drop in the ocean of their lifespans.

Azagoth made a sweeping motion with his hand, and the wall slid closed.

"So you just sit around all day and watch souls walk through a tunnel?"

A faint smile twitched on his lips. "That's just one of my duties. Come on. I'll show you around."

He took her down several winding hallways, pointing out various rooms that led to quarters for his *griminions*.

"What, exactly, are *griminions*?" She watched one of the troll-like creatures scurry through a doorway and disappear into the darkness.

"During the negotiations between Heaven and Sheoul over the creation of Sheoul-gra, it was agreed that I would be allowed to create a species of demon that could assist with the retrieval of souls."

"And you made creepy little skittery things?"

"Not...exactly. My design used imps and gentle Huldrefox demons as a base, combined with a species of demon that can see ghosts. Satan took out the Huldrefox and threw in extra imp. Now I have a bunch of Oompa Loompas with the intelligence of doorknobs." He shrugged as if trying to dismiss the almost undetectable fond note in his voice. "They're loyal little guys, though."

He kept walking, but she slowed him down several times to ogle the priceless weapons and art on his walls. He had tapestries and paintings believed lost to the ages, and weapons wielded by legends and kings. She wasn't sure how long it took them to get to the huge antechamber she'd walked through when she'd first entered the building, but as he explained some of the demon artwork, she only half-listened as she kept her eyes peeled for his *chronoglass.*

Disappointed that it was nowhere in the room, she followed him outside, with its blackened landscape and gray sky.

He looked out at the buildings surrounding his giant manor. "You can explore those at your leisure. Most of them are empty shells."

She eyed a pulsing vine hanging off one of the rooftops and made a note to avoid the native flora. She'd battled a lot of demons in her life, but she'd never spent enough time in Sheoul to get to know how creepy—or lethal—the vegetation was.

"Why are the buildings here, if they're unused?" she asked him.

A shadow darkened the emerald light in his eyes before disappearing a heartbeat later. "As humans built up their cities, I added buildings to match."

Okay, so that wasn't really an explanation, but she got the sense that if she asked for more, he wouldn't give it to her. "Why is everything here so...filthy?"

He dragged a fingernail down the surface of a pillar, leaving behind a thin line of white stone. "Sheoul-gra's soul is tied to mine. As I succumb to the malevolence that seeps out of Hell, so do the buildings."

So this was what thousands of years of demon-grade sewer leakage would do to a realm. No wonder there were angels employed full time to patch cracks between the human and demon realms. She could only wonder about the extent to which miniscule doses affected humans. But Azagoth had been exposed for thousands of years.

"When you first built this place, everything was white?"

He nodded. "And green. There used to be grass here. Trees. Flowers. Animals. Everything died over time."

She studied his profile, looking for any hint of emotion, but his face might as well have been carved from the same stone used to erect the buildings.

"I'm sorry," she said. "It must have been hard to see the realm you created waste away like that."

His expression hardened even more. "I made my choice." He spun on his heel and headed back inside.

Making a mental note that his realm's demise was a sore subject, she caught up to him as he strode inside the most amazing room yet.

It was a huge, cozy library with floor-to-ceiling shelves of books. A grand fire burned against one wall, and in front of it, a weathered leather sofa was angled so a person could lounge against the pillows and read by the light of the flames. In the center of the room was a recliner, and next to the chair was the object she'd been looking for.

She tried not to stare, but she'd never seen a double-sided version before.

"It's a *chronoglass*," Azagoth said, and she decided to keep the truth of what she knew close to the vest.

"It's amazing," she said truthfully. Framed by a gold rim, the pane of smoky mirrored glass stood at least ten feet tall and four feet wide, easily a third larger than either of the *chronoglasses* in Heaven. "Can you time travel?" Raphael had indicated that he couldn't, but she'd rather hear it from Azagoth himself.

"No."

"Then what do you do with it?"

"I use it to see what's going on in the world." In three graceful strides he moved in front of it. Instantly, the smoky color gave way to a clear view of the bustling streets of Paris.

Evidence of the recent near-apocalypse was visible in the scorch and pock marks on the sides of buildings and on the sidewalks, as well as the broken windows and twisted metal streetlamps and bike racks. But the signs of recovery were there too, in the open shop doors, speeding cars, and even a few tourists.

"But how do you choose the time period you want to see?" she asked.

"I can't." He reached out, a wistful smile playing on his lips as he traced a finger over a street sign. "I can only see what's current. Only those with time travel ability can choose to see events from the past."

"Can you at least choose the location?"

"That," he said, "I can do." He gestured to an odd black ball sitting on top of a stone stand. "It's sort of a mystical remote control."

She moved toward the ball, fascinated by this new discovery. She'd never heard of anyone using a *chronoglass* for anything but traveling through time. "How did you get all of this?"

"I made a deal with a fallen angel named Harvester. This was the first half of what she owes me."

Harvester, daughter of Satan? Wow. Her name had become household in the last few months. As the only fallen angel in history who had not only been restored to full angel status, but who had mated the most powerful angel in existence to become stepmother to the Four Horsemen of the Apocalypse, she was a rock star in Heaven. It was rumored that she still had to fight evil impulses, but according to most, that only made her an even better choice to be the Horsemen's Heavenly Watcher.

She skimmed her fingers over the *chronoglass's* shiny surface. "You do know that Harvester is a fully restored angel now, right?"

He tilted his chin in acknowledgement. "I'm aware."

Of course he was. For being trapped in isolation, he seemed to be well connected. "Were you also aware that she's mated to an angel named Reaver, who was recently promoted to Radiant status?"

His wry smile said he knew even more than that. "Of course. Were you aware that Reaver has an evil twin named Revenant, who was also raised to the Sheoulic equivalent of a Radiant?"

"He's a Shadow Angel?" she asked, stunned at the news. She'd known that Revenant was the Horsemen's evil Watcher, but she had no idea he was Reaver's brother—or that he was so damned powerful.

"Yes," he said. "It's been thousands of years since either Heaven or Sheoul had seen angels of their status." His smile turned malevolent. "Which means something big is about to happen. Just wait. It's coming."

At a tap on the door, they both looked up to see Zhubaal enter. "You have a visitor, my lord."

"Show him to my office," Azagoth said. As the fallen angel slipped away, Azagoth turned to her. "Feel free to explore my realm. No sentient being will harm you, but be wary of the plant life."

"It would be helpful if I had powers," she muttered.

In a surprising move that took her breath away, he was suddenly in front of her. Towering. Menacing. His aura practically dripped with a dark, magnetic energy that tugged her toward him. She actually took a teetering step forward.

His hand came up to cup her cheek in an astonishingly tender touch. Her pulse pounded in an erratic rattle through her veins, and desire spiked. How he could do that to her, she had no idea. She should have been immune to the charms of an arrogant, bossy male, given her experience with Hutriel.

Quickly, she banished her ex's name from her mind. He wasn't welcome here. She had enough to deal with already.

"In time, I'll allow you some access to your powers." His expression was still doing an imitation of the marble effigy on his desk, but his green eyes smoldered with intense heat. "But not until I'm sure you want to be here."

"I'm here, aren't I?" She sounded breathless and wanton, as if he'd been talking about sex, not getting her powers returned. *Idiot.*

He dropped his hand, and she felt the loss as a sudden chill on her skin. "Not the same thing."

No, she supposed not. "Is there any place that's off limits to me?"

"As my mate, what's mine is yours. You can go anywhere except the Inner Sanctum, where the souls are kept. It's a dangerous place for anyone, especially an angel."

"Gotcha." Sheoul-gra's Inner Sanctum didn't sound like a place she'd like to see anyway. Ever.

"Good." He glanced at his watch. "I have to go, but I'll catch up to you soon. I think we might have a lot to talk about."

She nodded, watched him leave, and then wondered what he'd meant by that. She didn't want to talk. Didn't want to be here.

Worst of all, she didn't want to be attracted to him.

Sadly, it was too late.

* * * *

The cloaked, hooded figure waiting inside Azagoth's office turned as he entered. The male angel, whose features were concealed by shadow, bowed his head in greeting.

"I hope you have some information for me, Jim Bob," Azagoth said, using the code name he'd given the angel over a century ago when Jim Bob had agreed to be Azagoth's spy in Heaven.

One of his spies, anyway. Azagoth had several, each useful in different ways. Some, like Jim Bob, came to him of their own free will, their reasons ranging from wanting the best for the Heavenly realm to having some secret, personal agenda. Others were unwillingly recruited thanks to intel Azagoth gained from the souls who came through Sheoul-gra. Azagoth didn't give a shit how his spies came to him, as long as they didn't screw him over.

Jim Bob, whose real name Azagoth didn't know, inclined his head again. "I was able to ferret out some background on your mate." He gathered the plain brown cloak more tightly around him, as if his jeans and German flag T-shirt would reveal his true identity. The paranoid moron.

Azagoth didn't give a shit who the guy was in Heaven. Mighty archangel or lowly desk-jockey Seraphim, it didn't matter. Still,

Azagoth would bet his right wing that Jim Bob was a high-ranking motherfucker, maybe of the order of Virtues or Principalities. The male radiated impressive power even here, where all power but Azagoth's was diminished.

"Lilliana is of the order of Thrones." Jim Bob's gravelly baritone took on a disdainful note, and the fact that he looked down on Thrones confirmed Azagoth's suspicion that the guy was very high-level, since Thrones weren't exactly serfs. "When she was an infant, her mother died in a time travel incident. Her father refused to take her in, and she was sent to the battle angel academy to be raised until it could be determined whether or not she possessed the time travel ability."

Interesting. The ability to travel through time was so rare as to be almost nonexistent. "And?"

"She tested positive." Jim Bob began to pace, his long strides carrying him across the room in a dozen steps. His heavy-ass work boots didn't make a sound. "At the age of fifty, she was taken out of battle angel rotation and sent to Time Travel Operations, where she worked for almost four centuries. She had a clean, if unremarkable, record of service until recently, when she was punished for stealing items from the past. Shortly after that, she went AWOL and didn't show up for work for months. No one could find her until she broke out of the *shrowd* in medieval England."

Azagoth was rarely taken by surprise, but that news did it. When angels traveled to the past, they did so within an impenetrable bubble known as a *shrowd*. The *shrowd* rendered them invisible and limited their ability to interact with the residents of the era. One of the most important and heavily enforced rules for time travelers was that they never leave the *shrowd*.

Maybe her infraction was what got her sent here. But why had she done it in the first place? Had she been running from something? He knew it was possible for angels to leave the *shrowd* in order to reside—or hide—in the past, but he didn't know how they avoided getting caught. Apparently, Lilliana didn't know either.

"Why did she break out of the *shrowd*?"

"No idea."

Disappointing. "What about lovers?" he asked. "Does she have any? Did she have to leave a male in Heaven to come here?"

Please say no. Not that he personally gave a hellrat's ass, but if he was going to have to put up with a crying, broken-hearted female for all eternity, he'd like a heads up and a lot more rum.

Jim Bob shrugged. "If so, she kept it quiet. The only relationship I found was with a male named Hutriel, but that ended decades ago."

Excellent. Azagoth stared into the fire as he contemplated everything he'd learned. When he looked back over at Jim Bob, the angel stopped pacing. "You look puzzled," Jim Bob mused.

"I'm just wondering why she wasn't destroyed for breaking out of the *shrowd.* Was mating me her punishment?"

"Perhaps."

How not helpful. Azagoth ground his molars in frustration. "Can you at least tell me if her ability to time travel was removed before she was sent here?"

"It was not."

Well, wasn't this all unexpected. He recalled how Lilliana had seemed so amazed by his *chronoglass*, so clueless about what it was and what he did with it, all the while knowing she possessed an ability that could activate the device.

It seemed as if his new mate had been keeping important information from him. Time to find out why.

And, perhaps, remind her that he dealt in death. Not forgiveness.

Chapter Five

Lilliana had no idea how she was going to get that giant *chronoglass* out of Sheoul-gra. For a few minutes after Azagoth left her alone, she'd tried to lift the thing, but it soon became clear that without her powers, she was going to have to drag it out. Which was going to take time and was going to make a lot of noise.

She'd have to plan this heist well.

She always thought best when she was walking, so she'd gone out to explore the buildings Azagoth had said were empty.

And they were...of people. Hellrats and other strange little demonic critters scurried around, and the pulsing, maggoty-pale vines had climbed walls and penetrated windows and doorways. As she wandered through structure after structure, she found evidence of what must have, at one point, been a bustling community.

One entire building had been dedicated to living quarters complete with private bedrooms. In another building, she found several long-empty community baths. There was even a huge hall filled with long tables and chairs. Wooden and stone food trenchers still sat at some of the seats, as if waiting to be filled.

Who had lived here? And why had they left?

It was all so eerie, and that was *before* she reached the Roman-style colosseum, its sandy basin littered with demon bones. Ancient weapons, none newer than about two hundred years old, hung from racks on the walls.

The soft thud of footsteps echoed through the structure, and it took all her years of training not to make a run for the nearest scythe. Panic in a strange place never ended in anything but death. In a controlled spin, she whirled around, breathing a sigh of relief when she saw Azagoth, his long strides eating up the distance between them with effortless grace.

But her sense of relief was short lived. His mouth was a grim slash, and his glacial, calculating gaze left her feeling trapped, as if he was a gladiator and she was a declawed, defanged lion. For a split-second, she reconsidered grabbing a weapon. Instead, she squared her stance and met him head on.

"I've been exploring your buildings," she said, going on the offensive. "Seems you left some information out."

"Your righteous anger falls flat, given that you withheld shit from me too."

"I don't know what you're talking about—" Suddenly, they were no longer standing in the arena. They were back in Azagoth's library, and as he gestured to the *chronoglass*, her gut twisted.

"You failed to mention that you can time travel."

Oh, shit. "It wasn't a secret." Not...really. The truth just complicated things. Things like trying to steal a *chronoglass*. "But out of curiosity, how did you find out?"

"A lot of people owe me a lot of favors," he bit out impatiently. "Now, why did you keep this news away from me?"

She swallowed. She'd always been a horrible liar. Every angel had to go through espionage ability screening as a youth, and she'd gotten a record low score. Nothing like being notorious for being *the worst* at something.

"Answer me," he demanded. "Is it because you thought you could run away? Breaking news, Angelcake, it won't work. This device only works for an hour at a time...unless you break out of the shrowd." He smiled, enjoying her discomfort. "Which is something you seem to be okay with."

She inhaled sharply. "What do you know about that?"

"Does it matter? If it makes you feel any better, I don't give a shit what crimes you committed in the past. But let's be clear on one thing; down here, you don't fuck with me. So tell me, are you planning to escape using the *chronoglass*?"

"That would be stupid. I'd be bringing Enforcers down on my head. I'd spend every minute looking over my shoulder for them. Eventually they'd find me and kill me." She folded her arms over her chest and glared. "And don't call me Angelcake."

"Enforcers won't find you if you cut off your wings." He ran his tongue over his teeth as if savoring the uncomfortable pause. "Angelcake."

Asshole. But the asshole was right. Any angel who cut off his or her wings became instantly undetectable to angelic senses. Any angel who would normally "feel" another angel's presence under certain variable circumstances wouldn't register her at all. Even face to face, an unobservant angel could very well believe the wingless angel was human.

"I'm not cutting off my wings," she assured him. "I hate pain, and seriously, why is this such a big deal anyway?"

"It's a big deal because you kept it from me for a reason. I want to know the reason. I don't tolerate deception. I'd tell you to ask my last assistant about my low tolerance, but his soul is busy being tortured and buttfucked in the Inner Sanctum." He laughed. "Buttfucked in the Sanctum. Get it?"

Apparently, the males of all species remained children no matter how old they got. "I get it. Sanctum sounds like rectum." She rolled her eyes. "So clever."

His smile remained, but his eyes were shards of ice. "Now, the truth. Why did you act like you barely knew what a *chronoglass* was while failing to tell me you could use it?" He snapped his fingers imperiously. "Let's hear it. My patience is wearing thin."

If he snapped his fingers again, she was going to break them. "Maybe I just wanted something for myself," she said. "I'm in a strange place, expected to mate with a strange male, and I have nothing of my own. Not even clothes, because *somehow* they've been delayed. So maybe I wanted an hour to myself now and then, outside of here." She glared. "Jackass."

Even though she'd called him a jackass, the shards of ice in his gaze melted a little, just enough to dull the sharp edges. "I can...understand that."

Holy shit, he'd bought it? Then again, it was the truth. If there had been no hope of getting out of this deal by stealing the mirror, she'd have felt exactly as she'd just said.

He stepped forward so suddenly she jumped. "Take me someplace."

"Excuse me?"

He stepped closer, but if he thought he could intimidate her with his height, he was an idiot. She'd gone through battle training with males far taller and bigger than he was.

None of those males, however, could hold a candle to Azagoth's lethal elegance and oozing sensuality. It was as if he had been born for killing and sex. The battle angel in her could appreciate the former. The female in her definitely appreciated the latter. And the thing that sucked was that she shouldn't be appreciating anything about him. He wasn't exactly an enemy, but neither was he someone she could afford to get attached to.

"Take me someplace," he repeated.

She tipped her head back to meet his gaze. "Ask nicely."

"Take me someplace...please."

"You could have at least made an *attempt* to make it not sound like an order."

Clenching his teeth, he ground out, "Will you please take me someplace."

Well, it wasn't quite what she was hoping for, but she doubted it would get any better. Besides, she was ready to get out of here for a while. "Fine," she said. "But you should know that I'll have full use of my powers once I'm outside your realm."

One corner of his mouth twitched. "Should I consider that a warning?"

"Just don't be surprised if you find yourself riding a bolt of lightning if you piss me off."

"I'm into kinky shit, so that works."

He gripped her palm, and she sucked in a sharp breath at the shock of awareness that shot up her arm. She stole a glance at Azagoth, but apparently he hadn't felt a thing, because he was as snarly-faced as ever.

Well...good. They didn't need to be having any kind of mutual "moments."

Although, really, it was a little insulting that he didn't react. At all.

Shoving aside her irrational annoyance, she reached deep inside for what angels in her field called the Triple T...the time travel tingle. Independent of her other, currently unusable, angelic powers, it started deep in her pelvis and spread outward, until it was as if she could actually feel time and space inside each and every cell. Now all she had to do was think of a specific time period...then a location...and there it was.

Instead of reflecting their images, the *chronoglass's* surface became a window, beyond which was an ocean of drifting desert sands.

"Ready?" At Azagoth's nod, she squeezed his hand tight and led him into the mirror.

Instantly, dry heat blasted them as their feet sank into the hot sand. Releasing Azagoth, she glanced around at the scenery. It was exactly as she'd known it would be.

Utterly desolate.

She'd dropped them in the middle of the Egyptian desert, where there was nothing but rolling dunes of sand. Only the cloudless azure sky added color to an otherwise monotonous field of beige.

Take that, Azagoth. He'd wanted to go somewhere outside of Sheoul-gra, so she'd brought him to the most boring, featureless environment she could think of.

Feeling smug, she pivoted around so she could soak in his disappointment.

Turned out, she was the one in for a letdown. Azagoth's eyes were closed, his face tilted toward the sun.

"Egypt," he sighed. "Damn, I miss the desert." Inhaling deeply, he smiled.

She gaped. "Seriously? You *like* this?"

"I miss...warmth." Gripping his collar, he yanked, ripping his shirt and popping buttons with such force that one pinged her in the forehead. "And the breeze...ah, damn, I miss the breeze."

He flung his ruined shirt to the ground, and good Lord, he was ripped. Muscles flexed under smooth, bronzed skin and made the multitude of incredibly lifelike tattoos plastered on his chest dance. She let her gaze rove hungrily over him, committing his body to memory, because she had a feeling no male would ever match Azagoth's savage beauty again.

He came off as detached and calm, but his ruthlessness as one of Heaven's most decorated and successful Interrogators was well documented. Humans, demons, and fellow angels alike died at his hand, but not before they endured a lot of pain.

Azagoth's skill with his hands extended to females as well, but instead of agony, they felt pleasure. His bedroom exploits were legendary, and now all Lilliana could do was wonder how many females had let their fingers play along the lines of the serpent tattoo that curled around his left pec. How many had dragged their tongues down the hilt of the sword on his breastbone, all the way beyond where the blade disappeared under his waistband. And how could Lilliana possibly touch him in ways no one else had?

Not that there would be any touching.

He kicked off his shoes and socks, tossing them aside without any care at all. Which made her wonder where he got his clothes. She hadn't noticed a bustling shopping mall in any of Sheoul-gra's outer buildings.

"What year is it?" he asked as he walked in circles, his gaze now transfixed on his toes sifting through the sand.

"I don't know exactly." She watched him bend over to scoop up some sand, and her mouth went as dry as the desert air at the way his slacks hugged his fine ass. Swallowing against the dryness, she continued. "I haven't been doing this long enough to aim for specific dates, or even specific years. I can usually get myself within a decade of my goal, though."

"A decade?" He straightened. "How long have you been doing this?"

She smiled wryly. "Why don't you tell me, since you know so much about me." When he said nothing, just looked up at the sky like he'd never seen it before, she went ahead and humored him. "Almost four hundred years."

Pivoting around, he looked her up and down the way a prospective buyer would examine a horse. "Sounds like a long time to still be off by ten years. Are you a slow learner?"

She stared, speechless for a second. "Am I a slow learner?" she practically sputtered. "I'm far ahead of most time travelers by this age, you arrogant ass."

"Huh. If your accuracy is that bad now, I'd hate to have seen you when you first started. You want to see the Battle of Gettysburg but find yourself running from dinosaurs. That would suck."

"It happens," she snapped. Because something *similar* had happened to her. But instead of the Battle of Gettysburg and dinosaurs, it had been the Battle of Almansa and saber-toothed cats. The worst part of it was that animals often could see angels inside the *shrowd.*

And it turned out that saber-toothed cats were freaking *mean.*

He laughed and slogged through the sand, his elation putting a severe damper on her exasperation. "Come on." He made a *follow me* gesture. "Let's walk."

"Are you kidding me?" She threw her hands up in the air. "There's nowhere to walk to. The nearest human settlement is a hundred miles away."

"So? Would you rather just stand here?"

She glanced longingly over her shoulder at Azagoth's library, visible through the rectangle portal that would allow them to go back at any time.

"Fine," she muttered as she jogged to catch up.

She supposed she could understand why Azagoth would want to stay in this giant cat litter box, given that he'd been shrouded in darkness for thousands of years. And really, it said something about him that he wasn't angry that the first place she'd brought him was the middle of nowhere. If anything, he was excited.

Even now, he was walking with his face to the sun, his arms outstretched, as if he was giving the desert a big hug. His hair, which had been perfectly combed before, was mussed by the breeze, and a hint of a smile gave him an irresistibly boyish appeal.

He looked over at her when she caught up, and his smile turned downright dangerous. Oh, not dangerous in the deadly sense. Dangerous in the, *I want to be flat on my back on a mattress with you*, sense.

Abruptly, he came to a halt.

Startled, she did the same. "What's wrong—"

Azagoth spun her, silencing her with his mouth on hers.

Stunned, she stood there like a dolt, her heart pounding so hard she felt her heartbeat in her lips where they were mashed against his. One big hand came around to tangle in her hair as Azagoth deepened the kiss, swiping his tongue along the seam of her mouth, tasting and testing until she felt her body sway against him.

Yes, definitely dangerous...

"Thank you," he murmured against her lips.

And then he was walking again, leaving her standing in the sand, knees weak and her insides quaking with the kind of arousal she hadn't felt in...well, ever. And he was sauntering away as if that kiss, brief as it was, hadn't affected him at all.

Muttering obscenities to herself...on the loud side, so he'd hear, she tagged along as he tread lightly across the endless expanse of desert, stopping every once in a while to just look up at the sky or gaze out over the sand.

It seemed like they'd only been wandering for a few minutes when the telltale pressure started in her chest. Their hour was coming up.

"It's time," she said.

Azagoth cranked his head around to peg her with his intense gaze. "For what?"

A gust of wind blasted sand in her face, and she had to spit out the grit before she could speak. "To go."

The light that had been sparkling in his eyes snuffed out. "So soon?"

"Soon? I don't know about you, but I could use a glass of something very wet and icy."

"I could go for something wet," he drawled, and oh, damn, the places her mind took that.

Pretending she hadn't heard a word, she reached for him. "I think the *chronoglass* will automatically suck both of us back into it, but to be safe, give me your hand."

For just a second, he hesitated, as if he wouldn't mind being stuck here, but in the end, he reluctantly took her hand. Instantly, the same warm awareness as earlier shot through her body, and just like before, Azagoth showed no hint that he felt anything at all.

Closing her eyes, she let her senses drift as the time travel pull made every cell in her body vibrate. The buzz grew more intense, until it felt as if she was being torn apart...and a moment later, they were back where they started, standing in front of the mirror, staring at their own reflections.

Azagoth looked at the shimmering surface, and she wondered if he saw the same sadness in his eyes that she did.

"Azagoth?" she said quietly. "What's wrong?"

All around her, the air crackled with a coming storm. "I have to go." His voice was little more than an inhuman drawl, steeped in rage and pain and a few other emotions she couldn't identify.

And then he was bolting out of the library, leaving her confused and alone.

The strange thing—besides his behavior—was that she was used to being alone. She was okay with it, had learned at an early age to rely only on herself and to be okay with her own company.

But for the first time in her life, she didn't like her own company.

And there was no way in hell that she wanted to analyze the reasons for that.

Chapter Six

Azagoth got the fuck out of the room. Away from Lilliana. Away from the female who had given him the gift of stepping outside of his realm for the first time in thousands of years. Who set his blood on fire when he'd taken her hand. And when he'd kissed her. Holy hellfire, today had been the best day he'd had in eons. Maybe in...ever.

He could still feel the sand on his feet and between his toes as he hauled ass to his office. The halls were empty, which was good, because right now he didn't trust himself not to disintegrate anyone who got in his way.

He hit the door at a dead run and slammed it closed behind him. With a thought, he shut down the soul tunnel and went straight to the fireplace.

The flames licked at his bare skin, but as usual, he felt nothing. How odd, given that the Egyptian sun had engulfed him in warmth.

Trembling all over, he gripped the mantel so firmly that the stone beneath his fingers gave way. He'd leave one hell of a set of handprints once he got himself under control.

But *could* he get himself under control? What the hell was happening to him? The moment he'd stepped from his library out into the desert and breathed the hot, dry air, something inside him had broken open, releasing a trickle of sensation he hadn't been able to identify. It had been familiar, and yet foreign, maybe what humans called déjà vu. Whatever it was, it had been pure and pleasant, a kind of joy that wasn't dependent on evil or violence or death.

But the moment he'd rematerialized inside his library, the sensation had morphed into something much less pleasant, as if the river of emotion seeping out of the fissure had become polluted. Tainted in the way only malevolence could do.

Hatred and pain and the desire to destroy something had overwhelmed him. He hadn't been prepared for the onslaught of feelings, and now his body was shaking and cramping like he'd overdosed on some human designer drug.

Closing his eyes, he made a futile attempt to corral his runaway emotions, to gather them up and stuff them back inside the icy tomb where they'd been interred for so long. He'd been such a fool to want to feel something again. How could he have forgotten that emotions were bad, bad things?

He growled at the sound of a tap on the door. "Go away."

The door whispered open, and he gripped the mantel even harder as his wings writhed beneath his skin. His true form, the one that literally frightened the piss out of most demons, was itching to break out and rip something—or some*one*—apart.

Soft footsteps padded inside, and he got a whiff of the warm citrus fragrance that was unique to Lilliana.

Instant, embarrassing hard-on.

Okay, so he couldn't rip her to shreds, but dammit, he wasn't ready to talk to anyone, let alone the female who had just drawn something from him he hadn't felt in forever.

This is your own damned fault. You wanted a mate, an angel who would warm you from the outside.

Yeah, well, he hadn't expected to be warmed from the *inside* too.

"Do you not understand the words, *go away*?"

He heard her drawn-out inhale, as if she was gathering her own temper. "You seemed upset. I wanted to make sure you were okay."

"I'm Azagoth, the Grim Fucking Reaper, king of my domain.

Of course I'm okay."

"What, so the Great Azagoth doesn't have feelings?" She made a noise that sounded suspiciously like a stomp of her foot. "Is the Great Azagoth also so rude that he can't talk to someone face to face?"

Irritated now, he rounded on her. "I told you not to come in."

She stiffened, but instead of defending her actions as he expected, she inclined her head. "You're right. I shouldn't have barged in and demanded something of you when you clearly want to be alone." Pivoting crisply, she started for the doorway.

"Wait," he blurted, his mouth operating independently from his brain. "I didn't mean to be a bastard."

The words came out stilted and unfamiliar to his own ears. How long had it been since he'd apologized to anyone? Thousands of years, probably. No wonder he was so rusty.

Lilliana turned around slowly. "What happened? You seemed so relaxed and happy when we were in the desert, like you were a normal person and not the Grim Reaper. Now you're extra...reapy." She cleared her throat. "Also, you've sprouted horns."

Of course he had.

She eyed him like he was a rabid hellhound, and when her gaze dropped to his feet, he barked, "What are you doing?"

"Checking for hooves."

He was pretty sure his horns grew larger. So did his dick.

Irritation that he couldn't control his own body, let alone his emotions, pissed him off even more. Made him...as she put it, *extra reapy*. Then she was walking toward him, her long, fluid strides kicking her slim hips out with each strut. The bare expanse of her belly became a focal point as she came closer, and suddenly, all the writhing, shifting feelings inside him narrowed into a single stream of lust.

Much, much better. Fury, joy, sadness, guilt...those were things he couldn't deal with. Lust, though...*that* he could handle, and handle very well.

"Look," she said as she halted in front of him. "It wasn't my fault that we had to come back. We used up the entire hour—"

A tap on the doorjamb cut her off, and they both looked over to the open doorway where Zhubaal stood, outfitted in leather and weapons.

Not a good sign.

"My lord, I had a meal sent to your dining room." He gestured down the hall. "And...you have another visitor."

"Send them away. I'm done for the day."

Zhubaal shifted his weight in an uncharacteristic display of unease. "Sir...it's Methicore."

Instant alarm shot up Azagoth's spine, and he instinctively stepped in front of Lilliana. "Is he alone?"

"Aye." Zhubaal's tone was grim. "I shackled him with Bracken Cuffs."

The cuffs, designed to neutralize supernatural abilities, weren't necessary, not when Azagoth was the most powerful being in his own realm, but with Methicore's history, it was a wise precaution. Plus, being shackled was humiliating, and Methicore deserved it. And worse.

"Send the bastard in."

Zhubaal bowed deeply and left. As soon as the door closed, Lilliana stepped closer. "Who is Methicore?"

"He's a vile excuse for an angel," he growled. "A pox upon his kind."

She frowned. "How do you know him?"

Azagoth inhaled deeply, doing his best to keep the monster throbbing inside him at bay. "I know him," he said thickly, "because he's my son."

* * * *

Bastard. A vile excuse for an angel. A pox upon his kind.

Azagoth's words about his own son completely obliterated any warm fuzzies Lilliana had begun to feel for him. It was too reminiscent of her own father's rejection of her. She'd been the product of breeding for a purpose, and when she'd approached him a quarter of a century ago in an attempt to get to know him, he'd made it very clear that he wanted nothing to do with her.

"I have a mate and sons now, and I don't need you barging into our lives and ruining everything."

In other words, his family didn't know about her. He'd kicked her out of his grand residence with instructions to stay away from him and his family.

Looked like Azagoth was no better than dear old dad. She should have known.

As Zhubaal escorted Methicore inside, anger at the way he was chained boiled up. She'd been shackled the same way only a few weeks ago, and the memory of being rendered helpless and at another's mercy closed in on her in a claustrophobic wave.

Methicore stopped a few feet inside the doorway, but Zhubaal remained outside, his hand hovering over a blade at his hip. Was this male truly such a threat? Or had Azagoth taken a page from her father's playbook? The moment her father had realized who she was, he'd summoned two underlings to flank her, as if she'd come to murder him instead of beg for acceptance.

"Father," Methicore drawled. "Did you take out your horns on my account? How special." He resembled his sire in height and coloring, but he was slimmer, and where Azagoth's eyes had glazed over with icy indifference, Methicore's burned with hatred.

She wasn't sure which was worse.

"Why are you here?" Azagoth's expression gave nothing away, as usual. "I told you to never return."

Oh, gee, Lilliana thought sourly. That sounded familiar. Azagoth and her father should get together for drinks and bond over woeful tales of their inconvenient bastard offspring.

"I wanted to tell you the news in person," Methicore practically spat.

Azagoth might as well have yawned, he looked so bored. Even his horns had disappeared. And he was still hoofless. "What news?"

"The kind that makes you fucking irrelevant." Methicore smiled darkly, the resemblance to his father becoming uncanny. "All Memitim are Ascending to full angel status as of today...and we've been given the ability to reproduce. You're done, asshole. No longer needed."

Surprise flickered in Azagoth's eyes, but it quickly snuffed out. "Is that all?"

"No." Methicore's grin widened. "Also as of today, *as of the second I leave*, access to your realm will forever be cut off to Memitim." He tapped his chest with pride. "My doing, of course. You'll never see any of your sons or daughters again."

Lilliana gasped in horror, but there was absolutely no reaction from Azagoth. Did he not care about his children at all? Slowly, as if this was all just so very ho-hum to him, he turned his back on his son and stared into the fire.

"I have no use for you," he said softly. "Begone."

Lilliana's heart crumpled like aluminum foil as a flicker of hurt flashed across Methicore's face. It was quickly smothered by a triumphant smirk, but she wasn't sure what he had to feel good about. Revenge was far more poisonous to the giver than the receiver. Besides, Azagoth didn't seem to be disturbed by the fact that he'd never see his offspring again, so Methicore's victory was hollow. She actually felt sorry for him.

Methicore shot Azagoth the bird and moved toward the door, pausing at the threshold. "Female." His eyes locked on her, and the calculation in them left her feeling more exposed than anything Azagoth had done so far. "You'll get nothing from him but a cock that's as frozen as his heart. Come with me, and I'll give you what he can't."

"Have a care, son." Azagoth's quiet voice held an ominous edge that seemed to make even the flames in the hearth shrink back. "For some species devour their young."

Methicore swept out of the office with a snarl. The moment the door slammed shut, Lilliana rounded on Azagoth.

"You *bastard*." She spat out the word with all the contempt she could muster. "How can you be so cruel to your own son?"

"Me? Cruel?" His hands formed fists at his sides. "I'm not the one cutting off access to my children."

"As if you give a shit."

"Do not," he growled, "presume to know me after a few hours of prancing around my realm."

Prancing? She'd never pranced in her life. "I don't have to know you to know your kind."

He swung around, his jaw tight and unforgiving. "My kind?"

"A breeder." The very word pissed her off. "A stud for hire who doesn't give a damn about the lives he creates."

He jerked as if she'd shot him with an arrow. She'd struck a nerve, hadn't she? "Shut. Up."

"Fuck you," she shot back. She hated being so crude, but something about this male and this realm brought out her bitchy side.

"Shut up," he ground out, "or I'll make you shut up."

He clearly had no idea how stubborn she was, something that had driven her kidnapper nuts. "You can't make me do anything."

He came at her, his gait loose yet predatory. "I can make you do *everything*."

Unbelievable. "Are you aware on any level whatsoever how arrogant you are?"

"This is my realm, angel. I *am* this realm. My reach extends beyond Sheoul-gra's boundaries to the deepest pits of Hell and the highest levels of Heaven. So yes, I'm aware of my self-confidence, and when I tell you that I can make you do something, I mean it."

You can't make me stay here. Oh, she couldn't wait to get out of this depressing place. "What will you do? Beat me into compliance? Torture me?"

He stopped in front of her, his gaze roving boldly over her, lingering on her breasts and bare skin of her belly. "Only a fool and a coward would harm his mate, especially if they have to co-exist for eternity." He bared his teeth in what she assumed was a smile. "I have other ways of getting what I want."

"Well, I hate to break it to you, but short of torture, you can't make me do anything."

His smile became downright wicked. "I can make you beg for the mere whisper of my breath on your skin. I can do things with my tongue that will make you scream with the exquisite intensity of it. And I can make you come so hard, for so long, that you'll pass out from pleasure."

"Sex," she said bitterly. "Typical male, thinking that's all females want." Never mind that she *did* want it. Lord help her, to experience an orgasm like that...oh, yes, please.

"Sex," he said huskily, "is only the beginning. I can make you a queen. I can give you an entire realm."

She snorted. "You mean this?" She made an encompassing sweep of her arm. "This cold, dreary realm full of death and *griminions* and fallen angels? Yeah, it's what every girl dreams of."

A tense black silence hung like a pall in the air, and she had a feeling she'd pushed him too far. Despite what he'd said about not harming his mate, she braced herself for a blow.

And one blow was all he'd get. Her power was muted down here, but she'd fight him until her last breath. Or she'd get the hell out of here and happily submit to the dissection team that would extract her time traveling ability.

But Azagoth didn't raise a finger. Instead, he dematerialized, leaving her alone. Again.

Chapter Seven

Azagoth materialized in his library, wishing he could scream in fury and agony. But all the emotion that had nearly crippled him earlier had found its way back into the desolate, frozen wasteland he called a soul. Although he supposed his soul had been sucked out of him a long time ago.

Snarling, he swiped a soda-bottle sized crystal chess piece off his desk and crushed it under his boot. Methicore had given it to him, a reminder that Azagoth was a king, and the world was his chess board.

Methicore should have remembered that.

Azagoth ground the heel of his boot on top of the piece, relishing the sound of destruction.

His son had betrayed him yet again. Not only betrayed, but destroyed every relationship Azagoth had forged with his sons and daughters. Not that he'd ever had much in the way of relationships, but at least he'd been able to visit with some of his offspring now and then. The ones who hadn't abandoned him when Methicore led the rebellion against him, anyway.

Funny how Azagoth had seen Satan's insurrection coming from a mile away, but he'd been utterly blind to Methicore's machinations. Then again, by the time his son had risen up against him, Azagoth's ability to sense deception had been dulled like a blade that had sawed too much bone.

And then there was Lilliana and her unwelcome observation about him. Calling him a breeder. *A stud for hire who doesn't give a damn about the lives he creates.*

The real pisser was that she was right. But not about all of it. He did give a damn about his offspring. He might not be able to feel true love for anyone or anything, but he *did* care.

He cared *too* much, and Satan had exploited that fact in order to get what he wanted from Azagoth.

The demon had never forgotten Azagoth's role in his expulsion from Heaven. Talk about holding a grudge. What a big, whiny baby. So Satan hadn't succeeded in taking over Heaven. He was King Shit of his own domain now. Who else could say that?

Oh, right—Azagoth could. Not that Lilliana gave a crap.

She'd given him the greatest gift of his life by taking him to the desert, but when he'd offered a gift of his own, the key to Sheoul-gra, she'd mocked him and flung it right back in his face.

This cold, dreary realm full of death and griminions and fallen angels? Yeah, it's what every girl dreams of.

How dare she, he thought, as he flashed himself outside his manor. How dare she reject anything that he, the Grim Reaper, offered? Females creamed themselves over him. They'd come to him by the thousands, begging for any scraps he'd throw their way. Granted, they were demons, but they'd been high-ranking, influential females from every species. Before her recent demise, even Lilith herself had approached him on multiple occasions to try to convince him that a union between the two of them would make them the most powerful couple in existence.

No thanks. He'd already been screwed by her. In more ways than one.

Frustrated, he kicked at the oily soil beneath his feet. It felt nothing like the sand in the desert. He looked into the distance at the dozens of buildings and beyond, to what used to be a forest filled with life, rivers, and lakes. Now there was nothing but gnarled tree trunks and stumps, dry creek beds, and one lake so stagnant that its toxic stench sometimes crossed the barrier between Sheoul and Sheoul-gra. Denizens of Sheoul's Horun region had affectionately named the affected area The Grim Reaper's Asshole.

It's what every girl dreams of.

Azagoth's heart went dead in his chest. Holy shit, Lilliana was right. Demons might think of Sheoul-gra as a treasure, but no one else, especially not an angel, would think that any of this was a gift.

What a fool he'd been. What a fucking dumbass.

He had nothing to offer Lilliana. Sure, he could give her great sex. Better than great. But beyond that? Nothing. His realm, which had once been teeming with activity and life, was dead.

The only thing for her to do down here was what Azagoth did; meet each evil soul as it came through the tunnel, and then decide its fate before sending it to the various levels of the Inner Sanctum to await reincarnation. Assignment to hard labor? A stint in Hades's dungeon? Maybe roasting in the Eternal Field of Flames or swimming in the Acid Pools of Agony?

And really, he should *not* have let Hades name shit in the Inner Sanctum. Azagoth wanted to beat the fallen angel every time he was forced to say, or even think, of the miserable area known as Feces-palooza.

Oh, hey, Lilliana, let me take you on a tour of your wedding gift. Yep, check out Disembowling Beach. We can honeymoon in Feces-palooza. And just wait until I take you to Boiling Piss Pond and the Fetid Razor Swamp.

Fuck.

Scrubbing his hand over his face, he decided he needed to rethink his strategy. If Lilliana was truly here because she was given no choice, eternity with him would, literally, be hell for her. He was a bastard who traded in death and pain, and while he liked to tell himself that he'd been corrupted by thousands of years of life in Hell, the truth was that even as an angel he'd been in the business.

Interrogators weren't exactly nice people.

Okay, so where did he go from here? First, he supposed, it might help to know why, exactly, Lilliana had agreed to mate him. Jim Bob had indicated that this was a punishment, but Azagoth wanted to hear it from Lilliana herself. Had she been given any choice in the matter at all? And if so, why had she agreed?

He couldn't do anything about Methicore and his idea of revenge...at least, not in the immediate future. But he could take care of what was happening right now in his home.

Home. What a joke. Home was a horror show of a necrotic

realm. Dream stuff, there.

As he contemplated his next move with Lilliana, he headed back inside and straight for the bedroom. He expected her to be waiting for him, but to his surprise, she'd climbed into bed, her chestnut hair spilling over the black satin pillowcase in a shiny wave. The clothes she'd been wearing were laid neatly on the recliner next to her wardrobe and, he noted, the sapphire silk baby-doll nightie was missing from the hanger.

Man, he wished he hadn't missed her putting that on. He could imagine her hard body loosely covered in luxurious material meant to caress her smooth skin, and when he added himself to the picture, the nightie became a shredded pile on the floor.

Mouth watering, but not for food, he made a quick detour to the kitchen to see if she'd eaten, and he was pleased to see that she'd made a huge dent in the Italian food Zhubaal had scored from one of Azagoth's favorite restaurants. Azagoth could cook, but one of his few pleasures was eating the best foods in the world, and Zhubaal had a knack for knowing exactly what Azagoth was in the mood for.

Too bad his mood for Italian had passed, because the three pasta dishes, steamed mussels, and tomato bisque looked amazing. What was left of it, anyway. Apparently, his angel had a hearty appetite.

The thought made him practically purr inside. He loved a female who could eat.

Returning to the bedroom, he eyed his erotic furniture, wondering if she'd show as much enthusiasm for sex.

How could she? She doesn't want to be here.

He shook off the thought. He'd make her want to be there. Sure, he didn't have a plan, but he had the power to bring anything she wanted into his realm. He could keep her content. Happy, even.

Keep telling yourself that, jackass.

With a growl of frustration, he stripped naked and climbed between the crisp sheets. She was lying as close to the edge of the mattress as possible, her back to him and the covers tucked under her chin. He closed the gap between them, easing himself close to her, but just short of touching. He didn't trust himself. If he touched her, he'd need to keep touching, and he wanted to give her time to adjust.

How gentlemanly of you. Yeah, well, his soul might be warped into something unrecognizable and his emotions all but dead, but his memories were fully intact and untainted by Sheoul's evil influence. He remembered his mother and how she'd been so timid and afraid of new experiences. It had hurt him to see, especially not knowing what had made her that way.

Those memories were what made him handle his nervous bedmates differently than he handled the others. While he might not actually *feel* sympathy for faint-hearted females, he knew he used to, before he came to Sheoul-gra. And despite the rumors, he had *never* taken a female by force or coercion.

He certainly wouldn't start with his mate.

"Lilliana?" he murmured. "I know you aren't asleep."

"What gave me away? The fact that my eyes are open?"

Apparently, the theme tonight was ornery. He could play that. "You have a sharp tongue, female." He caught a lock of hair in his fingers, and so much for not touching her. "May I suggest that you put it to better use?"

"May I suggest that you go to hell?"

"That insult has no bite, given that we're already here." Not technically, of course, since Azagoth's realm sat on a special plane between the human realm and the demon one, but the barrier between Sheoul and Sheoul-gra was extremely thin, allowing far too much leakage between them.

She sighed. "What do you want?"

Bracing himself on one elbow, he leaned in, inhaling the fresh rosemary mint of her shampoo. His cock stirred, and whaddya know, that scent was apparently an aphrodisiac.

"Tell me," he breathed into her ear. "Tell me why you're here."

"You really want to know?"

He inhaled again, this time catching the faint citrus spice of her skin along with the shampoo. She was a living, breathing dessert he couldn't wait to taste.

"I'm not in the habit of asking questions I don't want the answers to," he said, letting his lips brush the skin of her cheek.

She inhaled sharply, and the unmistakable aroma of arousal rose up all around her. His body responded with a primal surge of hunger, and his rapidly swelling cock went all *hellllooo, baby* on her backside.

Another inhalation, this time a little ragged. "I...ah, I was given a choice between being demoted and stripped of my abilities or mating you."

Azagoth had known the answer, but hearing her say it felt like a punch to the nuts. *Buh-bye, baby.* "And how difficult was your decision?"

The mattress creaked as she turned over to face him. Light from the fire danced on her face, softening her features, but making her eyes glow with a defiant glint.

"I'm sensing that there's a right and a wrong answer here, so why don't you go ahead and tell me which one I should pick." She propped herself up, matching his pose. "And why does any of this matter? I'm here. Isn't that enough?"

No, it wasn't. Being here wasn't the same as *wanting* to be here. If he had any emotions left in him at all, he'd be happy if just once, someone—anyone—truly wanted to be with him.

"It doesn't matter." Impulsively, he kissed her on the forehead before rolling away to leave her alone on her side of the mattress.

Weird, but this was the first time his massive bed didn't feel big enough.

Chapter Eight

Azagoth was gone when Lilliana got up the next morning. She experienced a fleeting twinge of disappointment, and then she buried her face in her pillow as she remembered feeling the press of Azagoth's erection against her butt. The velvety tip had nudged her solidly between her cheeks, spreading heat through her pelvis as her nerve endings sparked with awareness.

Everything about Azagoth and his realm might be polar-level cold, but his body was definitely in the triple digits.

How she'd been able to speak a single word, let alone entire coherent sentences after that was beyond her comprehension. Her heart had hammered so hard and erratically that she'd felt it in her spine, and her lungs hadn't been able to get enough air.

If things hadn't gone rapidly downhill right after that...nah. She'd have told him to roll over to his side of the bed and stay there.

While she lay on her side and stared at the spanking bench across from her.

Yawning, she started for the bathroom, slowing to give the bench a swat for keeping her awake for a good part of the night while she played out scenes in her head involving it and Azagoth. Inevitably, those scenes had turned ugly when she thought about the other females who had enjoyed a good spanking at his hand.

Sometimes, an imagination was a terrible thing.

His bathroom was the only truly light part of his manor that she'd found. Rough-cut white marble gave the room a masculine edge, but it was modern and elegant, and she could spend hours in the shower. Though she had to wonder why he needed five shower heads and two marble benches, but the heated floor tiles were a nice touch. How many females had he brought in here, anyway? She pictured him naked, water and suds sluicing over his muscular body, and suddenly the shower got a lot steamier.

Stop it.

Now he was on his knees, his tongue catching rivulets as they cascaded from her breasts to her abs.

Stop it!

In the next moment, she was bracing herself against the shower wall as he licked her sex, alternating quick flicks against her clit with long, firm strokes through her wet valley.

Stop. It!

Her blood quickened and her breaths came fast and hard as she drove her hand between her legs. In her mind, it was Azagoth's tongue circling her sensitive nub before thrusting inside her core, and when her climax took her a second later, it was Azagoth's name that whispered across her lips.

And damn, imaginary Azagoth was good. Her knees shook as she dried off, but the mouthwatering smell of bacon spurred her on. Once dried, she selected a pair of skinny jeans, boots, and a form-fitting violet sweater from the wardrobe, then followed the aroma of food to the kitchen.

Where she found a redheaded female in ripped-up jeans and a lacy fuchsia corset doing dishes.

"Breakfast is on the table," she said with a perky smile.

"And you are..?" She'd better not be one of Azagoth's bedmates. Not that Lilliana was jealous. Offended, yes. Jealous, hardly.

The female wiped suds off her cheek with the back of her hand. "I'm Cataclysm. Call me Cat."

"Azagoth failed to mention that he has a fallen angel for a cook."

"He hired me this morning. And I'm Unfallen, not True

Fallen."

Meaning she'd been expelled from Heaven, but she wouldn't be evil to the point of no return until she entered Sheoul and became a True Fallen.

"So you're trying to earn your way back into Heaven, huh? I can think of better ways to do that than working for the Grim Reaper."

She shrugged as she shoved a cast iron pan under a stream of hot water. "Life in the human realm with no angelic powers is dangerous for Unfallen. Here I'm protected from demons and angels alike. It's a good gig. I wasn't about to turn it down. Especially because suddenly, everyone is working overtime to drag Unfallens into Sheoul. I was almost caught twice in the last week."

Lilliana found a towel to dry dishes and stepped up to the counter. "Why the urgency?"

Cat snatched the towel from Lilliana and pointed to the table, which was loaded with pancakes, bacon, some sort of egg casserole, and mixed fruit. It was enough to feed half a dozen humans, but Lilliana figured she could down most of it herself. She'd always had a healthy appetite, and food was a guilt-free pleasure.

"Sit," Cat said. "And I don't know what's up, but everyone's scared. Just six days ago, one of my friends was dragged into Hell. When I saw her yesterday..." She shuddered. "She tried to force me into Sheoul. So, here I am."

As far as fallen angels went, Cat didn't seem too bad. Besides, Lilliana didn't have any room to judge, given her own disgraced status.

"So," she said, as she filled a plate with food. "What did you do to get the boot?"

Cat bowed her head. "I fell into temptation."

"Sex with a demon?" Lilliana slathered butter and syrup on the pancakes.

"A demon?" Cat wrinkled her nose. "No. Gross. Although...have you ever met a Seminus demon? Because if there's a demon out there who can tempt an angel..."

She fanned her face, and Lilliana rolled her eyes. Yes, the sex demons were legendary lovers who, as a species, had gotten more than one female angel kicked out of Heaven, but was having a half-an-hour-long orgasm really worth the risk?

Okay, maybe.

"Anyway," Cat continued, "do you know the Four Horsemen's ex-Heavenly Watcher, Gethel?"

The bite of fruit in Lilliana's mouth soured. "The evil bitch who wanted to start the Apocalypse by slaughtering one of the Horsemen's children? And who is now carrying Satan's baby? That Gethel?"

"Yes," she said wryly. "I see you know who I'm talking about. Anyway, I was her apprentice when she was still an angel. She made me do a lot of things that were questionable, but I did them anyway. Who was I to question the great Gethel, Heavenly Watcher to the Four Horsemen of the Apocalypse, you know? By the time I figured out that she was working for Team Evil, it was too late. I was in too deep."

"And you were punished by expulsion."

"Yep." She held up a pitcher of orange juice, but Lilliana shook her head. "So here I am. Thank you for giving me this chance. I was starting to get scared. It's very dangerous for my kind out there right now."

Footsteps signaled an approach, and a moment later Azagoth entered, looking scrumptious in black jeans, a forest green Henley, and Dr. Martens. His gaze traveled up and down her body, and her cheeks grew hot as her shower escapade roared back into her head.

"I see you've met your assistant," he drawled.

"Assistant?"

He swiped a grape from the fruit tray and popped it into his mouth. "Cataclysm is here to handle all your needs. Her chamber is down the hall."

"I...um...why?"

"Because Zhubaal has enough to do already." He went for a slice of apple next. "And you were right about my realm being no prize for someone like you. The least I can do is make this punishment of yours more tolerable. So for as long as you're here and you want her, Cat will be as well."

Okay, so now she felt like a piece of shit. Cat was here for her, so when Lilliana left with the *chronoglass*, Cat would be out of a job and a home, and she'd be vulnerable to anyone who wanted to hurt her or force her into Hell to complete her fall.

Dammit, she did not need this complication. She wanted to get out of here, and now she had Cat's future to consider.

"Well, thank you," she said as she pushed to her feet. "Did you come for breakfast? I'm just finishing up—"

"I came to ask if you'd take me someplace."

"Ask?" She snorted. "Is this going to be like last time?"

He swore, and yup, looked like they were in for a repeat of the drill sergeant routine. So she was shocked when he said, "Will you please take me someplace? I'd really like to get out of here for a little while."

"You're lucky I have nothing better to do," she said, only half-teasing.

She'd planned to spend the day in his library and wandering around his realm in search of anything that might help her get the *chronoglass* out. She doubted she'd find a moving dolly, but there were millions of items with the mystical power to render even the heaviest items much lighter. A lot of spells, too.

Azagoth led her out into the hall, where he started in the direction of the library. "We'll find something for you to do."

"Like what?" Walking next to him, she waited for a crude comeback like, "You can do me," but he didn't. He was serious.

"I don't know," he said. "But I was thinking of creating a new level in the Inner Sanctum, one appropriate for demons who aren't evil."

"All demons are evil. That's why they're demons."

He shook his head. "Just as there are angels and humans who are bad, there are demons who are good." He slowed to let a *griminion* scurry past. "There's good and bad in everyone, Lilliana. Some just have to work harder than others to overcome their nature."

She supposed that was true, but boy, did it ever fly in the face of everything she'd ever been taught in battle angel classes.

"What do you do with these 'good' demons now?"

"I send them to the first level, which is a vacation spot compared to the others," he said. "And I authorize their reincarnations first."

"Aw, look, there *is* some good in you," she teased.

He laughed. "Sending non-evil entities back into the world isn't out of the goodness of my heart. It floods Sheoul with neutrality, which means the truly evil demons will pay any price for me to authorize the reincarnation of evil souls." He winked. "I'm very open to bribes."

Charming.

"Why are you being so nice and talkative all of a sudden?"

"I wouldn't go so far as to say, *nice*, but you are my mate, and this is your realm now too. *Cold and dreary* as it is," he added. Ouch. He still had a bite, didn't he? "You need to have your own space and purpose."

Lilliana could just shake her head. How could someone who was so awful to his children be so thoughtful to someone he barely knew?

"People in Heaven think you're a monster, you know."

"I am." He pegged her with a dark stare. "Don't let my calm exterior fool you. There's a beast inside me that's capable of horrors you can't imagine."

She didn't doubt that.

They arrived at the library, where a fire was roaring in the hearth, but the temperature in the room was more akin to someone having left the freezer door open.

"Oh, and just FYI, something I forgot to mention last time." She shrugged like it was no big deal, but it kind of was. "There are a handful of fallen angels who can sense entries into the *shrowd*, and they make it their mission to destroy any angel who travels through time. It's rare that they find their target, but when they do..." She shuddered. She'd come up against them twice, and her mother had lost her life to the bastards.

"Any angel, fallen or not, who dares to challenge me will spend all eternity as artwork in my great hall."

She frowned, remembering all of the grotesque statues. The ones that looked like humans, demons, and...angels...in agony.

"Wait. So all of the sculptures in your..."

"Yes. Instead of sending their souls to Sheoul-gra, I bound them in statue. Some of them have been there for thousands of years. I'll bet they're quite insane by now."

"You can...you can even do that to angels? Even if they haven't turned evil? Their souls should automatically return to Heaven."

He shrugged. "I'm the Grim Fucking Reaper. This is my domain, and if I want to keep a soul, I can." He shot her a sideways glance. "I told you I'm a monster."

She'd be wise to remember that.

Because holy shit.

Inhaling the dusty tobacco scent of the library, she started toward the mirror, but something crunched under her feet. "I'm sorry." She sidestepped, cringing at whatever it was that she'd broken. It looked like a crystal chess piece.

"S'okay." He swiped the bits of crystal off the floor and tossed them into the trash. "It was broken before you stepped on it."

Realization dawned. "*You* broke it. Why?"

"It was a gift from Methicore," he said gruffly. "I want all reminders of him gone."

Her heart clenched. She'd sent a rare singing iris from Heaven's Covenant Mountain to her father once, hoping to open the lines of communication before their first meeting. When she'd finally met him face to face, he'd returned it to her.

Broken into three pieces.

"I don't understand how you can reject him so thoroughly." She searched his face for some sign of regret, but she saw nothing in his expression but disgust for his son. "What did he do to you?"

He looked startled that she'd ask. "Why do you want to know?"

"Weren't you just on the 'we're mates' trip a few minutes ago?" she reminded him. "Maybe we should, I don't know, talk?"

He swept some papers off his desk and into the trash can, covering up the broken chess piece. "Maybe I'll talk when you're ready to do the same."

"I've answered every question you've asked."

"Really?" Crossing his arms over his broad chest, he pegged her with a hard stare. "Then why don't you tell me why you're really here? Because something isn't adding up, Lilliana."

"I told you," she ground out. Was he never going to let this go? "I was given a choice between two evils. I picked this one."

"How sweet. But I know that. I want to know what made coming here more appealing than remaining in Heaven, even in the diminished capacity they offered you."

Oh, I figured it would be easy to steal your property, get out of here, and be restored to grace.

She probably shouldn't say that. She'd try another truth.

"Maybe I'm not ready to discuss my private humiliation with someone I just met."

A slow, bitter smile spread over his face. "Exactly."

"So your son is your private humiliation?" She probably shouldn't be pushing him on this when he'd made it clear he didn't want to talk, but dammit, she wanted to know what it took to make a father reject his own offspring.

"Private?" he laughed. "No, he's a very public humiliation." He gestured to the *chronoglass*. "Enough talk. I'm anxious to see where we're going. Somewhere warm, I hope."

"Sure," she said sweetly. "Let's go."

Chapter Nine

They stepped out onto a frozen wasteland with nothing but ice and snow as far as the eye could see. Not even the sky could offer color or texture. Gray, featureless clouds had turned it into a blanket of blah.

Lilliana watched Azagoth carefully for signs of annoyance that she'd brought him to someplace so cold and barren, but just like when she'd dropped them into the Egyptian desert, his expression conveyed awe and excitement. He wasn't at all pissed off. If anything, he lit up like the Christmas tree in Times Square.

"This isn't someplace warm, but I forgive you." Grinning like a loon, he extended his hands and let a flurry of snowflakes sift between his fingers. "I hate the snow," he said, but she never would have guessed that with the way he was acting. He even stuck out his tongue and caught a flake on the very tip. She hated that there was something very appealing...and sensual...about that.

"For someone who doesn't like the snow, you seem pretty taken with it."

"Because I haven't seen it in eons." He scooped up a handful, and with a sly grin, he beaned her with it. Right in the forehead. "Gotcha."

Sputtering, she wiped snow out of her eyes. "Really? How old are you?"

Bam! Another one hit her in the chest, and then he was running away from her, his boots slipping on the ice, but he never fell. She wanted to be annoyed, but his blatant joy was infectious. Smiling in spite of herself, she hurled her own snowball at him, using just a touch of angel flair to control its trajectory. Damn, it was nice being away from his realm and being able to use her powers again.

It nailed him in the back of his head.

"Payback's a bitch, Azagoth!"

His laughter rang out in the still Arctic air as he skidded and whirled. And then, and as far as she could tell, he went down intentionally to roll in the snow.

"This is amazing!" he called out.

Yes, it really was. How many people could say that they'd witnessed the infamously grumpy ruler of the dead romping like a child on a school snow day? All he needed was an inner tube and a hill.

Abruptly, he leaped to his feet and lifted his face to the gray sky. "Clouds," he said. "What a strange thing to miss." He swung around to face her, his big body as relaxed and loose as she'd seen it. "Before I fell, I used to make clouds in Heaven sometimes, mainly for a change from the blue sky. I made them orange, just for fun."

How could this male be the same as the one renowned for his ruthlessness as an angel? The history books she'd read had left out a *lot*.

"I made rainbow clouds," she said, encouraged to have finally found something in common besides a father-child hate relationship. "It was back when I was young and we were learning how to control our ability to think things into existence." Channeling a trickle of power, she painted a swath of primary colors across the sky before letting the gray drab take over again. "My instructor got all pissy and changed them to white, like everyone else's."

"So your rebel nature extends beyond taking me to the crappiest places you can think of?"

Busted. "I suppose."

"Rebels aren't exactly tolerated in Heaven." He grinned, a

heart-stopping, breathtaking grin that made her go hot right here in the middle of a deep freeze. "I like it."

Suddenly, another snowball came at her and popped her in the chest. She hadn't even seen him throw it.

"Oh, yeah?" With nothing more than a thought, she sent a huge wall of snow at him. His eyes flared, and for a moment she thought he'd flash himself out of the way, but instead he stood there, his expression almost blissful as it crashed over him like a giant wave.

As he shook snow out of his clothes and hair, he chuckled. And then, in a motion so fast she didn't see it, he was on top of her.

They went down in a tumble of limbs and snow, his body coming to a rest on top of hers as she sprawled on her back. She didn't feel the cold—not like most beings did, anyway. But she couldn't miss the stark contrast of the ice beneath her and the warmth of Azagoth's big frame above her.

"Did you really think you could get away with that?" He tweaked her nose, and she was momentarily speechless at the playfulness. This male with wild, windblown hair frosted with snow couldn't be the same guy who possessed the power to destroy souls. The same guy who had so coldly thrown his son out of his realm.

The same guy who had given her an assistant, free access to his realm, and pretty much the freedom to do whatever she wanted.

Maybe, just maybe, he wasn't all that bad.

Smiling up at him, she said, "Maybe I let you catch me."

One corner of his mouth twitched in an evil smile, and she knew she'd stepped into a trap of her own making. "Then you wanted to end up like this, did you?" Shifting, he settled more fully on top of her. His thigh slipped between hers, and she felt the blatant stab of an erection against her belly. "You wanted to feel my body against yours?"

No. Yes. Oh, dear Lord, she didn't know what she wanted. Not when he rocked his hips, driving that big bulge against her core. She sucked in a breath, and unbidden, her body arched upward to meet him. Her breasts pressed into his chest, and she wondered how they'd feel in his palms.

"I thought so," he purred. So arrogant. And really, so right. The bastard.

She bucked, but even she had to admit it was a half-hearted effort. Same as when she said, "Get off of me."

"I'll consider it." He dipped his head and nuzzled her throat.

The shock of his cold nose on her skin made her hiss, but a heartbeat later, his lips sliding along the curve of her neck made her moan. One of his hands tangled in her hair to hold her steady for his kisses, and the other came down lightly on her waist. His palm rubbed slow circles as it moved upward until his fingers brushed the underside of her breast, and a shock of desire shot straight to her groin.

It startled her how quickly need ignited her blood, and her heart beat so hard she could hear her pulse in her ears. Without thinking, she gripped his arms and drew him closer, until she could feel his nipples harden through his shirt. How long had it been since she'd given in to a male like this? Not since Hutriel, and even then, she'd never had the desire to bite every button off a shirt just to get to his powerful chest.

Then again, Hutriel had been all about "proper" lovemaking. And proper lovemaking meant an orderly removal of clothing, and afterward, there could be no lingering looks or touches. There was no penetration, just a tangling of bodies and limbs as you surrendered your soul to the merging. An instant, all-over body orgasm was the reward, an orgasm that could last for hours and leave you drained for a day.

Sure, it was awesome with a capital *A*. But for all the soul-melding, it wasn't especially intimate. Not on a physical level. And that was something she had desperately craved. Hell, she'd craved closeness of any kind after being denied it following her mother's death and her father's rejection.

Her father's *third* rejection.

Azagoth shifted, dropping his hand to her thigh and lifting her leg to his waist, putting her core in full contact with his erection. Ecstasy speared her, spreading through her sex and warming her so quickly that she might as well have been in a sauna, not in ten below Arctic temperatures.

Arching against her, he slid his hand beneath her shirt. Oh, damn, the skin-to-skin contact was decadent, but as he began to smooth his palm upward, she went taut. She shouldn't be doing this. Not when she was planning to leave. It wasn't fair to either of them.

You're worrying about him? The male who serviced seventy-two angels a year, plus the devil-only-knew how many demon females?

Yeah, she was kind of an idiot. But how could she feel such conflicting emotions all at once? How could she hate him but crave him? Want him but at the same time want to push him away?

The pull of the mirror rescued her from her own scrambled thoughts. She cleared her throat. "Are you still considering getting off of me?"

His voice was a silken whisper against her throat. "I'm considering getting you off."

Heat flushed her body. "We're going back in a few minutes."

"It can't be time." His mouth trailed upward, along her jugular, and shivers of pleasure shot through her. "We just got here."

It felt that way to her, too, and truth be told, she felt a twinge of disappointment herself. She'd meant to take him to the most horrible, boring place she could, and he'd loved it. She'd ended up having fun.

Total fail.

"Sorry, but—" She broke off, sucking air as his lips captured her earlobe. How could such a small thing feel so good?

"But what?" He traced the shell of her ear with his tongue. So. Very. Good.

The tug of the mirror intensified, becoming a buzz that drowned out all the pleasant things Azagoth was doing to her.

"But we have to go."

His head came up, and his gaze bored into hers. "I don't want to go."

Crazily, neither did she.

But the *chronoglass* had other plans, and a moment later, they were back in Azagoth's office, lying on the carpet.

He was still on top of her.

And his hand had moved to her breast. But the look on his

face said that he was anything but happy to be back. His eyes were wild, glinting with anger and what she thought might be confusion.

He'd freaked out last time when they'd come back, but she'd never found out why. She'd written it off as Azagoth being Azagoth, but twice now was too weird to ignore.

He looked down at her, fangs jutting from his upper jaw. Those things probably shouldn't be a turn-on, but then, she was rapidly discovering that there were a lot of things about Azagoth that shouldn't be sexy.

And *way* too many that should.

"Hey." She palmed his cheek, letting her thumb stroke the contour of his blade-sharp cheekbone. "What's wrong?"

"Not...used...to..." He broke off, panting, his lips peeled back in agony. "Emotion."

Emotion? How could he not be used to emotion? She'd seen him pissed as hell. She'd seen him smile. She'd seen him happy as a puppy in a meadow during their time travel jaunts.

But whatever was going on, it was clear he was in pain.

"Hey." She tilted his face down, forcing him to look at her. His gaze was glassy, tortured, and so very different from how it had been a moment ago. "I liked it better when you were kissing my neck." He groaned, his teeth clenched as if he was fighting with himself. Gently, she tapped on his cheek. "Focus. Come on, rein it in."

"Can't. Worse than...last time."

Shit. She'd seen something similar before, when she'd been a young angel in battle training. The male named Dreshone had been an empath with such strong abilities that it had been hard for him to function. He'd undergone a procedure to have his ability minimized, but the price had been a big one; his own emotions had been dulled, which had made him an extremely lethal warrior, but once per decade, he'd suffered a meltdown of uncontrollable emotion that had required lockup to prevent him from hurting anyone or himself.

But as far as she knew, Azagoth wasn't an empath, so what was going on?

"Azagoth, listen to me—" He snarled and started to push off of her, but she gripped his biceps hard and dragged him back down. "No. You aren't running again."

His deep growl rumbled through her body, reigniting the fire that had been burning her blood when they'd been lying in the snow. And wasn't it funny that his anger was turning her on as much as his lips had been.

"Don't...want to...hurt you."

Yeah, she didn't want that, either. "You won't. You've never hurt any of the angels Heaven sent to you over the centuries." News of that nature would have been the talk of the angelic airwaves.

"I never felt like...this."

Maybe time travel had an adverse effect on him. "Just focus," she said softly. "Focus on me."

His gaze locked with hers, and she saw the moment he went from furious to...well, furious *and* aroused. And she knew, in that moment, that no matter what happened next, nothing between them would be the same again.

Chapter Ten

Azagoth concentrated on the female beneath him, his body a mass of writhing, twisting contradictions. Like the last time he'd come back from time travel, he was reeling from emotions he couldn't handle.

Now it was happening again, only on a grander scale. The fissure that had opened inside him last time had cracked open further, leaving him overwhelmed with feelings. Joy, sadness, anger, jealousy. He wasn't even sure what event or person each emotion was attached to. It was just all bubbling out, as if thousands of years' worth of denied feelings were breaking free of their bonds.

This was what you wanted, asshole. You wanted to feel. Be careful what you wish for.

True enough. He'd been so cold inside for so long. And now he was cold *and* insane.

Distantly, he heard Lilliana talking. Felt her fingers digging into his arms. Felt her thighs clamping around his hips to hold him still. Felt her core pressed firmly against his raging erection.

Focus. He tried gathering the maelstrom of emotions together and forcing them down, back into the fissure. *Focus.* Reaching deep, he tried to separate out each one and associate it with an event, a person, anything to understand why he'd be so angry or jealous, but each time an image started to form, it scattered to the wind and was replaced by a black hole of fury.

Focus!

The female beneath him shifted, tugging him closer, rubbing her sex against his. Whether or not it was intentional didn't matter. He instantly locked up as his body took command of his mind and did the focus thing.

Of course, the focus was all in his dick. Whatever. He'd roll with it.

Zeroing in on Lilliana, he panted through the gnawing tension that made him feel as if he could explode into violence and death to become the corrupted monster that legend—and a few firsthand accounts—had made him out to be.

As he dropped his mouth to hers, a thread of guilt wove its way through the messy tangle of emotions that were fading to the background. He was using her. Doing to her what all the females before her had done to him. He'd been a stud for hire for Heaven, and demon females only came to him for bragging rights. Oh, sure, he fucked them well, but ultimately, all they wanted from him was sex. For pleasure or for other reasons, he was nothing but a lay and a means to an end.

And now he was using Lilliana to bring him out of an emotional overload he couldn't handle.

Also...what the fuck. When had he started having regrets or caring about anyone but himself? There was a reason he'd volunteered for Grim Reaper duty, and it sure as hell wasn't so he could go all Dear Diary about shit like being used.

Lilliana's hands were stroking his arms now, her slow, light touch soothing his mood but stoking his lust.

Focusfocusfocus...

"Azagoth," she whispered against his mouth, bringing him right back to the place he needed to be.

He slid his hand under her shirt again, caressing her smooth, taut skin as he kissed her quiet. But this wasn't enough. Not nearly enough.

With a growl, he gripped her shirt and tore through it as if it were paper. And glory be, like most angels, she wasn't wearing a bra.

Her gorgeous eyes watched him with curiosity and desire as he lowered his head to take one berry-red nipple into his mouth. Licking and sucking eagerly, he cupped the other breast, filling his palm with her warm flesh as he settled more fully between her thighs. His cock was aching like a sonofabitch behind his fly, and he shifted again so he could reach between their bodies and unzip. While he was down there, he yanked open the buttons on her jeans and drove his hand inside.

Lilliana gasped as his fingers found her center and stroked the silk fabric of her underwear.

"How many lovers have you had, angel?" He kissed the swell of her breasts and worked his way down her belly.

"One," she breathed. "Just one. And I don't want to talk about him."

Neither did he. Partly because he didn't want any other male to be here right now, and partly because he'd just had the strangest urge to arrange for that male's painful death.

Eager to wipe the bastard from her memory, he reared back on his heels and yanked her boots off, followed by her jeans and underwear. It was all done in a matter of seconds, and then his clothes joined hers on the floor, torn and wadded.

Ah, damn, she was gorgeous, sprawling naked in front of him like a feast to be savored. Her hair fanned out in silky waves on the Persian rug, her kiss-swollen mouth parted for her panting breaths, and her thighs spread just enough to catch a glimpse of the bare, glistening female flesh between them.

Her gaze dropped to his groin, and at the sight of his thick sex, her eyes flared. Oh, yeah, she wanted it.

Smiling, he wrapped his hand around his cock and stroked. The tip of her tongue came out to swipe her bottom lip, and he groaned at the sudden image of those lips wrapped around his shaft, that tongue flicking and laving.

Releasing himself, he leaned forward and cupped her intimately. Fuck, she was burning hot down there, and he groaned again as he pushed a finger between her folds. Every cell in his body was vibrating as he dragged his fingertip through her wet heat to that swollen knot of nerves that made her gasp.

He stroked, lightly at first, avoiding the sensitive tip. In moments she was panting and grinding, arching into him and riding his hand as her taut body chased the pleasure he was giving her. Holy hell, she was a wild thing, gripping him so hard her nails dug into his skin. He had to taste her. It wasn't a desire; it was almost a biological imperative.

Jacking his body off of her, he reared back, hooked his hands under her hips, and dove between her luscious thighs. He buried his face against her sex, reveling in how slick her flesh was against his mouth. He spread her wide with his thumbs as he used the flat of his tongue to lick right up her center.

She cried out as the tip of his tongue clipped her clit. He did it again, and she cried louder, her body quivering, her fingers clamped on his scalp to hold him exactly where she needed him.

She tasted like sugar cane and passion fruit, clean grass and crystal water, all things he hadn't seen, felt, or tasted in eons.

"Azagoth," she gasped. "I'm going to...oh, *yes*."

She bucked wildly, tossing her head back and forth, her body straining and her hips lifting off the floor as she came. *Beautiful*, he thought. So. Fucking. Beautiful.

Even before she came down, he mounted her, desperate to get inside and feel something besides the cold.

"Wait," she breathed, reaching for him. "Let me—"

Panting, crazy with need, he started to insert a finger to test her tightness...and froze.

Betrayal squeezed him like a vise, and all the emotions he'd managed to put away began to rise to the surface again.

"You lied," he croaked. "You're a virgin."

"No," she said firmly. "I've joined with a male in the way of angels."

Some might see the whole soul-sex thing as, well, sex, but even as an angel, he'd preferred the messy, downright dirty physical sex that humans had. So maybe she hadn't lied, but she hadn't been completely honest, either.

Sitting up, she palmed his chest, holding him with her gaze. "You're getting that crazy look again." She dragged her hand down, over his sternum, his abs, and finally, with a shaking hand, she grasped his cock.

"Shit," he gasped.

She had him now. He was hers for the taking, and as her hand began to move, so did his hips. He pumped into her closed fist, his hips pistoning back and forth as she worked him.

His head fell back, and he heard himself talking, swearing...he wasn't sure. All he knew was that stinging, molten heat was building in his balls and shaft, and when she squeezed him harder, sweat bloomed on his skin.

Sweat. He never sweated.

"Fuck," he breathed. "Oh, damn...Lilli..."

She sped up the pumping rhythm, and then her other hand joined the party, cupping his balls and rolling them in her palm.

"Tell me what to do," she whispered, but he didn't have the breath to tell her a damned thing. What she was doing was just fine.

"Just...ah...yes."

His climax was a spiraling, hot coil of bliss that, for a single, glorious moment, shattered the ice that had encased his soul for so long. He convulsed with the intensity of it, the absolute joy of truly *feeling* a release.

Watching her as she watched him set him off again, and another searing orgasm blew his mind and body apart.

As it waned, he folded his hand over hers and helped her ease him down as his hyper-sensitive cock jerked reflexively in her palm.

"Wow," she breathed. "I've never done that before."

His hand shook as he reached for a tissue on his desk. "What, you've never made a guy come with your hand?"

"My ex thought physical sex was repulsive."

"Your ex was a dipshit." Gently, he wiped his seed off her skin and then lifted her off the floor and carried her to the sofa in front of the fire.

Climbing onto the cushions next to her, he gathered her against him and tugged a blanket down over them both. She stiffened at first, and he understood that. He couldn't remember the last time he'd lingered with a female after sex. They came here for one purpose, and it wasn't to be cuddled.

He'd never longed for any kind of connection after sex either, so this thing with Lilliana...it felt foreign. And yet, it felt right.

And as she rested her hand on his chest, directly over his

heart, he *knew* it was right. Now he just had to figure out how to stop the emotional blowouts he kept having when they came back from time travel. Of course, if sex was the key to stopping them in their tracks, well, he supposed he could deal.

He just hoped Lilliana could, too.

Chapter Eleven

Azagoth didn't know how long they laid on his couch, bodies tangled together as they caught their breath, but eventually, Lilliana, her head on his chest, began to trace lazy circles on his abs. The intimacy of it—of all of this—left him in a state of awe and, truth be told, anxiety. Somehow, she was drawing emotion out of him, and he couldn't help but wonder how damaging that could be.

"Azagoth?"

"Hmm?"

"Why did you volunteer for this job?" Postcoital drowsiness permeated her voice, and he experienced a flicker of male pride that he was responsible. "To lose your angelic status and live among demons?"

He shrugged, knocking one of the pillows off the sofa. "Someone had to do it."

"Bullshit." Her fingers skated over his rib cage in an almost playful sweep. "I might be young, but I know that no one sacrifices freedom without a good reason."

He tucked one arm behind his head and gazed up at the wood-beamed ceiling. "Didn't you read everything you could find about me before you decided to become my mate? Surely you had an entire term devoted to me in history class."

"Three terms, actually." She drew the number 3 on his sternum. "You're quite the historical figure. The first term was devoted to your life as an angel known as Azrael and the events leading up to your expulsion, and the second and third terms were devoted to your life as Azagoth."

"I got three terms?" He grinned. "Nice."

But damn, the name Azrael brought back memories. And how odd was it that he preferred the memories he'd made as Azagoth over those that went with his Heavenly name?

"Yes, well," she said, "the history I learned painted you as an entitled playboy who chose to lose his wings because he'd rather rule an empty kingdom than follow others in paradise."

It figured that historians would twist the facts to fit whatever agenda they had. Angels were no more scrupulous than humans when it came to molding the truth into fact-based fiction.

"Then what's the point of asking why I chose this life if you already know?"

"Because only a fool believes everything they read or are told." She dragged the backs of her fingers up his sternum, and pleasant tingles followed in their wake. "So what's the real story?"

He supposed he owed her the truth, given what she was committing to. It was just so strange to owe anyone. *He* was the one who usually held all the I.O.U.s.

"I did it because I was tired of feeling," he said simply, because that's what his long-ass story boiled down to in the end.

Pushing up onto one elbow, she frowned down at him. "Feeling what?"

"Everything." He kept his gaze glued to a rough-cut beam overhead. "Did your history classes teach you that I was an empath?"

Her brow shot up. "But you were an interrogator with the Internal Corruption Investigation unit. Empaths aren't allowed. How can you torture people if you can feel everything your subject feels?"

"At the time, no one knew I was an empath. And it wasn't all torture," he said, maybe a little defensively. "Most of what I did for the ICI was ask questions. Being an empath gave me an edge when it came to detecting lies."

"Which is why you were the most successful ICI interrogator in history," she mused. "It was you who uncovered Satan's plot. You were unstoppable. Until you mysteriously quit and disappeared for a few centuries before returning to volunteer for the Grim Reaper gig."

Those few centuries had been the worst years of his life, so full of loneliness and regret. Funny how when you had no one to talk to, you relived everything you ever said and did, and when most of it wasn't pretty, you learned to hate yourself real fast.

"I quit because I was a cocky, spoiled, arrogant playboy, just like you said. I kicked ass at my job and I knew it, and then one day I got it wrong. I was so sure of myself that I mistook a young angel's fear for a family member for fear he'd get caught lying. Long story short, he was innocent, and he lost his wings because of me." He glanced over at her, expecting to see disgust on her face, but all he saw was curiosity. "Naturally, at the time I didn't blame my bad judgment on my arrogance. I blamed it on the fact that I wasn't a powerful enough empath. You know, if only I'd been even more empathic, I wouldn't have screwed up. So I did something stupid, a mystical spell went wrong, and one day I was the most empathic angel the world had ever seen."

She cocked her head, and her hair tickled his chest. "So what happened? You don't seem to be all that empathic to me."

"No kidding." There was a crack in the ceiling beam. He should get that fixed. "What happened is that my world went to shit. I couldn't be within a mile of a human or I'd feel everything they were feeling. Being within a hundred yards of an angel would drive their emotions and thoughts into my head like a knife. So I left ICI and isolated myself for two hundred years. It wasn't until a call was put out for volunteers to oversee Sheoul-gra that I realized I could do something useful again. The benefit being that here in the demon realm, my empathic ability doesn't work."

"I'll say," she muttered.

"What I didn't anticipate," he continued, "was that I'd lose more than my ability to feel what others feel. I've lost my ability to feel almost everything."

"You're saying you don't feel pain? Or anger? Or joy?"

"Anger stirs, but barely and not often. Otherwise..." He shrugged. "I've even lost my ability to feel heat. Only the ever-present biting cold. If not for the fire, I think my flesh would turn to ice."

"That's why the fire doesn't produce heat, isn't it? Because you absorb it all."

"Yes." He closed his eyes. "What I wouldn't give to be warm. Even when you took me to the desert, I could barely feel the sun on my skin." He took her hand and dragged it to his right pec, directly over the skull engulfed in flames tattoo. "These tattoos were designed to contain pain and emotion. I took them from one of the Four Horsemen, Thanatos, in hopes that I could access the pain. And for a while, I did." He sighed. "It was...glorious."

"Pain was glorious?"

He took a strand of her hair between his fingers. It was so soft, so different from the hard, cold texture of the world he'd created around him.

"I was happy to feel something...anything." Bringing the curl of hair to his nose, he inhaled her fresh scent. "But it didn't take long to drain the tats. Now they're as empty as I am."

"I'm sorry, Azagoth." Her pity put an end to this party, and he sat up with a curse. "Oh, no," she said, grasping his wrist. "What's wrong?"

He didn't need—or want—her sympathy. He'd made his bed and he'd lie in it. With her, preferably. But he did want her to understand that it wasn't her job to make him happy. Nothing and no one could do that.

"What's wrong is that none of this is fair to you," he said, breaking her hold so he could swing his legs over the side of the sofa and stare into the fire. "I wanted a mate. I didn't expect complications."

"So I'm a complication?"

He winced. "Not...you. This situation. I'm not usually impulsive, but I asked for a mate before considering what life down here would be like for her. A dark, creepy realm and a mate who can't feel anything. What a catch I am."

Oh, look, the pity party had started up again. Rock on.

"You're wrong," she said fiercely. "You can feel. I watched you in the sand and the snow, and I promise that what I felt coming off of you was sheer happiness. You felt that. I saw you. I *felt* you."

"And trust me," he said, "those were the best two hours of my life. Then we came back." He caught a glimpse of the *chronoglass* out of the corner of his eye, and he swore the thing mocked him. "When I was with you in the desert and Arctic, it felt as if the chains holding my emotions at bay broke. But the moment we return, all that emotion shifts to pain, like my body can't handle it."

"Maybe it can't. Your emotions have been bottled up for a long time. Maybe they're starting to break free." She shifted on the sofa so she was sitting cross-legged and facing him, the blanket tugged up to cover her all the way to her breasts. Shame, that. "You're empathic, but not down here, right?"

"Right. Except..."

"Except what?" She poked him in the thigh, startling him with her playfulness. "Tell me. I can handle it."

He scrubbed his hand over his face, knowing it probably wasn't wise to talk about other females when you were with the one you just made come.

Just spit it out.

"The only time I feel anything is when I'm fucking," he blurted. "And it's not even my emotions I'm feeling. It's the female's. So imagine how awesome it is to be servicing an angel who doesn't even want to be here. Who loathes me or is terrified. Yeah, it's great. But you know what the worst part of it is? Some small part of me is grateful even to feel their disgust and fear, because at least it's *something*."

Damn, that was some nice babbling, wasn't it?

He risked a brief peek at her, expecting to see revulsion, but all he saw was more pity. Which was somehow worse.

"Okay," she breathed. "So you can't feel your own emotions. But you *used* to have them down here, right?"

"Yes, thanks for the recap."

She huffed. "What I'm trying to say is that maybe this is the beginning of you starting to feel again. It started happening after the first time travel session, right?" At his nod, she continued. "So the time travel must be triggering it. Was it worse the first time or today?"

He thought about it for a moment. "Today, but you were a good distraction."

A shy smile turned up one corner of her mouth. "You're

welcome." The blanket had fallen to expose deep cleavage and the delicate swells of her breasts, but sadly, she tugged it up to her throat. "But I was afraid I was going to lose you again for a minute there."

"When?"

She turned as red as a Sora demon's ass. "When you, ah...when your finger discovered..." She cursed and blurted, "Why was my virginity such an issue for you?"

It was his turn to curse. He'd done so many stupid things in his life, and the virginity thing was one of them. She was going to think he was a serious idiot.

That's because you're an idiot.

"Remember I told you about how I did something stupid and became a stronger empath?" At her nod, he scrubbed his face again. If he had any emotions, he'd be embarrassed. "That something I did was a female. A succubus. A virgin succubus."

"Oh...shit." Angels weren't supposed to fornicate with humans, let alone demons, but of all the demons, succubi were the most forbidden. Virgin succubi were the worst of the worst, and if caught, the offending angel would pay dearly—perhaps even with his wings.

"*Shit* doesn't even begin to cover it," he said gruffly. "And I didn't know she was a demon at the time."

Lilliana smiled wryly. "Isn't that what they all say?"

Probably. But he'd prided himself on being too smart to fall for any demon tricks, especially those coming from succubi.

"I thought she was a human sorceress," he explained. "I'd made a few, let's say *shady*, inquiries through underground networks about a spell or a token that could increase empathic powers. She said she could help. She was the perfect mix of vixen and maiden, and I fell for it."

"Wait...if you were an empath, why didn't you sense the fact that she wasn't human?"

"Because most breeds of succubi can project false emotion and mask their true identities with aphrodisiac magic. Virgin succubi, in particular, are impossible to detect as demons."

Lilliana shifted, and the sound of the blanket rasping against her naked body made his sex stir again. Quickly, he swiped his pants off the floor and threw them on.

"A succubus's virginity is priceless," she said as she watched him dress. "The moment her barrier is broken, a massive wave of power is released. People pay outrageous sums to deflower a virgin succubus and reap the benefits of that power. So why would she just give it to you when you didn't even know what she was?"

He sank back down on the couch. "Because when an angel deflowers a virgin succubus, she absorbs a huge amount of his power in return. Now, picture a succubus who possesses abilities generally available to angels." At her expression of horror, he laughed bitterly. Yeah, she got the picture. "Thanatos once accused me of being the Horsemen's father. I played it off like he was way off base, but the truth is that I did fuck Lilith." He remembered how sweet she'd been. How delicate. How fucking good she was at deception. "It was Lilith who granted me my wish to be more empathic. She was the virgin."

Lilliana sat back hard against the back of the couch, as if her body would no longer support her.

"Oh...wow." Her hand clutched the blanket so tightly that her knuckles were white. "So that's how she became so powerful...powerful enough to trick Reaver into sleeping with her and fathering the Horsemen."

"Everything comes with a consequence. I took her virginity and got what I wanted, but I also set into motion the events that almost led to the Apocalypse. She absorbed many of my powers, turning her into the most powerful succubus to ever live. Then she seduced Reaver, and the Four Horsemen of the Apocalypse were born."

"Holy crap." Lilliana flopped onto her back, eyes wide and staring at the ceiling. "You know, my life has been very boring compared to yours."

Unexpectedly, he laughed, a flat-out, genuine laugh as he stretched out beside her once again.

It was then that he noticed it. His lungs seized and his body trembled, and it took forever for his brain to process the reality as he stared into the fire.

For the first time in thousands of years, he felt the warmth from the flames.

Chapter Twelve

It turned out that when someone informed you that they had deflowered the most infamous succubus in history and set off what would become major apocalyptic events, you shut down. At least, Lilliana did.

She'd lain there with Azagoth in surprisingly comfortable silence, her mind spinning with more questions. But eventually, she dozed off, and when she woke, Azagoth was gone. But fresh clothes had been laid out on the table next to the sofa, and next to the clothes was a tray containing a turkey sandwich, a bowl of fruit, an assortment of cheeses and crackers, and two decadent desserts. She decided she'd eat the caramel cheesecake first, and save the fudge truffle cake for last.

Whoever brought the food and clothes had also set out a pitcher of ice water, a pitcher of pomegranate juice, a bottle each of red and white wine, three different types of beer, two cans of cola, and a can of Sprite. Apparently, Azagoth wanted her to float out of here.

She looked around for the clothes he'd stripped off her, but they were gone, and a blast of heat bloomed in her cheeks at the memory. He'd been intense. Primal. A male drowning in a need he couldn't satiate without a female.

The moment she'd seen him suffering in emotion he couldn't

contain, all she could think about was making it better, and when the tension inside him had shifted from confusion and violence to sex, she hadn't hesitated. Not until the moment of truth, when it looked as if intercourse was imminent.

She'd panicked a little, not because she was a virgin, but because somehow joining with him like that would make things real between them, and she wasn't ready to go there. Not when she was still planning on leaving.

So it was probably a good thing he'd freaked about the virginity thing, but criminy, the reason for his spaz attack had blown her mind. He'd been seduced by the most infamous succubus in history. He'd *deflowered* the most infamous succubus in history.

Holy shit.

His actions had kicked off pretty much everything that had happened in the human, demon, and angelic worlds up until now. No wonder he'd taken this job. Even without the empathic curse that had driven him here, she'd bet he'd have volunteered anyway, purely out of guilt.

The overload of events and information from today turned her brain foggy, so she gave it a rest while she dressed and ate. The fudge truffle cake turned out to be almost as decadent as the orgasm Azagoth gave her, and she decided she definitely needed another piece later.

A piece of cake...or of Azagoth? Maybe she could have her cake and Azagoth too.

The thought made her blush as she finished eating, and then she went through his books for something to help her get the *chronoglass* out of here.

For the second time, the thought screamed through her in a blast of remorse.

Truly, Azagoth had been good to her. The big, scary Grim Reaper had done nothing but be nice. Oh, sure, he'd been a jackass at first, but then, she'd been a little hostile too. And to know that he'd been down here so long, unable to feel anything...it broke her heart.

Granted, being unable to feel was probably what kept him sane. Having to deal with evil twenty-four seven would make anyone who was sensitive to emotion crazy.

Several hours later, she'd found nothing helpful, and a small part of her was glad.

As she shoved the last book she'd thumbed through back onto a shelf, Cat poked her head through the doorway, and Lilliana jumped, startled by her own guilt. "I didn't mean to scare you," Cat said. "Can I bring you anything more to eat or drink?"

"Thank you, no." She studied the other woman, wondering just how intimate the relationship between them should be. Azagoth had hired her, but Lilliana could really use a friend down here.

Problem was, she didn't know how to go about it. She'd never had many friends. Time travelers had a tendency to illicit distrust in others. Lilliana's supervisor claimed it was because, deep down, others knew they wouldn't be able to resist the temptation to change history, and there was nothing angels hated more than reminders that they were so flawed.

Finally, Lilliana just threw it out there. "I was thinking about taking a walk. Would you like to join me?"

Cat grinned, flashing petite fangs that came standard issue for both Unfallen and True Fallen angels. "I'd be happy to."

"Really?" Lilliana blurted. "Why?"

Flames from the hearth cast an orange light on Cat's red hair, creating a gentle halo around her head, and for a moment, Lilliana could picture her as a full angel, her green eyes glinting with impish humor.

"I owe you and Azagoth for saving me," she said simply. "I like it here."

"You...*like* it?"

She nodded. "Very much. No one is hunting me, the *griminions* aren't bad once you get to know them, and Zhubaal is kind of hot."

Okie-dokie, then. They walked outside into the ever-present gray blah, and even though the chill in the air didn't bother her, she rubbed her arms. Everything outside of Azagoth's manor just *looked* cold and inhospitable.

"I've been exploring the surrounding buildings," she said to Cat. "They were once occupied, and there's a lot of stuff that was left behind."

"Who used to live here?"

"I have no idea," Lilliana said. "Azagoth has been a little tight-lipped."

"He's very odd. But in a good way," Cat added quickly. She said something else, but Lilliana's concentration had taken a sudden detour.

"Cat." She gripped the other female's shoulder, shutting her up. "Do you see that?"

Cat followed Lilliana's gaze to a patch of ground near the fountain in the center of the courtyard. "That's weird. Why would that one bit of land be—"

"Green," Lilliana whispered. "It's grass."

As they stood there, bright green blades of grass popped up, expanding outward, swallowing up the blackened earth as it went. When the grass reached a scraggly, leafless gray bush, color began to push up the thick, dead stems, and at the very tips of the branches, little pink buds popped out.

"What's going on?"

"Emotion," Lilliana breathed. "It makes sense. Azagoth said it himself. *I am Sheoul-gra.*" He'd said he'd been corrupted by evil, his emotions stripped away. And now, with his emotions starting to open up, his realm was reflecting that. Holy shit. "Where is he? I have to show him this."

Cat cringed. "He gave me a message for you. I forgot. I'm sorry I didn't tell you right away."

"It's okay." As she spoke, Lilliana couldn't take her eyes off of the transformation taking place in front of her. "What's the message?"

"He said he had to go to the Inner Sanctum. He didn't know when he'd be back."

Lilliana finally looked over at Cat. "Did he say why?"

"All I know is that a seriously yummy guy with a blue Mohawk came to visit, and they left together."

"Ah. That would be Hades." Too bad she hadn't been there to meet him. She was curious about the fallen angel who Azagoth had appointed as his Soul Keeper.

"*The* Hades?" Cat asked. "Wow. He's like a rock star. Does he come up from the Sanctum often?"

"I have no idea." Lilliana started walking, giving the new green patches a wide berth. Stepping on the fresh new life struck her as a jerk thing to do.

"Do you think Azagoth would let me see the Inner Sanctum?"

Lilliana jerked in surprise. "Why would you want to? By all accounts, it's a cesspool of suffering."

"I want to be reminded of why I want to earn my way back into Heaven."

Lilliana nearly tripped over her own feet. Overdosing on evil seemed like an extreme way to keep yourself on the straight and narrow path, but she supposed it was better than the alternative.

They wandered through the buildings Lilliana hadn't gotten to the other day. She'd planned to search for something to help with the *chronoglass*, but she was so curious about everything that searching for something specific took a backseat to simply exploring. They found classrooms complete with history books—human, demon, and angel. They found indoor and outdoor training and sports facilities. They even found what appeared to have been gardens. What *was* this place?

"This is such a waste," Cat said sadly. "These buildings were meant to be filled."

Yes, but with who? Or what?

Eventually, they made their way back to the main building, but Azagoth hadn't yet returned. Lilliana helped Cat cook dinner, and while they ate, Cat insisted that they watch a movie called *Magic Mike*. There hadn't been any magic, but *dayum*...Lilliana would never look at a male stripper the same way again.

As the credits rolled, Cat gathered their dinner plates. "I think I'm going to see if Zhubaal wants some company," she said with a sly smile that all but announced her lusty intent. "And maybe if you're lucky, Azagoth will be back soon."

Strangely, Lilliana hoped so. Not because the movie had pushed every one of her horny buttons, but because she was actually starting to like the guy.

He's an asshole father.

Okay, there was that. But what if he wasn't entirely to blame for whatever had gone down with Methicore? Now that she had a little distance, she could see a bit more clearly, and the guy had definitely struck her as a bit of an ass. But what could he have done to deserve the things his father had said to him?

Her own father's harsh words clanged in her ears as she showered and put on her nightgown and robe. Had she tried too hard to build a relationship with him? Had she not tried hard enough?

Frustrated by the questions she asked herself way too often, she shoved a pile of clean, folded clothes inside the wardrobe. The box holding the necklace Azagoth had given her tumbled out, and the shiny silver chain skittered across the floor.

Picking it up, she admired the delicate little key pendant and finely-wrought clasp. He'd given it to her with an order to wear it, but she hadn't, and he hadn't nagged her about it or gotten angry. But then, with his emotional void, she supposed he wouldn't have thrown a fit about it. Still, it had seemed important to him.

And it really was pretty...

She fastened it around her neck, and the cold silver warmed instantly on her skin.

As she climbed into bed, it didn't escape her notice that Azagoth's body did the same thing.

Chapter Thirteen

Azagoth hadn't come home last night.

Inexplicably irritated, because yeah, why *wouldn't* someone be upset about getting an uninterrupted night's sleep, Lilliana skipped breakfast and stormed into his office, expecting to find him there.

Nothing. The fire roared in the hearth and his computer was humming softly, but the soul tunnel was closed and Azagoth was nowhere to be found.

Even more annoyed now, she went to the library, but he wasn't there, either. Fine, she thought as she stared at the *chronoglass*. She should use it. Go someplace without Azagoth, just as he'd done.

But even as she thought it, she knew she wouldn't do it. In all her years of existence, she'd never seen such unfettered joy in anyone, and she'd certainly never given it. Being able to give someone a gift like that made her feel good. Really good.

The door burst open and over six and a half feet of dangerously handsome male strode into the library. Black military-style pants and a black turtleneck made Azagoth seem even larger, sleeker, and deadlier, but then, he'd never come across as anything less than one hundred percent lethal grace. Raw power radiated from him like heat from one of Sheoul's lava lakes.

His eyes smoldered as he took in her jeans and pink tank top, and she felt the blood rush to her face at the memory of the last time he'd looked at her like that.

It was yesterday, when he'd made her come, right here where she was standing.

"Morning."

"Yes," she grumbled. "It is."

He cocked a dark eyebrow. "Something wrong? Is Cat not working out? I can find someone else—"

"No!" she said quickly, and then dialed it back a little. "No. I like Cat."

"Then what's bothering you?"

She hesitated. At what point in their relationship should she start questioning his whereabouts? Her relationship with Hutriel had never reached that point. He'd blown his lid the first time she'd asked him why he was late for their dinner date, and after that, she'd only asked to piss him off. Which it did. Every single time.

"Lilliana?" he asked softly. "Are you going to tell me what's going on?"

Feeling a bit like a fishwife, she blurted, "Where have you been?"

"Didn't Cat tell you? I went to the Inner Sanctum with Hades."

"She told me," Lilliana assured him. He'd mentioned not being one for second chances, and she definitely didn't want to get Cat fired. "But I didn't expect you to be gone all night. Why did it take so long?"

His expression turned grave. "I had business to take care of."

"That's it? Just...business?"

"I'm the Grim Reaper, Lilli. I have business with demons sometimes."

Lilli. He'd called her that yesterday too, when she'd had her hand curled around his erection, her palm stroking the stiff length as he moaned in ecstasy.

"Fuck," he breathed. "Oh, damn...Lilli..."

No one had ever given her a nickname. Warmth suffused her, but she let herself linger on the name only for a moment before getting back to the subject at hand.

"What in the world can dead demons do for you?" she asked.

"Newly acquired demons have information I want and need. It's how I make bargains and find new souls to take. Trust me, you don't want details."

No doubt he was right. Still... "If I did want details, would you tell me?"

"Yes." He gave her a look that chilled her to the bone, and she knew for sure she didn't want to know the particulars of what he did with the souls. "But please don't ask."

You got it, buddy.

She wasn't sure where to go from there, but Azagoth seemed to have no such problem. He strode over to her, hauled her against him, and laid a kiss on her that had her melting into him like softened butter.

"I missed you," he whispered huskily against her lips. "All I could think about was getting back to you and finishing what we started here in the library. You made me feel, Lilli. For the first time in...fuck, I don't know, I felt something other than the cold."

Oh, yes, she felt it too, in the bulge nudging at her center. Instantly, her breasts grew heavy and a warm rush of wetness blossomed between her legs.

"Azagoth?" she murmured, as he kissed a hot path from her mouth to her ear. "Have you been outside?"

"No." He nibbled her earlobe and her knees nearly gave out. "Why?"

He didn't know about the new growth out there, the signs of hope that were sprouting out of the black ash of his realm. But it wasn't enough to tell him...she wanted to show him.

"No reason." She moaned as he traced the shell of her ear with his tongue. "Maybe we could take a walk?"

Pulling back, he looked down at her. "A walk? Here?" He jerked his head toward the *chronoglass*. "How about somewhere more interesting. Where to today?"

She hadn't actually thought about it. The last two journeys had been designed to thoroughly annoy him, but he'd been ecstatic. She no longer wanted to fool around like that. He deserved better.

"Maybe you should suggest a time and place," she offered. "Surely there's someplace you want to go."

With tenderness that shocked her even though he'd been nothing but gentle with her, he grazed a knuckle over her cheek. "I've been locked inside my realm for thousands of years. Anywhere you take me is going to be amazing."

She snorted. "Oh, I doubt that. London during the Black Death was a drag." Taking his hand, she guided him to the mirror. "Where do you want to go?"

"A beach," he said without hesitation. "On the Oregon coast. I've always wanted to see the tide pools." He squeezed her hand. "No, wait. Let's do that tomorrow. I feel like going somewhere tropical."

Ooh, tropical. She'd been a tropical waters girl since she'd tasted her first coconut. "I know just the place." An image appeared on the mirror's surface, blue waters and golden sand beckoning. Clinging tightly to Azagoth's hand, she stepped into the *chronoglass* and out into a sultry breeze.

Azagoth inhaled, and his entire body relaxed, as if the sun and air had drained every last drop of tension from him. "Where are we?"

"It's a private resort in the Caribbean." She gestured to the cliffs around them. "And this is a private alcove." Overhead, birds sailed on the currents, and in the distance, fish jumped out of the waves and made splashes as they hit the crystal water.

"It's perfect," Azagoth said. "If mortals come here, will they see us?"

"Nope. We're invisible to them. In reality, we are just as much here as they are, and we can manipulate objects. But when we do something that changes the world around them, their reality warps to fit our needs."

He kicked off his boots and sighed as his bare feet dug into the sand. "That makes no sense."

Time travel was complicated, with thousands of natural and mystical laws to fit every situation. It had taken her hundreds of years to learn just a fraction of them. She'd have to break her explanation down to the most basic level.

"Okay, let's say I take the last French fry off some guy's plate at Denny's. He either won't remember that there was a French fry there, or he'll believe he ate it. That's the angelic warp in action. Or maybe I steal someone's car. The angelic warp will wipe any witness memories away, and the owner of the car will report it stolen. But as long as I'm inside the vehicle, the angelic warp will keep it visible yet...unnoticeable...until I get out of the car. But that's exactly why we're supposed to be observers only, and we get in a lot of trouble if we mess with humans. The Powers That Be don't like human memories to be messed with unless absolutely necessary." Which was hilarious, given that The Powers That Be had no problem with messing with the memories of angels.

"Can humans ever see you?"

Her gut dove to her feet. "Yes. When you break out of the *shrowd.* That's why it's forbidden to the extreme."

"How does Heaven find out when it happens?"

"The second you break out, alarm bells shriek in the Time Travel Department. Approximately sixty seconds later, a team of angels will flash to the location of the breakout, and if the offending angel is still there, they either kill the responsible party or arrest them. Depends on the circumstances. Obviously, this doesn't happen very often."

He bent to pick up a shell, and she unabashedly ogled his backside. "How many times has it happened since you've been time traveling? I mean, besides you."

"What?" Damn, he had a fine ass. "Oh, right...just once." Except she *was* the once.

He rubbed his thumb over the shell's smooth curves, and her breasts tingled, as if they wanted in on that action. "What happened to him?"

"It was a her. And her fate is still up in the air." She pointed to a massive vessel on the ocean horizon. "There's a cruise ship. I could take you on one of those sometime. They have the most incredible lavish buffets, bars, activities, and ship-borne viruses."

"Sounds delightful."

She loved his understated sense of humor. "You know what would be delightful? Cocktails. Hold on." She flashed to a nearby beach bar and used a frowned-upon but not forbidden trick of planting a suggestion in the bartender's ear. A few minutes later, she was flashing away with two Mai Tais, complete with little umbrellas.

But when she materialized on the beach where she'd left him, she found only a pile of clothing. Then she heard splashing.

It was all she could do to not roll her tongue out like a welcome mat when she saw Azagoth naked and hip deep in the surf, his face turned to the sun and his hands dragging through his wet hair. Holy mother of hotness, he was sex on legs. If there had been people here—and they could see him—he'd have every woman on the beach drooling.

As it was, the only drooling going on was coming from Lilliana.

She watched him dive into a wave, his sinuous body barely rippling the surface as he arched like a dolphin. His long, muscular legs and spectacular ass glinted in the sunlight before disappearing into the ocean. He surfaced a few yards out, laughing in pure, unadulterated pleasure.

Lilliana had spent her entire life in Heaven amongst angels with a zest for living, but she'd never seen anyone come alive the way Azagoth did every time they passed through the *chronoglass*. It was as if he was a different person, and Lilliana really, really liked that person.

"Come on, angel!" he called out. "Water's great!"

"Nuh-uh," she teased, holding up the drinks. "Ice'll melt. Guess I'll have to drink them both."

She took the tips of both straws between her lips, and in an instant, Azagoth was in front of her, naked, dripping water, and gloriously aroused.

"If you really want to suck on something..." He waggled his brows, and she rolled her eyes, but the truth was that she enjoyed this playful side of him, and she loved that it brought out the playful side of her, too.

It was becoming harder and harder to think about leaving.

Shoving those thoughts into the back of her mind, she thrust Azagoth's drink at him. "Suck that, Soul Boy."

He narrowed his eyes. "Did you just call *me*, the Grim Fucking Reaper, *Soul Boy*?"

"I did," she teased. "What are you going to do about it?"

His voice became a low purr. "I do think I'll have to spank you."

A shiver of unabashed want trekked up her spine. "Promise?"

Three days ago, she wouldn't have believed she'd be flirting with Azagoth. Heck, she wouldn't have believed she'd be flirting with anyone. Hutriel had been too serious for flirting, and she'd been too busy since they'd broken up to even think about seeing anyone else.

"Mmm." His noncommittal response left her practically squirming with uncertain anticipation.

Azagoth's gaze never left her face as his lips closed on the straw. He sucked down the drink, his Adam's apple bobbing with each swallow. When he'd drained every last drop, he tossed the empty glass to the ground and stepped into her.

"Swim with me." His hand came up to her throat, and then froze. "My necklace," he murmured. "You're wearing it."

"It's beautiful."

His eyes darkened with emotion so pure and powerful that she felt it wrap around her heart like a warm blanket. "You honor me by wearing it by choice, not by command," he said softly. "But you don't have to wear it."

Her hand shook as she rested it on his. "I wanted to."

A rough, primitive sound rolled like thunder from inside his chest. His mouth came down hard on hers, and she met him with equal aggression, tangling her tongue with his and nipping at his lips.

As if a dam had broken, need flooded her body, swift and urgent. She'd known lust before, but this was wild, the kind she'd thought might actually be a myth.

She lifted her thigh to his hip and arched her sex against his. She just needed to get out of these pesky clothes—

Abruptly, the hair on the back of her neck stood up and a shrieking alarm clanged around inside her skull.

Oh, shit.

They weren't alone.

Chapter Fourteen

The vibration that skittered over Azagoth's skin was almost orgasmic. In Sheoul-gra, evil was everywhere, permeating everything so thoroughly that unless a being was off-the-charts evil, he barely noticed.

But here in the human realm, evil stood out like a hell stallion in a herd of donkeys.

Reluctantly, he pulled away from Lilliana and turned to meet the source of the malevolent vibes.

Two fallen angels, both looking like they'd stepped out of a *Mad Max* movie, were walking toward them, their crude leather armor streaked with dried blood, their hands wrapped around sharp, wicked-looking swords. Teeth, bones, and scalps hung from their belts, and he didn't even want to know what was stuck between their teeth and crusted to their boots.

These were true killers, fallen angels so corrupted by darkness that murder was all they lived for. He didn't know what made some fallen angels turn into mindless beasts, but he encountered their type every once in a while when they came through his soul tunnel. They were defiant, antagonistic, and they scoffed when he threatened to send them to the worst places in the Inner Sanctum.

Later, much later, when Azagoth went to check up on their misery, they were different people. The information they willingly spewed had given him some of his greatest blackmail material.

Next to him, he felt Lilliana charge up her powers, but he could already tell that these two fucktwats coming toward them were stronger than she was. No problem, because he was going to take them apart in a matter of—

A lightning bolt slammed down in a surge of light, and the fallen angel on the left lit up like a neon sign. His scream joined the crash of the surf and the calls of the seabirds overhead. Stunning ruby-tipped black wings sprouted from Lilliana's back, arching high against the blue sky as she threw her hand out, sending another strike that knocked the enemy to the ground, his skin reddened and steaming.

Azagoth grinned. His female was a warrior. Time to finish off these fucks and have some victory sex.

"Okay, boys," he growled. "Time to die."

He let loose a barrage of fire bombs...at least, he tried to. The weakly little sparks died before they got ten feet from his fingertips. What the hell—

The non-crisped fallen angel snarled, and suddenly, Lilliana was slammed by an invisible force so powerful that she hit the rocky cliff thirty yards behind her. Blood spattered on the stones, and she crumpled to the sand in a broken lump.

Rage burned Azagoth's throat like he'd swallowed burning tar, and with a roar, he let out the beast he'd become, the thing that hid beneath his skin. As his bones popped and his features contorted, the fallen angel that attacked Lilliana streaked toward her, his gore-crusted weapon raised.

"No!" Azagoth's voice, so warped that he didn't recognize it, didn't faze the bastard.

Power sang through Azagoth as his wings erupted from his back. He shot into the air and came down on top of the fallen angel, his black, serrated talons ripping into the guy's flesh with the ease of a spoon through gelato.

A weapon struck him, and pain blasted through his chest, but he ignored it as he snapped his jaws closed on one thick arm. The limb tore away with a satisfying rip, and the fallen angel's scream was absolute music.

He lost himself to the sounds, tastes, and smells of the

battle...until he heard another fight taking place. Out of the corner of his eye, he saw the fried fallen angel engaged in combat with Lilliana. Her summoned fire sword was holding up against the fallen angel's elemental staff, but Azagoth wasn't taking any chances.

With a final roar, he stabbed his claws through the guy's rib cage. The dude's scream came out gurgled as his blood filled his mouth. Tightening his grip, Azagoth yanked his hands apart, ripping the fallen angel in half.

At the same time, he raised his scaly tail and aimed the poisonous bone spur at the tip at the charred son of a bitch. As Crispy swung his staff at Lilliana's head, Azagoth struck. The tail spike skewered the fallen angel at the base of the skull, piercing the brain stem and delivering a lethal dose of toxin into his nervous system.

If the physical trauma didn't kill him, the poison would.

Crispy fell to the ground, body spasming, mouth open in a silent scream as white foam boiled out of his throat.

Awesome.

Lilliana stood there, eyes wide as she stared at the two dead fallen angels. They went even wider when she finally got a load of Azagoth. Her fear was palpable, shivering through him as if it was his own. Just days ago, he'd have been ecstatic to feel her emotions, no matter what they were, simply because he hadn't felt anything at all in so damned long.

But he hated that he was scaring her, and for the first time since becoming the Grim Reaper, he felt shame.

"I'm sorry," he said, his voice smoky and rough as it cleared his massive jaws and teeth. "It takes a few minutes to turn back."

She swallowed. Nodded. And then she made her summoned sword and wings disappear.

"It's okay," she breathed. "But I gotta say, you are one scary-ass bastard."

"You say the sweetest things," he rumbled.

She dropped her gaze to the dead fallen angels. "You really don't mess around, do you?"

He grinned, and then quickly hid it, because in this dragon-demon mash-up form, a grin was probably terrifying. "The beauty of all of this is that I get to see their souls again when they come through my tunnel later."

As if on cue, *griminions* materialized from out of nowhere and streaked to the bodies, which had just started to disintegrate.

"Hey, fellas," he said. "Feel free to play with these bastards while you're waiting for me to open the tunnel."

Their excited chatter sounded like squirrels on crack. They were cute little buggers sometimes.

He watched as the souls of the fallen angels rose out of their rapidly decaying bodies, only to be shackled by the *griminions* and ushered away in a poof of gray smoke. Their screams lingered in the air a little while longer.

"Did you see that?" he asked. "That was cool." Lilliana looked at him like he was crazy. "What? I've never seen souls rise and my *griminions* show up for the harvest. I'm always on the receiving end of the soul reaping."

Lilliana grimaced. "Let me repeat the scary-ass bastard thing." She held out her hand as if to touch him. "May I?"

He shrugged, making his twelve-foot leather wings flap in the breeze. Tentatively, Lilliana skimmed her fingers over the scaly skin of his forearm, and a strange rumble he'd never heard bubbled up from his skeletal chest. It took a moment to figure out what it was.

A purr. He was purring.

Lilliana didn't seem to be disturbed by the noise in the least, and if anything, she'd moved closer, was now running her hand up his arm to his shoulder.

"Is this okay?" she asked softly? "I'm not hurting you or anything, am I?"

"Hurting...*me*?" He stared down at her in amazement. He could bite her head off right now, before she could even blink, and she was worried that her sensual touch was hurting him?

"Well, you do have blood on you."

"It's not mine." The initial injury he'd taken from the non-crispy fallen angel had healed already, leaving only a thin, foot-long scar across his torso. In another five minutes, even that would be gone.

"Good," she murmured. "Can you change into this form at will?"

"Yes. But it comes out on its own when I'm angry." Not that he was angry often, given his numbness to emotions. But his inner beast took advantage of even mild anger now and then. "It came out this time because I don't seem to have any powers in this realm."

"It's the *shrowd*," she said. "Only angels with the ability to time travel can use their powers here."

"You could have mentioned that earlier," he muttered.

"Sorry," she said, even though she sounded anything but contrite as she explored the corded tendons in his neck.

He closed his eyes, marveling at the sensation of a female touching him so...reverently. Sweet, savage hell, that felt good. Between the jacked-up high of the battle and Lilliana's feathery touch, a lance of lust shot through him.

And then, to his abject horror, his cock got interested in everything Lilliana was doing. With a hiss, he spun around, desperately trying to will his body to shift back.

"Azagoth?" Her hand came down between his shoulder blades, in the sensitive expanse just below his wings. "Are you okay?"

"Just...give me a minute."

Her hand fell away, and for a long, painful moment, he thought he'd offended her. But then she strode past him on her way toward the surf. A few feet away, she looked back over her shoulder with an impish smile on her face.

"I'm going swimming. Join me if you want to." She stripped as she walked, shedding clothes in a trail on the sand, and he was panting before her feet hit the water.

Suddenly, he didn't give a shit what he looked like. He needed that female, and he needed her now.

* * * *

Lilliana had only gone shin-deep in the water when she heard a whoosh and a splash behind her. Turning, she faced Azagoth, still in his beast form.

Damn, he was scary. At least two feet taller and a hundred pounds heavier than his usual form, he was the epitome of what humans would call a demon. From his massive, elongated jaws and serrated talons, to the black horns that jutted from his forehead and curled up over his skull, he was the stuff of nightmares.

No doubt he'd become those fallen angels' worst nightmare. And to make it all worse, they couldn't escape him in the afterlife, either. She almost felt sorry for them.

Almost. One of them could have been the bastard who'd killed her mother. So if Azagoth wanted to spend weeks in the Inner Sanctum with them, she was okay with that.

It occurred to her that she was thinking into the future, but this time, she couldn't get worked up about it. Not now. Not with this magnificent creature in front of her.

Azagoth's deep chest was heaving as he stared at her with intense, red eyes, and she probably should have been terrified, but after the initial shock of seeing him like this wore off, she'd been fascinated. He was beautiful in the way a cobra was, sleek and graceful, primitive and deadly.

He was also very, very turned on.

She tried not to stare. She really did. But Azagoth The Sleek and Deadly was sporting a baseball bat between his legs. Morbid curiosity made her want to touch it, to see if she could close both hands around the thickness.

"I can feel the change starting to happen," he rumbled. "So if there's anything you want to...explore...now's the time."

Oh, what the hell. This wasn't a stranger. It was Azagoth, even if he didn't look like he usually did, and if she was even *considering* staying with him, she had to accept all of him.

Stepping closer, she took his length into her hands. He hissed in pleasure as she gently stroked the ebony head and feathered her fingers down the rigid shaft. Sweet mother of sin, he was huge, so thick around that the tips of her thumbs and fingers barely met as she grasped him in both hands. When she reached the base of the smooth column, she dipped one hand lower, to his scrotum, and yup, there were the baseballs to match the bat.

"You're, um, well endowed," she whispered, her tongue so dry she could barely speak. Probably because all of her moisture had gone south, and even as her mouth dried up, her sex became soaked.

Was she really turned on by this? Her aching breasts and throbbing pelvis said yes.

Azagoth's big body trembled, and as she watched, his form crumpled in on itself until he was back in his usual form, panting, his eyes wild.

He stumbled back, averting her gaze, and alarm rang through her.

"Azagoth?" She moved toward him, but he turned away, leaving her to stare at his bare back. "What's wrong?"

"No one...no one has ever touched me like that."

"I can't believe no one has touched your penis."

He inhaled raggedly. "No, I mean, no one has touched *me* like that. Not in my demon form. Weren't you afraid I'd hurt you?"

"Why would I be? You were *you* in there. You weren't some mindless beast." She laid her hand on his shoulder. "Am I wrong? When you're in that form, can't you control yourself?"

His muscles flexed under her palm. "I'm in complete control unless I'm killing. But even then, my focus is limited to the one I'm fighting."

"See? That's why I wasn't afraid to touch you."

"But this is what thousands of years of corruption has done to me. I'm hideous."

"Not to me," she said softly.

He moved in a blur. One second he was staring at the sand, and the next, he was pressed against her, his arms wrapped around her back and shoulders, his hands digging into her hair. His lips came down on hers in a fierce, hot meeting of mouths.

"Lilli," he whispered, "thank you."

She had no idea what he was thanking her for, and it didn't matter. At this moment, she needed everything he could give her. It was as if she couldn't bear another second without him inside her.

Throwing her arms around his shoulders, she lifted herself up so her thighs wrapped around his waist and his sex rubbed against her core. He groaned into her mouth, the very male sound of need reverberating all the way to her breasts.

Arching, she used her entire body to stroke him, her sex grinding against his, her breasts rubbing over the smooth skin of his chest, her belly creating hot friction against his abs. Dear, sweet

Lord, she was going to come right here, right now.

He took her down to the wet sand, where tiny waves lapped at her skin as he positioned himself over her. This was different than it had been in the library, when he'd been wracked with emotion he couldn't control. Now he was using his cool self-restraint to devastating effect, kissing and nibbling down her neck as he rocked slowly between her legs, his shaft sliding between her folds in languid thrusts.

She clung to him, digging her nails into his shoulders as he dragged his mouth lower to kiss her breasts and lave the stiff peaks with his tongue. Closing his mouth over one, he sucked, drawing upward with such delicious pressure that she groaned and arched, seeking more and at the same time, thinking it was way too much.

"I love how you respond to me," he murmured against her skin. "I love the sounds you make. The way you smell." He pushed her breasts together and licked up the deep valley between them. "The way you taste."

A gentle wave pushed between their bodies, lapping at the hot place where their bodies met, and she groaned again.

"If we had time, I'd lick you everywhere," he said, giving each breast a kiss. "But I can do that later."

She couldn't wait, but he was right. They had only minutes now, and she was anxious to feel him deep inside her, to know what his weight would feel like as he pumped against her.

"Please," she whispered. "I'm so ready." A sudden thought popped into her lust-soaked brain, and she gripped him fiercely. "Protection?"

He dragged his tongue up between her breasts. "I can turn my fertility on and off." He gave her a cocky smile. "It's one of the advantages of being me."

"Very handy," she admitted before giving his hair a playful tug. "Now, show me some more advantages."

"You got it." Reaching between their bodies, he guided his cockhead to her entrance. "This will hurt, sweetheart," he said. "But only for a second." He planted a gentle kiss on her lips. "If I could bear it for you, I would."

Tears stung her eyes. How could a male with such a fierce reputation be so caring? Azagoth was constantly surprising her, and she wondered how many more he had in store for her.

"I'm pretty tough," she croaked.

"That," he said softly, "is very clear."

He brought his thumb to his mouth and dragged his tongue across the tip before returning his hand between their bodies again. She felt a light, buzzing stroke over her clit, and she sighed with pleasure.

His thumb circled the pulsing nub as he pushed his penis against her opening. Sensation burst through her pelvis, making her dizzy with need. The pain came then, sharp and searing as he slammed his hips forward, breaking her barrier and filling her so full she thought she'd die.

But almost instantly the pain was gone, replaced by pleasure so wondrous she gasped.

Azagoth froze, his arms trembling. "I'm sorry," he rasped. "Are you okay?"

"Oh, yes," she said. "This is incredible."

"It only gets better." Dipping his head, he kissed her throat.

Then he began to move, and she nearly screamed at the ecstasy. Oh, dear Lord, this was exquisite. Every time he nearly pulled out, she tensed up, afraid of losing that amazing feeling of fullness. Every time he thrust deep again, she clenched, as if doing so would keep him there.

"You're so...fucking...tight," he ground out. "And you keep...ah, yes, squeeze me harder...fuck, yeah."

"Azagoth," she breathed. "More. I need more."

She felt him smile against her neck. "So do I, baby. So do I."

He picked up his speed, pumping harder and faster, until she was sliding forward with each thrust. All around them, the tiny waves lapped at their bodies, licking between her legs in her most sensitive spots, until it felt as though Azagoth's cock and tongue were both working her in sync with his thumb.

Groaning, she rolled her hips to take him even deeper, to get him moving faster...anything to ignite the climax building at her core.

It came in a detonation of ecstasy so intense she saw lights behind her eyes as her consciousness practically exploded from her body. She might as well have been shooting through time and space.

Azagoth lifted his head to stare into her eyes as he held himself above her, his body flexing and surging, the sunlight glinting off the fine sheen of sweat and seawater coating his skin.

"Mine," he growled, the tendons in his neck straining with each word. "You. Are. Mine."

His words triggered another orgasm, and she screamed as it took her even harder than the first one. Throwing back his head, he joined her with a feral shout that was surely heard in the Heavens. He drove into her with such power and erotic savagery that she left a deep groove in the sand as he propelled them forward, but she didn't care. Her climax kept her spiraling out of control, mindless with pleasure.

Finally, he jerked, his body spasming as the last of his hot jets spilled inside her.

Now she knew the reason she'd held on to her virginity. It might not have been a conscious thing, and maybe it was even fate. But whatever had kept her virginity intact, she now understood why.

She was meant for Azagoth.

Chapter Fifteen

Azagoth hated that they had to return to his realm. Especially just seconds after the best sex he'd ever had. He'd barely withdrawn from Lilli's wet heat when the pull of the *chronoglass* dragged them back into the cold darkness of Sheoul-gra.

But this time, the well of emotional turmoil didn't writhe out of control like before. This time, he was able to grasp each one and wrestle it into submission as he wrapped Lilliana in a blanket and carried her to his shower, where he spent half an hour washing her.

And another half an hour making love to her on one of the benches.

He loved listening to her come. Loved tasting her as she orgasmed in his mouth over and over. And when he'd entered her again, it had been like the whole world was right.

For the first time since creating his realm, it now truly felt like home.

Even better, the necklace he'd given her hadn't been needed. Oh, it was still beautiful on her delicate, creamy skin, but its true purpose hadn't played a role at all.

When he'd decided he wanted a mate, he'd been concerned that he and the female would need an emotional connection, something he couldn't give her, nor she him. So he'd had the jewelry special made to operate within Sheoul-gra to transmit thoughts and emotions from his mate to him. He'd hoped he could feel her. Understand her.

All of that was happening naturally, and damn if that wasn't a miracle.

"I have a surprise for you, Soul Boy." Lilliana said as she slipped her feet into flip-flops. She'd chosen a pair of shin-length white pants and a bright orange T-shirt, all of which would have been perfect for the beach earlier. He wondered if she was still basking in the tropical glow.

Because he sure as hell was.

"I like surprises," he said. "Good ones."

Smiling, she took his hand and led him out of the bedroom. "It's a good one."

He let her lead him outside the palace and onto the stone steps. "Where are we going—" He broke off with a breathless gasp.

The landscape had transformed. It still looked like a nuclear blast had devastated the area, but signs of rebirth and recovery were everywhere. Green grass was punching up through the blackened soil, and colorful buds were sprouting from tree branches that were no longer gnarled and as dark as licorice. The pulsing vines climbing the buildings had withered and died, replaced by grape vines that were spreading even as he stood there.

He stood, speechless, as a breeze, something he'd not experienced here in centuries, brought a light floral scent with it. He couldn't remember the last time the air out here had smelled of anything but decay.

"How," he croaked. "How did you do this?"

"I didn't. I think it's connected to your emotions. As you start feeling them, your realm is reflecting that."

Of course. The place had died as he'd grown more and more corrupted by evil, until there was nothing left. His domain had been as dead as he was, but now that he could feel life pulsing inside him once again, the world around him was feeling it too.

But Lilliana was wrong on one point. "You did do this, Lilli," he said, as he framed her face in his palms. "Without you, this wouldn't be happening. This *is* your doing."

Lowering his mouth to hers, he kissed her softly, drinking in the sweetness that was Lilli's soft, welcoming lips.

"Thank you," he murmured. "You've brought more to my world in a few days than anyone has given me in a lifetime."

She went taut, and he was about to ask what was wrong when the sound of a clearing throat interrupted his thoughts.

"My lord."

"Dammit, Zhubaal—"

"It's Hades," Zhubaal said from where he stood on the temple's bottom step. "He has another situation."

Fuck. Ever since Azagoth had authorized the reincarnation of Lucifer's soul—at Satan's insistence—things in the Inner Sanctum had been chaos. Now every fallen angel wanted to be reincarnated, born as an *emim*—the non-winged but still powerful offspring of two fallen angels. The demon souls in the Inner Sanctum were antsy, sensing Lucifer's coming birth, something that could affect all of the realms...demon, human, and Heavenly...in game-changing ways.

The doors at the top of the stairs blasted open, and Hades strode out, his face and bare chest streaked with blood. His seizure-inducing color-shifting pants were oddly clean, but his boots were covered in stuff Azagoth didn't want to guess at. His blue Mohawk was pristine, though. The dude never let anything mess up his hair.

"Did he tell you?" Hades growled. "Riots. I'm dealing with riots. I think it's time you went Grim Reaper on a few asses."

"I'm sorry, Lilli," he sighed. "I have to go."

"Duty calls." She smiled sadly, and he shouldn't be thrilled by that, but he was. She was sorry to see him go. How great was that? Most people would sell their souls to get him out of their lives. Literally.

"I'll be back soon," he swore. He'd take care of whatever Hades was whining about, and afterward...there was something he needed to do. With his emotions coming back online, he wanted to connect with his children. Oh, thanks to Methicore, seeing any of them in person would be impossible...for now. But the bastard couldn't take away his ability to care for them, and maybe even to love them.

Because now he knew he could love. Knew it for sure.

He was in love with Lilliana.

Chapter Sixteen

Two days passed without Azagoth. Two days in which Lilliana did nothing but worry. She'd done her best to keep busy, helping Cat with cooking, reading in the library, and her favorite, tending to the new plant growth outside.

Not once did she try to find a way to get the *chronoglass* out of Sheoul-gra. She figured she still had three weeks to decide if she was truly staying, and when it came down to it, she simply didn't want to think about leaving. Without the *chronoglass*, returning to the Heavenly realm would end in a life of lobotomized misery. With it, she could continue with the life she'd had, but really, what kind of life was that? She'd been busy but lonely. Happy but not content.

Could she be content here?

And where in the hell was Azagoth, anyway? Should she be worried? She didn't think he could be in any danger, but suddenly, a million scenarios spun through her head, many involving hostile takeovers in the Inner Sanctum. Azagoth was the ultimate power down here, but what if Hades and all of the demons trapped in the Sanctum rose up against him? Could he be held prisoner? Maybe even killed?

Okay, so now she'd gotten herself into a panic, and when Zhubaal passed her in the hallway as she was on her way to Azagoth's office, she grabbed his arm.

"Has Azagoth returned?"

Zhubaal snarled at her. "How should I know?"

"Isn't it your job to keep track of him?"

He yanked out of her grip. "He doesn't always inform me of every move he makes."

"Can you at least tell me if he's okay?"

"Of course he's okay." Impatience dripped from his voice. "He's Azagoth."

Zhubaal was really ill-tempered. She hoped Cat didn't get involved with him. "Does he go away like this a lot?"

"Sometimes."

So not an answer. "Okay, let's try this. Why is he there? What's going on?"

"It's not my place to share."

"Yeah? Well, he's my mate, so you *will* share."

A slow, sinister smile spread across his face. "You truly want to know?"

"No," she snapped, her patience worn out, "I asked because I don't want to know. What are you not telling me?"

His smile grew broader. "He went to the Inner Sanctum to visit a lover."

"What?" Her heart clenched. "Why?"

"Why does anyone visit a lover?"

Instant, crushing hurt left her dazed and sick to her stomach. "I don't believe you," she croaked.

He shrugged. "Ask him yourself when he gets back. Her name is Rhona."

Spinning around like he couldn't wait to get away from her, he took off, leaving her shaking with rage and jealousy. After all she and Azagoth had been through, after his assurances that she'd changed his life and helped him, he could do this to her?

He's Azagoth. He's evil. What the hell did you expect?

No, this was wrong. Zhubaal was lying. He was, after all, a fallen angel, and everything that came out of their mouths was suspect.

Still, tears stung her eyes as she jogged toward Azagoth's office. She had to see him. Had to find out if there was a way to get into the Inner Sanctum. Maybe a *griminion* could help.

But as she passed the entry to the great hall, she caught movement out of the corner of her eye.

Doubling back, she peeked through the doorway. Relief flooded her when she saw Azagoth standing in front of a huge stone she'd thought was a weird piece of boring art. But now it was transparent, its surface flickering like a TV screen.

A spy stone. Interesting. The things were fairly common, but few had the power to use them. She should have known Azagoth would be one of the few.

Frowning, she inched closer. What was he watching? There appeared to be a beach in the background, and as the screen narrowed and focused, a female in a skimpy swimsuit leaped for a volleyball.

The female, a curvy redhead, sent the ball sailing back over the net. She landed gracefully, her perky breasts bouncing all over the place and drawing every male eye around. Azagoth smiled, and Lilliana's throat burned. With a wave of his hand, the picture changed, this time focusing on a dark-haired female in tight yoga pants and a sports bra as she jogged through what looked like Central Park in New York City.

Azagoth's smile grew wider, and Lilliana's throat burned more. He reached out, touched his finger to the female's face, the reverence in his expression leaving Lilliana flushing miserably.

Suddenly, the picture went blank, and he strode off toward his office. Must be a bigwig soul coming through the portal. Lilliana wondered what kind of baddie was bad enough to drag him away from the females he'd been lusting after.

The bastard.

Irrational rage such as she'd never felt before, not even when her kidnapper threatened and abused her, singed the edges of her control. As if flames were searing her from the inside, she exploded in a fury that blackened her vision and her thoughts.

With a snarl, she rushed forward on a collision course with the stone. She hit it with her shoulder with as much force as she could muster. The thing tilted, teetered, and started to right itself.

"No!" Azagoth's furious voice startled her, but she'd committed, and now she was going to finish her mission.

She shoved the stone before it fell back into place, and with a crash, it hit the floor and shattered into a million pieces. A godawful roar echoed through the room, vibrating the air and making every statue, every portrait, tremble. Even the floor beneath her feet bucked, throwing her off balance as she raced toward the exit.

She didn't make it.

An icy hand clamped around the back of her neck, and suddenly she was being slammed onto the ground. As the stone floor came at her face, everything went black.

* * * *

Lilliana came to lying on the couch in Azagoth's office. He was sitting across from her in his desk chair, forearms braced on his knees, head hanging loosely on his slumped shoulders.

"Why did you do that?" he asked, his voice softer than she would have expected.

Azagoth had spread a blanket over her, and as she scooched into a sit, she shoved it away, not wanting any of his kindness right now. "You swore you wanted me."

"I do." He was still looking down between his spread knees, his tone even and showing no signs of anger.

Was he truly calm, or was he simply back to being unable to feel emotion? If the latter, he could be on the verge of killing her and she wouldn't know until it was over and she was nothing but a soul waiting to be reaped.

Or turned into one of his stone statues.

She shuddered. "If you want me," she shot back, "then why did you go to the Inner Sanctum to see a lover? And why were you looking at other females?"

His head came up sharply, his green eyes blazing. "A lover? You mean Rhona? Did Zhubaal tell you that?" At her nod, he cursed. "She hasn't been my lover for over a century. She seduced Methicore, and he killed her for it. I went to see her to get information."

Abruptly, Lilliana felt nauseous. If he was telling the truth, she'd just made a huge fool of herself.

Holding her stomach, as if that would stop the rolling that

threatened to spill her breakfast, she asked, "What about the females you were watching in the stone?"

"They were my daughters," he said roughly. "That stone is—*was*—the only way I could see what was happening in my childrens' lives."

Oh...oh, shit.

Her breath came raw and scorching in her throat. "I thought...I thought you didn't care about them. Methicore said—"

"Methicore is a bastard who coveted what I have," he snapped. "This place used to be teeming with life, but he ruined it all."

This place? She'd known it used to be green and full of creatures, but...she inhaled a sharp breath. "Your outbuildings...someone used to live there."

"Your powers of observation are unsurpassed," he drawled.

Ignoring the well-deserved sarcasm, she continued. "You said you built them to create a unity of sorts with the human world. But you built them for people, didn't you? Who?"

"Memitim." A blast of cold came from him, and she tugged the blanket over her again, not because she was cold, but because she needed a shield between them, even if it was just a flimsy piece of flannel. "For any who wanted to stay here."

"You let them live here?"

"Let them? I *wanted* them here. They don't have the powers normal angels have, and they can't live in Heaven until they've Ascended to become full angels, so they're vulnerable to demons in the human realm. I gave them a safe place to live and to train for their duties."

"Then why did they leave?"

"Rebellion." Reaching over to his desk, he swiped the ever-present bottle of rum off a stack of papers. "I gave them sanctuary. A place to gather in safety and prepare for their eventual Ascension. I'd intended for Methicore to become my apprentice, to take over Sheoul-gra one day."

She blinked. "But you're immortal. You don't have to give this up."

He laughed bitterly. "Give this up? Really? Do you think I like being isolated? Would you want to spend all eternity alone?" He took a swig from the bottle and then heaved it into the fireplace. It shattered, the alcohol exploding in a massive *whoosh.* "I wanted out. That's why I've spent my entire time down here trading in information and death. I figured that eventually I'd find someone with the knowledge to get me what I wanted." His expression became a mask of rage through which she saw flickers of his inner beast. "Then, a few centuries ago, Methicore decided he wanted to overthrow me. He and hundreds of his brothers and sisters tried to kill me. Turned out they would rather rule this realm than play guardian to humans who need them."

She couldn't even begin to understand how it felt to be betrayed by your children like that. Especially after he'd offered them a safe place to live and gather as a family. What a bunch of ingrates. She'd have given anything to have a family.

"Not all of them rebelled," he continued. "A handful stuck around to serve in this realm until a few years ago, when the first Horseman's Seal broke. It was chaos for them then. Their assigned humans were all in danger, and they were too busy to return to this realm. Many died. None came back. What little life was left here died."

Now Lilliana felt suddenly chilled, and she gathered the blanket more snugly around her. "None?"

"One of my daughters, Idess, visits, but only when there's an urgent matter. I can only hope that Methicore's plan to keep everyone away won't extend to her. She gave up her angel status to be with a Seminus demon mate, so Memitim rules shouldn't apply."

"You really love your children," she murmured.

He looked at her with bloodshot eyes. "I didn't," he said in a strained voice. "I felt mild affection for them. Until now. Until you unlocked the box of emotions I thought was sealed tight. Now I love them." He picked up a jagged piece of rock, and with horror she realized that it was a chunk of the spying stone she'd broken. "And now I'll never see them again."

Oh...God. She swallowed, desperate to keep breakfast down. "You can get another stone, right?" Her voice was shaky, hollow, shot to hell.

"Yes, but they only work to spy on those who have given their permission. By now, Methicore has probably poisoned them all against me."

"I'm sorry," she whispered. "I'm so sorry. I've never felt jealousy before, and I didn't know how to handle it. That's not an excuse, I know, but please believe me when I say I'm sorry." She took a deep breath and met his gaze, desperate to make him see her regret. "And I'm very sorry that I judged you as a father. I think I carried my issues over to you."

He narrowed his eyes. "Your issues?"

"My father...he was..." She started to say, "Like you," but Chaniel was nothing like Azagoth. "He was a sperm donor. Nothing more. After my mother died, he wouldn't have anything to do with me. The bastard left me to be raised an orphan at the battle angel academy."

"He what?" Azagoth's jaw clenched so hard she heard bone pop. "I hope he has since pleaded for your forgiveness. And that you told him to fuck off."

She almost laughed at that. No way she'd have told him off. She'd have taken any scrap he'd have given her. "He refuses to see me."

Azagoth's eyes sparked crimson. "He doesn't deserve to be a father. He wouldn't deserve even a viewing stone."

The reminder of the stone she'd broken made his expression go hard and flat again, and she shoved to her feet, prepared to fall to her knees and beg his forgiveness if that's what it took. "Azagoth—"

"Don't." He bounded from his chair and away from her. "I can't deal with you right now."

He might as well have driven a stake through her heart, that's how badly his words hurt. "Do you want me to leave?" she asked, before realizing he didn't know she had a thirty-day window.

"Even if you could, no." He smiled sadly. "I told you I want you, and that hasn't changed. If anything, I want you even more. You're all I have left." He backed up, lifting his hands in an almost defensive gesture. "But stay away from me. Just for now."

With that, he slammed out of the office, and that's when she lost it.

So much for breakfast.

Chapter Seventeen

Lilliana paced across the twenty-foot diameter pentagram at the base of the portal out of Sheoul-gra, trying to work off the events of yesterday and the sleepless night alone in the giant bed, with reminders of other females all around her in Azagoth's sex furniture. Without him there, all she could think about was how he'd used each and every item, and how she'd yet to banish those ghosts from the bedroom.

Now it might be too late.

Azagoth had disappeared after leaving her in his office, and according to Zhubaal, he'd gone to visit his "lover" again.

She'd punched him. Right in the nose. She'd believed Azagoth when he told her about his past relationship with Rhona, and Zhubaal wasn't going to plant doubt in her head again.

Zhubaal was very clear on that now.

She only wished she could be as clear on how she felt about the situation she currently found herself in.

She had messed everything up. Thanks to her impulsiveness, she'd severed Azagoth's last connection with his children. And thanks to her deception, he'd grown to care for her, and if she was honest with herself, she had to admit that she cared for him, too.

She hadn't intended for any of this to happen, hadn't considered the collateral damage involved in her grand plan to abscond with the *chronoglass*.

If she left now, it might be the best thing for him. After all, their relationship was based on lies. She couldn't handle it anymore. She'd reached a tipping point, one that was very close to toppling. She had to commit—to either staying...or leaving.

"Hi Lilliana."

Startled, Lilliana whirled around. An Adonis-faced angel stood in the center of the pentagram, his crisp business suit as flawless as his distinguished salt-and-pepper hair and olive skin.

"Hutriel," she gasped.

"It's good to see you."

She wished she could say the same, but she really did not like her ex. "Why are you here?"

His periwinkle eyes flashed imperiously. "I come with news from Raphael."

Oh, shit. She had a sneaky suspicion she wasn't going to like this news. "Well, spit it out."

He stiffened in that haughty way of his. "I'm an angel of the Order of Virtues. I outrank you by three Orders. In addition, I'm an angel of good standing, while you..." He sneered at Azagoth's manor. "You are a shameful wrongdoer undeserving of my company. You will address me with respect."

"I give respect when it's earned," she said bluntly. "You lost mine a long time ago, and I don't see it happening again soon, Rod of God."

He used to love to point out that his name meant, "*rod of God*", as if it made him important. He was a rod, all right, but he probably wouldn't appreciate the alternative use of the word.

The egotistical rod.

"I don't like your attitude," he ground out.

"And I no longer care what you like or don't like." She crossed her arms over her chest. "So tell me why you're here or go away."

His mouth pursed so tight she thought his teeth would break. "Raphael wants to know what's taking you so long."

"I have a month. It's only been a few days. Tell him to hold his horses."

Rod of God's eyes nearly bugged out of his head. "That's an archangel you're speaking about."

"He hasn't earned my respect either. So why don't you march your suck-up self back to Raphael and tell him..." Tell him what? That she'd changed her mind? *Had* she changed her mind? For sure? "Tell him I need more time. And I could use some help, as well. With my limited powers, the *chronoglass* is too heavy to move."

"That's not his problem."

"No, it's yours," she said. "You're the one who has to go back and tell him to bite me."

"You're very brave down here in Azagoth's realm. Will you be so mouthy once you're face to face with Raphael in his chambers?"

She'd deal with that when—and if—she stole the *chronoglass*.

"I don't know. Will you be so mouthy when you're face to face with Azagoth?"

He snorted. "It's really too bad you're not going to stay here. You deserve him."

"How do you know I'm not staying?"

He laughed, a full-on belly laugh. "Come now, Lilliana. I know how you like your freedom. It's why you left me, isn't it?"

She shrugged. "Mostly I left you because you're a controlling asshole. It's funny how Azagoth is talked about as if he's a soulless monster, but he's been better to me in a few days than you were in a hundred years."

"Good...Lord," he breathed. "You actually like him. You're *falling* for him." He stared at her, horror spreading over his perfect features as the truth of her situation began to solidify in his mind. "You've fucked him, haven't you? You...whore."

"You haven't changed a bit. Still a judgmental dick." Done with him, just like she'd been all those decades ago, she spun around and started toward the building. Walking away was as easy this time as it had been then. "Tell Raphael to suck an egg."

He moved in a flash to snare her wrist and yank her back to him. Teeth bared, he snarled. "Find a way to steal the *chronoglass*, Lilliana. Raphael feels that giving you too much time has made you slack off. You now have two days to do it."

She inhaled sharply. "What?"

"Two days, Whore of Sheoul-gra." His eyes flared with exaggerated astonishment even as his fingers dug painfully hard into her flesh. "Oh, you don't like that name? Because that's what everyone is going to call you if you stay here. So get your ass in gear, or—"

A roar shattered the air, and suddenly Hutriel went airborne in a bloody explosion. A fine pink mist hung in the air as his wrecked body hit the ground inside the portal's pentagram ring.

Lilliana pivoted toward the owner of that bloodcurdling roar, and her heart slammed hard into her rib cage. Azagoth, fully eviled-out, was pounding down the stairs three at a time, his massive, sharp teeth bared, his wings extended, his eyes glowing with crimson death.

"You dared to touch my mate?" His words were warped, guttural, and dripping with murder. He snarled, and Hutriel screamed as dozens of bones in his body snapped. "You. Will. Die."

"Azagoth, no!" She leaped to intercept, but Hutriel, still inside the portal circle, disappeared in a glittery shower of sparks, barely escaping with his life.

He rounded on her, but his voice had tempered. "Who was he?"

"Take off your demon face," she said in a low, soothing tone, "and we'll talk."

His nostrils flared, and a muffled, soft growl rumbled in his chest. He stared at the empty space where Hutriel used to be, his clawed hands flexing as if he was regretting the missed opportunity to rip the angel apart.

"Come on," she urged quietly. "Shift back."

Azagoth remained like that for a few seconds, and then he paced in a circle for a minute, until finally, he morphed back into his usual body. As he turned back to her, his tall, elegant form outfitted in black slacks and a matching button-down, she couldn't help but think that the civilized clothing only heightened the awareness that underneath it all, he was death in human skin.

"Who. Was. He."

"He was my ex," she replied. "Hutriel."

Azagoth's nostrils flared and his eyes flickered with red sparks. "Why was he here?"

Oh, because he needed to tell me to hurry up and steal your chronoglass.

"He wanted to wish me good riddance," she said, hoping he

didn't notice the tremor in her voice. She hated lying to him, but at this point, the truth was only going to cause more pain, and she couldn't do that to him again.

She'd done enough of that already.

"He grabbed you." Once more, flickers of his inner beast formed as shadows in his expression. Quickly, she took his hand and pulled him to her, drawing him hard against her body, where she'd needed him to be since yesterday.

"We fought." She slid her hand behind his neck and massaged him there, digging deep into muscles so tight they felt like bricks. "It's what we do. But I don't want it to be that way with you."

"He touched you. I can...*smell* him." With a growl, he hauled her even closer to him as he dipped his mouth to her ear. "I need to be inside you. I need to mark you. Brand you. Make him disappear forever."

Oh...oh, damn. "Yes," she whispered.

And with that, she knew for sure she wasn't leaving.

Chapter Eighteen

Azagoth was in a state of animalistic need. The desire he felt for Lilli was so basic, so primal that, just like his killing urge, he knew better than to fight it. He swept her up and headed inside his manor on a direct course for his bedroom, and Hades help anyone who was stupid enough to get in his path.

Only one *griminion* came close to making that mistake, but he leaped out of the way with a squeak and scurried into his living quarters as Azagoth stalked down the hall. Lilliana's lips were kissing hot paths along his neck and jaw, driving him insane. When he reached the bedroom, he kicked open the door, not caring that it cracked down the middle.

Once inside the bedroom, he set her on the floor, but when he lowered his head to kiss her, he caught another whiff of her former lover. Possessive anger lit him up as he gripped the flirty purple sundress she was wearing and ripped it in half.

"You've had a very busy couple of days, haven't you?" He dropped the shredded dress to the floor and hooked his finger under the delicate lace of her panties. "Meeting with your ex, destroying my viewing stone, punching Zhubaal in the face."

"I'm not sorry about Zhubaal," she said. "He's a jerk. And I certainly didn't invite Hutriel for a visit." She laid her hand over his and pushed it deeper inside her underwear, until his fingers brushed her cleft. "But I swear, I'm so sorry about the spy stone."

He let his fingers play a bit, stroking over the flawless hills of her sex. Countless years of bedding angels had taught him that gentle touches while talking soothed the savage beast—both his and theirs.

"What led you to think I wanted someone besides you?"

"Zhubaal said...it's not important. And then I saw you looking at females," she said, going breathless as he slipped a finger between her folds. "Then there's all of this sex furniture stuff. You used it on other females, and I have to just sit here and look at it."

He supposed he understood that. If the situation were reversed and he'd been subjected to constant reminders of Hutriel the Silver-haired Douchebag, he'd be on edge, too.

"I'll toss it. All of it." He dropped to his knees and used a fang to slash her underwear open. Damn, he'd never get tired of the sight of her like this. Bare. Her flesh parted just enough to invite his tongue. "After," he growled as he put his mouth to her waiting sex.

She allowed him a single, mouthwatering lick before stepping away from him. "No. You want to erase Hutriel, and I want to do the same with all of your females." She marched over to the St. Andrew's Cross, her glorious backside swinging. With a lithe spin, she put her spine to the wood and snapped her wrists into the restraints. "Do it. Let's banish all of our demons. You know, figuratively."

He inhaled in an attempt to get a bead on where her emotions were, but all he got was a blast of lust that made his knees wobble as he came to his feet.

Real smooth, buddy. Real fucking smooth...

It was crazy how this female had torn down his defenses, made him feel things he hadn't felt in a long time. Or ever.

He looked around at the bedroom, at all of the equipment he kept, and suddenly he didn't want Lilliana's exquisite skin touching any of it. He'd used it for a purpose he'd never again need it for. It had to go.

Well, maybe the spanking bench could stay.

Summoning all his control, he unbuttoned his shirt. Slowly. Taking his time while Lilliana hung from the St. Andrew's Cross, her breasts rising and falling faster and faster every time a button popped.

"Do you want to know why I have all of this stuff?" he asked.

Licking her lips, she nodded.

He inhaled deeply, hating that his breath was shaky. He didn't want to admit this, but she needed to hear it, and he wanted to make sure she never doubted him again.

"Heaven sent me seventy-two females a year."

"Yes," she ground out. "I know that. All of Heaven knows that."

He probably shouldn't like the note of jealousy in her voice, but hey, he was evil.

Turning away, he stared at the Monet on the wall. "Seventy-two females who didn't want to be here. Much like you." Silence churned between them as the truth of what he'd said thickened the air like a rancid stew. "Well, that's not entirely accurate. Usually two or three of the bunch were eager to experience me. The rest..." Pivoting back to her, he waved his hand dismissively. "The rest closed their eyes and prayed. Literally *prayed.* Do you have any idea how unpleasant that is?"

"I can't imagine," she said softly. "But what does that have to do with all of this...stuff?"

"I told you that I couldn't feel any emotions of my own, but I discovered that the more they felt, the more I felt. Remember when I told you I took Thanatos's tattoos just so I could feel something?" At her nod, he continued. "The only other time I could ever feel anything was when I was inside an angel. The more she was worked up, the better for both of us." He trailed a finger over the wood near where Lilliana's wrist was circled by the leather cuff. "All of this allowed me to play until even the most timid female begged for my cock."

She growled. "I did *not* need to hear that."

Oh, yeah, he fucking loved that little twinge of jealousy. "And I didn't need to see Hutfuckriel touching you." That wasn't fair and he knew it, but the fact that he was actually experiencing jealousy was awesome. Right now, *every* emotion was awesome, simply because he could feel them at all. "But that's over. All of it is over, isn't it?"

"Yes," she whispered.

"Good. Now, let's try something more deserving of your behavior." He released the restraints.

"B-behavior?"

Smiling, he took her by the shoulders and swung her around to the spanking bench. He bent her over, locking her wrists into the cuffs. His cock strained behind the fly of his pants, and he unzipped, springing it from its fabric prison.

"Are you ready?" he asked as he took his erection in his hand and gave it a few strokes.

He was dying for this, but he wanted her to be dying for it, too, the way she'd been on the beach and in the shower. But instinctively, he knew this was a cleansing of sorts, a way for them to banish their pasts. He wanted intimacy. He wanted the sex to mean something.

This could be a new start for them both.

He stroked himself as he gave her a swat on her perky ass. She hissed, but as he rubbed the pink handprint on her ivory skin, she pushed into his palm.

"Yes," she moaned. "Please."

"Another then," he murmured, swatting her harder.

This time she whispered a soft, "Oh, yeah. More. We are so keeping this bench."

He gave her three more slaps in rapid succession, and his cock thickened to the point of exquisite pain as her ass reddened and grew hotter with every blow. Her arousal was like an airborne aphrodisiac, entering his lungs and spreading through his body like wildfire.

"Azagoth," she pleaded, her breathless voice pushing him to the edge of his control. "I need to come."

"You got it." He positioned himself behind her and nearly moaned at the way she lifted her hips in anticipation. Her juices glistened between her swollen folds, and when he cupped her mound, her honey coated his fingers.

Still stroking himself, he slid his fingers into her slit and rubbed back and forth. She whimpered, pushing into his hand as far as the restraints would allow.

"Don't worry," he whispered. "I'll release you. We'll start this way, but I want to end with you on your back. I want to look into your eyes when I come."

She cried out, so close to orgasm he could feel the tremors building between her legs. Gently, he eased his thumb into her silken opening.

"When you first came here, did you think we'd end up like this?"

"Never." The honesty in her voice was tinged with an odd note of remorse. Did she feel bad about not wanting to come here?

Didn't matter. What mattered was that she was here now, and he had all eternity to show her that she'd made the right decision to join him in Sheoul-gra.

His cock throbbed as he pressed it against her slit. Very slowly, he nudged the head inside her, her slippery desire easing the passage into her tight channel. Suddenly, her emotions slammed into him, a mixture of yearning and guilt. He shook his head, wanting them gone. He could feel now; he didn't have to borrow her emotions.

But they wouldn't subside. What the hell? He gripped her hips, holding both of them steady as he struggled to clear his head.

A glint of silver caught his eye, and suddenly, it all made sense.

The key pendant. Designed to transmit strong emotion, it was doing exactly that.

Another blast of her guilt hit him hard enough to make him groan. He needed to remove the necklace and use the rest of the night to assuage whatever regrets she had. He never wanted her to have a negative emotion again.

He'd get her a new pendant. One that wasn't enchanted.

You only have thirty days to get out with the chronoglass before we close the door on Sheoul-gra, and you're stuck with Azagoth forever.

He froze as Lilliana's thoughts, her very memories, slammed into him like a lava troll's meaty fist. Stunned, he could only stare blankly as the unbelievable truth pinged around inside his head and clawed at his heart. She'd betrayed him. She'd lied from the very beginning.

The warmth that had been nudging at his flesh, that had been starting to thaw his body, iced over.

"Damn you," he rasped, his voice as raw as the wound she'd

just inflicted. "You came here to steal the *chronoglass*."

"Azagoth...no...wait—"

"Damn you!" Snarling, he gripped the necklace and yanked hard. The delicate chain snapped, and tiny links flew everywhere. Before she could say another word, he flipped the switch on the cuffs and released her.

"Get out." Bypassing the ripped garment on the floor, he threw open her wardrobe, ripped a sunny yellow sundress from a hanger, and hurled it at her. And wasn't he a gentleman for making sure he kicked her to the curb with undamaged clothing.

Idiot.

Lilliana caught the garment with shaking hands. "Please, just listen—"

"Listen?" he shouted. "*Listen?* To what? More lies? You've deceived me from the moment you crossed the threshold into my realm. You destroyed the only connection I had with my children, and now I find out you've lied about why you came here."

Pain, sharper than any he'd ever experienced, cleaved through his heart and he nearly doubled over. How could she do this to him? How could she betray him like this? She'd used him, exploited his desperation, just like Lilith had all those years ago.

"Get the fuck out of my realm," he gritted through clenched teeth. "and tell the archangels that if they dare to send another angel to me, for any reason, I'll send that angel back in pieces." He bared his teeth and advanced on her, forcing her to scramble backward toward the door. For the first time since she'd stepped foot in his realm, he got off on her fear. Craved it. Reveled in it. "Go. Before those pieces are yours."

* * * *

Lilliana tried to not cry as she fled down the hall toward the building's exit, tripping and careening off walls as she attempted to put on the dress while running at full speed. She'd screwed up badly. She'd hated Azagoth in the beginning, but he'd been nothing but good to her. And once she'd understood his lack of emotions, his coldness had not only made sense, but had been understandable.

She should have told him the truth the very moment she realized she was having second thoughts about why she'd come here. Instead, she'd swept her deception under the rug and hoped he'd never find out.

Fool. Of course he found out. This is his realm. He knows all. Sees all.

Wait...how *had* he found out?

Not that it mattered. What was done was done, and as the tears rolled down her cheeks in hot streaks, she cursed Raphael. Hutriel. Herself.

"Lilliana!"

Cat's voice rang out as Lilliana shoved open the door to outside. Only the knowledge that Cat might very well be screwed out of a job halted Lilliana in her tracks.

Cat jogged over. "What's wrong? Where are you going?"

"I'm leaving," Lilliana said. Well, she tried to say it, but the sobs muffled her words. "I'm sorry, Cat. I'm so sorry. Your job—"

The fallen angel threw her arms around Lilliana and hugged her tight, which only made her cry harder. "Screw the job. I don't want you to go."

Get your head on straight. Pull yourself together for her sake. You can fall apart later.

Easing back from Cat, Lilliana dabbed at her wet face with the hem of her dress. "Listen to me. Stay out of Azagoth's way for a while. If he fires you..." Lilliana couldn't believe she was about to say this, given the fact that she was an angel and this went against everything angels believed, but things had changed since she got here. *She* had changed. "There's a demon hospital called Underworld General. Go there. Try to get a job. You'll be safe from the fallen angels trying to drag you into Sheoul."

Cat nodded, her eyes filling with tears. "Don't go."

A tormented roar, barely muffled by the building, rang out, stirring up a malevolent wind that reeked of rot and danger. "I have to." She squeezed the female's hand. "Promise me you'll do as I said."

Cat's bottom lip trembled. "I promise."

Breathing a sigh of relief, Lilliana released Cat. "Be safe. And thank you for everything."

Hastily, before Azagoth made good on his word to send her to

Heaven in pieces, Lilliana flew down the stairs and hit the ground running. As she stepped into the portal that would transport her out of here, she looked out over Azagoth's kingdom.

All the new life, all the vibrant color and fresh air, was dying. Her last thought before the portal whisked her away was about Azagoth.

If his realm was dying, what was happening to him?

Chapter Nineteen

Azagoth stood in the library amongst shattered glass, his body trembling, his heart aching, his soul screaming. Pain surged through him in great waves that threatened to make him black out, but fate was a cruel bitch, and he remained as alert and sensitive to agony as ever.

His Lilli had betrayed him. Had plotted to steal his *chronoglass* and leave him. He looked down at the shards on the floor. Now she'd never get it. In a great fit of irrational fury, he'd destroyed it the way she'd destroyed him.

He could still feel her, and crazily, *stupidly*, he hoped she'd go to their bedroom and wait for him. Maybe try to convince him that he was wrong about her. That she loved him and couldn't leave.

He wasn't sure how he'd react to that, but a big part of him would be relieved.

Suddenly, something inside him extinguished, as if a flame had gone out. Or as if his breath had been forcefully expelled from his lungs.

Lilliana was gone.

Agony overwhelmed him. His breath scorched his throat with every desperate inhale. She'd left him, and his world was crumbling around him. Literally. The building was shaking, books falling from their shelves, cracks popping in the walls.

With a great roar, he fell to his knees. He screamed in utter misery, and only later realized he was screaming her name.

* * * *

Lilliana spent a full day in Heaven. Now she was down to twenty-two hours before Raphael's ticking time bomb was set to go off and she'd have to submit to the time-travelectomy procedure.

Or she'd be shut inside Sheoul-gra forever.

With a person who wanted to tear her to pieces.

So far, she'd been able to get around without anyone knowing she was back behind the pearly gates, and hopefully no one had gone into the Time Travel Department's artifact room yet.

Twenty-two hours.

She took one last look at the cottage she'd called home, at the eclectic decor from time periods all over the human world. She'd either never see this place again, or she'd return with no energy or passion for life.

But then, she didn't need to have her time travel ability ripped away for the latter to happen.

Twenty-two freaking hours.

Taking a deep, bracing breath, she flashed herself out of Heaven and to as close as she could get to Underworld General Hospital, which turned out to be its underground parking lot.

There weren't many cars, but there was a blond male in a black paramedic uniform scrubbing out the inside of one of two black ambulances near the entrance. Lilliana had no idea what had happened inside the vehicle, but it looked more like a mobile slaughterhouse than a rolling medical unit.

"Excuse me."

"What?" came the gruff response.

"I'm looking for someone named Idess."

"Inside."

How helpful. "I can't go inside." No angel could enter the demon hospital, thanks to some sort of anti-angel ward. Apparently, no one could commit violence inside, either, thanks to another spell. Those wily demons had thought of everything.

"Guess you're out of luck."

Okay, now she was getting irritated. Stepping to the side of the rig, she slammed her fist into the center of the Underworld General symbol, leaving one hell of a dent.

"Luck is irrelevant," she said. "I can't enter the hospital, and I need help. Is it not your job to render assistance?"

Very slowly, he turned around, his fangs and silver eyes flashing. Surprise flickered at the sudden realization that he was a dhampire, a rare vampire-werewolf cross. She'd studied them in their Scottish homeland during one of her time travel assignments. She'd be fascinated to meet one in person if she wasn't so annoyed. And in a serious time crunch.

"*Medical* assistance," he said. "Are you bleeding to death, having a cardiac incident, or suffering from a splinter in your little finger? No? Then fuck off."

Steam built in her veins. Tales of Underworld General staff arrogance reached the farthest corners of Heaven, but she'd always thought they were exaggerated. Turned out, not so much.

She slapped her palm against the side of the rig again, using a bit of angel power to make the sound crash through the enclosed parking lot like a sonic boom. Dhampire boy jumped high enough that he nearly brained himself on the roof.

"I'm approximately one insult away from rendering you down to a greasy stain of dhampire fat on the asphalt, so hear me, and hear me well," she said, using the same power to make her voice resonate all the way to the paramedic's marrow. "This is about Idess's father. If you're at all aware of who he is, if you've only heard *whispers* regarding his identity, you will drop that bottle of cleaner and fetch her. Now."

The male, whose name tag read *Conall*, studied her for a moment. "You could have lead the conversation with the threat and saved us both a lot of time, not to mention damage to the rig." He leaped out of the truck, and as he strode away, boots clapping on the pavement in heavy thuds, she swore she heard him mutter, "Fucking angels."

She waited impatiently, watching a few vehicles come and go through the hidden portal in the lot's concrete wall. Finally, just as she was contemplating climbing into the ambulance and turning on the siren, Conall returned with a stunning female whose caramel hair had been piled on top of her head in a messy knot.

"I'm Idess," she said. "You're here about Azagoth?"

Lilliana glanced over at the paramedic, who stood protectively by Idess. "Can we have some privacy, please?"

Idess nodded at the dhampire, and after shooting Lilliana a look that promised pain if she caused trouble, he hopped inside the ambulance and went back to his gruesome work.

"Your father needs you," Lilli began. Might as well get to the point. "One of your brothers, Methicore, arranged to have Sheoulgra cut off to all Memitim. His viewing stone is broken, and he has no way to contact his children, let alone see them. I think you're the only one who can access his realm now."

"Methicore," she hissed. "That son of a bitch has been causing trouble for centuries." She eyed Lilliana. "How do you know all of this? Who are you?"

"I was supposed to mate him."

Idess's eyes flared. "Supposed to? Wait...*mate* him? What about the seventy-two angels? What the hell is going on?"

"I'll explain it all later. Right now your father is in trouble, and I don't have much time. I need your help. *He* needs your help."

For a long moment, Idess stood there, staring at Lilliana. Finally, she said, "Why is this important to you?"

No matter what she said, she was going to sound stupid, so she might as well put it all out there. "Because he deserves a chance to be happy. And...I love him."

Conall's head whipped around and he stared at her like she was insane, but Idess merely looked curious.

"Are you trying to win him back?" she asked.

Lilliana shook her head. "I would love a second chance, but even if that doesn't happen, I want to fix what I broke, and you're the only person who can help me do that. Please. Not for me, for him."

Idess glanced at her watch. "My lunch break is in ten. Let's grab a bite somewhere and figure this out." She gave Lilliana a wary glance. "How do I know this isn't a trick? No offense, but a lot of angels have turned out to be..."

"Lying assholes?"

Idess snorted. "Yeah."

"Do you know Reaver?" When Idess nodded, Lilliana breathed a sigh of relief. "He can vouch for me."

Idess's expression lit up. "If Reaver is cool with you, then so am I. Welcome to the family, Lilliana."

Lilliana appreciated the welcome, and the family thing sounded awesome. But she doubted it would happen. Hell, she was lucky Azagoth hadn't killed her. There was no way he'd forgive her.

Betray me and you'll see exactly how unforgiving I can be. There are no second chances.

Chapter Twenty

Azagoth stood in the courtyard outside of his palace, staring into the murky waters swirling around in the black-streaked fountain. What had, for a few short days, been pristine white was now smeared with sooty residue. The once-crystal water had stagnated, its surface so thick with slime that it resembled industrial sludge.

His belly hurt and his heart ached, and his throat was raw from screaming. He missed Lilliana as much as he hated her. No, that wasn't entirely accurate. He missed her more than he hated her. And truth be told, he didn't hate her...he hated what she'd planned to do.

"Father."

The familiar voice came from out of nowhere, and he wheeled around. Idess stood on the stone pathway that led from the portal, dressed in jeans and a fitted violet silk blouse with matching strappy sandals. The desire to hug her damned near made him tremble.

But so did the fear that she was the rotten icing on the cake, here to tell him to fuck off like everyone else. Bracing himself, he waited.

"I spoke with Lilliana," she said, and his heart shot into his throat. "She's worried about you."

He snorted. "She should be worried about herself. After the

archangels relieve her of her time travel ability, she's going to be miserable." He should be happy about that, but no, the thought of her suffering only dragged him deeper into the pit of despair he'd dug for himself. "How is it that you spoke with her?"

"She came to me at Underworld General. She told me what Methicore did. And she gave me this." Idess reached into her purse and withdrew a polished sapphire globe about the size of a softball. "She stole it from the Time Travel Department."

"What is it?"

"It's a miniature viewing stone. It's practically useless to Heaven because it requires permission from those you want to spy on...and who in their right mind consents to that?" She shrugged. "But somehow Lilliana convinced hundreds of my brothers and sisters to give permission. It's not the same as them being able to visit, but it's better than nothing. Some of them even sent messages and invitations to contact them. They're all about Skype."

He had no idea what to say, even if he could speak. His voice was gone, clogged by the emotion in his throat. Idess handed the shiny ball to him, the solid weight of it sitting heavy on his soul. Lilliana had done this even after the way he'd treated her?

You treated her that way because she lied to you. She deceived you.

Somehow, none of that seemed to be important right now, which was strange, because he had *never* treated betrayal lightly. Had anyone else done what she did, they'd be gracing his great hall right now, frozen in a screaming statue.

"Father," Idess said softly. "I know this is none of my business, but I think you should cut her some slack."

He rolled the globe around in his palms, strangely comforted by the fact that Lilliana had once held it in her own graceful hands. "You don't know what she did." His voice was humiliatingly hoarse.

"Yes, I do. She came down here to steal the *chronoglass* and return to Heaven." Idess dropped her bag on the ground and gazed out at the devastated landscape. "Did she ever tell you why she was given the choice to come here or have her ability taken away?"

"She broke out of the *shrowd*."

"Yes, but did she tell you why she did that?"

He frowned. She'd always skirted around the issue or changed the subject, never lighting on talk of her punishment or the *shrowd* for long. "No, she didn't."

"She did it because she was taken prisoner by an angel named Stamtiel. He forced her to travel into the past to search for some sort of holy object he could use to wrest power away from one of the archangels. She refused, even when he tortured her."

His breath burned in his throat, and his voice turned smoky with the depth of his anger. "He tortured her?"

"Badly. He wrecked her, Father. To save herself, she agreed to do his bidding, but it was a trick. She went into the past and then broke out of the *shrowd* in hopes that angels would rescue her. They did, but they were angels from the past. What she did was highly illegal, and it caused a lot of problems. Memories had to be wiped, and getting her back to the present was a long, involved process that required more memory alterations."

"So she was punished for escaping her torturer?"

Idess nodded. "You know how Heaven operates. Rules are rules, and they can't be broken for any reason."

Bastards. "Why would she tell you all of this but not tell me?"

"She didn't tell me. I asked Reaver to do a little digging, and he discovered all of that. The reason she didn't tell you is that she doesn't remember the worst of it."

"Why not?"

"She was in bad shape," Idess explained. "The angels knew she needed to be punished, but even they felt sorry for her, so they altered her memories. She knows she was kidnapped and that she escaped, but she has no recollection of the horrors Stamtiel inflicted on her." Idess pursed her lips in disgust. "Father, she came here to steal your property, but somehow, she managed to fall for you, and given her past, even if she can't consciously remember it, that's kind of a miracle."

He squeezed his eyes shut, but his vicious actions replayed on the back of his eyelids. "I'm such a fool."

"Males always are," she muttered.

"Did you give your..." He held up the orb, afraid to even ask if she'd consented to allow him to check up on her from afar.

For a moment, Idess looked perplexed. "Why would I?"

"You're siding with Methicore, then."

She grimaced. "Hardly. I didn't infuse my permission into the globe because I'm not Memitim. I can visit your realm anytime I want to. And if you want to see me, send one of your *griminions*. Or heck, send an e-mail. I'll come, Father."

He gaped at her. "You'd visit me? For no reason other than that I requested it?"

"Of course." She shrugged. "I didn't know you wanted me here or I'd have come more often. And when my son is born, I'll bring him, too."

He sucked in a sharp breath. "You're pregnant?"

"Soon," she said. "With all the apocalyptic crap that happened recently, Lore and I wanted to wait until we knew we wouldn't be bringing a child into a shitty world. It's still shitty, but between Lore's family, the Horsemen, and Reaver and Harvester, I know my son will have a powerful, loving family to depend on. And, of course, you."

He hugged her, something he'd never done before. It was awkward and stiff at first, but when she relaxed into him, an emotional earthquake rocked him. This was his first true connection with one of his children, and he hoped it wouldn't be the last.

He tried not to think of the children he might have had with Lilliana as he reluctantly pulled back.

"Thank you, Idess," he said, his voice thick with the force of what he felt for her. "You've already done so much, but I have one favor to ask of you."

"Anything."

"Tell her...tell her I love her."

Idess stepped away. "I can't do that," she said, and his heart sank. "But you can tell her yourself."

She turned, and he followed her gaze to the steps of his mansion, where Lilli was standing...in a flowing white gown, just as she'd been dressed when she'd first arrived. Her hair was long and loose, the way he liked it, and peeking out from under the hem of the gown were her bare toes, painted bright cherry red.

He closed the distance between them in less time than it took to blink. Then he stood there like a dolt on the step beneath hers. He'd had so much to say to her just a few seconds ago, and now he was completely blank.

"Hi," she said.

He couldn't even manage that. Dolt.

"Um..." She cleared her throat. "I'm not sure where to start. I originally came here with every intention of stealing your *chronoglass* and leaving." Her eyes grew liquid, and it took every ounce of restraint he had not to reach for her. "And then I...I started falling for you. I put off taking the *chronoglass* so I could stay, and then I changed my mind, but by then..."

"By then it was too late," he finished. God, he was an ass. "I'm sorry too," he croaked. "I should have let you explain. I should have listened. Instead, all I could think about was how I'd let another female deceive me. I went back to that dark place from so long ago, and it wasn't fair to you. Please forgive me, Lilli. Please."

A tear dripped down her cheek. "Only if you forgive me."

He caught the tear with his finger, and damn, it felt good to touch her again. "It doesn't matter. None of it matters." His heart thumped against his rib cage. "Tell me you're here to stay. Tell me—"

She silenced him with a kiss. When she pulled away, she was smiling. "The window for me to leave closed sixty seconds after I got here."

He stepped back and nearly fell down the stairs. "Lilli, damn...you took a huge risk. What if you'd gotten here and I was in a rage? Or if I never forgave you?"

"Then I'd spend the rest of eternity making it up to you." She grinned. "I can be pretty persuasive. It wouldn't have taken an eternity. Besides, I figured I could hold that hour a day of time traveling over your head."

He grimaced. Ran his hand through his hair. Looked down at his shoes. They were dirty. "Ah...about that. I sort of destroyed the *chronoglass*."

"You *what*?"

"I know. I'm an idiot. I just—"

Abruptly, she gripped his arm in a bruising hold. "Azagoth! Look."

Cranking his head around, he took in the new splendor of his realm. His daughter was gaping in disbelief as the scorched earth once again sprouted with lush, green grass. The gnarled, charred trees straightened, their blackened bark peeling away to leave healthy wood in its place. Leaves unfurled along branches that stabbed up into an infinitely blue sky. And all around, the fountains spewed crystal water against the backdrop of pristine white buildings.

"That's your doing, Lilli," he breathed, his love for her flowing through his veins and through the realm. "This is all because of you."

She sidled up close, drawing him to her with arms around his waist. "We've been over this. It's you. Because you can feel again."

"Yes," he said, as he dipped his head to kiss her, "I can feel." He could feel everything now. Love. Joy. Tenderness. Against the soft warmth of her lips, he whispered, "But all of the beauty infusing my realm is simply a reflection of what I see when I look at you."

Chapter Twenty-One

Eight days had passed since Lilli returned to Sheoul-gra, but to Azagoth, the realm now seemed like Heaven.

He could tell she missed being able to time travel, but maybe he could arrange for an artifact that would allow her to get out of here every once in a while. He'd heard that some objects, such as the one her torturer had possessed, could transport the user to a very specific time and place.

Better than nothing, he supposed.

He'd been keeping her busy with plans for the newest Inner Sanctum level, and it wouldn't be long before construction would start. She'd also been tending to the new growth in the realm, but soon she was going to need a definitive purpose. He just hadn't figured out what. He definitely didn't want her involved in soul reaping or visiting any of the Inner Sanctum levels.

A tap on his office door brought him out of his planning, and he hoped it was Lilli, in from outside for a lunch break and, if he was lucky, a little between the sheets action. Or on the floor action. Or against the wall action. Or maybe if he was very lucky, she'd done something deserving of a spanking.

He wasn't particularly picky.

"Come," he called out.

The door burst open, and the Four Horsemen's Heavenly

Watcher, Harvester, swept in, dressed in super-skimpy attire as usual. Her mate, Reaver, must love her barely-there black leather miniskirt and thigh-high boots. Azagoth needed to get that outfit for Lilliana, ASAP.

"Azagoth." Harvester brushed her long black hair back from her face. "I assume you're calling in that favor I owe you?"

"I am." He sat back in his chair and folded his hands across his abs. "I need an angel to be dead."

She gave a haughty sniff. "You do realize I'm not a fallen angel anymore. I can't go around killing angels for fun. Not that I wouldn't like to, mind you. But sadly, Heaven frowns on angels who assassinate other angels."

"You will handle this," he said, allowing a thread of warning to weave into his voice. "When I allowed you into the Inner Sanctum to rescue Reaver, you agreed to bring me one item and one person of my choice. Stamtiel is my person."

She narrowed her eyes. "Stam? Heaven has been looking for him for years. Do you know where he is?"

He nodded. His network of spies and people who owed him favors had made fast work of his request to locate the bastard. "He abused Lilliana. I want his soul."

"Can't you send your *griminions* out to give him a heart attack or something?"

"Come now, Harvester. You know they can only kill demons and evil humans." And even then, there were rules he had to follow.

"Hmm." Tapping her chin with one blue-lacquered nail, she appeared to consider that. "Swear to me that if I agree, I will be free of my debt to you."

A strange request, since that was the deal they'd struck already, but what the hell. "I swear."

"Then I agree." She shrugged. "So how are things going with your...what should I call her...prisoner?"

He looked past her shoulder at the female just now entering the office. "Why don't you ask Lilli?"

Lilliana strode inside, giving Harvester a polite, but forced, smile. "Hello."

"Lilliana, this is Harvester."

Lilliana checked up short, as if she'd hit an invisible barrier. "H-Harvester," she stammered. "I, ah, know your Reaver." Wincing, she shook her head. Damn, she hadn't even been this flustered when she'd met him. "I mean mate. I mean, I know your mate, Reaver."

Harvester cocked her head and studied Lilli. "Have you fucked him?"

Lilliana choked. Maybe he should tell Harvester to stop messing with her, but this was kind of amusing.

"N-no." Lilli waved her hands vehemently. "We're just friends."

"Oh," Harvester said brightly. "Then you can keep your head. And geez, don't be so nervous. Also, you should probably know that it was your friendship with Reaver that got you sent down here."

"What?" Lilli blurted breathlessly. "How?"

Harvester's smile was sour. "Raphael and Reaver have a...past. Now that Reaver has been raised to Radiant status, he's far more powerful than Raphael, and he can't strike at Reaver the way he wants to, so he's finding other ways to punish him. When you did Reaver's Christmas shopping, it gave Raphael a reason to go after you." Her tone turned apologetic, something Azagoth had never heard from the notoriously prickly angel. "You got caught in the crossfire. I'm sorry."

Lilli looked down, and for a long moment, Azagoth feared the worst. That she was wishing she'd never gotten involved in a power struggle between an archangel and a Radiant.

But when she looked up again, there was fire in her gorgeous eyes. "A couple of weeks ago, this would be upsetting news. But today? I think I'm very fortunate that Raphael has it in for Reaver."

Harvester rolled her eyes, but Azagoth's heart got all stupid happy. Then a thought occurred to him.

"Harvester," he began, "if you knew why Lilliana was sent here, then you must have known about Stamtiel."

Now her eyes went wide with exaggerated innocence. *"Moi?"*

He stared, and she huffed.

"Okay, fine. Yes, I knew. And I suspect that Raphael was involved in Lilliana's kidnapping as well. Stamtiel was Raphael's friend until he went rogue. Raphael denies that they are still friends, but he's also a lying bastard. I'd bet my shiny new halo that Raphael put Stamtiel up to kidnapping Lilliana, but I think her escape wasn't part of the plan. In any case, I'd already intended to destroy the bastard for what he did to her. You didn't need to call in my debt to you."

Now her odd request earlier, that her debt would be paid if she killed Stamtiel, made sense. If he'd known that she was already planning to kill Stammy, he wouldn't have wasted the request on her. Well, fuck. But he had to admire her cunning.

She turned to Lilliana. "I also knew you didn't sleep with Reaver. I was screwing with you. That, I'm not sorry for. Now," she said, "if we're through here, I have an angel to hunt down."

"See Zhubaal in his office." Azagoth stood. "He'll give you the information you need to find the son of a bitch."

Harvester nodded in farewell. "Oh," she said, as she strode out the doorway, "I almost forgot. Reaver left you a present outside."

The moment Harvester was gone, Lilli turned to him. "A present?"

Azagoth groaned. "I had Hades hold Reaver in the belly of a giant demon in Sheoul-gra's Sanctum for three months. The present is likely not a good one." He took her hand. "Let's go see what we're in for."

Once outside, he inhaled the air, thick with the fragrance of apple blossoms. He still couldn't believe the transformation. And then he saw it. Movement in one of the trees.

"Doves," Lilliana whispered. "There are doves in that tree." She pointed excitedly. "And rabbits. Look over there!"

"Animals." He stared in awe. He hadn't seen anything but demon critters since he'd come here. "But they can't survive here. Not with the demon animals."

Cat appeared next to them. "I helped Reaver bring in the animals," she said, but he barely heard, too stunned by this new turn of events. Reaver should hate him, and yet...he was helping to make sure Lilliana was going to be happy here.

"He brought some other Unfallens to help clear the realm of demon creatures," Cat continued. "And we brought in several wolverines to help with the smaller things. And one of the Horsemen's mates, Cara, said she'll loan you a hellhound too, if you need it."

"No hellhounds," he said quickly. "They'll eat the Earth animals."

"She said she can tell it not to," Cat's voice held a note of admiration. "Apparently, they listen to her."

Still, a hellhound would be a last resort. The things were vicious, unpredictable and, frankly, they were assholes.

Harvester exited the building and trotted down the stairs. "Are you two dense? The animals aren't the surprise."

"You're such a pleasant person," he muttered.

She grinned. "Right?" She glanced over at Lilliana. "Do you think you could make use of that?"

Lilli blinked. "Of what?"

Harvester pointed at the portal, and Lilliana gasped. "A *chronoglass*! Oh, my God. Where did you get it? *How* did you get it?"

Harvester held up her hands in a *not-me* gesture. "It was Reaver's doing. Idess overheard Azagoth say he broke his, and when she told Reaver, he made it a mission to secure one. I'm pretty sure he stole it from the Time Travel Department, but hey, it's yours now."

Lilliana broke away from them and dashed to the *chronoglass*, where she hugged it. Actually *hugged* the thing.

"Thank you, Harvester." He lowered his voice, even though Lilli was out of earshot. "I know you don't owe me anything anymore, but if you happen to run into an angel named Chaniel, I would consider it a personal favor if you would beat the crap out of him."

"Who is Chaniel?"

"Lilliana's father."

One shoulder rolled in a shrug as she started for the portal. "Consider it done."

Lilliana let go of the *chronoglass* long enough for Harvester to transport out of there. The angel waggled her fingers at them as her body started to dematerialize. "See ya."

Lilliana and Azagoth lingered for a few minutes after Harvester left, both so enthralled with the amazing work the

Unfallens were doing. Azagoth still couldn't believe that not only had Reaver arranged all of this, but that people were actually volunteering to help clean up his realm.

"Azagoth?" Lilli squeezed his hand.

"Hmm?"

"Why do you think Unfallen are suddenly being grabbed and dragged to Sheoul?"

"I don't know." He watched a cottontail rabbit do some kind of spazzy hop and sprint. "Fallen angels have always made doing that a sport."

"But according to Cat, they're being hunted." She looked over at the unused buildings. "I was thinking that since the buildings aren't being used..."

Of course! His Lilli was brilliant. Besides giving her a purpose and the Unfallens a safe place to live, it would breathe even more life into the place.

"That's a great idea," he said. "And bonus, there'll be a lot of people who will owe me in the future." She gave him an exasperated look. "What? I'm evil."

She heaved a long-suffering sigh, but the faint smile on her glossy lips gave her away. "I don't think you're half as evil as you believe yourself to be. Come on," she said, tugging him toward the *chronoglass*. "Let's get it into your library. And then, I think we deserve a vacation."

"Where to?"

"Anywhere in the world you want to go."

There were so many places for him to choose from, but when it came down to it, he didn't need to leave to discover the world.

Lilliana *was* his world, and finally, for the first time in his life, he was content right where he was.

* * * *

Six months flew by before Lilliana knew it. Of course, in the grand scheme of an angel's life, six months was like a thousandth of a second.

And that's what it had felt like.

Even on the bad days, when Azagoth had to deal with some

new, intense emotion he wasn't prepared for, time flew by. She didn't feel the need to escape into the *chronoglass* every day, and in fact, she and Azagoth hadn't gone anywhere in a week.

She loved her life in Sheoul-gra, and as long as she didn't visit the Inner Sanctum, she could almost pretend Sheoul-gra was a paradise.

A paradise full of *griminions*, fallen angels, and demons who came and went as they worked out deals with Azagoth.

Demons aside, she wouldn't give up her life here for anything. She was even doing good work with the nearly one hundred Unfallen angels who now called Sheoul-gra's outer buildings their home.

Every day she helped them to improve themselves and work their way toward making up for whatever sin had gotten them kicked out of Heaven. When they became discouraged, she reminded them that Reaver, now one of the most powerful angels in existence, used to be Unfallen. It was rare that a fallen angel could earn his or her way back into Heaven, but it happened, and she wouldn't give up. Not on the Unfallens. Not on anything.

This was her realm. Her future. And Azagoth was her mate. She was made for him and he for her.

And as she lay next to him in the huge bed where they both slept in the middle, she fingered the new, *un*enchanted key necklace he'd given her and realized that freedom wasn't about wide, open spaces. It was about being able to make choices.

And she chose Azagoth.

Forever.

Hades

Author Acknowledgments

Every story presents unique challenges for an author, and every story makes the author appreciate those who help to make a book the best it can be. For the most part, Hades played nice, but I need to thank Liz Berry, Kim Guidroz, and Pamela Jamison for all their hard work in whipping Hades into shape. I love you, ladies! I just wish Hades hadn't liked the whipping so much…

Chapter One

The road to Hades is easiest to travel. —Diogenes Laertius

Enjoy the trip, because the stay is going to be hell. —Hades

If Cataclysm had to clean one more toilet in this demon purgatory known as Sheoul-gra, she was going to jump in and flush herself down.

She'd always assumed that when angels got kicked out of Heaven they got to do fun fallen angel stuff. Like terrorize religious people and drink foamy mugs of Pestilence ale with demons. But no, she'd gotten stuck wiping the Grim Reaper's ass.

Okay, she didn't actually wipe Azagoth's ass. And if she did, his mate, Lilliana, would have had something to say about it. And by "say," Lilliana meant "behead."

Cat reconsidered that. Lilliana, who was still, technically, a fully-haloed angel, wouldn't do anything quite so drastic. Most likely. But Cat still wouldn't want to get on the female's shit list. Anyone who pissed off Lilliana pissed off the Grim Reaper, and that...well, Cat could think of nothing worse.

Except maybe cleaning toilets.

Stop whining. You took the job willingly.

Yes, that was true, but she'd only agreed to serve Azagoth because she wanted to earn her way back into Heaven, and doing that required her to A) keep her nose clean, B) avoid entering Sheoul, the demon realm humans often referred to as Hell, and C) do something heroic to save the world.

Easy peasy.

She snorted to herself as she carried a tray of dirty dishes from Azagoth and Lilliana's bedroom, her bare feet slapping on the cold stone floor that covered every inch of the ancient Greek-style mansion. He'd surprised Lilliana with breakfast in bed this morning, which was something Cat would have been shocked by a few months ago. Who would have thought that the Grim Reaper was such a softie?

She supposed she should have known better after he gave her a job and a place to live so she didn't have to worry about some jerk dragging her, against her will, into Sheoul for fun or profit.

No, Sheoul was off limits to her. Entering the demon realm would complete her fall from grace and turn her into a True Fallen, a fallen angel with no hope of redemption. As an Unfallen, she had a little wiggle room, but even so, very few angels had ever been given their wings back. In fact, she knew of only two

One of those two, Reaver, was now not only an angel, but one of the most powerful angels to have ever existed. His mate, Harvester, had also spent time as a fallen angel, but her circumstances were unique, and while Cat didn't know the whole story, she knew that Harvester had saved Heaven and Earth, and she deserved every one of her feathers she got back.

The thought of being made whole again made Cat's useless wing anchors in her back itch. Her luxurious mink-brown wings were gone, sliced off in a brutal ceremony, and with them, her source of power. She totally understood why an Unfallen would cross the barrier between the human and demon realms to turn themselves into True Fallen and gain new wings and new powers. But was the evil upgrade worth it? Cat didn't think so.

"Cat!" Azagoth's voice startled her out of her thoughts, and she nearly dropped the tray of dirty dishes as she looked up to see him striding down the hallway from his office.

In the flickering light cast by the iron wall sconces, he didn't look happy. He also wasn't alone.

Hades, Azagoth's second-in-command and the designated Jailor of the Dead, was walking next to him. No, not walking. With the way his thigh muscles flexed in those form-fitting black pants with every silent step, it was more like prowling. His body sang with barely-leashed power, and she shivered in primal, feminine response.

Son of a bitch, Hades was hot. Hard-cut cheekbones and a firm, square jaw gave him a rugged appearance that bordered on sinister, especially when paired with a blue Mohawk she'd kill to run her palm over. But then, she'd kill to run her palms over all of him, and she'd start with his muscular chest, which was usually, temptingly, bare. Not that she'd complain about what he was wearing now, a sleeveless, color-shifting top that clung to his rock-hard abs.

She tried not to stare, but really, even if she'd stood in the middle of the hall with her tongue hanging out, it wouldn't have mattered. He never looked her way. He never noticed her. She was nothing to him. Not even worth a glance. Those cold, ice-blue eyes looked right through her. And yet, this was a guy who laughed with Lilliana, pulled pranks on the other Unfallen who lived here, and played with hellhounds as if they were giant puppies. Giant, man-eating puppies.

Azagoth stopped in front of her. "Cat? You okay?"

She blinked, realized she'd been lost in a world of Hades. "Ah, yes. Sorry, sir. What is it?"

"Have you seen Zhubaal?"

She nodded. "He was heading toward the dorms about half an hour ago. I think he said he was going to be teaching some of the new Unfallen how to be an asshole or something."

Hades barked out a laugh, and she caught a glimpse of two pearly-white fangs. She used to think fangs were repulsive, but if Hades wanted to sink his canines into her, she'd gladly bare her throat and invite him in. She tapped her tongue against her own tiny fangs, the smaller versions that Unfallen grew a few days after being de-winged. For the most part, she'd gotten used to them. She didn't even bite her lip anymore.

"Z is finally teaching them something he knows all about," Hades said.

There was no love lost between those two, but Cat had no idea why. She did, however, know why she thought Zhubaal was an ass. Not that she wanted to think about it, let alone talk about it. She just had to hope that no one else knew.

Because humiliating.

"Thank you, Cataclysm," Azagoth said, dipping his dark head in acknowledgment. "I hear you've been helping out with the Unfallen, as well. Lilliana says you advised them to use their Heavenly names instead of their Fallen names. You know that's forbidden, right?"

Anxiety flared, but she lifted her chin and boldly met his gaze. "Not in Sheoul-gra. The rules are different in your realm. I figured that if they use their Heavenly names here, it'll remind them to stay on the right track if they want to earn their way back into Heaven."

Hades's gaze bored into her, the intelligence in his eyes sparking. No doubt he was wondering why she hadn't taken her own advice, but thankfully he didn't have a chance to ask.

"Very smart." Azagoth's approval gave her a secret thrill, and then it was back to minion-chores as usual when he said, "By the way, my office could use some attention. It's a little...messy."

Azagoth brushed past her, and was it her imagination or did Hades linger for just a moment? Every inch of skin exposed by her blue and black corset tingled, and she could have sworn his gaze swept over her, appreciative and hot. But then he was as cold as ever, walking next to Azagoth as if she didn't exist and never had.

With a sigh, she dropped off the dishes in the kitchen and grabbed her bucket of cleaning supplies before heading to Azagoth's office. Once inside...well, he wasn't kidding when he said he'd left a mess.

She ran a cloth over the stone and wood walls, wiping down the blood mist from whatever demon Azagoth had vaporized. And it must have been a big demon.

Apparently, he didn't obliterate demons often; there was a price to pay for destroying souls. But when he did, the mess was considerable.

She went through two bottles of cleaner and dozens of rags before the office no longer resembled a slaughterhouse, and man, she was going to need a long shower. Relieved to finally be done, she started to gather her supplies when a dark spot on the wall behind Azagoth's desk caught her eye. Cursing, she swept her cloth over the stain, scrubbing to make sure she got every sticky bit of gore. But dammit, blood had gotten into a crack, and...she frowned.

Putting down the rag, she traced the crack with her finger, squinting at what appeared to be a round recess in the wall. What the heck was it? Driven by curiosity, she pushed slightly. There was a click, followed by a flood of light coming from behind her.

Oh...shit.

She turned slowly, and her gut plummeted to her feet.

A huge chunk of wall had disappeared, revealing a portal from the human and demon planes. A stream of griminions filed through, their short, stocky forms escorting the souls of demons and evil humans into the realm of Sheoul-gra. The creepy little griminions chittered from under their black, monk-like hooded robes as they marched the souls, whose bodies in Sheoul-gra were as corporeal as her own, through the cross-sectioned tunnel, only to disappear into another portal that would take the demons to their final destination—Hades's Inner Sanctum.

"No!" she shouted. "Stop! Azagoth hasn't approved the transfers!"

But they didn't stop. They kept emerging from the right side of the tunnel and disappearing through the shimmering barrier of darkness to the left. Panicked, she pushed on the lever again, but the griminions kept marching. She wiggled it, pushed harder, punched it, and finally, with a whoosh, the portal closed, leaving only a solid wall in its place.

Cat swallowed dryly, her heart pounding, her pulse throbbing in her ears. Maybe she hadn't screwed up badly enough for anyone to know. Maybe no one would notice the souls that got through to the Inner Sanctum without Azagoth's approval.

And maybe she'd just earned herself a place in the Grim Reaper's hall of horrors, the Hall of Souls at the mansion's entrance, where statues made out of the bodies of his enemies were on display for the world to see.

What made it all worse was that the people encased in those statues weren't dead.

On the verge of hyperventilating, she slumped against Azagoth's behemoth of a desk and forced herself to breathe slowly. How did she keep screwing up? And not just screwing up, but royally screwing up. Just last week she'd broken one of Azagoth's centuries-old Japanese swords. And a month before that, she'd spilled pineapple soda all over a priceless rug woven from demon sheep wool by Oni craftsmen.

"Did you know that, unlike pineapple soda, fallen angel blood doesn't stain demon wool?" he'd asked in a dark, ominous voice as she'd scrubbed the rug. And no, as a matter of fact, she hadn't known that.

When she'd said as much, he'd merely smiled, which was far, far worse than if he'd just come out and said that if she fucked up again, her blood would definitely not stain that damned carpet.

Soda, however, did stain, just like he'd said.

It seemed to take hours before she stopped trembling enough to gather her crap and flee the office, and thankfully she didn't run into Azagoth on her way to her quarters. She did manage to catch another glimpse of Hades as he rounded a corner though, the hard globes of his ass flexing under the tight, midnight black pants.

Maybe she could try talking to him someday. Try saying something more coherent than, "Hi, Mr., um, Hades. Or do you prefer Jailor? Or Lord? Or...?"

He'd looked at her as if she'd crawled out of a viper pit. "Hades," he rumbled. "Easy enough."

And that had been the sum of their conversation. Their only conversation. Ever.

Did he think she had freaking halo pox or demonic measles? And why was she dwelling on this anyway? He was clearly not interested in her, and she had more important things to worry about.

Like whether or not Azagoth was going to not stain his carpet with her blood when he found out that she'd allowed unauthorized souls to enter the Inner Sanctum.

Chapter Two

Hades had a lot of names. Lord of the Dead. Keeper of Souls. Jailor of the Baddies. Asshole.

He owned them all. Ruled his piece of the underworld with an iron fist. Feared nothing.

Correction. He feared nothing except the Grim Reaper. Azagoth was the one person who had proven time and time again that he could turn Hades's underworld upside down and shake it like a snow globe.

So Hades generally despised the monthly meetings between him and Azagoth, but thankfully, this latest one had been refreshingly brief and light on fault-finding. Which was good, because Hades's brain had been occupied with images of Cat.

He remembered the first time he'd seen her when she came to work for Azagoth a few months ago, remembered how drawn he'd been to her energy. She was new to life on this side of the Pearly Gates, and while most newly fallen angels were either terrified or bitter, she was neither. According to Lilliana, Cat was curious. Eager to learn. Enthusiastic to experience new things.

Hades could teach her a new thing or two.

Except he couldn't, could he? Nope, because the curvy redhead was off-limits to him, and panting after her like a hellhound on the trail of a hellbitch in heat would only end in pain.

Pain that would likely come at the end of Azagoth's hand, and Hades had long ago learned that pissing off his boss was stupid beyond stupid...beyond stupid.

Still, it grated on him that he'd been read the riot act about Cat when he was about ninety-nine percent sure Zhubaal had bedded her. So what was up with *that*? Z was a cranky sonofabitch with a short fuse and a stick up his ass, but somehow *that* mongrel was good enough for Cat?

So fucked up.

Hades took one of three portals dedicated to travel between Azagoth's realm and the Inner Sanctum back to his residence, and as he materialized inside his living space a tingle of mayhem skittered over his skin. How...odd. Sure, hell was all about mayhem, but this was different, and it had been different for a few months now. Before, there had always been a balanced mix of order and chaos. Organized chaos. Chaotic organization.

Even here, in Sheoul-gra's Inner Sanctum, where the souls of dead demons came to play until they were born again, there was order. Rarely, there was chaos.

At least, chaos used to be rare. But now that Satan had been imprisoned and Sheoul was no longer under his rule, all hell had broken loose—literally. Sheoul was now operating under a new regime, with a dark angel named Revenant as its overlord, and not everyone was happy about the new leadership situation. Just as with humans, demons didn't accept change easily, and the tension surrounding Revenant's takeover had bled over into Sheoul-gra.

Completely unacceptable.

The tingle began to sting, as if Hades was crawling with hornets. Resisting the urge to rip off his own skin, he stepped into his personal portal next to the fireplace. Like Harrowgates that transported demons around Sheoul and the human realm, some of the portals inside the Inner Sanctum had been built to travel only between two locations, while others could transport a person to one of multiple places by manipulation of the symbols inside the portal's four walls. But Hades could also operate them with his mind, allowing any portal to take him anyplace within the Inner Sanctum he wished to be. Or, like now, to get where he needed to be, he merely had to concentrate on the sensation of mayhem wracking his body, and a moment later, the portal opened up.

He wasn't at all surprised to find himself in a burned-out sector of the 5th Ring, a vast, dreary realm of fog, heat, and despair that contained the evilest of the evil. Before him, demons scattered into the mist the moment they recognized him.

Most demons, anyway. A few stood their ground, their defiance admirable, if not foolish.

A demon who had been a professional torturer before he was killed several years ago by Aegis demon slayers blocked his path. Here, demons could choose their appearance, and this bastard had chosen his former skeletal Soulshredder form, his grotesque, serrated claws extending from long fingers.

"Move." Hades slowed, but he didn't stop. He didn't have time for this shit. His skin burned and his insides vibrated, alerting him to some sort of violent disturbance nearby. And it had to be a whopper for him to have felt it from inside his home on the other side of the Inner Sanctum...which was roughly the distance from one earthly pole to the other.

"Fuck you, Soul Keeper."

Surprise jolted him; few were brave—or stupid—enough to challenge him. But Hades kept his expression carefully schooled. Tension was running high right now, and he couldn't afford to let anyone think he was losing control of the Gra.

From two-dozen feet away and without breaking his stride, Hades flayed the demon with a mere thought. Stripped him of his skin like a banana. The demon screamed in agony, and Hades let him. That noise would carry for miles, warning everyone within earshot of the consequences of fucking with him. Sure, Hades could have "killed" him, but the demon's soul would simply have fled the old, broken body and taken a new form. Handing down pain was much more satisfying.

Hades continued on his way, his boots crunching down on charred bone and wood, and as he strode by the Soulshredder, the demon stopped his annoying screaming long enough to croak, "You...will...fail."

Hades ignored him. Because really? Fail at what? His job was pretty simple and straightforward. All he had to do was keep demon and evil human souls inside the Inner Sanctum until the time came when, or if, they were born again. *How* he kept them was entirely up to him. He could leave them in peace, he could torture them, he could do whatever he wanted. Failure? That was ridiculous. There was nothing to fail *at.*

Really, this place was boring as shit most of the time.

Leaving the asshole behind, he threaded his way past the kind of horrors one would expect to find in a place where the evilest of evils lived, but the bodies, blood, and wrecked buildings didn't even draw his eye. He'd seen it all in his thousands of years down here, and nothing could faze him.

Not even the hellhound crouched in the shadows of the gnarled thorn tree gave him pause. The beasts could cross the barrier between Sheoul-gra and Sheoul, and for the most part, Hades let them. He kind of had to, since their king, Cerberus, had taken it upon himself to be the self-appointed guardian of the underworld—specifically, Sheoul-gra. For some reason, hellhounds hated the dead and were one of the few species that could see them outside of Sheoul-gra. Inside Sheoul-gra, they got their rocks off by ripping people apart. As long as they limited their activities to the 3rd, 4th, and 5th Rings, where the worst of the demons lived, he didn't give a crap what the fleabag hounds did.

Ahead, from inside the ruins of an ancient temple, came a chorus of chanting voices. *Ich tun esay. Ich tun esay. Ich tun esay alet!*

He frowned, recognizing the language as Sheoulic, but the dialect was unfamiliar, leaving some of the words open to interpretation. Somehow, Hades doubted his interpretation was correct and that the chanters were talking about opening a dime store.

He tracked the sound, and as he approached the reddish glow seeping through a doorway in the building ahead, the hair on the back of his neck stood up. What the hell? He hadn't been creeped out or afraid of anything in centuries. Many centuries.

Ich tun esay. Ich tun esay. Ich tun esay alet...blodflesh!

What. The. Fuck.

Something screamed, a soul-deep, tortured sound that made Hades's flesh crawl. Something was very, very wrong.

Kicking himself into high gear, Hades sprinted into the fire-lit, cavernous room...and then he skidded to a halt, his boots slipping in pools of blood on the stone floor. A hundred demons from dozens of species were gathered around a giant iron pot hanging over a fire. Inside the pot, a Neethul demon's screams died as his body bubbled in some sort of acidic liquid.

"*Stop!*" Hades didn't give a shit about the demon. What he did give a shit about was the ritual. In Sheoul-gra, all rituals were forbidden and came with a penalty of having one's soul disintegrated, so they didn't happen often. Oh, Hades had come across one or two loners performing religious rituals now and then, but this kind of massive gathering and ceremony? This was a first.

And, by Azagoth's balls, it would be the last.

The mass of chanting demons turned as a unit, their creepy smiles and empty eyes filling him with a sickening sense of doom. Alarm shot through him, and in an instant, he summoned his power and prepared to blast every one of these freaks into the Rot, the prison meant for the worst of the worst, where suffering was more than legend, and where the only release came when Azagoth destroyed your soul.

With a word, he released his power. At the same moment, one of the demons overturned the pot of acid. The liquid, mixed with the goo of the dissolved Neethul, splashed on the floor in a whoosh of steam. Suddenly, as if Hades's power had hit an invisible wall, it bounced back at him, wrapping him in a cocoon of blackness.

As he was transported by his own spell to the prison all demons feared, he heard the chant again. *Ich tun esay alet!*

Oh...shit. This time, he understood.

The demons weren't trying to open a dime store. Somehow they'd acquired a forbidden object or person of power and were attempting to open Sheoul-gra's very walls, to allow millions of souls out into the human and demon realms.

They were looking to feast.

Chapter Three

Hades had no trouble freeing himself from the Rot, although he'd had a hell of a time trying to convince one of the guards, a fallen angel named Vype, that he wasn't a demon in disguise.

Once he'd talked the guy down, Hades gathered a handful of his fallen angel staff and returned to the site of the demonic ritual. Within a few hours, they'd captured two of the demons who had been there. They'd changed their physical appearances, but Hades could see through their costumes to their souls. Idiots.

After delivering them to the Rot, he went immediately to Azagoth, who was surveying his library's vast shelves of books, some of which vibrated as his gaze landed on them. Hades hung back, a lesson learned after being bitten by one of Azagoth's rabid tomes. Who knew books could bite? Vicious little bastards.

Hades cleared his throat to announce his presence. Azagoth didn't even turn around, simply barked out a curt, "Sit."

The Grim Reaper's voice didn't leave room for argument. But then, it rarely did. So Hades took a seat in the leather chair...leather made from the finest Molegra demon hides.

Azagoth took a seat on the plush sofa across from Hades and reached for a tattered book on the armrest. "So," he said. "What's going on in the 5th Ring?"

Hades didn't bother asking how Azagoth knew. No doubt one or more of Hades's wardens were agents for Azagoth. The guy's spy network extended from the deepest pits of Sheoul to the highest reaches of Heaven.

"Hell if I know," Hades said. "But whatever it is, it's bad. I caught a bunch of assholes performing a forbidden ritual powerful enough to deflect my power and blast me to my own fucking prison."

One of Azagoth's dark eyebrows shot up. "I assume you took care of the situation."

"Once I got myself out of my own jail, yeah. I only found two of the offenders, but I've got 'em strung up and awaiting your questioning. I believe they got their hands on something from outside. The power they wielded was like nothing else I've felt."

"Dammit," Azagoth breathed. "You're losing control—"

"My ass," Hades snapped. "The Gra is becoming overloaded with evil souls. You need to stop reincarnating only non-evil demons and start working on the baddies. Get them back to Sheoul where they belong. I've been spending way too much time moving Ufelskala Tier 4 and 5 demons to Rings less equipped to handle that kind of malevolence."

The Ufelskala, a scale developed to categorize demons into five Tiers based on the intensity of evil inherent to their species, was also one of the tools Azagoth used to sort demons into the five Rings of the Inner Sanctum. Not that the guy couldn't send anyone to any Ring he wanted, but in general, he followed the information laid out in the Ufelskala.

"The 1st and 2nd Rings are clearing out," Azagoth said. "As per Revenant's orders, I'm reincarnating a lot of the non-evil demons on those levels. So do some creative reassigning."

Not only would that be a lot of work, but it would require bringing in more fallen angels to oversee Rings that were going to contain a lot more evil demons, and no fallen angel volunteered to work in the Inner Sanctum. Not when they weren't allowed to leave and their powers were limited. They'd have to be...recruited. By force.

"Sir, this is bullshit," Hades growled. "What the everloving fuck is Hell's new overlord doing?"

Azagoth flipped open the book. "That's not for you to question."

Hades burst to his feet. "My hot ass," he snapped. "I never

thought I'd say this, but at least Satan kept order and balance in Sheoul. This new douchebag—"

Burning pain ripped through him, and only belatedly did he realize that he'd been struck by a bolt of hellfire that had streamed directly from Azagoth's fingers.

"Here's the thing," Azagoth said calmly. "Satan didn't give a shit what anyone said about him. But Revenant? He's putting down everyone who speaks out against him. Hell, he's laying out anyone he even *suspects* might rebel."

"That's because he's a paranoid fool. Learning his true identity has made him weak." Apparently, Revenant had grown up in Sheoul believing he was a fallen angel, when the truth was that he had always been a Heavenly angel. How could a true angel, no matter how tarnished his halo, expect to be ruthless enough to rule Hell?

"And yet, he managed to defeat and imprison not only Satan, but Lucifer, Gethel, and the archangel Raphael as well." Azagoth snapped the book closed with a heavy thud. "Respect him."

"He couldn't have done it without help from his brother," Hades muttered.

"Maybe not. But keep in mind that he and his brother have each other's backs. Don't piss off either one of them. Together they are far more dangerous than Satan ever was."

Hades actually liked Revenant's brother, Reaver, who happened to be one of the most powerful Heavenly angels to ever exist. Reaver had spent a little time in the Inner Sanctum as Azagoth and Hades's prisoner, and really, even when the guy had been in pain, he'd been pretty cool.

But Revenant could suck Hades's balls.

The thought of having his balls sucked made an image of Cat flash in his head, which, granted, was way better than thinking of Revenant. But still, off-limits was off-limits. Dammit.

"Yeah, whatever," Hades said, resisting the urge to roll his eyes. "Ever since Rev took over as King of Hell, the Inner Sanctum has been a war zone."

"Which is, in part, because he requested that I only reincarnate Ufelskala Tier one and two demons."

"And the result of that idiotic order is that my domain is

filling up with majorly evil fuckheads who only want to cause trouble."

Azagoth's dark eyes flashed as his patience with Hades wore thin. But then, he'd never had much patience to begin with. "Deal with it. Now. Your rebellions are leaking over into my part of Sheoul-gra, and the archangels are starting to get twitchy."

"The *archangels* are starting to get twitchy? I'm the one trapped down there with demons who are desperate to get out."

"Then keep it from happening."

Keep it from happening? As if Hades had just been laying around on a beach and drinking margaritas while the Inner Sanctum went up in flames? "What the fuck do you think I've been doing for thousands of years?"

There was a long, brittle silence, and then Azagoth's voice went low. And maybe a little judgmental. "There have been escapes."

"Very few, and never more than one at a time. And come on...there were special circumstances in each case." No demon could escape on his own, not when demons had no power in Sheoul-gra. Escape required energy or objects from an outside source, which was why visitors were very rarely allowed inside the Inner Sanctum. A single feather from an angel could be used in spells to destroy barriers or kill a target. One seemingly harmless vampire fang had once given a Neethul the power to reincarnate himself without Azagoth's help.

"Still, you must be extra vigilant." Azagoth dragged his hand through his black hair, looking suddenly tired. Good. Hades shouldn't be carrying the stress of all of this by himself. "I've never seen Sheoul so unstable."

Vigilant. *Vigilant*, he'd said. As if Hades was a total noob at this. But instead of saying that, he merely gritted his teeth and offered a tense smile. "Yes, sir. Anything you say, sir."

"Good. Now get out. And do not fail me again."

* * * *

Somewhere outside Azagoth's Greek-style mansion, a bird of prey screeched. Cat loved hearing it. Not long ago, Sheoul-gra had been a dead realm, a physical manifestation of Azagoth's emotional state. Dark and dreary, the "Gra," as it was sometimes called, had resembled a toxic wasteland that couldn't support any animal or plant life that wasn't straight out of Hell itself.

But Lilliana's love had changed Azagoth, and with it, his realm.

Now, when Cat strolled outside the palace, the grounds and buildings surrounding it teemed with life, from the lush grass, leafy green trees, and sparkling water, to rabbits, birds, and even the occasional fox or deer.

Smiling, she put down her feathered duster and headed from Azagoth's pool room toward the mansion's entrance, and as she rounded a corner, she collided with a body.

A huge, muscular body.

Hades.

An instant, hot tingle pricked her skin as she leaped backward, crashing into something behind her. She heard something break, but at the moment, it didn't matter.

This was the first time she'd touched Hades. The first time her ability to sense good and evil as a physical symptom on the surface of her skin had triggered. At least, it was the first time with Hades.

She'd always suspected he'd give off an intense blast of evil, but she hadn't expected the evil to be tempered by a ribbon of goodness. She also hadn't expected to be so...aroused by the vibes he gave off. Then again, merely looking at him aroused her, so why wouldn't touching him do the same?

He stood there, bare-chested and wearing a skin-tight pair of silver pants that showed every ropey muscle and presented that impressive bulge at his groin like a gift. Criminy, he might as well be naked. She *wished* he was naked.

"E-excuse me," she squeaked.

He looked down at her, one corner of his perfect mouth tipped up in a half-smile. Which was a first. Everyone seemed to get smiles but her.

"You broke Seth."

She blinked. "What?"

He nodded at something behind her. She turned and gasped

in horror at the black, waxy hand lying on the floor and the now-handless statue next to it. "Oh, shit. Azagoth is going to be pissed."

This was his Hall of Souls, a giant room filled with mounted skulls and fountains that ran with blood. It was also where people who did especially vile things—or who made Azagoth *really* angry—were turned into tortured statues. Inside, they were still alive, screaming for all eternity. And she'd just given one an amputation that must be agonizing.

She scrambled to replace the hand, but Hades just laughed. "Don't worry about it. Seth was a demon who passed himself off as an Egyptian god back in the day. He tortured and killed thousands of children. He deserves worse than anything Azagoth or you could do to him."

She stared at the statue, the naked body twisted in whatever agony Azagoth put him through before turning him to stone, his mouth open in a perpetual scream.

"Children?"

"Children."

Sick bastard. She dropped the hand, grabbed Seth's tiny penis, and snapped it off. "I hope he's feeling that."

Hades's booming laughter echoed around the chamber, and she swore the crimson liquid in the center fountain stopped flowing for a heartbeat. "I'll bet you just made every poor stiff in here fear you more than Azagoth. Awesome."

She dropped the nasty appendage next to the hand. "Yeah, well, I'd probably better find some Superglue before he notices."

Hades nudged the pieces with his boot. "I'll take care of it. I'm the one who ran into you, and besides, I live for this kind of thing."

The note of mischief that crept into his voice made her suspicious, and she narrowed her eyes at him. "What have you got up your sleeve? You know, if you had sleeves."

"Don't worry," he said with impish delight, "I know what to do with a cock." He shifted his gaze to her, giving her a roguish once-over that heated her skin even more than touching him had. "So, what's got you in so much of a hurry? Hot date?"

Flustered, because this was the first time he'd spoken to her like she wasn't diseased, she stood there like an idiot before finally blurting, "I heard a bird."

He looked at her like she was daft. "And that's significant...why?"

Heat flooded her face. She must be as red as a Sora demon's butt. "They have wings." Geez, could she sound any dumber? "I guess I miss mine."

"If you miss them that much, you could just enter Sheoul." Massive black, leathery wings sprouted from his back and stretched high enough to brush the ceiling. Blue veins that matched his hair extended from the tips to where they disappeared behind his shoulders, and now that his wings were visible, the veining appeared under his skin, as well. It was as if he were a marble statue come to life.

Cat's breath caught in her throat as she took in his magnificence. He'd transformed, and for the first time, she could see why the demons in the Inner Sanctum would kneel before him.

I'd kneel, she thought, *but for far different reasons.*

That image burned itself into her brain, and she wondered if her face went even redder. Then, to her horror, she found herself reaching out to skim her fingertips along the edges of his wings. He went taut, but her body did the exact opposite as shivery, wild sensations jolted her system and coiled between her thighs. Damn, this male was a danger to everything that made her female, and she stumbled back on unsteady legs.

"Sorry," she whispered, hoping her voice didn't betray her lust. "Like I said, I miss them. I want them back, but I want to get them by earning my way back to Heaven, and I can't do that if I become a True Fallen."

"Not joining me on the dark side, huh?" Now that she was no longer touching him, he'd relaxed, probably relieved that the crazy, horny Unfallen was keeping her hands to herself. Shrugging, he put away his wings, and the veins under his skin faded away. Good, because her fingers might have been all about his wings, but her tongue had wanted to trace every vibrant vein on his body. "Suit yourself. More evil cookies for me."

Shooting her a wink, he sauntered off toward one of the

portals that allowed travel between Sheoul-gra proper and the Inner Sanctum. Cat watched him—and his drool-worthy butt—until he disappeared around a corner.

Outside, the bird of prey screeched again, but now that she'd seen Hades's wings, she wasn't sure anything else could compare. As she contemplated her next move, she eyed the castrated statue and, unbidden, her mind popped an image of the bulge in Hades's pants. She glanced down at the sad little male appendage on the floor and laughed.

Nope. No comparison.

Chapter Four

It had been three days since Cat had opened the portal from the human realm and allowed souls into the Inner Sanctum, and as far as she knew, nothing catastrophic had happened. Maybe no one had noticed. After all, there were millions of souls imprisoned in Sheoul-gra. So what if a handful had slipped through without Azagoth's stamp of approval?

Rationalizing the whole thing didn't make her feel a lot better, so she took out her frustration on the floor of the Great-Hall-slash-Hall-of-Souls at the entrance to Azagoth's mansion. Why the hell did she have to polish the obsidian stone by hand, anyway? Did Azagoth not believe in buffing machines?

Okay, in all fairness, he'd never told her to clean the floor. The big jobs, like landscaping outside and maintaining the floors inside, had been assigned to the dozens of Unfallen who, like Cat, had come to live in the safety Sheoul-gra provided to those caught in the gap between Heavenly angel and True Fallen. But footprints on the floor drove Cat nuts, and today, some jackass had tracked in dirt and grass, completely ignoring the new mat she'd placed at the entrance that said, in bold red letters, WIPE YOUR DAMNED FEET.

She thought the play on "damned" was funny, given that almost everyone who came to Sheoul-gra was some sort of demon. Hades had gotten the joke, had laughed when he saw it. She still smiled when she thought about it.

She shot a fleeting glance over at the statue of Seth, which still hadn't been repaired, but at least the two body parts were missing. Maybe Hades was trying to fix them. *Hopefully*, he was trying to fix them.

A tingle of awareness signaled the arrival of a newcomer into the realm – it was kind of cool how anyone who resided in Sheoul-gra developed a sensitivity to the presence of outsiders. It was usually Zhubaal's job to meet visitors, but he was busy, so she leaped to her feet.

Happy to toss her cleaning supplies aside for a few minutes and always curious about who was paying a visit, she hoofed it out of Azagoth's mansion to the great courtyard out front, where the portal from outside was glowing within its stone circle.

And there, striding toward her, was a magnificent male with a full head of blond, shoulder-length hair and a regal stance that could only mean he was a higher order of angel. As a lowly Seraphim, she'd rarely seen angels ranking higher than a Throne, but there was no doubt that this male was at the very top. Perhaps even a Principality, one rank below an archangel.

"E-excuse me, sire," she said, her voice barely a whisper. "Can I help you?"

The big male nodded, his blond mane brushing against the rich sapphire blue shirt that matched his eyes. "I will see Azagoth."

"I'm sorry, but he's busy—"

"*Now.*"

Mouth. Dry. A lifetime of fear of higher angels made her insides quiver, even as she realized that Heavenly angels held no power here. Inhaling deeply, she reached for calm. As a fallen angel in Azagoth's employ, she was actually more influential in Sheoul-gra than this new guy was.

Somehow, that thought didn't make her feel any better.

"This is not your realm, angel," she said sternly. "You can't just poof in here and demand an audience with Azagoth."

"Is that so." The male's voice was calm. Deadly calm. *Scarily* calm.

"Yes. That is so." She was proud of the way her voice didn't quake. Not much, anyway.

A slow smile curved the male's lips, and if it hadn't been so terrifying, it would have been beautiful. "I don't want to cause trouble for you, Cataclysm. So either fetch him or take me to him. Those are your only choices."

"Or?" she asked, and how the hell did he know her name?

Suddenly, the air went still and thick, and massive gold wings sprung from his back, spreading like liquid sunshine far above them both. "Guess."

Holy...*fuck*. He was...he was...a Radiant. An angel who outranked even archangels. And since there could be only one Radiant in existence at any given time, that meant that this was Reaver, brother to Revenant, the King of Hell. That alone would have been enough to terrify her, but making things worse, much worse, was the fact that she had lost her wings because she'd been in league with an angel who had not only betrayed him, but who had attempted to kill his infant grandchild.

Cat's knees gave out, but before she hit the ground, Reaver caught her, landing her on her feet with one arm around her to hold her steady. Instantly, her skin became charged with his Heavenly energy, the magnitude of it rendering her almost breathless.

It was too intense, scattering her thoughts in a way that touching Hades hadn't. As an angel, she'd touched other angels, but it had never been like this. As a fallen angel, she'd had skin-to-skin contact with Lilliana, and while the female had given off a slight positive energy buzz, it hadn't been anything like what she was experiencing with Reaver.

Maybe the fact that she was a fallen angel had made the sensation of goodness too overwhelming for her. Or maybe the intensity had to do with the fact that Reaver was a Radiant. Whatever it was, it made her want to throw up, the way eating too much of a rich food did.

"You okay?" he asked, his voice low and soothing.

She couldn't say a word. But her inability to speak was more than just her reaction to his touch. He was a rock star in the angel world. Beyond a rock star. He was...*the* rock star. *The* angel.

And she'd nearly destroyed his family.

"What the fuck?" Azagoth's voice rang out from somewhere behind her. Dazed, she turned her head to see him walking toward them, his gaze boring into Reaver. "You know that when a high-ranking angel steps foot into my realm, I feel it, right? Like, migraine feel it."

Legs wobbly, she stepped away from Reaver. "Sir—"

A wave of Azagoth's hand silenced her. "I've got this. Reaver is a friend."

"Friend?" Reaver asked, incredulous. "May I remind you that you ordered Hades to hold me in the belly of a giant demon, where I was slowly digested for centuries?"

Cat couldn't believe it when Azagoth rolled his eyes. He wasn't usually so casual with Heavenly angels. But then, Reaver *had* sent gifts for him and Lilliana. "It was three puny months."

"Yeah, well, it felt like centuries," Reaver muttered.

"Good." Now *that* was more like Azagoth. "Are you here to see Lilliana?"

Reaver shook his head. "Unfortunately, I'm here to see you. There's a soul in Sheoul-gra I need to be released."

"Demon?"

"Human."

Azagoth cocked a dark eyebrow. "Really. And why should I do that?"

"Because he shouldn't be there. Your *griminions* took him before his soul could cross over."

"Even if they'd made that mistake, I'd have caught it," Azagoth said, and a knot formed in Cat's stomach.

"You missed this one."

"Impossible."

A bird chirped in the distance, its cheery song so out of place in the growing tension surrounding Azagoth and Reaver. Cat couldn't help but think that the old, lifeless Sheoul-gra might have been a better setting for the confrontation happening right now between these two powerful males.

Reaver stared at Azagoth, his expression darkening with anger. "Seriously? You think Heaven would make that kind of error?"

"You think *I* would?" Azagoth shot back. "In thousands of years, have I ever allowed a non-evil human soul into Sheoul-gra?"

Oh, no. The knot in Cat's belly grew larger as her little incident three days ago filled her thoughts.

"Mistakes happen."

As Azagoth growled, Cat started to sweat. *She* was responsible for the innocent soul being sent into the holding tank. It was the only explanation.

"I don't make mistakes." Azagoth spoke through teeth clenched so hard that Cat swore she heard one or two crack.

"Then someone else did," Reaver said. "I don't give a shit who's at fault. What I do give a shit about is the fact that there's a human soul in the Inner Sanctum who doesn't belong there, and we want him back before he's harmed or someone realizes he's not evil and they use him to break out of Sheoul-gra."

"Um...excuse me," Cat interrupted. "But this person you're talking about...he's a soul, not a physical being, at least not on Earth or in Sheoul, so how could he be used to help demons escape?"

"Here, as in Heaven, his soul is solid," Reaver said. "A soul-eating demon could absorb him, or his soul could be harvested and liquefied to use in spells." As the horror of what could be happening to an innocent human sunk in, Reaver turned back to Azagoth. "You fucked up big time."

Azagoth snorted. "Bite me."

"You have one week."

"And I repeat—"

"Reaver!" Lilliana's voice rang out, and a moment later, she flung herself into his arms. "It's so good to see you."

They started to chat, giving Cat time to slink away. Holy shit, what had she done? Azagoth had given her a purpose, a home, and safety, and she'd just gotten him into some serious hot water with Heaven.

And that poor human. She'd seen firsthand how traumatic dying could be for humans. Even in Heaven it sometimes took them months to adjust, especially if their deaths were violent or sudden. But to die and then find yourself trapped in hell with no idea why or what you'd done to deserve it?

She shuddered as she shuffled along the stone path toward Azagoth's palace. She had to fix this, but how? Maybe she could find the human herself. Her ability to differentiate between human and demon souls from great distances would be an advantage for her, so maybe, just maybe, she could fix this quickly. If she could get in and out of the Inner Sanctum before anyone noticed she was gone, surely Azagoth would forgive her. It was even possible that the archangels would consider the rescue a good enough deed to allow her back in Heaven.

No one noticed her moving away from the group, so she took the steps two at a time and hurried through the massive doors. The moment she was away from prying eyes, she could no longer maintain her cool composure. She sprinted into action, running so fast through the corridors that she skidded around one corner and nearly collided with the wall on her way to Azagoth's office.

As expected, the office was empty. Terrified, but hopeful that what she was about to do would right a lot of wrongs, she hurried to the lever she'd accidentally opened, the one that had started this whole mess.

Next to the lever that opened the soul tunnel was a switch she'd seen Azagoth and Hades use to gain access to the Inner Sanctum. When she flipped it, a section of the wall faded out, allowing a view of a dark, shadowy graveyard set amongst blackened, leafless trees on the other side.

For a moment, she hesitated. In Heaven, she'd always been the first of her brothers and sisters to take risks, to step into the unknown. But none of them had ever faced anything like this. To them, taking risks meant speaking up at meetings or chasing a demon into a Harrowgate.

Her two brothers and two sisters would shit themselves if they ever stood where Cat was right now.

The thought gave her a measure of comfort and even made her smile a little. So, before she changed her mind, she took a deep, bracing breath, and stepped through the portal. Instantly, heat so thick and damp she could barely breathe engulfed her. Each breath of fetid air made her gag. The place smelled like rotting corpses. And the sounds...gods, it was as if people in the graves were moaning and clawing at their coffins.

Why would anyone *be* in the coffins?

Fear welled up, a suffocating sensation that seemed to squeeze her entire body. This was a mistake. A horrible mistake. She had to go back. Had to confess what she'd done to Azagoth. Panicked, she spun around so fast she nearly threw herself off balance.

Hurry, her mind screamed. Then it froze mid-scream.

The portal was gone.

Frantic, she searched the wall for a lever of some sort. Or a button. Or a freaking spell that would allow her to use a damned magic word.

"Open sesame?" she croaked.

Nothing.

"Let me out."

Nada.

She pounded on the wall where the door had been. "Open the damned portal!"

The sounds coming from the graves grew louder, and her throat clogged with terror.

She was trapped.

Chapter Five

Cat spent what seemed like forever trying to find a way back to Azagoth's realm, but the solid wall, which reached upward into a pitch-black sky as far as the eye could see, was apparently endless. So was the graveyard. Why was there a graveyard here, anyway?

Even stranger, the headstones, all different sizes, shapes, and materials, were unmarked. At least, they weren't marked with names or dates. Some had been carved with what appeared to be graffiti, and others were scarred by writing, mainly in the universal demon language, Sheoulic. Several were warnings to not enter any of the five mausoleums that seemed to be randomly placed around the sprawling cemetery.

Unfortunately, she'd heard enough about the Inner Sanctum to know that the mausoleums were the gateways to the five levels, or Rings, as they were officially called, that housed the demons Hades watched over. She had to enter. But which one? None were marked in any way that would indicate which Ring they led to. Was she supposed to just choose randomly and hope she'd picked the right one? Ugh. Yet another reason she wanted to go back to Heaven. There, everything was clearly marked.

She eyed the five mausoleums and finally decided on the closest one. Before she entered though, she found a heavy piece of wood she could use as a club if needed. When she'd lost her wings, she'd lost all innate defensive weapons, but they wouldn't have done her any good down here, anyway.

She really should have thought this out a little better.

Your impulsiveness is going to get you in trouble someday.

Her mother's words rang in her ears, and so did her siblings' echoes of, "Told you so," uttered just before her wings had been sliced off.

Cat stared at the mausoleum's iron grate door. Apparently, not even losing her wings had taught her a lesson.

Cursing herself—and throwing in some choice words for her siblings—she pushed open the door, cringing at the rusty creaking noise that made the things in the graves screech. The inside was dark and dusty, but anything was better than the foul dampness of the graveyard. It was also smaller than it appeared to be from the outside, about the size of a phone booth.

The door slammed shut behind her, and she nearly screamed at the clank of the metal hitting the stone. An instant later, it swung open by itself, and she stepped out into a featureless, sandy desert. There was nothing but pale yellow sand and gray sky. Nothing moved. There was no breeze, no sound, no smell...what the hell was this place?

Okay, this might have been a mistake. She spun around to go back to the graveyard and a different mausoleum, but like earlier when she first left Azagoth's library, she found nothing but empty air where the doorway should have been. Panic rose up, but before she could form a coherent thought, she heard a noise behind her. A chill shot up her spine as she slowly turned.

Heart pounding, fingers digging into the wood club, she squinted into the distance, and that's when she saw it—a shimmer in the air that slowly solidified into a number of blurry shapes. And then the shapes took form, and her heart slammed to a sudden, painful stop at the blast of evil that struck her.

At least fifty demons of several different species formed a semicircle around her, a wall of fangs, claws, and crude, handmade weapons. The crowd parted to allow one of them, a seven-foot tall, eyeless thing with tiny, sharp teeth and maggot-colored skin, to come forward. In his slender, clawed hand, he held a chain, and on the other end of that chain, crawling on all fours like a dog, was a human male, his hair matted with blood, his skin bruised and bleeding, one ear missing.

This was the very human she'd come for. Relief quickly gave

way to guilt and horror at what had been done to him. And at what might *still* be done to him. To both of them.

"Aren't you a tasty thing," the maggot demon slurred, his voice mushy and sifted through sharp teeth.

Terror, unlike anything she'd ever experienced, clogged her throat. Oh, she'd been afraid before, plenty of times. But this was different. She'd never faced so many demons, and she'd certainly never done it while holding only a stick of wood as a weapon.

Raising her club, she found her voice, shaky and squeaky as it was. "Demon, I am a fallen angel on a mission from Azagoth himself," she lied. "You are to hand over the human immediately."

Maggot-man laughed. "Foolish *kunsac*." Her Sheoulic was rusty, but she was pretty sure he'd just called her a rather nasty slang term for a demon's anus. "You bluff. And you will die." He grinned, flashing those horrid teeth at her. "But not before we get what we want from you."

Another demon stepped forward and made a sweeping gesture toward the others. "What we *all* want from you."

What they wanted from her? How had they even found her?

They came at her in a rush. She swung her club, catching one in the jaw hard enough to knock a few teeth out, but as she swung again, something struck her in the head. She tasted blood and heard a scream, but only later did she realize that the scream was hers.

* * * *

"My lord."

Inside one of the hundreds of tiny cells in the Rot's lowest dungeon levels, Hades turned away from the broken body of one of the two demons he'd captured three days ago. Silth, the fallen angel commander in charge of the 5th Ring, stood in the doorway. "Tell me you've located the rest of the insurgents."

Silth inclined his blond head in a brief nod. "Yes, but—"

"I trust you've dumped them into the Rot's acid pit?" That was one of Hades's favorite punishments. The demons would splash around as their bodies were dissolved slowly and painfully, until only their souls remained.

That was when things got fun. Exposed souls were delicate, and the acid was even more agonizing on their raw, tender forms. The demons would take another physical body, and then the acid went right back to work, starting the cycle again. It usually didn't take more than a few days before the bastards started talking.

And if that didn't work, dropping them into one of the graves in the cemetery for a couple of decades would.

"Of course." Silth shifted his balance nervously, making his chain mail rattle, and Hades stiffened. "A situation requires your attention."

A dark, slithery sensation unfurled in Hades's gut at both Silth's words and the grim tone. "Tell me."

"The entire 5th Ring is becoming unstable, and the violence is spreading into the 4th Ring. Intelligence indicates that a large-scale escape from Sheoul-gra is in the works."

"Bullshit." Hades kicked at the straw on the floor and watched a hellrat scurry into another filthy pile. "There's no way they could gather enough power to accomplish something like that."

Silth, who Hades had personally chosen as the 5th Ring's warden because he was an evil sonofabitch who liked pain and feared nothing, suddenly looked as if he'd rather be anywhere but here. He even took a step back from Hades, as if he expected to be slaughtered.

Which meant the guy had some fucking bad news.

"Somehow," he growled, "they got hold of an Unfallen."

Hades blinked. "An Unfallen? Like, a living, breathing fallen angel? How? Azagoth wouldn't have allowed anyone inside without telling me." No way. Any living being who was given access to the Inner Sanctum had to be escorted and contained to prevent exactly what appeared to be going on right now in the 5th Ring.

"I saw her myself," Silth said.

"Her?" Hades frowned. "Who?"

"I know not. I caught but a glimpse," Silth said, reverting back to what Hades like to call his "medieval speak." The dude had fallen from Heaven in the late 900's and had spent way too much time messing in human affairs and picking up their annoying habits. "When I captured one of the rebels, he admitted that she was an Unfallen being used in a ritual that would break down the Inner Sanctum's walls."

The hellrat poked its head out of the straw and took a bite out of the unconscious demon on the floor. They were cute little buggers.

"Something's still not right." Hades tore his gaze away from the rodent. "It would take more than a single Unfallen to unleash the kind of magic that would destroy the Inner Sanctum's boundaries. What else do they have?"

"Unknown. But I fear that if we don't act now, it won't matter if the walls fall or not. The uprising is spreading, and if it reaches all of the levels..." He trailed off, knowing full well that Hades understood the seriousness of the situation.

A large-scale rebellion might not result in the destruction of the Inner Sanctum's walls, but it would force Azagoth to halt the admission of new souls into the Inner Sanctum, resulting in a backup that would affect both the human and demon realms. Azagoth had even theorized that a large enough riot could blow out the inner barriers that separated Azagoth's realm from the Inner Sanctum, resulting in a wave of chaos that would destroy everything Azagoth held dear.

Not that Hades gave a shit what Azagoth held dear, but any threat to Azagoth was a threat to Hades, as well. If Azagoth fell, so would Hades, no matter how connected he might be to the Biblical prophecy laid out for Thanatos, the Horseman known as Death.

And I looked, and behold a pale horse; and he who sat on it was named Death, and Hades followed with him.

Yeah. That.

Hades had already helped out the Four Horsemen on several occasions, but he had no idea what was in store for him down the road. No doubt, it wouldn't be good. The Horsemen had a way of getting themselves into trouble.

Hades brushed past Silth and started down the narrow, torch-lit hall, the fallen angel on his flank. "Where are the insurgents holding the Unfallen?"

"My boys and I battled them on the 5th Ring's Broken Claw Mountain." Silth paused as they stopped at the armory, where Hades grabbed a leather harness loaded with blades fashioned from materials found in the Inner Sanctum. Anything from outside was strictly forbidden except inside Hades's home. "The survivors fled into the canyon with the female. I believe they're holed up there."

Hades snorted. "You think they're what, cornered? Waiting to be slaughtered?" Testing the edge of a bone blade, he shook his head. "They have a plan."

"You think it's a trap?"

"Hell, yeah, it's a trap." He grinned because as shitty as the turmoil in the Inner Sanctum was, there was a bright side. Thousands of years of monotony had worn thin, but now there was a little excitement. Something to challenge him, to make him feel alive.

He thought of Cat and how, when she'd run into him in Azagoth's Hall of Souls, he'd had a moment where he'd felt more alive than he had in centuries. It had been enough to make him forget, just for a few minutes, that she was off-limits to him. His pulse had picked up, his body had hardened, and he'd wanted so badly to wrap himself around her and revel in skin-on-skin contact.

But that wasn't going to happen, so he'd have to settle for the next best thing.

A good old-fashioned fight.

Chapter Six

It turned out that Silth hadn't been exaggerating when he'd said that the 5th Ring was in chaos. In the canyon where the Unfallen was supposedly being held, Hades found himself having to fight his way through hordes of demons simply to get within sight of the staging area where the leaders were chanting and dancing and sacrificing demon critters for their blood.

As Hades and his team of fallen angels battled an endless stream of demons, he kept an eye out for the idiot Unfallen who had somehow landed herself in a shit-ton of trouble. Because even if the demons didn't kill her, Hades would.

And he was going to have fun doing it.

He threw out his hand, sending a wave of disruptive power into the crowd of demons in front of him. They blew apart as if they'd been nuked, leaving a path of meat and blood ahead of him. Hellhounds rushed in to feast and snap at the souls rising from the ruined bodies. It wouldn't be long before they reoriented themselves and generated new flesh-and-blood bodies again, so Hades had to hurry. Although only Hades and his fallen angel wardens possessed supernatural powers down here, the demons still had size, strength, teeth, and claws in their arsenals, not to mention sheer numbers. If Hades and his team were overwhelmed, things could get bad. Real bad.

Worse, he'd gone back to his place to contact Azagoth only to find that communications were down, and they must have been for hours. Azagoth always sent a message for a status update at precisely midnight, but for the first time in thousands of years, there was nothing. He probably should have popped into Azagoth's office to see what was up before charging into battle, but dammit, the Grim Reaper's Darth Vader-ish warning to not fail him again was still sitting on his mind like a bruise, and he didn't feel like poking it. Still, it might have been helpful to know how the hell an Unfallen had gotten into the Inner Sanctum.

Whatever. Regrets were for douchebags.

"There!" Silth pointed to a crude wooden crucifix near the site where animal blood ran thick from a stone outcrop in the cliffs. "The Unfallen."

Hades sprinted toward the crucifix, dodging a volley of spears raining down from demons perched on the rock outcroppings of the canyon's walls. He wished he could use his wings, but flying would make him more of a target. For now, he was safer in the enemy crowd.

He kept his eye on the crucifix as he ran. From this angle, he could make out the slim body of a female hanging limp from the crucifix, arms tied to the cross-board, her head falling forward, her face hidden by a mop of bright red hair. A spark of recognition flared, but it snuffed like a squashed firefly as an axe struck him in the head. Pain screamed through him as shards of bone from his own skull drove into his brain.

"Bastard" he snarled as he wheeled around to his attacker, a burly Ramreel with a black snout and glowing red eyes. "You fucked up my Mohawk." At least, that's what he thought he'd said. The words were garbled. Clearly, the bone shards had also fucked up the part of his brain that controlled speech.

One eye wasn't working, either, but his ability to draw and quarter a demon with a single thought was still intact, as he proved a heartbeat later.

Head throbbing as flesh and bone knit back together, Hades made a run for the Unfallen female. Lightning flashed overhead, and electric heat sizzled over his skin. That lightning wasn't natural. He looked past the giant wooden crucifix, and his hackles raised.

An Orphmage, one of the most powerful sorcerer-class demons that existed, was moving toward the female, a bone staff in his hand. And from the staff, tiny bolts of lightning surged.

Impossible. *Im-fucking-possible.* No one but Azagoth, Hades, and his wardens could wield power here. No one. Not without a source from outside the realm. He supposed the demon could be drawing energy from the Unfallen, but she wouldn't have enough for the kind of magic he was brandishing.

No, something much, much bigger was in play here.

Hades lunged, sending a stream of white-hot electricity at the demon. The Orphmage flipped into the air, avoiding Hades's weapon like he did it all the fucking time. As he landed, he whirled, and in a quick, violent motion, he stabbed the Unfallen in the chest with the sparking end of his staff. She screamed, a sound of such suffering that it somehow drowned out the violence of the battle and reduced the cries of the wounded to muted whispers in the background.

Hades froze. He finally recognized that voice. And that hair. And, as her scream began to fade into a tortured rasp and her body went limp, he recognized her clothes. Faded, torn jeans. Black and emerald corset. Bare feet.

Cat never wore shoes.

The Orphmage stepped back, his head covered by a burlap hood, but Hades could make out a sinister grin stretching his thin lips into a hideous slash. He raised his staff to strike Cat again. With a roar, Hades hurled a series of fireballs at the demon even as he charged toward him. Somehow the demon blocked the fire, but the force of their impacts against his invisible shield still knocked him backward with each blow.

In Hades's peripheral vision he saw one of his wardens go down, his body going one way, his head going another, and dammit, Geist might have been a sadistic tool, but he'd served Hades well for nearly a thousand years.

Quickly, Hades put the dead fallen angel out of his mind and charged up the rocky slope, using his mind to continue throwing shit at the Orphmage. A crude arrow punched through Hades's arm, and as he yanked it out, several more pierced his legs and back. Gritting his teeth against the pain, he hauled himself up the incline and leaped onto the plateau where demons had been making their sacrifices and where Cat was hanging limply from the crucifix.

"Cat," he breathed. "Cat!"

He ran toward her, ignoring the volley of projectiles raining down on him. Pain wracked him, blood stung his eyes, and his battery of powers was draining, but none of that mattered. He had to get to Cat. She was only about thirty yards away, but it felt like he'd run miles by the time he unsheathed a dagger and sliced through the ropes holding her captive.

Awkwardly, he threw her over his shoulder and reached out with his senses to locate the nearest portal. It wasn't far, but naturally, a horde of well-armed, giant demons were standing between him and the way out.

"Hellhounds!" he shouted into the flashing sky. From out of nowhere, two inky canine blurs shot up the side of the canyon toward him. "Make a path!"

Instantly, the hellhound veered toward the group of demons and went through them like bowling balls through pins. Hades followed in the beasts' wakes, reaching the portal as a demon with a missing arm swung a club at him. With relish, Hades sent a blast of power into the bastard's head, exploding it in a fabulous gore-fest.

The portal swallowed him, and an instant later, panting and exhausted, he stepped out of the 5th Ring's mausoleum at the graveyard. He flew the short distance to the wall where portals to and from Azagoth's part of Sheoul-gra were laid out and triggered by only his and Azagoth's voices.

"Open," he barked. Nothing happened. Frowning, he tried again. "Open."

Again, nothing. What the hell? Reaching out, he smoothed his hand over the dark stone surface. It felt the same as always, so why was it not opening?

"Open!" Gods, he might as well have been talking to a wall. He snorted. Sometimes he cracked himself up. "Damn you, fucking *open!*"

Given that the passage was the only way to get out of the Inner Sanctum, this was not good. Had Azagoth sealed the door on purpose? Was this a weird glitch? Or had the demons in the 5th Ring had something to do with this?

Hades wasn't sure which scenario was the better one.

Cat groaned, and shit, he needed to get her someplace safe where she could recover from whatever the Orphmage had done to her. And as soon as she was able to talk, she had some serious explaining to do.

Chapter Seven

Everything was gray. Light gray. Dark gray. And every shade of gray in between.

Cat blinked. Where was she? Squinting, she shifted her head from side to side. She was lying down, apparently inside some sort of lidless stone box. It was huge, about the size of a king-size bed, and like a bed, it had blankets and pillows. Who the hell slept in a giant box?

She sat up, but she was so weak that it took two tries, and as she peered around the room, her head spun.

"Ah, Sleeping Beauty awakens."

Cat turned to the owner of the voice, and she would have gasped if her breath hadn't clogged in her throat. Hades? What was he doing here? Of course, it might help to know where "here" was. "Here" appeared to be a room constructed from the same stone as the box she was sitting in. Iron sconces on the walls gave off a gloomy light, but the fire in the hearth kept the place from being completely horror-movie chic.

"Where am I?" Her voice sounded cobwebby, which seemed appropriate, given that the room looked like a tomb.

"My place." Hades walked over to the far wall where a pot steamed over the fire's roaring flames. He was shirtless today, and the light from the fire flickered over his skin, the shadows defining every glorious muscle as he went down on his heels and ladled something into a cup.

Gods, she was confused. Why was she here? What had

happened? The last thing she remembered was being in Azagoth's office...no, wait. She'd gone to the Inner Sanctum to find a human. But everything was pretty cloudy after that.

She rubbed her eyes, which were as blurry as her memories. "What happened to me?"

Hades came over, moving in that way of his, like a panther on the hunt. Not even the chains on his massive black boots made a sound when he walked.

"That's my question for you." He held out the cup, which was really more of a bowl. That looked suspiciously like the top of a skull. "Drink this."

She eyed the contents as she took the bowl, nearly splashing the clear yellow liquid on her hand. It seemed safe enough, wasn't full of floating eyeballs or anything.

"Smells good," she said as she put it to her lips. "What is it?"

"It's a healing broth. Made it myself from the skin and bones of a Croix Viper."

Cat tried not to gag even though the liquid actually tasted decent, like spicy chicken soup. "Thank you." She tried to hand it back, but he shook his head.

"Drink it all. It'll heal the rest of your wounds."

She looked down at herself, but there wasn't a mark on her. Her jeans were dirty, and there were splashes of what might be blood on her feet, but it didn't appear to be hers, and otherwise, she seemed to be in great shape. "What wounds?"

He picked up one of several blades he'd laid out on a crude wooden table and began wiping it down with a rag. "You were pretty messed up when I found you. I have the capacity to heal minor physical damage, but the other stuff is beyond my ability."

"The other stuff?" She watched him slide the blade into a leather harness hanging off a chair.

"Psychic wounds," he said gruffly. "The kind you get when an Orphmage thrusts his magic stick in you."

She drew a sharp breath. "Magic...stick?"

"Not *that* kind of magic stick. Seriously, you ever seen an Orphmage's junk?" He snorted. "I figure they use their staffs to compensate for their tiny dicks."

She'd have laughed if she wasn't so confused about why she

was here and what had happened to her. She hadn't spoken to Hades much, but she'd seen how he interacted with others, and she loved his sense of humor. He was so inappropriate and nothing like the people she'd dealt with in her sixty years of life in Heaven. She was pretty sure most angels had *magic sticks* up their asses.

"Maybe I could get out of this..." She looked around at the box she was sitting in. "This...um, coffin? Am I in a freaking coffin?"

"It's actually more of a sarcophagus." He grinned. "Cool, huh?"

Actually, yeah. Hades, guardian of the demon graveyard, had a sarcophagus for a bed. He really lived the part, didn't he?

He offered her his hand, which she took, relishing the hot static buzz that skittered over her skin as she allowed him to help her to her feet and out of the giant coffin. And man, his hand was big. And strong. And it made her wonder what his fingers would feel like as they caressed her skin.

This was the second time they'd touched. She liked it. Wanted more. Being this close to a male was rare and strange, and aside from the unfortunate incident with Zhubaal, she'd never really had more than casual contact with the opposite sex. In Heaven, many angels were all "free-love" and "if it feels good do it," but Seraphim tended to be conservative, determined to use ancient practices like arranged matings in order to preserve the inherent abilities that made Seraphim unique among angels.

She'd always thought Seraphim customs were a drag, even though her parents hadn't been as militant as most others. Even so, just before she'd been booted from Heaven, they'd started to nudge her in the direction of suitable mates.

Now she was on her own, curious, and frankly, she was horny. Her brief encounter with Zhubaal had been ill-conceived and had only left her more sexually frustrated. Although, if she were honest with herself, she could probably lay some of her frustration at her own feet since she hadn't been shy about asking Lilliana about sex with Azagoth.

Lilliana had been shocked at first, but they'd grown close, and soon Azagoth's mate was confiding in Cat, sharing what they did in the shower, with the spanking bench, out in the woods... Cat shivered at the thought of doing some of those things with Hades.

The desire to feel more than the buzz she was getting through their clasped hands became a burning need, and she stepped closer to him, drawn by his bare chest and thick arms. If she could just smooth her palm over his biceps or abs—

Abruptly, he released her and leaped back, almost as if she'd scorched him. A muscle in his jaw twitched as he stood there, staring down his perfectly straight nose as if she were an enemy. And yet...there was an undercurrent of heat flowing behind the ice in his eyes.

Could he read her mind? And if he had, wouldn't her naughty thoughts have made him want to touch her more? She didn't know much about the males of her species, but she knew it didn't take much to get them interested.

"Make yourself comfortable," he said gruffly. "I don't have a lot of visitors, so..." He shrugged as he gestured to one of two chairs in the small space.

Right. So...pretend that neither one of them had been affected by the brief moment of...well, she didn't know what to call it. Maybe avoidance was for the best.

She cleared her throat in hopes of not sounding like a moron. "This is your home? I wouldn't have expected you to live in a one-room...what is this? A crypt?"

"Ding, ding," he said, his voice dripping with sarcasm but not malice. "Give the girl a prize. More snake soup, maybe?"

She held up her still-full bowl. "Thanks, but I'm good." The crackling fire drew her attention to the carved gargoyles on the ends of the mantel and the faded painting of angels battling demons in a cemetery hanging above it. Okay, maybe Hades was taking the graveyard guardian thing a little too far. "So, why do you live in a crypt? Surely you could have a mansion if you wanted."

"You'd think, right?" He gestured to the chair again. "Sit."

It didn't occur to her to not obey, so she sat carefully in the rickety chair that must have been put together by a five-year-old child. As far as she could tell, it was constructed of branches and strips of leather.

Hades folded his arms over his massive chest and stared at her until she squirmed in her highly uncomfortable seat. As if her discomfort was exactly what he was waiting for, he finally spoke.

"Tell me, Cat. What did you do to piss off Azagoth, and why would he send you to the Inner Sanctum without telling me?"

Shit. She was a terrible liar, and she had a feeling that Hades would see through a lie, anyway, but the truth...man, it was probably going to get her punished in a major way. She stalled by sipping the snakey soup.

"Also," he pressed, not missing a beat, "what do you know about communications being down and the door between Azagoth's realm and the Inner Sanctum being locked?"

She choked on the broth. "It's locked for you, too?" At his nod, her mouth went dry. This was bad. Really bad. "I tried to go back, but I couldn't. I thought I screwed something up."

"You screwed up, all right," he said, "but you couldn't have gone back. Only Azagoth or I can operate the doors." He tossed a log on the fire. "Why did you come here?"

Dread made her stomach churn, as if the soup had morphed back into a snake in her belly. "Before I answer your questions, I need to ask something."

"Sure," he drawled, arms still crossed over his chest. "Why the fuck not."

Well, that didn't sound promising. "Azagoth has the ability to destroy souls." She shuddered at the very idea, at the sheer *power* one must possess to undo what God himself had done. "Do you?"

One corner of his perfect mouth tipped up. "You worried?"

"A little."

"Seriously?" He lost the smile. "What the fuck did you do?" His eyes narrowed, becoming shards of angry ice. "Azagoth doesn't know you're here, does he? You entered the Sanctum without his knowledge. Holy shit, Cat, do you know what I'm supposed to do to intruders?"

She could guess, but she really didn't want to. The bowl in her hands started to tremble. *Calm down. He probably won't kill you. Probably.*

"Cat!" he barked. "At least one of my wardens is dead because of you, so I need some answers. *Now*."

She couldn't look at him, so she concentrated on her feet and said softly, "I accidentally let some souls into the Inner Sanctum."

"Accidentally?"

"Of course it was an accident," she snapped, annoyed that her motives were in question. "Who in their right mind would open the tunnel without Azagoth's permission? I didn't even know *how* to open the thing. I was cleaning, and I accidentally—"

"Okay," he interrupted. "I get it. It was an accident, but that doesn't explain why you're here."

She set the bowl on the edge of the coffin and blew out a breath. "I wanted to fix my mistake. I know it was stupid. I changed my mind, but the portal closed and I couldn't get back."

"So you traveled to the 5th Ring?" he asked, incredulous. "What kind of dumbass move was that? What the fuck were you thinking?"

"I was thinking that I needed to find the human," she shot back, feeling a little defensive. She might be impulsive, and she might not have made the best decision ever, but she had been trying to make things right. "But I swear, I'd barely stepped out when demons surrounded me."

"That's because you're different. You are, for lack of a better word, alive. They can sense your life-force in a way my wardens and I can't." He scowled. "Wait. Human?" He moved a little closer, and she suddenly felt crowded. "What human?"

Ah, yeah, this was where things got really sticky. And bad. "One of the souls that got through...it was human."

"So?" He picked up another of his wicked knives off the table and ran his thumb over the blade. "Evil humans are admitted to the Inner Sanctum every day. The souls you allowed through would have made their way to one of the five Rings...which isn't a catastrophe. Eventually we'd have figured out that they were in the wrong place. *If* they were in the wrong place. So why did you worry about it? Because you were afraid of Azagoth's wrath? Not that you shouldn't be afraid," he threw in. "He peeled me once. *Peeled me*. Do you know what it feels like to be fucking peeled? I'll give you a hint. It's not as fun as it sounds."

Er...she didn't think it sounded fun at all. And geez, she knew Azagoth could be terrifying, but she'd also seen his tender, caring side, and she'd never known him to be needlessly cruel. Then again, by all accounts, Lilliana had softened him considerably. Cat wouldn't have wanted to know Azagoth pre-Lilliana.

"I'm...not sure how to respond to that." But she was sure as hell more afraid of Azagoth than ever. "I mean, yes, I was worried about Azagoth's reaction, but the problem is that the soul was mistakenly brought here. He's human, but not evil. He was reaped by mistake."

"A mistake? How do you know all of this?"

"Because Reaver paid a visit to Azagoth. He wants the human back in a bad way."

Hades went silent, spinning around to pace, his heavy boots striking the floor with great, tomb-shaking cracks. "When did this happen? When did you send the human into my realm?"

She didn't *send* the human into the realm, but she wasn't about to quibble about terminology at the moment. "Three days ago." She reconsidered that, since she didn't know how long she'd been held captive by the demons. "Could be a little longer."

Hades let out a low whistle as he ran his hand over his Mohawk. "Damn, Cat. Just...fuck."

"I know," she said miserably.

"No, you don't know. It all makes sense now. The ritual I came across a few days ago. The Orphmage wielding power. The human was fueling all of it. The damned human is why all of this shit is happening, and with the comms down, Azagoth had no way to warn me."

"What shit?"

"The riots down here. The rebellion." He hurled the knife to the table. The tip of the blade punched into the wood and vibrated, the noise filling the small space with an eerie echo. "The magic."

She shook her head, completely lost. "I don't understand. There have been riots? What magic?"

"The magic that severed communication with Azagoth and sealed the exits out of the Inner Sanctum."

"Sealed? Not just locked? Like, there's nothing you can do?" She couldn't believe that. How could one dead human cause so much trouble? "You're Hades. Surely—"

"No, Cat. That's what I'm trying to tell you. The exit is sealed. We're stuck here, and if the demons are clever enough, they can use the human to reveal the location of my home as well. And once that happens..." He trailed off, and she swallowed. Hard.

She knew she shouldn't ask, but as the psychotic angel she used to work for once said, she was "fatally curious." "Once that happens...what?"

"We'll be overrun by millions of the evilest demons on the Ufelskala scale. They'll kill us, Cat, and if we're lucky, they'll only spend a couple of days doing it."

Chapter Eight

Hades could not believe this shit. In his thousands of years of presiding over the hellhole that was the Inner Sanctum, not a single soul had entered by mistake. Both he and Azagoth had been very careful about who—and what—passed through the barrier. The consequences of the smallest foreign object or unauthorized person entering the Inner Sanctum was precisely why not even his fallen angel wardens were allowed to leave once they started work here. Hades himself couldn't bring anything in, except under certain circumstances, and only with Azagoth's permission.

Made it tough for a guy to get a pizza.

And now, in a matter of days there had been at least two unauthorized entrances, and the full extent of the resulting damage had yet to be seen.

Cat shoved to her bare feet, which were decorated with purple nail polish. Cute. He'd been ordered not to touch her sexually, but would sucking on her toes count?

"So you're saying that we have no recourse?" Her hands formed fists at her sides, and he wondered if she was attempting to keep from punching something. "There's no way to contact Azagoth?"

"I've been trying. My phone has no signal, and even our old methods of communicating through ensorcelled parchment and blood isn't working. I'd been wondering why Azagoth has been so quiet."

"You have a phone down here?" She glanced around as if seeking said device. "A phone that works?"

"I know you haven't been a Heavenly reject for long, but never underestimate the ability of demons to hijack and tweak human advancements." He gestured to a cabinet in the corner. "I have TV, too. Do *not* mess with me on *The Walking Dead* night."

Her delicate, ginger eyebrows cranked down in skepticism. "Are you saying that demons are smarter than humans?

"I'm saying that demons think outside the box and are a lot more creative." He shrugged. "Plus, most of them aren't limited by stifling moral values."

Cat appeared to consider that, her blood-red lips pursing, her pert, freckled nose wrinkling as she thought. "Okay, so we find the human. They must be using his non-evil energy to fuel the spell that cut off the Inner Sanctum from the rest of Sheoul-gra."

He liked that she was thinking this through without freaking out. And as stupid as her decision to enter his realm might have been, he had to admit it was bold—and brave. How many people would have done the same? And how many could have gone through what she had and still be not only mentally intact but willing to keep trying to fix their mistake?

"Maybe," Hades said. "But what did they want with you? Do you know?"

She closed her eyes, her long lashes painting shadows on her pale skin. "I'm not sure. I thought they were going to hurt me, but if they did, I don't remember much of it."

Good, because Hades remembered enough for both of them. Oh, he hadn't witnessed everything that happened to her, but he knew she'd taken a beating at some point. He still couldn't get the bruises and welts that had marked every exposed inch of her body out of his head.

A growl threatened to break free from his throat as he thought about it. Even as he'd laid her carefully in his bed and channeled healing waves into her, he'd sworn to hunt down every one of her attackers and introduce them to his favorite knives.

"Did they say anything to you?" he ground out, still angry at the memory of what had been done to her.

She licked her lips, leaving them glossy and kissable, and he was grateful for something to concentrate on besides her now-healed injuries. "The Orphmage talked about using me to usher in a new world order. Or something crazy like that."

"That sounds about right. Orphmages *are* crazy. But it's a mad scientist kind of crazy that's dangerous as fuck because they can make their insane ideas come to life." Which actually sounded pretty awesome. "Man, if I ever get to be reincarnated, I want to come back as an Orphmage."

"Fallen angels can only be reborn to other fallen angels," she pointed out, as if he didn't know that. "Also, you're twisted."

"Which doesn't stop you from panting after me every time you see me at Azagoth's place." He got a kick out of the way her face went bright red, and he wondered if she was going to deny it.

He wasn't an idiot; he'd seen the way she looked at him. The way she got all flustered when he was near. He loved it. Had come to crave the attention whenever he was visiting Azagoth. He supposed that intentionally seeking her out just so he could get a reaction he couldn't return in kind was a form of self-torture, but hey, torture was what he did, right?

"W-what?" She sputtered with indignation. "I don't do th—"

"You do."

"Don't."

"Do." He laughed. Felt good, but not because he didn't laugh a lot. He just hadn't had a laugh teased out of him by a female in a long time. "It's okay. There's no shame in wanting me. I *am* hot, after all."

She huffed, making her breasts nearly spill out of the tight black and emerald corset she wore. "Whatever," she mumbled. And then she smiled shyly. "I didn't think you noticed."

He nearly swallowed his tongue. He'd been teasing; he hadn't expected her to be bold enough to admit to wanting him. Time to change the subject, and fast, because he wasn't entirely sure he had the willpower to withstand any coy come-ons. He hadn't been with a female in years, not since the last time Azagoth let him out of Sheoul-gra. Everyone inside the Gra, including demons, were off-limits to him, and always had been.

That's what you get when you mess with the Grim Reaper's family.

Yeah, he'd brought his punishment on himself, but fuck,

he'd made that mistake thousands of years ago. Hadn't he paid his debt by now? He'd asked Azagoth that very question just recently. As it turned out, Azagoth had a long memory, held a grudge, and wasn't the forgiving type.

Shoving thoughts of past mistakes aside, he changed the topic. "So what made you think you could enter the Inner Sanctum and find the human?"

Disappointment at the subject change flashed in Cat's jade eyes, but she covered it with a casual shrug. "I possess a particularly powerful ability to sense good and evil."

"You still have it? Even after you lost your wings?"

She glanced around the room, and instead of answering, she asked, "You got anything to drink? You know, that isn't made from snakes?"

"Sure thing." With a flick of his wrist, the wall behind the TV slid open, revealing a small kitchen that looked like something straight out of *The Flintstones.* Except he had demon-installed electricity. Yay for refrigeration and hot stovetops.

"Huh," Cat said. "I did not expect that. You got a secret bathroom, too?"

"Other wall." As he walked to the kitchen, he heard the wall behind him slide open, heard her murmur of approval.

"Happy to see the shower. Not so happy to see a...what is that, a toilet *trough*?" Her dismayed tone amused him. "That looks like something pigs would eat out of."

"I'm old-fashioned." His amusement veered quickly to shame as he reached into the cupboard for his only two cups. As he plopped them onto the pitted stone counter, he cursed his stark living conditions. They'd never truly bothered him before, but now, seeing how he lived through Cat's eyes had lifted the veil a little, and he didn't like it at all. So instead of going for the rotgut moonshine made right here in the Inner Sanctum, he reached for his prized bottle of rum that Limos, one of the Four Horsemen, had given him three decades ago. "Rum okay? And you haven't answered my question."

"What question? Oh, right. Um, yes, rum is fine, and as far as my ability, it's not as strong as it was before I lost my wings, but I can still feel the difference between good and evil from a greater distance than most haloed angels or True Fallen."

As he splashed a couple of fingers of rum into each cup, he realized that for all of the times he'd seen Cat and asked questions about her during his visits to Azagoth, he knew very little about her. Oh, he'd heard the story of how she fell from grace, how she'd associated with Gethel, the turncoat angel who sold her soul to have Satan's child. He also knew Cat had been brave enough to admit to her mistakes instead of trying to cover them up.

Admirable. Not the route he'd have gone in her situation, but hey, he'd never been a shining beacon of light even when he'd still rocked a halo.

Swiping up the cups, he turned back to her. Damn, she was beautiful, standing in the middle of his living room, barefoot, her jeans ripped in several places, a narrow strip of flat belly peeking between her waistband and her top. But the real showstopper was her hair, that glorious, wavy ginger mane that flowed over her shoulders and breasts in a tangle of wild curls. She looked like a warrior woman plucked from Earth's past, and all she was missing was a sword and shield.

And all he was missing was a brain because those were thoughts he shouldn't be having. He strode back to her and handed her a cup.

"So, with that kind of specialized ability," he began, "what did you do in Heaven?"

"You mean, what did I do before I started working for a traitor who got me booted out of Heaven?" Her voice was light, sarcastic, but there was definitely a bitter note souring the soup.

Of course, if he'd been tricked into nearly starting an apocalypse, he'd be bitter, too.

"Yeah." He raised his sad little bone cup in toast. "That."

She gave him an annoyed look. "I'm a Seraphim. What do you think I did?"

As a Seraphim, who Hades knew was one of the lower angel classes despite what human scholars thought, she would have been required to work closely with humans. "Guardian angel stuff?"

She snorted. "Seraphim don't work in the Earthly realm. We

mainly do administrative work for humans who are newly crossed over."

He hoped it wasn't too rude to cringe, because he did. "Sounds boring as shit."

"It is," she admitted. "But because my ability to distinguish good and evil was so strong, my work was a little more interesting."

She was interesting. "How so?"

"Well, all humans are a blend of good and evil, but they're mostly good. They almost immediately cross over to Heaven when their Earthly bodies die." She sank down in the chair again, gingerly, as if it would splinter. It might. Hades had made it himself, discovering in the process that he was a better Lord of Souls than he was Lord of Furniture. "The evil ones are collected by Azagoth's *griminions* and brought here. But if there's any question at all about their level of evil, *griminions* are supposed to leave them alone so they can either remain in the human realm as ghosts or cross over to Heaven on their own. People like that are a very specific mix of equal amounts of good and bad. And others, the ones humans call sociopaths, are even more complicated."

Huh. Hades had never really thought about that. Yes, he knew there were more shades of good and evil than there were stars in the sky, but it never occurred to him that there would be those who walked such a fine line that they would be difficult to place in either Heaven or Sheoul.

"So you worked with the oddballs?"

"We called them Neutrals. Or Shuns." She sipped her rum, her freckled nose wrinkling delicately at that first swallow. "And yes, my job was to feel them out, I guess you'd call it."

He'd like to feel *her* out. It was probably best not to say as much. "How did you do that?"

She smiled and gestured to her bare arms and feet. "Our skin is our power. We can't discern good and evil the way animals, some humans, and other angels do, like a sixth sense. For us, awareness settles on our skin. That's why I cover as little of myself as I can get away with, and what clothes I do wear need to be tight, or sensation can't get through and I feel like I'm suffocating."

Now *that* was interesting. He'd never met anyone who shared his affection for form-fitting clothing. Most people thought tight clothes were binding, but Hades had long ago found that garments that fit like a second skin were more freeing and allowed him to feel the world around him. The air. The heat or cold. The touch of a female...when he could get it.

He took a swig of his rum. "So did you perform your job naked?"

Her eyes caught his, held them boldly, and damn if he didn't stop breathing. He'd been teasing; she was not. "Some of my colleagues did." She reached up and twirled a strand of hair around her finger, and he swore it was almost...playful. "I preferred our standard uniform of what humans would call a tube top and miniskirt."

He pictured that and got instantly hard. But then, he liked her in the ripped jeans and belly-revealing corset she was wearing now, too. He watched her lift the cup to her lips almost in slow motion, watched her throat work as she swallowed.

Damn. He threw back the entire contents of his cup, desperate to get some moisture in his mouth. "And what does good and evil feel like?" he rasped. "On your skin, I mean?"

"I'll show you." She moved toward him, every step popping out her hips and making her breasts bounce in a smooth, seductive rhythm. His mouth went dry again, but then it began to water as she reached out and placed her palm in the center of his chest.

Very slowly, she dragged her hand along the contours of his pecs, her touch so featherlike that he barely felt it, and yet, he was hyper-aware of every move her hand made, every centimeter of skin her palm passed over.

"Goodness and light," she said softly, "is like bathing in Champagne. It's tingly and effervescent. It wakes you up even as it relaxes you."

"Like sex," he murmured. "With someone you like."

"With someone you like?" She blinked. "Why would you have sex with someone you *didn't* like?"

A rumbling purr vibrated his chest. "Baby, it's like fighting, but with orgasms."

"And less blood, I suppose."

"Not if you're doing it right." He waggled his brows, and she rolled her eyes. "So what does evil feel like to you? If good feels good, then does evil feel bad?"

"That's the funny thing." She inched closer, adding another palm to his chest, and he gripped the cup so hard he heard it crack. More. He needed more. And damn her for making him crave it when he'd been perfectly fine being alone for all these years. "It's as seductive as good, but in a different way." She shivered delicately. "It's hot. If good is like bathing in Champagne, evil is like bathing in whiskey. There's a burn, but it's almost always a lovely burn."

Yeah, he felt that lovely burn where she was touching him. As she talked, it spread across his chest and into his abdomen, then lower, to his pelvis and groin. Everything tightened and grew feverish with lust.

"Seems to me," he said in a humiliatingly rough voice, "that bumping up against evil would be an incredible temptation for angels like you."

"It is," she purred. "Which is why we aren't allowed to leave Heaven except under certain circumstances, and even then, we must have an escort. It's one of the reasons I know I can't ever enter Sheoul. To become a True Fallen would be to have my full powers of detection restored, and I'd be skewed toward evil. The few Seraphim who have become fallen angels are like drug addicts, seeking out the most evil beings they can find, to serve them, to just be near them."

He wondered how having a Seraphim fallen angel as a warden in the Inner Sanctum would play out. Then Cat dragged her palms down his chest to his abs, and he forgot all about everything except what was happening right now, right here in his home.

"And what do you feel when you're near me?" He knew he shouldn't ask. Knew he was encouraging something that shouldn't be encouraged, but holy hell, he was starving for female contact. Maybe this little bit would be enough.

And maybe he was lying to himself.

Closing her eyes, she inhaled. "Like I want to climb your body like a tree so you can wrap yourself around me."

Hot...*damn.* He wasn't sure if the rum had gone to her head or if she was affected by his inner evil, but what she'd said made him want desperately to play giant oak for her so she could do whatever she wanted with his hardwood.

Giant oak. Hardwood. Man, he cracked himself up sometimes.

His amusement fled as her fingers brushed his waistband and reality crashed down on him, splintering the tree fantasy. She was clearly not in the right state of mind to understand the consequences of getting physical with him, while he understood far too well.

Cataclysm is off limits to you.

Azagoth's deep voice echoed inside Hades's ears. He'd gone to Azagoth a few months ago, hoping he'd grant Hades permission to see Cat. Hades would have been happy to just talk to her, to get to know her, but Azagoth had been immovable. And then, when Hades had asked Azagoth why, after thousands of years of service, he couldn't even take a walk in Sheoul-gra's lush forests with Cat, the unsatisfying answer had been, *You know why.*

Yeah, he did. *And what if I disobey?*

Do you remember the last time you disobeyed me?

As if Hades could forget. The very memory still made Hades's testicles shrivel. Reluctantly, he stepped back from Cat, but she moved with him, her hands splaying on his torso as they caressed him in slow, sensual circles.

So. Fucking. Good.

Gods, he felt like he'd been deprived of air for so long that he no longer knew how to breathe, and now someone was offering him an oxygen mask but he wasn't allowed to take it.

"Is this really what you want?" He forced the question from his mouth, because dammit, this was really what *he* wanted. He just wanted to take a breath. "To get me worked up?"

"Didn't you just accuse me of panting after you?"

He had. He'd been teasing, but there was nothing funny about this anymore. Her flirtation had been cute and flattering, but it had to stop. For both of their sakes.

"Yes," he drawled, reaching for the cockiness that had served him well when things got too serious. "But to be fair, all females do."

A slow, seductive smile curved her mouth, and it took a lot more restraint than he cared to admit to keep from dipping his head and kissing her senseless. "I'd tell you that you're arrogant, but I'm sure you already know that. And I like it."

Man, he had no idea how to handle this little vixen. She seemed both innocent and experienced, and he wasn't sure which was the truth.

Maybe it was time to find out.

Chapter Nine

Cat's heart was pounding so hard that she wondered if the surrounding tissue was going to be bruised. After months of trying to catch Hades's eye, she had him all to herself. She had his ear, his eye, and with luck, she'd have him in that coffin-bed.

Yes, there were pressing matters to attend to, but in this moment, they were in background because all she cared about was the foreground. And what a foreground it was.

The problem, she realized, was that she had no idea how to proceed. Things with Zhubaal had gone disastrously wrong, so she didn't want to repeat the mistakes she'd made with him. She just wished she knew what, exactly, she'd done.

Gods, this had better not be a replay of her incident with Z.

Closing her eyes, she let herself feel Hades's unique blend of good and evil on her skin. She'd made the comparison of good feeling like sparkling wine, while evil felt like whiskey, and Hades was a swirling mix of both. Carbonated whiskey. Might taste funky, but her skin felt alive with a tingling heat that spread to her scalp, her toes, and everything in between.

It was especially concentrated in her feminine parts.

So delicious.

"Hades—" She'd barely gotten his name off her tongue when his mouth came down on hers.

"Is this what you want?" he growled against her lips. "I'm not one to question motives when it comes to females who are willing to fuck me, but you have me confused as shit."

She wasn't confused at all. Zhubaal...he'd been an experiment. A means to an end. Oh, she'd liked him, she supposed. He was gruff and rude, but he was never cruel. At least, not that she'd seen.

But Hades was unique. From his clothing to his hair, he blew other fallen angels out of the water. And where most other fallen angels were all serious and dour, Hades was playful, even silly at times. Once, when Thanatos, one of the Four Horsemen of the Apocalypse, had come to Sheoul-gra with his toddler son, she'd watched Hades chase the squealing boy through the courtyard before tackling him gently and then tickling the boy's belly with his Mohawk.

She'd been fascinated to see a legend like Hades, a male whose job it was to make life miserable for millions of demons, handle a child with such tenderness. And he did it with such exuberance, without a care who was watching. How many times had she seen male pride get in the way of fun, as if enjoying life and showing emotion was wrong or weak?

No, it took strength to live the way Hades did and still be able to laugh at a joke or enjoy a child's giggle.

That was the fatal moment in which Cat had decided that she needed to get to know Hades a little better. It was also the moment in which she decided she wanted to feel that blue stripe of hair tickle *her* sensitive spots.

Before she could tell him as much, he spun her, put her hard into the wall, his body against hers. She gasped at the feel of his erection as it pressed into her from her core to her belly. Oh, sweet Heaven, how was that going to feel inside her?

"Most females want me because I'm a monster." He arched against her, and she moaned at the erotic pressure against her sex. "Is that your game? Fuck the underworld's most notorious jailor and earn some bragging points?"

A note of bitterness crept into his voice, but she couldn't tell if he was bitter because of what he was...or if he was bitter because he thought she only wanted him for bragging rights. Either way, it made her want to hug him.

Not long ago, she'd have thought him a monster, but even if she hadn't seen him playing with a child or pilfering bread from

Azagoth's kitchen to feed the doves, Lilliana's stories about Azagoth's redemption had touched her. Azagoth had been perched on the precipice of the kind of evil one couldn't come back from, but Lilliana had lured him away from the ledge. Oh, there was still darkness in him—the kind that had made Cat sick for days after accidentally touching him. She had a feeling that if anything ever happened to Lilliana, Azagoth would fall into that black, evil hole and would never return.

But Hades, for all his evil deeds and all the malevolence that surrounded him, had somehow avoided becoming toxic. So, no, he wasn't some sort of fiend, and he wasn't going to convince her otherwise.

She lifted her leg and wrapped it around him, trying to get closer. Trying to get some friction going on. "I don't believe you're a monster."

He scraped his teeth over her ear. "Why not?" he growled, so softly that the crackling flames from the fire nearly drowned him out.

She could have told him the Thanatos story. She could have told him how beautiful he was when he laughed with Lilliana. She could have mentioned the time she saw him smiling as he watched a couple of foxes playing on the edge of the forest just outside Azagoth's mansion. But for some reason, she wanted him to know why her opinion of him was so personal.

"Because I worked with Gethel," she whispered. "She was a traitor who plotted with Pestilence to slaughter a newborn baby and start the Apocalypse."

He brought one hand between them to feather his fingertips across the swell of her breasts, and she went all rubbery in the knees. "So you're saying that in comparison, I'm a saint."

"No." She nipped his lip. "I'm saying you are nuanced. You're evil, but there's good in you, as well."

"You don't know that."

"Expose more of my skin, and I will."

She felt his chest heave against hers. Once. Twice. And then, as if he'd given himself permission, he reached around behind her and ripped her corset off. Thank Heavens she'd chosen the one with the Velcro closure today.

"Now tell me," he breathed into her hair, "do you feel me?"

"Yes," she moaned, undulating her entire body, desperate to get as much skin-on-skin contact as possible. Her nipples, so sensitive they were almost painful, rubbed against the hard planes of his chest. She hadn't known they could ache like that.

"Shit," he rasped. "Too much. This is too much."

Too much what? It wasn't *enough*, as far as she was concerned. "I like touching you."

"No one ever touches me." He took a deep, shuddering breath that somehow sounded...pained, and not in a good way. "Nothing but the wind and rain ever does."

Wind and rain? Was that why he often went bare-chested? He liked the feel of something caressing his skin because people wouldn't? Or maybe he wouldn't let them?

She couldn't imagine living like that. She liked to touch and be touched. To show him how much she enjoyed it, she shoved her hand between them and found his erection as it strained against his pants.

Oh...my. She could feel every ridge and bump through the thin fabric as she ran her fingers along his length. Her strokes, made awkward by her inexperience and their position, still managed to elicit a tortured moan from him. The sound emboldened her, and she gripped him more firmly. His thick length pulsed, the hot blood pounding in her palm, and his shout of pleasure filled the room.

Then, suddenly, he was standing near the portal door and she was slumped against the wall, which was the only thing holding her up. How had he moved so fast? More importantly, *why* had he moved so fast?

"I have to go." For a split second he looked frazzled, his chest heaving, his nostrils flaring. Then he smiled, a cocky lopsided grin that did *not* fit the situation. "Hanging with you was great, but I have people to torture and shit. You can..." He looked around the room. "I don't know. Clean or something."

"*Clean?*" Sure, she was still disoriented from the fog of lust and the surprise of him breaking it all off so quickly, but still...*clean?* "I work for Azagoth. Not you."

He shrugged. "Then sleep. Cook. Watch TV. Whatever. Just

don't leave this crypt."

"But I have to find that human."

Reaching behind him, he palmed the symbol carved into the portal door, and it flashed open, turning into a shimmering arch of light. "I'll do it."

She pushed away from the wall, hoping her wobbly legs would hold her up. "I can help."

"No." His tone was harsh, but he softened it as he continued. "The demons were using you for something. Until I know what, we can't risk you being out in the general population. Stay here. I'll be back soon." Before she could protest, he stepped through the portal and disappeared.

"Bastard," she shouted after him.

She swore she heard laughter echo from out of the portal.

* * * *

Lilliana strode through the halls of the building that, just a few short months ago, she'd thought of as her prison. Now it was her home, and the male who ran it was the love of her life.

She found him in his library, standing in front of the fire, his big body outlined by its orange glow. He didn't turn when she entered, even though she knew he'd heard her approach. Coming up behind Azagoth, she wrapped her arms around his waist and pressed her cheek against his broad back.

"Hey."

He covered her hands with his. "My love," he purred. She adored that, how he saved certain tones and words for her and her alone. "What's up? I thought you were busy with the new Unfallen recruits."

"I was, but I couldn't get Cat off my mind."

"Cat? Is she okay?"

She sighed. "I don't know. Have you seen her?"

"Not today." His voice rumbled through her as he spoke. "But I've been busy trying to figure out why Hades won't respond to my messages and why the fucking portals to the Inner Sanctum are sealed."

Yeah, Azagoth hadn't just been busy with that mess—he'd

been obsessed. Something was terribly wrong in the Inner Sanctum, and with Heaven breathing down his back over the human stuck inside, Azagoth had been going nonstop. Between researching ways to open the portals and requesting help from the best demon engineers alive, he'd barely had time to eat, let alone sleep.

"You haven't made any progress, I take it?" He made a hellish sound she was going to take as a no. "I'm sorry," she whispered, and that fast, he relaxed a little.

"S'okay." Within the cage of her arms, he turned to her, his gaze intense but concerned. "Now, what's going on with Cat?"

"Did you send her on an errand to the human realm?"

Concern creased his forehead. "No. What's this about? Is she missing?"

"For two days." She stepped away from him, needing room to pace off her nervous energy now that she knew her friend was truly missing. "I didn't worry until today because you sometimes send her off with messages or to fetch things. But she's never been gone this long."

"And you've looked everywhere? The forest? The dorms? The old buildings? You know how she likes to explore."

True. Lilliana had never seen anyone so inquisitive and curious about the world around her. When Cat had first arrived, her constant, prying questions had irked Lilliana until she realized that Cat was simply trying to learn and experience.

"I've scoured all of Sheoul-gra," Lilliana sighed. "I suppose she could be hiding, but there's no reason to do that."

"Maybe she got tired of working here."

She shook her head. "She feels safe here. And even if she did decide to leave, she wouldn't have done it without saying good-bye first." A bad feeling tightened her chest. "Could someone have hurt her?"

He stiffened a little, just a slight shift of his broad shoulders, but Lilliana knew him well enough to recognize genuine unease. "You think one of the Unfallen living here has done something to her?"

God, she hoped not. It had been Lilliana's idea to use the old outer buildings to house Unfallen who didn't want to enter

Sheoul, who wanted a chance to make amends for whatever had gotten them booted from Heaven. If one of them had harmed Cat, she'd never forgive herself.

"I don't know," she said. "But I'm telling you, she wouldn't have gone this long without telling one of us. And Sheoul-gra is huge. I searched for her, but there are a lot of places where a person could hide a body or hold someone captive."

Azagoth's eyes went stormy, and Lilliana was very glad the tempest of fury wasn't aimed at her. "If anyone has dared to so much as *touch* a female under my protection," he growled, "I will create a 6th Ring in the Inner Sanctum just for them, and I will fill it with every nightmare they've ever had. They will spend eternity alone, running from the things that scare them most, and just when they think they can't take it anymore, *I* will become the thing they run from."

She shivered. And how twisted was she that she found his threats sexy? Not long ago she'd have thought him a fiend. Okay, he was still a fiend, but only to those who deserved it...and with them, he showed not a shred of mercy. Not even Lilliana would dare get between him and someone he set his vengeful sights on.

So Heaven help anyone who touched Cat, because Azagoth sure as hell wouldn't.

Chapter Ten

Cataclysm spent the next few hours rummaging through Hades's house-crypt. It was probably all kinds of rude to sort through his things, but it was also all kinds of rude to get her worked up and then suddenly back out, tell her to clean his dusty tomb, and then take off. So she didn't feel too bad about snooping through his stuff.

And what interesting stuff it was. Hell, his entire crypt turned out to be a treasure trove of mystery. In addition to the hidden kitchen and bathroom, there was an office, but instead of it being concealed behind a wall, it had been camouflaged by sorcery. His desk, a blocky monstrosity that appeared to have been carved with a pocket knife, sat just inches away from the rickety chair she'd sat in, but she never would have seen it—or bumped into it—if she hadn't picked up the hollowed-out book she found on a shelf. The simple act of opening the book had revealed the hidden desk and file cabinets.

Unfortunately, the cabinets were locked, presumably by more sorcery. But the contents of his desk were more than enough to keep her occupied. She found building plans for an expansion of the 1st Ring, an accounting of the prisoners in some fortress called the Rot, and a list of every fallen angel warden employed in the Inner Sanctum. Then there were the knickknacks on his desktop.

She ran her finger over an egg-sized stone carving of a hellhound, laughing every time she touched its tail because the carving would come to life and snap at her before freezing again in its snarly, crouched stance. Then there was a framed photo of a blue lake nestled between snowcapped mountains. It was beautiful, but why did he have it?

As she went to put it back on the desk, she bumped her elbow, and the picture fell to the floor. Glass shattered, sending shards skidding all over the place.

Shit. Hades was going to kill her.

As she scrambled to clean up the mess, the portal Hades had gone through opened. Of course. Apparently, Hades had the same impeccable timing as Azagoth when it came to her breaking stuff.

"I'm sorr—"

"Who are you?" The deep, unfamiliar voice made her yelp in surprise.

She leaped to her feet, and her surprise veered to terror. A huge male strode into the room, his craggy face shadowed by a filthy, hooded cape that flapped over boiled leather armor as he walked. The necklace of teeth around his neck and the string of ears dangling from the belt around his waist said he was pretty damned comfortable with cutting things off, and she hoped the gore-crusted halberd he carried in one gloved fist wasn't going to be the weapon he used to cut *her* things off.

"W-who are *you*?" she asked, her voice trembling as fiercely as her hands.

As he strode toward her, crusty stuff fell off his boots with every step, and wasn't it crazy that she wanted to yell at him for leaving a mess?

"I'm a warden in the 4th Ring, and you"—he seized her by the throat—"you are an intruder."

"No," she gasped, and then she just tried to breathe because he squeezed harder, cutting off her voice and her air.

His lips peeled back from blackened teeth and a wicked set of fangs as he put his face in hers. "The 4th and 5th Rings are in chaos, and do you know why? There are reports of unauthorized beings in the Inner Sanctum, and it looks like I caught one of them." He grinned, and if she hadn't been struggling to breathe, she'd have screamed. "Do you know what we do to intruders, female? I dare you to imagine the worst because I promise the reality will look far, far more horrible."

His meaty fist filled her vision, and then there was blackness.

****

Hades was balls deep in a demon horde. The 5th Ring had literally been set on fire, and all around, smoke and flame erupted from crude bombs and fire arrows.

He and every 5th Ring warden had been fighting for hours, and they hadn't come any closer to finding the human. Reports of violence were coming in from the 3rd and 4th Rings, as well, and just moments ago, Silth had brought extremely troubling news.

He'd found a weak spot in the membrane that separated the Inner Sanctum from the rest of Sheoul-gra. If the spot wasn't shored up, and fast, demons would overrun Azagoth's realm, which could result in a catastrophic destabilization and allow the souls to escape, flooding human lands.

At least Cat was safely ensconced in his home, although he'd come to realize there was nothing "safe" about her. She might have been an angel once, but he wouldn't be surprised if there was a little succubus in her family tree.

He whacked an ugly-ass demon on its scaly head with his battle-ax and shot a lightning bolt at another. The bolt bounced around the crowd of demons, taking out another dozen before it fizzled away. Shit, this sucked. He'd always liked a good fight, but this was on a scale he hadn't seen since...well, ever.

Panting with exhaustion, he took advantage of the brief reprieve from charging demons. They were all around him, but they were busy fighting wardens, so he figured he had about thirty seconds to breathe.

"My lord!" A towering warden from the 4th Ring powered his way through the crowd and jogged over, his sword dripping with blood. "Malonius sent me with a message. He needs you at the Rot right away."

"Do *not* tell me we're dealing with prison riots, too," Hades growled.

The warden, Rhoni, wiped grime out of his eyes with the

back of his gauntleted hand. "No, sir. He captured an intruder."

He frowned. "Someone else was able to get into the Inner Sanctum?"

"Apparently, sir."

Yes. The portals must be operating again. Azagoth must have realized something was wrong and had people working on the problem from his side. Finally. Now he could get Cat back where she belonged.

An uncomfortable sensation caught tight in his chest. He wasn't ready to give her up yet. Sure, he couldn't have her, not in the way he wanted, but now that he'd gotten a taste—so to speak—he wanted more. Her bravery and impulsiveness fascinated him, and her unique blend of artlessness and seductiveness enchanted him. He loved the way her kisses were eager but unpracticed, and her emotions were so unguarded. Such a rare thing for a fallen angel.

Yes, she was newly fallen, and no doubt she'd lose that innocent patina eventually, but only if she was exposed to ugliness. Something inside him wanted to protect her from that ugliness, the way he'd protected humans back when he'd been an angel.

Back then, he'd gone too far in his desire to protect the innocent, and it had cost him his wings and his soul. But how far would he go to protect Cat?

He knew the answer immediately. He'd stop at nothing. Which meant that, if the portals were open, he had to send her back. With only one exception, the Inner Sanctum was ugly, and Cat deserved better. She deserved to not lose her shiny.

The whisper of a spear passed too close to Hades's ear for comfort, jolting him back to the ugliness around him. The kind he needed to protect Cat from.

"How are things in the 4th Ring?" he asked.

"They're bad," Rhoni said, "but not this bad."

Hades clapped the guy on the shoulder. "Get back to it. I'll head to the prison."

Extending his wings, he launched into the air, spinning and diving to avoid projectiles. The icy burn of some sort of weapon ripped through one wing, but a few heartbeats later, he punched through the portal and was striding down the Rot's dark, damp halls to the processing center where all guests were interrogated before being sent to either a cell or a torture chamber. When he arrived in the chilly antechamber, Malonius greeted him.

"She's in Jellybean," he said, his breath visible in the freezing air. "Seems her greatest fear is spiders."

From its pulsating walls to its seeping ceiling, Jellybean was a room that fed on fear and came alive when someone was locked inside. Once it got hold of someone's fears, it made them real. He'd once seen the room fill with jellybeans while the demon inside screamed in terror...hence, the name of the room.

Malonius had shoved an orange bean up the guy's nose, and the demon had confessed all of his considerable sins. *Freaking jellybeans.*

"Wait. She?" Hades asked, every internal alarm clanging as what Malonius said sank in. He opened his mouth, but whatever he was about to say fled when he saw the pile of clothes on the table behind the other fallen angel.

A pair of faded, ripped jeans and a corset.

Cat.

Fuck! Wheeling around, he tore out of the room and charged down the hall, his pulse pounding in his ears even louder than the strike of his boots on the stone floor. Holy hell, if she was hurt, someone was going to pay in blood and bone and pain, and Hades was going to be the one to collect.

Up ahead, a warden stood guard outside Jellybean. "Open that fucking room!" Hades shouted.

The guy jumped, fumbled at his side for the key, but before he could unlock the door, Hades was there. He wrenched the key from the warden's hand and knocked him aside.

His fingers shook as he jammed the heavy iron skeleton key into the lock, but somehow he managed to open the door. He whipped it open, and a wave of spiders of all species and sizes skittered out, spilling over his boots.

"*Dach niek!*"

The Sheoulic command put the room to rest, and the arachnids disappeared. He burst inside, and his knees nearly gave out at the sight of Cat huddled in the corner, naked and shivering.

Her arms covered her head as she rocked back and forth on her heels. Bruises marred her pale skin, and fury made his blood steam.

"Cat." He knelt next to her and laid his palm gently on her shoulder, cursing when she flinched. "Cat, it's me. It's Hades."

A shudder wracked her body, and she made a sobbing noise that pricked him in the heart he'd long ago thought immune to pretty much anything emotional.

He lowered his voice, shooting for something that might resemble soothing. "The spiders are gone. They weren't real. It's okay."

Very slowly, her arms came down, and she peeked at him through splayed fingers. Her bloodshot, red-rimmed eyes were a punch in the gut. "Hades?"

"Yeah." He cleared his voice of the hoarseness that had crept into it. "It's okay, I promise."

She lowered her hands, but her gaze shifted and her eyes went wide as the sound of footsteps indicated that someone had come into the room.

"My lord," Malonius began, his voice pitched with fear, proving he wasn't completely stupid. Clearly he realized he'd fucked up in a very, very big way. "I found her in your crypt...she'd ransacked the place...I thought—"

"I know what you thought," Hades snapped. He didn't turn to look at the male because if he did, he wouldn't be able to control the murderous rage pounding through his veins. "And that's the only reason you aren't hanging by your entrails right now."

As much as he wanted to blame the warden for this, it was ultimately Hades's fault. He hadn't thought to tell all of his staff about Cat, but that was a mistake he wouldn't make again.

"Tell the others," he said. "Tell them that this Unfallen is mine, and she's not to be harmed, or ogled, or even fucking *breathed on*."

"Yes, sir." Malonius tossed Cat's clothes to Hades, and a heartbeat later, they were alone again.

"Cat? I'm going to take you home...ah, I mean, to my place."

He started to pull her into his arms, but he jerked back at the sight of the gore streaking his arms. Cursing, he looked down at himself, realized he must look like he'd showered in a slaughterhouse. The fact that he was covered in blood wasn't the most unusual thing ever, but after what Cat had just been through, she didn't need this, too.

So much for protecting her from the ugliness of the Inner Sanctum.

Guilt churned inside him like a living thing, and this thing had teeth. It gnawed at his heart and clawed at his soul because this could have been prevented.

Cat's teeth began to chatter, so he let the guilt monster feed as he gathered her in his filthy arms and tucked her against his grimy chest and got her out of there, snarling at everyone who got in his way. Or who looked at her naked body. Or breathed in his general direction.

He reached the exit portal in record time, but as he stepped inside, he wondered what else could possibly go wrong.

Chapter Eleven

Face buried against Hades's powerful chest, Cat clung to him with all her strength, which seemed to be in short supply. She couldn't stop the shaking, but when Hades held her tighter and whispered comforting things in her ear, the wonderful whiskey-fizz sensation he gave off wrapped around her like a warm blanket and helped ease the trembling a little.

She didn't open her eyes to see where they were going. She didn't care. As long as she wasn't trapped with spiders in that horrible room with pulsing walls and the faint sound of a heartbeat, she was thrilled. Besides, she trusted Hades. He'd given her no reason not to. More importantly, he worked for Azagoth, and no one in their right minds would do anything to intentionally harm anyone in the Grim Reaper's employ.

Hades let out a hardcore curse, grumbled, and cursed again. She didn't look. Whatever had pissed him off wasn't something she wanted to see. He started moving again, and then suddenly, she felt a cool, fresh breeze on her bare skin. The scent of freshly mown grass and flowers filled her nostrils, and riding on the raft of air was the faint tang of the ocean.

Where in the world were they? Had they escaped the Inner Sanctum?

Still, she didn't peek, not even when he spoke to someone in Sheoulic, dashing her hopes that they'd gotten free. A few moments later, she heard a door close, and the mouthwatering aroma of roasting meat and baking bread finally had her cracking her eyelids.

Her mother had always joked that nothing could make her come running like the ring of the dinner bell, and it was so true. She loved food. Loved to cook. She secretly enjoyed when Azagoth or Lilliana asked her to whip them up something in the kitchen, even though they had several full-time chefs. Sometimes she even helped out in the kitchen that served the dozens of Unfallen who lived and trained in Azagoth's realm.

She wondered how long it would be before she could do that again.

"Where are we?" Her throat, raw from screaming, left her voice shredded.

Holy eight-legged hell, she hated spiders. And, as she'd discovered in that horrible room, demon spiders made every species of arachnid in the human realm seem like cuddly puppies.

"We're with friends. They're letting us take their house for as long as we need." Hades's hand stroked her hair gently. "I'm going to put you down on the bed. Is that okay?"

She nodded, and he set her down carefully on a mattress she suspected had been filled with straw. Before she was even out of his arms, he covered her with a blanket and tossed her clothes onto a small table next to the bed.

They appeared to be in some sort of Tudor-era hut that, while being primitive in comparison to modern-day standards, was pristine, as if brand new. The furniture and decor was simple but elegant and had clearly been fashioned by talented hands. A small, doorless bathroom had been built into one wall, but like Hades's place, the toilet was crude, a mere hole in a stone and wood box she was guessing emptied through some sort of pipe and away from the home.

He sank down beside her on the mattress. "I'm sorry about what happened. I'll be having a little chat with Malonius later."

"Don't," she said, surprising herself. Earlier, she'd cursed that male from here to Mars until she had to stop cursing in order to scream. "He caught me going through your things. I can see why he thought I was an intruder." She shuddered. "The spider room was overkill, though."

"You're a lot more forgiving than most people would

be...wait, going through my things?" His voice was teasing and light, so unexpected, and so welcome. How did he know exactly what she needed?

"I was bored. And I wanted to get to know you better." She rolled her bottom lip between her teeth, wondering at what point curiosity became intrusion. "I saw the picture on your desk. The lake in the mountains. Is it someplace special?"

He grunted. "Crater Lake. I've always thought it was one of the most beautiful places in the world, and I need a reminder now and then. Especially since most of the Inner Sanctum is craptastically ugly."

That was so...sweet. And again, unexpected. Who would have thought that the guy who operated a demon holding tank would want something beautiful near him?

"I'm going to go get something for you to eat." Hades reached over and squeezed her hand, but when he glanced down at the way their fingers were entwined, he jerked away from her. "Sorry...I'm covered in...I was fighting before I went to the Rot...fuck." A blush spread over his cheeks as he popped to his feet. "Will you be okay by yourself?"

"I'm not afraid of a little dirt and blood," she said tiredly, "and I'm not a child who can't be left alone." That said, she still checked out the room for spiders. And she couldn't get that infernal heartbeat to stop echoing in her head.

"I know." There was an odd note in his voice...admiration, maybe? The idea that he, a powerful Biblical legend, admired anything about her, a disgraced Unfallen with few survival skills, gave her a boost of much-needed energy. "I'll be right back."

She waited on the bed, the scratchy wool blanket wrapped tightly around her. Soft voices drifted back and forth from the other room, and a few minutes later, he returned with a pottery mug and a bowl of steaming meat and bread swimming in gravy. Her stomach growled fiercely, and she didn't feel the slightest embarrassment when she snatched the plate and crude metal spork from him.

Completely setting aside polite manners, she shoveled a bite into her mouth and chewed. "Oh, damn," she moaned. "This is amazing. But I'm not going to ask what kind of meat it is."

He chuckled as he set the mug on the stand next to the bed. "I can tell you that it's not demon snake."

"Good," she muttered. "I've had enough of that for a lifetime." She took another bite, chewed, swallowed. "So why aren't we at your place?"

"Because Malonius locked the portal to my crypt to protect it, and I can't open it without him. I can break through his lock eventually, but I didn't want to waste time. Besides, I figured you'd be more comfortable here."

She licked gravy off the spork and decided she wanted the recipe. "Where is here?"

"We're in hell's version of Cloud Cuckoo Land."

"Say what?"

"Don't you watch movies?" He shook his head, making waves in his Mohawk. "We're in a recently-built realm Azagoth and I created for demons who don't really fit into any of the five Rings."

She frowned. "But I thought the Rings coordinated with the Ufelskala."

"They do." He moved over to the window and peered out, his expression watchful but not tense, which relieved her more than she'd care to admit. She'd always thought of herself as being tough, but the last couple of days had tested her resolve, and she was ready for a break. "But the 1st Ring didn't seem suitable for all good demons. There was no reward for demons who have done more than simply exist. Who have contributed to society for the greater good."

As an angel who spent her entire life in Heaven, she'd been raised on stories of the depravity of demons, so while she had no trouble believing that there were demons who were "less evil" than others, she wasn't convinced that "good" demons existed.

"Good demons?" she asked, not bothering to hide her skepticism. "Really?"

He turned away from the window, his big body partially blocking the eerie orange light from outside. "You said yourself that humans come in a wide range of good and evil, so why wouldn't demons? God has always wanted balance, so for every evil human, there exists a good demon."

Cat scooped up a bit of bread and gravy. "Makes sense, I guess. But what kinds of good demons are you talking about?"

The muscles in his shoulders rippled as he shrugged, and her pulse kicked. When she'd clung to him earlier, her lips had been *right there*. She could have kissed him. Licked his skin to see if it tasted as smoky as it smelled.

At least, she could have done all of that if she hadn't been occupied with trying to keep from curling up into a weeping ball of spider-trauma.

"Kinds like the ones who work at Underworld General Hospital." He propped one booted foot against the wall behind him, his pose casual, but deadly energy remained coiled beneath the surface, so tangible that Cat swore she could feel it dance on her skin. He might say they were safe, but he was prepared for anything. So *he* might not feel safe, but she did. Nothing was going to get past him.

"Or the ones who live among humans and do nothing more than try to fit in," he continued. "Before this expansion, they went to the 1st Ring, which is still a pretty hellish experience. Here demons can actually enjoy their time until they're reincarnated. Which, thanks to Revenant being Sheoul's new overlord, happens pretty quickly."

Someone who looked human walked past the window, a ball in his hand. Hades didn't even glance at the guy, but Cat had a feeling he was well aware of every step the male took.

"I'm curious," she said after the guy disappeared. "In Heaven, humans choose their appearance, but everyone can still 'see' each individual as the person they'd always known, even if they knew them on Earth as a twelve-year-old boy, but in Heaven they appear as a twenty-five-year-old female. Is it the same here?"

Hades dipped his head. "Essentially. Demons in the Inner Sanctum do choose their appearances, but people don't always recognize them. I think it's because they're rarely born twice as the same species."

Huh. It hadn't occurred to her that a Seminus demon wouldn't be born again as a Sem. "How does that work?"

He cocked an eyebrow. "Do you really want to talk about this?"

"It's your fault," she said around a mouthful of bread. "You piqued my curiosity."

"Well then," he said with a lopsided grin and an impish glint in his eyes, "I guess I'll have to satisfy your…curiosity."

Oh, yes, please. Satisfy anything you want.

She swallowed about a million times to keep her mouth from opening and those exact words from falling out.

Hades didn't seem to notice the lustful distress he'd caused, continuing his demonic reincarnation lesson as if he hadn't just teased her with sexual undertones. "Demons here are generally reborn as a member of a species that fits within their soul's Ufelskala, but every once in a while a level one will be reincarnated as a species that rates a five, or vice versa. It's why you'll sometimes encounter a Soulshredder that wants to help others, or a Slogthu that likes to kill."

That made sense, she supposed. Anomalies happened in every species on Earth, so why not in Sheoul? "So how does all of this work? How do you keep everyone in line?"

"That's the reason the Rings are all based on the Ufelskala. No matter your score, you can travel to any level that is higher on the scale, but never lower. So an Ufelskala Tier Two demon can travel between the 2nd, 3rd, 4th, and 5th Rings, but they can't go to the 1st Ring. And no one from any Ring can come here."

She considered that for a moment. "But as you said, the Ufelskala scale is based on a species' level of evil as a whole, and not every individual is representative of their breed."

"Which is why Azagoth and my team review every person who comes through the gate." Hades bent over and yanked off his boots. "Now, if you don't mind, I need to clean up."

She scooped up another bite of gravy-soaked bread. "Go for it." Oh, wait...was he going to use the open—*very* open—bathroom? He strode over there, his fingers working at the ties on his pants. Oh, boy, he was going to—

He dropped his pants, and she nearly swallowed her tongue along with the bread. With every silent step, the muscles in his legs and ass flexed, making her fingers curl with the desire to dig into his hard flesh.

Hades hit a lever, and water streamed from a wide slot in the stone wall. He stepped beneath the steaming waterfall, closing his eyes and dipping his head back. He was a living, breathing work of art. Angel and demon all wrapped up in a package of physical perfection. Her mouth watered, but now it had nothing to do with the food. She wanted something much more tasty.

Wanted it desperately. And the thing was, lust had driven her wants before, but something had changed. Yes, when she looked at him, lust was a writhing, burning entity inside her, but there was also a flutter of attraction to the male inside that magnificent body.

But did he want her? He'd spent months avoiding her—or, at least, it seemed that way. And back at his crypt, he'd taken off just when things had gotten hot. But things *had* gotten hot. And he'd sort of flirted a couple times, the way he had a moment ago when he talked about satisfying her…curiosity. So there *was* something there. Right?

She needed to know for sure. Her curiosity had always driven her, even when she should have minded her own business, but a wereleopard couldn't change its spots, could it?

Gathering all her courage, she stood, letting the blanket fall to the floor. His back was turned to her, so he didn't see her moving toward him, her pulse picking up speed with every step.

"Need help washing your back?"

He whirled around, eyes wide, his lips parted in surprise. A blush crept up his neck and into his face as his gaze traveled the length of her body. Between his legs, his sex stirred, swelling and lengthening as he took her in. Between *her* legs, she went wet, and she hadn't even stepped under the water yet.

"I...ah...I'm doing fine by myself..." It was adorable how flustered he was. Big bad Hades was completely off balance. She was so taking advantage of that.

"You missed a few spots." Stepping into him, she gripped his biceps and forced him back around. The tingly, whiskey heat of him immediately sparked on her skin, giving her that contact high that had been so incredibly seductive back at his crypt.

She soaked up the sensation as she palmed the hard bar of handmade soap and began to wash him, starting on the back of his neck and working her way down. Damn, his body was firm, his skin smooth. She'd never touched a male like this, and she made a mental note to do it again. Hopefully with Hades.

Intrigued by this new experience, she committed everything to memory, like the way his muscles leaped under her touch. Like the way the water and suds sluiced over hard flesh that rolled with every one of his rapid breaths. Like the way his fingers dug into the stone wall as if he was trying desperately to hold himself upright.

"Cataclysm," he said roughly. "This might not be the best idea."

Pulse fluttering in her veins, she dropped her hands lower, skimming his buttocks as she scrubbed in wide circles.

"Why not?" She hoped her words came off as light and teasing, that the sound of the water hid the tremor of insecurity. What if he rejected her again?

Taking a deep breath, she went lower, so she was gliding the soap over his firm ass and hips.

"Because."

His voice, husky and dripping with male need, made her bold. "That's not a reason," she murmured as she tucked the soap in the crack of his butt and slid her hand downward, her fingers reaching between his legs—

His hand snapped back to grasp her wrist, and then he was turning into her and pushing her back against the wall. "I think," he said, as he pressed his body against hers, "that it's my turn."

Yes! He did want her!

Dipping his head, he captured her mouth as he wrested the soap out of her hand. His kiss was hotter than the water pouring on them, and his hands, oh, sweet hell, his *hands*. They roamed her body with finesse, his touch alternating between light and firm, teasing and let's-do-this-thing serious. Every pass of the soap over her breasts and buttocks made her groan, and when he dropped the bar and dipped his fingers between her legs, she cried out in relief and amazement. She'd never been touched so intimately before, but now she was glad she'd waited. Hell, she'd have happily given up her wings for this one, beautiful moment.

"You like this," he said in a deep, guttural rasp. "I like it too. I shouldn't, but I do."

There was a strange note in his voice, a tortured thread of...regret? Before she could think too hard on that, he did something sinful to her clit, and she nearly came undone. His fingers slid back and forth between her folds, the pressure becoming firmer as her breath came faster. He changed the rhythm every few strokes to rub circles around her sensitive nub or to slide the pads of his fingers past her opening, hitting a sensitive spot she didn't know she had.

"Please," she begged, not even sure what she was begging for. She wanted everything he could possibly do to her, and thanks to Lilliana, Cat knew a *lot* of things were possible.

He smiled as he kissed a path from her mouth to her jaw and down her neck. Arching her back, she let her head fall against the stone wall to give him as much access as he wanted. He grunted in approval and nipped her throat, the tiny sting adding fuel to the fire that was building inside her.

Another pass of his fingers had her panting and pumping her hips into his hand. Then he slipped one inside her. Yes, oh, damn...*yes!*

He worked her for a moment, wringing sighs and moans from her before adding another finger. The burn of her tissue stretching yielded to pleasure within a couple of heartbeats, and she surrendered herself to his masterful play.

His fingers pumped as his thumb circled her clit, and too soon she exploded, her first climax with a male coursing through her body in an uncontrolled free fall. When she still had her wings, she would sometimes climb high into the air, tuck in her wings, and let the fall take her skimming close to mountaintops and deep into canyons. The orgasm Hades gave her was like that. Freeing, life affirming...and dangerous.

She knew herself well enough to know that for her, sex and emotion would be tightly linked. It was a horrible character flaw, one that had the potential to hurt badly. She supposed it was a good thing Zhubaal had rejected her, but now she thought that maybe Hades should have, too.

He brought her down slowly, his touch growing lighter as she became sensitive to every waning sensation.

"You're so beautiful." His smoky voice rumbled through her

like a second climax, sparking a new wave of pleasure skimming across her skin. "God, the sounds you make when you come."

"I need to hear you," she said, taking him in her fist. "Let me."

He gasped, his body going rigid as she squeezed his erection. She'd never touched one before; she and Zhubaal hadn't gotten this far. Not even close. The skin was so silky, the shaft textured with veins she wanted to trace with her tongue.

Suddenly, he seized her wrist and shoved her hand away. Confused, she glanced up at him. He didn't meet her gaze as he backed out of there, leaving a trail of puddles on the wood floor. "I have to go."

What the hell?

"Don't do this again." She shut off the water. "Please, Hades. What's wrong?"

Someone knocked on the door, and she swore he jumped a foot in the air. "Who the fuck is it?" he yelled.

"Silth. I have news you're going to want to hear."

The urgency in Silth's voice said the news wasn't good, but Hades seemed relieved. Was he happy for an excuse to get out of the bedroom? "I'll be out in a second." He didn't bother drying off, simply jammed his feet into his pants. He didn't look at her as he said, "In this part of the Inner Sanctum, and only this part, you can clothe yourself in whatever you want, with just a thought. But the second you leave, the clothes will disappear."

Cool, but clothes were the least of her concerns right now. "Can you slow down for a second?" She reached for one of the folded cloths on the shelf next to the shower. "We need to talk."

"Talk," he said sharply, "doesn't seem to be what you want from me." He held up the hand that had, just moments ago, given her so much pleasure. "I gave you what you wanted, didn't I?"

Stung by his sudden, inexplicable anger, she lashed out. "No, you didn't. Not even close. You think I sit around fantasizing about your *hand?*"

Said hand formed a fist at his side. "Sorry to disappoint, babe." He yanked open the door with so much force that the iron handle broke. "But I'm sure Zhubaal will be happy to give you whatever it is you fantasize about."

"Wow," she said quietly. "I can see where your reputation as a master torturer comes from. You know exactly where to plunge your dagger, don't you?"

He jerked as if she'd struck him, and then he stormed out, leaving her to her fantasies. Which, right at this minute, included smacking Hades in his stubborn, infuriating head.

Chapter Twelve

What the fuck have I done?

Snarling, Hades slammed the bedroom door and strode into the hut's living room, his hard cock pinching in his pants and his regrets piling up with every step.

He never got this moody, but right now he was strung tighter than a vampire stretched on the Rack in the Rot's dungeon. Sexual frustration combined with the anger from the situation with Cat and the bullshit going on in the Inner Sanctum had damned near reached critical levels. He considered himself to be a pretty laid-back, easygoing guy, especially for a fallen angel, but damn, when he was with Cat it was as if he was mining desires and emotions he'd kept buried, and now he'd hit a vein that ran thick with fury and hopelessness.

It had been centuries since he'd last succumbed to the kinds of feelings that usually signaled an impending catastrophic bout of self-destructiveness.

He either wanted to kill something, or he wanted to fuck something...and the latter something was Cat.

Stupid, Hades. It would be so fucking stupid to start a relationship that can't go anywhere, not to mention the fact that Azagoth will break you in half like a wishbone.

Oh, but didn't he already board that stupid train when he made her the brunt of his anger at not being able to make love to her? She hadn't deserved any of that. Then he'd made it worse by bringing up Zhubaal, which had only served to throw jealousy and shame into the toxic mix brewing inside him right now.

He'd hurt her when he'd sworn to protect her. He'd done what he did best; find a soft spot, slip a blade in it, and give it a good twist.

Fucking idiot.

Water dripped down his back, reminding him of how Cat's gentle fingers had caressed him in the shower. He'd felt like a map and she was the explorer looking for interesting places to go. He'd wanted so badly to let her. Her touch was a gift, a connection he hadn't had with anyone since before he fell. Even then, his relationships hadn't been serious. He'd been young and impulsive, and females had been a fun distraction from his crappy job and his priggish, cold parents.

Since his fall, the few females he'd been with had been sexual partners and nothing more. How could they be anything more when the total of his time outside of Sheoul-gra could be measured in hours instead of days?

Gnashing his teeth, he stopped in front of Silth and tried to keep his tone civil. "What is it?"

"We captured the Orphmage who was holding the Unfallen female you rescued," he said, and Hades's heart leaped. Finally. Maybe he would get to kill someone after all.

"He's alive, I take it."

"Yes, sir." Silth fingered the hilt of the sword at his hip, his chain mail armor tinkling softly as he moved. "We have him at the Rot. But I had a chance to interrogate him at the site where we captured him."

"He talked?"

"After I reached into his chest cavity and started breaking off ribs."

"Nice." Hades nodded in approval. "So what did he say? Did you get the human?"

"No, sir. But he did say that when he jammed his staff into the Unfallen, he released an enchantment inside her."

Hades's heart stopped leaping. "Her name is Cat. And what kind of enchantment?"

"The kind that drains her life force."

Oh, fuck. His heart started beating again, but in an erratic, schizy rhythm. "For what purpose?"

"To open holes in the barriers between the Inner Sanctum and Sheoul, as well as the barrier between the Sanctum and Sheoul-gra."

Not unexpected, since demons were always trying to get out of the Inner Sanctum to wreak havoc as ghosts in both Sheoul and on Earth. But they'd been trying to do that for eons, so what made this attempt different?

"I'm still not clear on how that would work," he said. "What role does the human play in this?"

"They're draining him, too. Both the Unfallen, ah, Cat, and the human are timed to drain at the same time."

Hades's gut was starting to churn. "And how much time do we have before this event takes place?"

"Approximately twenty hours. But it could happen sooner if both the human and the Unfallen are beheaded simultaneously. When their souls flee their bodies, perforations will appear in the barriers, and demons will escape."

Holy shitmonkeys. "Find a hellhound," Hades said. "Quickly."

Silth's upper lip peeled back, revealing two shiny fangs. Like pretty much everyone else, he hated hellhounds. "Why must I track down one of those filthy mutts?"

"Because I need a message delivered to their king. Tell the hellhound that we need Cerberus's help. We can use every hellhound they can spare to find the human."

Silth's curse told Hades exactly how he felt about dealing with the beasts. "And if that fails?"

"Then we'll need the hellhounds to patrol the borders. We can't let a single demon escape, let alone millions of them."

And there was no way he could let Cat die.

"There's one other thing, sir."

Of course there was. "What is it?"

"The enchantment inside the Unfallen...it can be used to track her whereabouts."

Mother. Fuck. "She can't be left alone."

"Do you want me to stay with her?"

Oh, hell, no. Silth was a nasty motherfucker, but he was

movie-star handsome and had an insatiable sexual appetite. He wasn't getting near Cat, who had shown herself to be very open about her own sexual appetites.

Gods, she was a dream female. Beautiful and kind, if a little reckless, and when it came to being physical, she wasn't shy...and yet, there was that pesky innocence about her that intrigued him.

And made him crazy, as his outburst in the bedroom had proven.

"My lord?" Silth prompted, and Hades realized he'd gotten lost in his thoughts. "Shall I stay with her?"

"No," Hades said quickly. "I've got it for now. Send the message to Cerberus, and then contact me once we have hellhounds searching the Rings. Cat can help look for the human, but I don't want her out there until we have the hounds for protection."

Silth gave a shallow bow and took off, leaving Hades to wonder what to do in the meantime.

One thing was certain, he wasn't going to tell Cat any of this. She'd been through enough already. Now he had to figure out how to stay with her while not giving into his desire for her. Somehow, he had to pretend that being with her was easy, no big deal, when the truth was that being with her without being inside her might be the hardest thing he'd ever done.

Chapter Thirteen

The longer Hades was gone, the angrier Cat got.

Yes, she understood he was handling business. And given the state of...everything, it was probably serious business. But the way he'd backed out of the shower and run out of the room had been insulting. Of course, his insults had been insulting, too.

Was he playing a game with her? Was he getting a good laugh over the Unfallen panting after him while he remained distant? Was she just a toy for his amusement?

Cursing to herself, she finished drying with the rough linen cloth she'd assumed was meant to be a towel, and then she tried out the "thought clothes" Hades had mentioned. Instantly, she was clothed in jeans and a corset identical to the real ones on the bed. Huh. She changed the colors, turning the corset to bright orange and the jeans to black.

Neat.

But maybe she should try something different. Something that would knock Hades off balance. He thought she should go to Zhubaal to get what she wanted, so maybe she should show Hades exactly what he'd be missing.

But what?

If you want to get a male's attention, give him something to look at.

Lilliana had told Cat that while picking out an outfit to distract Azagoth from some sort of bookwork he'd been poring over a few weeks ago. Hours later, if the spring in Azagoth's step had been any indication, Lilliana's choice of clothes had been spot on.

What the hell, Cat thought. She replicated the outfit, going for a red leather miniskirt and a leather bra top, finishing it off with matching stilettos. Looking down at herself, she smiled. Let Hades resist *that.*

As if on cue, he opened the door. But to her frustration, he didn't so much as glance at her as he crossed to the window.

"Silth found the Orphmage." He brushed back the curtains. "It shouldn't be long before he gives up the location of the human."

Great. Terrific. She should probably say something about that, given that she'd kicked off this entire mess when she came to the Inner Sanctum to find the human.

Instead, she opened her mouth, and something else came out. "What is up with you?" she snapped. "I have been flirting my ass off, and you act like I'm trying to sell you stewed maggots."

"Hey," he said with a wave of his hand. "Don't knock stewed maggots. With enough spices and tomatoes—"

"Argh!" She spun away from him, too angry to continue this. And she hoped like hell he didn't notice her nearly break her ankle on these stupid shoes that clearly didn't work to catch his attention. Nothing did. Maybe it was time to give up and stop being pathetic. "Never mind."

A hand clamped down on her shoulder, halting her in her tracks. A heartbeat later, Hades was in front of her, his expression serious. "Trust me, I'm not immune to your...feminine wiles."

"First of all," she said, shrugging away from his touch, "I don't have any wiles. Second, you're a big, fat liar."

"Baby, you're *wearing* fucking *wiles.*" He grabbed her wrist, and before she could resist, he ground his erection into her palm. "And does this feel like I'm immune? Did I look like I was immune when I was in the shower and you were stroking me?"

Holy shit. She stood frozen to the spot, her hand cupping Hades's massive erection. Finally, she looked up at him, her breath catching in her throat at the glow of heat in his eyes.

"I—I don't understand. If you want me, why have you been such a colossal asshat?"

One corner of his mouth twitched in a smile. "Asshat? I like that."

With a huff, she stepped away from him. "It wasn't a compliment."

"Your hand was on my dick. Anything you said would have been a compliment."

How had he gone from being a jerk to being all charming so quickly? "You still haven't answered my question."

"You want the truth?" Reaching up, he ran his hand over his hair and blew out a long, tired breath. "You're off limits to me."

"Off limits?" she asked incredulously. "Says who?"

"Azagoth."

She scowled, searching her brain for a reason Azagoth would say that, but she came up blank. "Why would he tell you I'm off limits?"

"You mean, why would he tell me that when he didn't seem to give a shit that Zhubaal fucked you?"

Ouch. Flustered, she opened her mouth. Shut it. Opened it again. "That's not what—" She cursed. "How did you know about me and Zhubaal? What did he say?"

"He didn't say anything. That bastard is as tight-lipped as a Ghastem."

Seeing how Ghastems had no mouths...yeah. "Then how did you know? And why do I have to keep asking the same question twice?"

He shrugged, his bare shoulder rolling slowly. "Dunno."

She was going to kill him. "How. Did. You. Know?" she ground out.

"*Griminions* love gossip. Those little suckers live for it. When they aren't collecting souls, I'm pretty sure they hold tea and knitting parties or something."

Hmm. Maybe the reason things with Z had been so disastrous made sense now. Because he'd taken her to his chambers, but then he'd refused sex with her. She'd been pissed, but what if the reason for his reluctance was because Azagoth had forbidden him to be with her?

Sighing, she wished away the shoes and padded barefoot to the wooden chair at the end of the bed. "Is he punishing me, do you think? I keep breaking stuff, and I've missed some cobwebs in corners, and once, I even tracked ashes through his library." She sank down on the chair, her stomach churning. "He's going to send me back to the human realm, isn't he?"

She'd be in danger there, defenseless, easy prey for angel-hating demons and True Fallen who made it a sport to drag Unfallen into Sheoul. Even worse, she'd lose Lilliana as a friend. And she'd never see Hades again. At least, not until she died and came back to the Inner Sanctum as a soul waiting to be reincarnated.

Groaning, she rubbed her eyes with the heels of her palms. She could lose everything, and wasn't that a laugh given how little she actually had. Feeling suddenly very vulnerable, she wished herself new clothes that covered everything. She didn't even mind the suffocating feeling of having so much skin hidden. Right now, the clothing was much-needed armor.

"He's not punishing you," Hades said, his gaze fixed somewhere outside.

"How do you know? Obviously I've angered him somehow."

"Trust me, if he was angry with you, you'd know." He shook his head. "No, Cat, this isn't about you. It's about me." Reaching up, he rubbed the back of his neck. "I'm the one he's punishing. All females in Sheoul-gra are off limits to me, including servants and his daughters. And trust me, when the Grim Reaper tells you his daughters are off limits...you listen. I looked at one of them too long, and he impaled me. Big stick right up the ass and out of the top of my skull. I still pucker when I think about it." His tone was light, breezy, as if his pain was no big deal, but when his gaze caught hers, she sucked in a harsh breath at the sadness there. "I want you, Cat, and if all it would cost me was a pointy stick up the ass, I'd pay that price. But it wouldn't stop there. And I don't know what price you'd have to pay, as well."

Stunned by his admission, she just sat there, unsure what to say. All she knew was that Hades wanted her after all, and that should have made her happy, but the only thing it did was make her miserable.

* * * *

So much for playing it cool.

Hades felt like a total jackass. He shouldn't have said anything about his punishment, about wanting Cat, about anything at all. The only way he stayed sane was to let everything slide off him like lava rolled off a Gargantua.

He wondered if the owners of this hut had alcohol stored somewhere. He could use a drink. Or ten.

"Hades?"

He gazed out the window at the lily pad-choked pond out back and braced himself for a bunch of pity. "What?"

"Is that why you live in the Inner Sanctum? Because Azagoth doesn't want you to be tempted or something?"

"Nope." He watched a crowd of people tossing a ball around in a nearby yard. He hated this place. It was too...human. Too bright and cheery. It reminded him that his life was all gloom and doom and asshole demons.

"So you choose to live in the Sanctum? In what's little more than a hovel?"

He turned back to her, drawing a quick, surprised breath at her clothes. While he'd been looking out the window, she'd changed into tights and a long-sleeved, form-fitting T-shirt. There were even socks on her feet. Since her skin was a gauge for good and evil, she must not want to feel those things. She must not want to feel *him*.

Not that he blamed her, but he still felt a pinch of hurt that made his voice sharper than he'd intended. "What, you were expecting a palace?"

She stared. "You live in a crypt and sleep in a coffin. They make these things called beds now."

What a joke. "Azagoth limits my comforts. You know what I miss most about that? Peanut butter. And chocolate. Limos introduced me to them when they first appeared on the human scene, you know? I always raid Azagoth's kitchen while I'm on that side, but usually I fill up on shit like pizza and Doritos."

Cat had been reaching for a miniature wooden arrow on the shelf next to her, but now she froze, her brows cranked down in confusion. "Azagoth won't even let you bring decent food to your place?"

"Oh, he will. He just won't help me get it. I have to call in favors. Or blackmail people. Limos brought me gelato once, but it was melted by the time Azagoth let it through."

Cat gasped. "That's awful."

He laughed. "It was gelato. Hardly a global disaster."

"Azagoth is an asshole," she snapped. He probably shouldn't love that she was angry on his behalf. "Why is he doing all of this to you?"

"Long story."

She picked up the arrow and gently stroked her fingers over the smooth surface. "Well, we don't have much else to do while we're waiting for the Orphmage to give up the human."

He could think of a lot of things they could do. If he wasn't forbidden by Azagoth to do them.

Anger and frustration threatened to boil over. He'd put up with Azagoth's asshattery for thousands of years, but now...now it felt like he was at a crossroads, at a place where he couldn't stand it anymore. Hadn't he paid for his sins for long enough?

Growling to himself, he stormed out of the bedroom and searched the hut for liquor. Soft footsteps followed him, but he ignored Cat as he popped the cork out of a clay jug of what smelled like extremely potent bloodwine.

Cat drifted into his peripheral vision as she checked out the knickknacks on the walls. Demons loved their wood and bone carvings. "So how did you end up here, anyway?"

He chugged a few swallows of the tart bloodwine, relishing the hot tingle as it burned its way down his throat. "You're a fallen angel, too. You know all about dirty laundry."

A wisp of pink swept across her cheeks. "My fall wasn't entirely my fault."

"You're still going with that story, huh?"

Her chin lifted. "It's true. I told you how it happened."

He snorted. "And Seminus demons hate sex."

She snatched the jug from him and took a swig. He had to hide an amused smile when she coughed. "So you own your fall?" she wheezed as she sat down at the kitchen table.

"Yup." He took back the jug. "I fucked up royally." He brought the container to his lips, pausing to say, "You really want to hear this? You want to know how I got here?"

At her nod, he lowered the jug. He hadn't told anyone this. It wasn't that he gave a crap who knew. It was just that he never really talked to anyone. Not about himself or his life. This was new, and he wasn't sure it was a good thing.

Finally, he propped his hip on the table edge. "When I was still an angel, my job was to process new humans arriving in Heaven after they died on Earth. It was boring as shit, and every time someone came through who had been slaughtered by another human, it pissed me off. So I started spending my time in the human realm, stopping sinners before they committed sins."

"Stopping them? How?"

"At first, I caused distractions. Earthquakes, sudden rainstorms, swarms of mosquitoes, whatever it took. Then I came across some vile bastard in the act of raping a young woman. I didn't think, didn't pause. I flash-fried him with a lightning bolt. And the weird thing is, I didn't feel an ounce of guilt. I knew I was going to be punished because, with very few exceptions, angels aren't supposed to kill humans."

He expected her to show some revulsion, but she merely propped her elbows on the table and leaned forward like a kid hearing a bedtime story. "Did you? Get punished, I mean?"

He shook his head. "Nope. Guess no one was paying attention. So the next time I found an evil human committing an atrocity, I whacked him. Damn, it felt good." So. Fucking. Good. "And that's where it all went wrong."

"Ah," she murmured. "You liked to kill."

Damn straight, he had. "It didn't take long before I wasn't just killing evil humans, but bad humans." There was a difference, a very *important* difference. Evil couldn't be repaired. Couldn't be forgiven. But bad could. "I made no distinction between those who were evil and those who were just assholes. I felt the need to punish, and I was made bolder by the fact that I didn't get caught. Not until I went after a son of a bitch who was famous for his torture methods. Turned out that he was Primori."

"Primori are people whose existence is crucial in some way," she mused, and then her eyes shot wide. "Which means he had a Memitim angel to protect him. And all Memitim..."

"Are Azagoth's children," he finished.

"Oh, shit."

"Yeah." He took another healthy swig from the jug. "The Memitim dude came out of nowhere, and we got into a nasty fight that ended with him dead."

"What did you do?"

Despite the fact that this had taken place over five thousand years ago, Hades's gut sank the way it had way back then when he'd realized what he'd done. He'd killed a fellow angel. Nearly killed a Primori. And worse, he hadn't cared all that much. His concern had been for himself, and for thousands of years, nothing had changed.

Until now. Now his greatest concern was making sure Cat was safe. His own fate was unimportant.

"I knew I'd get caught," he said, "so I ran for a while. Lost myself in the human population. But my parents were both professors of Angelic Ethics, and I'd had their teachings drilled into me since birth, so when the angels started closing in, I figured I'd earn points for turning myself in voluntarily." He curled his lip. "Turns out, not so much. I was relieved of my wings, but instead of being given a new name and booted out of Heaven, I was handed over to Azagoth."

At first, he'd thought the archangels's decision to let him keep his name and send him to Azagoth had been done purely to make the Grim Reaper happy, but once the Biblical prophecy tying him to the Four Horsemen appeared, he understood that he was meant for more than just being Azagoth's plaything.

Not that being a Biblical legend had helped him avoid pain. At all.

"Wow." Cat's already pale skin went a shade paler, making her freckles stand out on her nose and cheeks. "I'm shocked that he didn't kill you."

"Azagoth doesn't kill people." Hades reconsidered that. "Mostly. He's a big fan of eternal torment." No, Azagoth didn't take the easy way when it came to revenge. Or justice. He definitely wasn't the forgiving sort. "He needed someone to run the Inner Sanctum, so he gave me wings and power, making me the only Unfallen in history to be able to enter Sheoul without becoming a True Fallen." He smiled bitterly. "But he also made it his mission to make my life a living hell. And for thousands of years, he did."

She sat back in her chair, her lips pursed in thought. "Is your living situation part of that?"

"Yup." He shrugged. "He's only recently started letting me out of the Inner Sanctum for short periods of time. It's only been in the last fifty years or so that he allowed me to have luxuries from the outside if I can get anyone to bring them to me."

"Like the ice cream Limos brought you."

The pity creeping into Cat's voice made his jaw tighten. "Yeah."

"But you said you can go outside now. How often?"

"I've left Sheoul-gra five times in the last hundred years, and it cost me each time." Even when the Four Horsemen had gotten him sprung to help with a massive battle a few years ago, he'd paid dearly despite the fact that he'd fought for the good guys. For that, Azagoth had taken away Hades's only real friend, a demon who had been living in the 1st Ring for two thousand years. Azagoth had reincarnated him, leaving Hades with only his asshole wardens for company.

"So I'm guessing you don't do much dating if you can't leave, huh? You said females in Sheoul-gra are off limits, but what about here in the Inner Sanctum?"

He laughed. But it was a bitter, hard sound, even to his own ears. "Everyone is off limits to me, Cat. My wardens can screw whoever they want in the Inner Sanctum, but me? Remember the peeling thing I told you about? Yeah. Celibacy and me became really fucking intimate."

"You must have been so lonely," she said softly.

He blinked. Lonely? That thought hadn't occurred to him, and he didn't think it would occur to anyone else, either.

Although, now that he thought about it, yeah, there had always been a strange tension inside him that he couldn't identify. That he'd always written off as being sexual in nature. But now that he'd spent time with Cat, it was killing him to know that it was only a matter of time before he lost her company and her soothing touch. Fuck, he couldn't think about it, because if he did, he'd lose it.

Redirecting his thoughts, he flipped back to his default setting of deflection. "I don't know if I was lonely, really, but I was definitely horny."

She muttered something that sounded suspiciously like, "I know the feeling."

A scream from outside jolted them both to their feet. He rushed to the window and signaled for Cat to stay back, out of sight of anyone who might have a ranged weapon.

"What is it?" she asked. "What's going on?"

Awesomeness, that's what. Turning to her, he grinned. "Ever seen *The Lord of the Rings* or *The Hobbit?* You know how the giant eagles always turn up to save the day?"

She jammed her hands on her hips. "Are you going to tell me that big birds are helping to search for the human?"

Outside, people were still screaming. "Better. The hellhounds have arrived."

"Hellhounds eat people," she pointed out.

"Hilarious, right?" He held out his hand. "Come on. I'll introduce you."

"To the hellhounds?"

"Not just the hellhounds," he said, grasping her hand in his. "To the king himself. Let's go say hi to Cerberus."

Chapter Fourteen

Cataclysm had seen a lot of scary shit in her life—most of it in the last few days—but the massive, two-headed beast standing outside, surrounded by hounds that were as large as bison but still half his size, was one of the most intimidating creatures she'd ever come across.

Black as night, with glowing crimson eyes and teeth that would make a shark jealous, Cerberus used one massive paw to rake deep grooves in the grass. Steam rose up from the damaged earth, turning everything around it to ash.

"Hey, buddy," Hades said. "'Sup?"

The two heads snapped at each other before the left one put its ears back and lowered to eye level. A deep, smoky growl curled up from deep in the beast's chest.

Hades turned to her. "He said his brethren are sweeping the Rings for the human, and he apologizes in advance for any accidents."

"Accidents?"

"Most hellhounds hate angels, fallen or otherwise. Ol' Cerb here barely tolerates *me*. So we can expect some casualties among my warden ranks." He picked up a stick and threw it, and two of the hellhounds took off in a blur of black fur. "Also, he didn't really apologize. It was more of a description of how he thinks they'll taste."

She couldn't tell if he was serious or not, and frankly, she didn't want to know.

Cerberus's other head made some snarling noises, and Hades snarled back. The two of them went back and forth, until finally, Hades held up his hand and turned to her again.

"I...uh...I failed to mention something earlier."

She glared at Hades. She hated being kept in the dark about anything. "Dammit, Hades, what did you not tell me?"

"The Orphmage who captured you is using your life force to fuel the spell that will open the Inner Sanctum's barriers. He did the same thing to the human. Cerberus thinks that if we can get you close enough to the human, you'll be able to detect him. It should also unlock the doors between the Inner Sanctum and Azagoth's realm. Basically, the mutt wants to use you to track the human. Funny, yes? How it's the opposite of in the human realm, when humans use dogs—"

"I get it," she blurted. And criminy, could this situation get any worse? "But I can't believe you were keeping this from me. My life force? Seriously?"

"I'm sorry," he said, but he didn't sound very contrite. "I didn't want to worry you. Especially not after I was such a dick to you earlier."

Well, at least he admitted to being a dick. "I'm not worried," she explained. "I'm mad. We need to be out looking for the human. I have to fix this so the world isn't overrun by demon spirits and so Azagoth won't expel me from Sheoul-gra." She watched the hellhounds grab the stick and start a game of tug-of-war. "And fixing this could go a long way toward earning my way back to Heaven."

Hades's head jerked back as if he'd been slapped. "Why the everloving fuck do you want to go back to people who kicked you to the curb?"

"Heaven is my home," she said simply.

Even with the growls and snarls coming from the hellhounds and the shouts of people yelling at the beasts from a safe distance, Hades's silence was deafening.

Finally, he said quietly, "Seems to me that home is where the people who want you are."

For some reason, his words knocked the breath out of her. "And who would that be?" she asked. "Azagoth? I clean his house. And not very well. Anyone can do that. He's probably going to fire me anyway, once he learns that I was the one who got the human sent here in the first place. Lilliana? I consider her a friend, and I hope she feels the same about me, but she'd be fine without me. The other Unfallen living in the dorms? Sometimes I cook for them. They'd miss my brown butter vanilla bean cake, but aside from that..."

She shrugged as if it was all no big deal, but the realization that she was so insignificant hurt. Making matters worse was her status as an Unfallen. She had no powers, no status, no identity. Maybe she should have entered Sheoul and turned herself into a True Fallen. At least then she'd have wings and power.

But the cost would have been her soul.

Suddenly, Hades's hands came down on her shoulders. "*I* want you, Cat. I want you more than I've wanted anything since I fell."

Her heart pounded with joy, but a blanket of sadness wrapped around it, muffling the happiness. "And what good does that do either of us if Azagoth is so bent on revenge?"

"Cat—"

She pulled away from him. "Don't make things worse. We need to find the human, and I need to get back to Heaven. Can we do that, please? Before all of my life is drained?"

A chill settled in the air, so noticeable that even the hellhounds looked around to see where the cold front was coming from. Cat didn't bother searching.

An icy glaze turned Hades's eyes cloudy and his expression stony. Blue veins rose to the surface of his skin, which had lost a few shades of color, the way it had back at Azagoth's mansion when he'd shown her his wings. A darkness emanated from him, making her skin burn, and it struck her that this was the Hades who came out to play when things went to hell. *This* was the Jailor of the Dead. The Keeper of Souls. The Master of Torture.

"Tell me, Cataclysm." His voice had gone deep, scraping the craggy bottoms of Hell's fiery pits. "How did you get your name?"

Oh, God. *He knew.* Humiliation shrunk her skin. "It doesn't matter. We should go." She spun around. The door to the hut was just a few steps away—

A hellhound blocked the path, drool dripping from its bared teeth. Clearly, Hades wasn't done with this conversation, but she wasn't going to give him the satisfaction of turning around to face him.

"Did you choose your name?" She jumped at the sound of his voice, so close to her right ear that she felt his breath on her lobe.

"You know I didn't," she ground out, her humiliation veering sharply to anger that he'd chosen to go there. But then, he was the Master of Torture, wasn't he? He'd proven earlier that he knew where to strike in order to extract the most pain from a victim, and names could be an extremely sensitive subject for fallen angels.

When an angel lost his or her wings, they usually got to choose their new names. Heck, a fallen angel could rename themselves over and over, although they were never to use their angel names again. . . except inside Sheoul-gra.

But sometimes, the archangels chose a person's fallen angel name. As a punishment, or an insult, or a lesson...whatever their motivations, when they selected a name for a disgraced angel, it forever rendered one unable to refer to oneself as anything but the name the archangels chose. If they'd wanted Cat's new name to be Poopalufagus, she would be compelled to use it. Hell, she couldn't even *speak* her angelic name if she tried...and she had. The name always got clogged in her throat.

"Why did the archangels choose to call you Cataclysm?" His lips grazed her ear as he spoke.

"Because I was a disaster." Her voice cracked, and she hated herself for it. Hated Hades for making her revisit the worst moment of her life. Hated him more for forcing her to confront a truth she wasn't ready to face yet. "I helped nearly end the world, and they wanted to remind me of it forever."

Silence stretched, and she sensed Hades withdraw. When he finally spoke, his voice was back to normal, but somehow, she knew that nothing would be normal ever again.

"And those are the people you want to go home to." He brushed past her and shooed the hound out of the way. As he threw open the door to the hut and gestured for her to enter, he smiled coldly. "Then, by all means, let's not waste any time getting you back there."

* * * *

Hades spent over twelve hours with a pack of ravenous hellhounds and one fiercely silent female as they searched the 5th Ring for the damned human. Granted, he hadn't felt like talking, either, because ultimately, what did he and Cat have to talk about? Her desire to go back to Heaven, to people who saddled her with a name that would haunt her forever? His selfish desire to prevent that?

Ultimately, there was nothing he could do to convince her not to go back to Heaven if she was given the chance. She didn't want to be here, and even if she did, they couldn't be together. Not if Azagoth was still determined to punish him.

He looked over at Cat, who was standing about thirty yards away on a cliff above a river of lava. In the distance, a blackened volcano spewed smoke and steam as reddish-orange veins of molten rock flowed down its sides. She was dressed in her jeans and corset, and when Hades made clear they were going to be dealing with scorching terrain, she'd agreed to wear a pair of boots loaned to her by a the demons whose hut they'd stayed in.

Hellhounds surrounded her, keeping her safe. The demon canines were unabashed killers, but when given something to protect, they took their job seriously. There was nothing on the planet more loyal than a hellhound. There was also nothing more ravenous, as the half-dozen hellhounds tearing apart some hapless demon nearby proved.

Hades signaled to Silth, and the guy jogged over from where he'd been using a divining rod, fashioned from the thighbone of the Orphmage who had captured Cat, to locate the human. The stupid mage had refused to talk, so they'd gone with Plan *B*. Or, as Hades called it, Plan Bone.

"My Lord?" Silth asked as he climbed the jagged lava rock hill to get to him.

"The hounds want to phase us to another region." Which

was awesome because Hades hated this one, despised the heat and the smell. The only upside was that few demons lived here. Which made it a potentially great place to store a human. "But I want you and a few hounds to stay."

"You suspect something?"

Hades couldn't put his finger on it, but there was a sense of wrongness here that went beyond simply not liking the area. They hadn't found anything suspicious, but—

"Hades!" Cat came running toward him, hellhounds on her heels. "I think I can feel the human."

One of the hellhounds with her had something in its mouth, and as she drew to a halt in front of Hades, the hound playfully tossed it at her. She caught it, yelped, and dropped it.

"Hey," Hades said, "he likes you. He just gave you the finger." Of some kind of demon.

She gave him a look of disgust. "How can you joke about that? It's not funny."

"Nah," he said. "It kind of is."

"Gross." She kicked at the digit, and the hound snatched it up, swallowing it in short order. She grimaced and then rubbed her arms. "Like I was saying, I'm sensing something nearby. It's a feeling of good, which shouldn't be here, right?"

"In the 5th Ring? No way." His pulse picked up as the idea that they might be close sank in. "It's gotta be the human. Can you narrow it down to a direction?"

She shook her head. "It's weird, like a thread of good woven into a massive evil cloth. There's too much evil around it to get a bead on it."

"Uh...boss?" Silth held up the wobbling divining bone. "Got something."

As Hades watched, the thing went from barely moving to vibrating so intensely that Silth had to use two hands to hold on.

"Shit." Hades wheeled to the hounds. "Call for backup! Now—"

An arrow punched through his chest. Agony tore through him, but as a hail of arrows fell on them, all he could think about was getting Cat to safety. A fierce, protective instinct surged through him as he took her to the ground and covered her with his body while the hellhounds charged an army of demons pouring out of fissures in the ground that hadn't been there a moment ago.

"Son of a bitch!" Silth, pincushioned by a half a dozen arrows, shouted in anger and pain, but he didn't go down. Palming his sword, he leaped into the fray.

"Let me up," Cat yelled against Hades's chest. "The human is close now. If I can get to him—"

"They're trying to draw you out." He held her tight, cocooning them both in his wings as he peeked between hellhound legs. "They need to behead you both simultaneously to open the holes in the barrier."

"*Behead* me?" she screeched. "Maybe you could have shared that little factoid sooner?"

"Maybe," he said, keeping it light to hide how fucking terrified he was for her. "But nah." He signaled to one of the hounds who had arrived at the hut with Cerberus, a scarred son of the hellhound king Hades knew only as Crush. "Take her to the graveyard. If I'm not there in ten minutes, take her back to the hut."

"What?" Cat punched him in the arm and struggled to her feet. "No. I can help!"

He didn't have time for this, but he gripped her shoulders and shook her. "There are thousands of demons coming at us, all with one goal; to behead you."

"But what about you? If you're not there in ten minutes—"

"Then I'm dead." Before she could say another word, he kissed her. Hard. And he poured as much emotion into it as he could. Because whether they won the battle or not, this would be the last kiss they shared.

Quickly, he stepped back and signaled to the hound. A heartbeat later, the beast was gone, and with him, Cat.

Even above the sounds of battle, he heard her scream, "*Noooooo*," as she faded away.

Chapter Fifteen

Cat and the hellhound materialized in the weird graveyard where she'd started this bizarre journey.

Damn Hades! She eyed the mausoleums that corresponded with the five Rings, but even as she zeroed in on the one she'd originally entered that went to the 5th Ring where the battle was going down, the stupid hellhound got in her way. It even snarled at her.

"You're an asshole," she snapped.

It cocked its big head, raised its pointy ears, and looked at her as if it was expecting her to throw a stick or something. Then it burped. And dear God, what had the thing eaten today? She tried not to gag as she turned around and searched the wall for the opening to Azagoth's realm. Yes, she knew it was locked, but it couldn't hurt to try. It wasn't as if she had anything better to do, since clearly, the gassy hellhound wasn't going to let her go back to the 5th Ring.

Hurry, Hades.

His kiss still felt warm on her lips. Her skin still burned from his touch. She missed him, and they'd only been apart for a couple of minutes. What would happen when—and if—she finally got out of here? How could she deal with knowing he was just a doorway away?

Maybe it would be better if she got to go back to Heaven. He wouldn't be a temptation to her anymore. And besides, being accepted back into Heaven meant her family would take her back, right? Her friends would forgive her. She could forget the terrible things they'd said as she'd been dragged to the chopping block.

Traitor.

Satan's whore.

You're no daughter of mine.

You sicken me.

Yes, she could forget. With enough demon bloodwine, anyway.

An electric tingle charged the air, and the hairs on the back of her neck stood up. She pivoted around as Cerberus materialized, his black fur shiny from blood, one of his massive jaws clenched around a broken, bleeding human.

And dangling limply from the second set of jaws was Hades.

Oh, shit! She sprinted to the giant hellhound, who dropped both bodies to the ground. Sinking to her knees, she gathered Hades's lifeless body in her arms.

"Hades? Hades!" She shook him, but there was nothing. He wasn't even breathing. How could this be? How could he be dead? He couldn't be, right?

"He's only mostly dead."

She wrenched her head around to see Azagoth striding toward them, a trail of *griminions* on his heels.

"M-mostly dead?"

"Haven't you ever seen *The Princess Bride?*"

It took her a second to realize he was making a joke. Mr. Serious, the Grim Fucking Reaper, was *joking.*

The opening in the wall must lead to an alternate reality.

The *griminions* gathered up the human and scurried back through the doorway where Lilliana was waiting.

"Come on," she called out. "Leave Hades to Azagoth."

Cat hesitated, and when Azagoth barked out a curt, "Go," some secret, dark part of her rebelled. She'd just spent what was likely days in a hell dimension with a male who wanted her, a male she wanted, and the person who was keeping them apart wanted her to leave.

Screw that.

She held Hades tighter and boldly met Azagoth's gaze. "I'm staying."

Azagoth's eyes glittered, but his voice was calm. "What I'm about to do won't work if I'm not alone with him, so if you want him to live, you'll go."

Lilliana held out her hand. "Trust him."

Swallowing dryly, Cat nodded. Very gently, she eased Hades's head onto the ground, stroked her hand over his hair, and said a silent good-bye.

Why was this so hard?

"Azagoth," she croaked. "The human and I…the demons enchanted us, and unless it's broken—"

He cut her off with a brisk hand gesture. "Whatever was done to you will lose its power when you leave the Inner Sanctum. So go. *Now.*"

Sensing he'd reached the limits of his patience with her, she reluctantly shoved to her feet. She managed to keep it together until she was inside Azagoth's office. The moment the door closed, she started bawling, and Lilliana pulled her into a hug.

"I'm so glad you're okay," Lilliana said, and was she crying too? "I knew something was wrong days ago, and then when we tried to operate the doorway to the Inner Sanctum and it wouldn't work, we feared the worst." She pulled back just enough to eye Cat, as if making sure it was really her, and then she hugged her again. And yes, she was crying.

"I'm sorry," she murmured into Lilliana's shoulder. "I screwed up, and when I tried to fix it, I only made things worse."

"It's okay," Lilliana said. "We can hash it out later." She wrapped her arm around Cat's shoulders and guided her toward the door. "Let's get you cleaned up and fed. You must be exhausted."

Cat cranked her head around to the closed portal door. "But Hades—"

"There's nothing you can do for him. Azagoth will update us when he can."

Cat wanted to argue, to rail against being led away, but Lilliana was right. "What about the human?" she asked as they walked toward her quarters. "What happened to him?"

"The *griminions* took him to the human realm where he'll be met by angels and escorted to Heaven."

Good. When most humans died, their souls crossed over to the Other Side on their own, but this poor guy had gone through the worst nightmare imaginable, and if anyone deserved a Heavenly escort, it was him. He'd definitely be sent to a Special Care Unit where humans who died as a result of trauma went to allow them time to adjust. Cat had a feeling he'd need an eternity. She just wished she could do more for him.

Cat was so lost in guilt and worry about Hades that she barely noticed when they arrived at her small apartment. The fragrance of her homemade crisp apple potpourri snapped her out of her daze, and she wasted no time in showering off the remains of the Inner Sanctum. She tried not to think about the fact that Hades was part of that. Gone was the smoky scent of him on her skin. Gone was his touch. His kisses.

She tried not to cry again as she dried off and dressed.

When she was finished, Lilliana was waiting with a tray of food and a pot of hot tea.

"Thank you," Cat said as she took a seat. The food looked amazing, but she couldn't eat. Not until she knew Hades was okay. "It's weird to have *you* serve *me*."

"It's what friends do," Lilliana said. "Also, Azagoth sent word that Hades is fine." Cat nearly slid off her chair in relief. "Like he said, Hades was only mostly dead." She grinned. "I've made Azagoth watch *The Princess Bride* about a million times now. He bitches and moans, but he laughs every time."

That was hard to imagine. "What does 'mostly' dead mean?"

"It means that Hades was killed, but *griminions* grabbed his soul and brought it straight to Azagoth." Lilliana shoved a cup of tea at Cat. "If Azagoth can get a soul to a body fast enough, he can sort of...reinstall and jumpstart." At what must have been Cat's expression of amazement, Lilliana nodded. "Yeah, I didn't know about that until today, either." She propped her elbows on the table and leaned in, her amber eyes glowing with curiosity. "So. What's going on between you and Hades?"

Cat wasn't going to bother asking how Lilliana knew. It was probably written all over her face. She stalled for time though, sipping her tea until Lilliana tapped her fingers impatiently on the table.

"Nothing," Cat finally sighed. "There's absolutely nothing going on with Hades." Saying those words made her heart hurt far more than she would ever have suspected.

"Why? Doesn't he share your feelings?"

"That's not the problem." Man, she was tired. She shuffled to the bed and sank down on the edge of the mattress. "The problem is your mate."

Lilliana's hand froze as she reached for a grape on the platter of food. "What do you mean?"

"You should probably ask him." Cat's lids grew heavy, and she felt herself sway. "Why am I so sleepy?"

"The tea." Lilliana helped ease Cat back on the bed. "It's made from Sora root. It'll help you rest."

Rest would be good. Maybe in her dreams she and Hades could finally be together.

* * * *

The thing about dying was that it made a guy think about his life. What he'd done with it. What he could potentially do with it in the future. And as an immortal, Hades's future could be really long. And really lonely.

The thought of living one more day the way he'd lived the last five thousand years made him want to throw up as he prowled the length of his crypt until he swore the soles of his boots cried out for mercy.

Azagoth had left him hours ago with all kinds of assurances that Cat wouldn't be harshly punished for what she'd done. But Azagoth's idea of "harsh" was a lot different from Hades's. Well, not usually, but for Cat, definitely.

Hades just hoped Azagoth hadn't suspected that anything had gone on between them. Technically, Hades hadn't gone against Azagoth's orders, but the Grim Reaper wasn't a fan of technicalities. And if he did anything to punish Cat for what Hades had done, Hades would fight that bastard until he was too dead to fix.

Snarling, Hades threw his fist into the wall. Never, not in his entire life, had he felt this way about a female. Hell, he hadn't felt this way about anything. Oh, he'd always been passionate about meting out justice, but this was a different kind of passion. This was an all-consuming desire to be with someone. To be something better *for* that someone.

He hadn't known Cat for long, but in their brief time together, he'd shared things he'd always kept private. He'd given comfort and had been comforted. He'd wanted, and he'd been wanted back.

She wants to go back to Heaven, idiot.

Yeah, then there was that. The chances of going back were extremely slim, given that in all of angelic existence, only a handful of fallen angels had been offered the opportunity. But just the fact that she wanted to go was troubling.

Oh, he understood. Who would choose to live in the grim darkness of the underworld when they could flit around in light and luxury? But dammit, Cat was wanted down here. Could he make her see that?

Closing his eyes, he braced his forehead on the cool stone wall he'd just punched. Pain wracked him and not just because he'd broken bones in his hand and they were knitting together with agonizing speed. That pain was nothing compared to the ache in his heart.

He needed to be with Cat, but how? He supposed he could try reasoning with Azagoth. Sometimes the guy wasn't completely unbending. Especially now that he had Lilliana. She'd leveled him out, had given him a new perspective on life and relationships.

But would it be enough?

Because one thing was certain. If Hades couldn't have Cat in his life, then Azagoth had saved it for nothing.

Chapter Sixteen

Cat dreamed of Hades.

It was so real, so sexy, that when she woke, she was both heartbroken to find herself alone in bed and turned on by the things they'd done in her dream. She let her hand drift down her stomach, her mind clinging to the images that had played in her head like an erotic movie. She could almost feel the lash of his tongue between her legs as her fingers dipped beneath the fabric of her panties.

Oh, yes. If she couldn't have him right now, in her bed, she could at least—

Someone knocked on the door, and then Lilliana's voice filtered through the thick wood. "Cat? Are you awake?"

Cat groaned. "No."

Lilliana's soft chuckle drifted into the room. "Azagoth wants to see you in his library."

A cold fist of *oh shit* squeezed her heart, and so much for her libido. It was more dead than Hades had been yesterday.

"I'll be right there," she called out.

It took her less than five minutes to dress in a pair of cut-off shorts and a tank top—she wanted as much skin exposed as possible in hopes that she could sense Azagoth's level of anger in the form of evil. Not that knowing would help her any, but it could at least mentally prepare her for disintegration or something.

Gut churning, she hurried to his library, finding it empty. She took a seat in one of the plush leather chairs, and just as she settled in, Azagoth entered.

She trembled uncontrollably as he took a seat. "Hades told me what happened," he said, getting right to it. "I know that letting the unauthorized souls into the Inner Sanctum was an accident. What I don't know is why you didn't tell me when it first happened. We could have prevented all of this."

"I know," she whispered. She tucked her hands between her knees as if that would stop them from shaking. It didn't. "I should have. But I was afraid. I thought I could fix it on my own, but then I got trapped and couldn't get back...it was all a big mistake."

One dark eyebrow shot up. "A *mistake?* It was a colossal fuckup that could have caused destruction on a global scale. And after the recent near-Apocalypse, having millions of demonic spirits loose in the human world would have damned near started another one."

Her eyes burned, and shame in the form of tears ran down her cheeks. "Are you going to kill me?" Or worse, give her a place of honor in his Hall of Souls, where she'd scream forever inside a frozen body. She wasn't going to ask about that, though. No sense in giving him any ideas.

Azagoth gaped. "Kill you? Why would you think I'd kill you?"

Was he kidding? "You're sort of known for not giving second chances. And for disintegrating people who piss you off."

He appeared to consider that. Finally, he nodded. "True. I've never denied that I'm a monster." He jammed a hand through his ebony hair and sat back in the chair, his emerald eyes unreadable as he took her in. "You're a terrible housekeeper, Cat. You're always breaking and misplacing things, and I doubt you even know what a vacuum cleaner is—"

"I'll do better," she swore. "I'll try harder and work longer hours. Please don't—"

"Let me finish," he broke in. "Like I said, you're a terrible housekeeper. But you're an excellent cook. Zhubaal and Lilliana have watched you with the Unfallen, and they both agree that you're also a great teacher. You're eager and enthusiastic, and I don't think I've ever seen anyone try as hard as you do to get things right. It's that quality that led you to fix the mistake you made by letting the human into the Inner Sanctum. I admire your determination, and I like having you around. So no, I won't kill you. Besides," he muttered, "Lilliana would mount my head on a pike if I did that."

Cat sat, stunned. He admired her? Liked having her around? Even more unbelievable, the Grim Reaper was *afraid* of Lilliana. "I—I don't understand. What are you going to do to me?"

"Nothing. I think you've punished yourself far more than I ever could." He smiled, barely, but for him, that was huge. "I can hire someone else to clean if you'd rather do other work in Sheoul-gra. Just let Lilliana know, and she'll arrange it."

Relief flooded her in such a powerful wave that she nearly fell out of her chair. She could barely function as Azagoth came to his feet in a smooth surge. "I'm glad you're back, Cataclysm. Lilliana was inconsolable."

Inconsolable? Warmth joined the flood of relief. Lilliana truly cared about her. Oh, Cat had had friends in Heaven, but no one had worried about her. Okay, sure, they didn't worry because Heaven was a pretty safe place, but even when she'd gone to work with Gethel, no one had expressed concern. When she'd been found guilty of colluding with a traitor in order to start the Apocalypse, her friends and family had been sad, angry, and embarrassed, but to say that they'd been distraught or inconsolable would be a huge overstatement.

"Thank you," she said, her voice thick with emotion. "But before you go, can I ask you something?"

He gave a clipped nod. "Ask."

She cleared her throat, more to buy a little time than to get the sappy emotion out of her voice. "I want something from you." Azagoth cocked a dark eyebrow, and she revised her statement. "I mean, I would like something from you."

"And what's that?"

"Let Hades have some furniture."

Clearly, Azagoth hadn't expected that because the other eyebrow joined the first. "Furniture?"

"He's been sleeping on a hard-ass slab of stone and using

scraps of who knows what for other furniture. He made his own playing cards from bits of wood."

"So?"

She shoved to her feet, ready to go toe-to-toe with him over this. Hades deserved as much. "Don't you think he's been punished enough?"

"You know what he did, yes? You know he slaughtered my son?"

"I'm aware," she said gently...but firmly. "I know that must be painful for you. But I'm also aware that he's been paying for that for thousands of years."

Crossing his arms over his broad chest, Azagoth studied her. His green eyes burned right through her, and she wondered what he was searching for. "He wouldn't ask for these things. So why are you?"

"Because it's the right thing to do."

"Is that all?" he asked, and her stomach dropped to her feet. *He knew.*

"I care for him," she admitted. "And he deserves better—"

"Than how I'm treating him?"

Oh, hell, no, she wasn't falling into *that* trap. "Better than how he currently lives."

When Azagoth smiled, she let out the breath she didn't realize she'd been holding. "Fine. He can have whatever he wants for his home."

She almost pointed out that his home was a damned crypt, but she figured that would be pushing it. So for today, she accepted the victory.

But she wasn't done. Hades had fought for her, and now it was time for her to do the same for him.

First, though, she had someone to see.

Chapter Seventeen

"Can I talk to you?"

Cat stood in the doorway of Zhubaal's office in the Unfallen dorms, her stomach churning a little. She really didn't want to be having this conversation, but curiosity had always been her downfall. Like a real cat.

Zhubaal had been gazing out the window at the courtyard below where several Unfallen were playing a game of volleyball, but now he turned to her, his handsome face a mask of indifference. "About what?"

"I want to know why, ah..." Man, this was awkward. "That day, in your chambers..."

Leaning against the windowsill, he crossed his booted feet at the ankles and hooked his thumbs in his jeans' pockets. "You want to know why I refused sex with you."

Her cheeks heated. That had been a seriously humiliating thing. "Yes. Did I do something wrong?"

"You didn't do anything wrong. I had my reasons."

She probably shouldn't ask, but... "Can you tell me those reasons?"

He stood there for a long time, his expression stony, his mouth little more than a grim slash. Finally, when it became clear that he wasn't going to say anything, she shook her head and started to turn away.

"It's okay," she said. "I had no right to ask."

She headed down the hall, made it about ten steps when he

said, "I'm waiting for someone."

Oh. She pivoted around to him as he stood just outside his office door. "Someone you know? You have a lover? A mate?"

He averted his gaze, and she realized that in all the months she'd known him, this was the first time he'd shown any vulnerability. "Not exactly."

Not wanting to ruin the moment, she took a few slow, careful steps toward him, approaching the way she might a feral dog. "Did...did Azagoth warn you to stay away from me?"

"No."

That seemed strange, given that he'd read Hades the riot act. "Why not?"

Gaze still locked on the floor, he replied, "Because he knows about my vow."

"What vow?"

"That," he said, his head snapping up, "is none of your business.

Touchy. But now she was curious. What kind of vow? She recalled his interactions with the resident Unfallen and all the visitors to the realm and realized that she'd never once seen Zhubaal with a female.

"Are you gay?"

He snorted. "Hardly."

Come to think of it, she'd never seen him with a male, either. So what was his deal? He was waiting for someone...someone specific? Was his vow—

She inhaled sharply. "You...you're a virgin, aren't you? You rejected me out of honor."

His gaze narrowed, and his lips twisted into a nasty sneer. "Do not confuse my lack of sexual experience with innocence or kindness, and especially not honor. Not when you tried to use me to rid yourself of your own virginity."

"I didn't know. I'm sorry. I'll just go now. But Zhubaal...I hope you find whoever it is you're waiting for."

As she hurried away, she swore she heard a soft, "I hope so, too."

* * * *

Zhubaal watched Cat disappear around a corner, his heart heavy, his body numb. She had been his single moment of weakness, the only one in nearly a century.

It had been ninety-eight years since his beloved angel, Laura, had been cast out of Heaven. Ninety-eight years of searching for her in Sheoul and getting his own Heavenly boot in the ass in the process.

Cat had come to him in a moment of weakness, on a day when he'd despaired that he'd never find Laura. But even as he'd kissed Cat, touched her, started to undress her, Laura had filled his thoughts.

As young angels, he and Laura had made a blood-pact to be each other's firsts, and he'd kept that vow, even after she lost her wings. He'd searched for her, eventually losing his own wings, but still, he remained faithful. And then, even after he discovered that she'd been slaughtered by an angel, he'd held onto that pact like a toddler with his comfy blankie. After all, her soul had been sent to Sheoul-gra, and he'd figured he could find her there, even if he had to get himself killed to do it.

At least they'd have been together in the Inner Sanctum.

But fate had intervened in the form of Azagoth, who had needed a new assistant, which gave Zhubaal access to privileged information about the residents of the Inner Sanctum.

Then fate threw him a curve ball.

He was too late.

Laura had, indeed, been a resident of the Inner Sanctum's 1st Ring. Until Azagoth reincarnated her thirty years ago.

Pain stabbed Zhubaal in the chest. His Laura was out there somewhere. She was a different person with a different name, but she was still his, and he wouldn't break his vow until he found her.

Unfortunately, he was now bound to Azagoth with a vow just as binding as the one he'd made with Laura. He could leave Sheoul-gra, but only for a few hours at a time, which made searching for Laura—or whatever name she went by now— next to impossible. Especially since Azagoth refused to give any specifics regarding her status, her parents, or even her species.

As a fallen angel, she should have been born only to a fallen angel to become either *emim* or *vyrm*, but Z had learned long ago that there were very few rules that couldn't be broken. For all he knew, his Laura could be feeding on offal and lurking in garbage piles as a Slogthu demon.

The big question was whether or not he'd recognize her. Surely their bond had been strong enough that he could see his Laura in whoever she'd become. And if she'd had the rare good luck of retaining her soul-memory, she could remember bits of her previous life. If so, *she* might even be searching for *him*.

Sighing, he went back inside his office, but he didn't feel like working anymore. He wanted to be out in the world, scouring the realms for Laura. He was a fool and he knew it, but dammit, he'd made a vow, and even if he couldn't have the angel he'd fallen in love with, he wasn't going to break the pact with someone he didn't love. He'd hurt Cat, and he felt a little bad about that, but he hadn't loved her. Cat deserved better. Laura deserved better.

He wasn't sure what he deserved, but he knew what he wanted.

He was just losing faith that he'd ever get it.

Chapter Eighteen

Cat spent the next two days plotting ways to convince Azagoth to lighten up on Hades. Lilliana had volunteered to help, and Cat gladly took her up on her offer. The trick, Lilliana said, would be to make him think it was his idea. As Cat had suspected, he could be incredibly thick-skulled when it came to certain things, like offering second chances.

She opened the door to her apartment, intent on paying Lilliana a visit. But instead of facing an empty hall, she found herself standing mere inches away from Hades. Heart pounding with surprise and excitement, she stared.

"Hades," she gasped. God, he looked good, so good he stole her breath. Wearing nothing but form-fitting, color-shifting pants and black boots, he filled the doorway, his massive shoulders nearly touching the doorframe. "What are you doing here? You'll get in trouble—"

He was on her in an instant. His mouth came down on hers as he swept her into his arms, crushing her against him. His hand came up to tangle in her hair, holding her in place for the erotic assault. Forbidden, shivery excitement shot through her, and her core went molten.

"I don't care," he said against her lips. "I need you. I *burn* for you."

She moaned, her heart soaring at his words as he pushed her toward the bed. But as her knees hit the mattress and they both fell onto the soft covers, she wedged her hands between them and pushed him off.

"I can't," she said, and oh, how it hurt to say that. "I can't watch you suffer because of me."

Hades cupped her cheek in his warm palm. "I was going to go to Azagoth first, but I know him. He'll say no."

"All the more reason to not do this." She heard the sound of the plea in her voice, the weakness in the face of Hades's desire. She needed to be stronger, but she wanted him so badly she shook with the force of it.

He leaned forward and brushed his lips across hers in a feathery, tender kiss. "All the more reason to do it. How does that old saying go? Better to seek forgiveness than ask permission from some asshole who's going to tell you no?"

Damn him, this wasn't funny. "Hades—"

"Shh." He silenced her with another kiss. This one deeper. Harder. "Just this once, Cat," he murmured. "I need this to hold onto when I'm alone at night."

She might have argued some more. She might have shoved him away. She might have done a lot of things if he hadn't slid his thick thigh between her legs as he untied her corset and freed her breasts. If he hadn't dipped his head to take one aching nipple into his mouth.

"Hades," she moaned.

He opened his mouth fully over her breast, his hot breath flowing over her skin as he worked the buttons of her jeans. His tongue teased her as he dragged it low, under the swell of her breast before laving attention on the other one.

Against her thigh, she felt his immense arousal pressing into her, a hot, unyielding presence that she'd never felt in the one place she needed it to be. Arching, she twisted so his erection settled between her legs, but her damned jeans and his pants—

As if Hades was thinking the same thing, he reared up and made fast work of removing her pants. "I love that you don't wear shoes," he said, his voice all breathless and needy. "Nothing to catch your jeans on."

He tossed them to the floor, kicked off his boots, and then stripped away his own clothing, leaving him beautifully, gloriously, naked. His cock jutted upward from the plump sac between his legs, the broad head glistening at the tip. Unbidden, her hand reached out, but he seized her wrists and pinned them over her head as he stretched his body over hers.

"Not yet," he said as he nuzzled her neck. "If you touch me, I'm a goner. Embarrassing, but true."

Okay, she'd let him off the hook. For now. But later, she wanted to touch him. Smell him. Taste him. She had a lot to learn, and she was going to use whatever time they had wisely.

"There you go," he murmured. "Relax. Close your eyes. I'll make this good for you."

Relax, huh? It was weird how her body felt wound tight and liquid at the same time. In the dark behind her eyelids, she imagined the expression on his face as he kissed his way down her body.

His tongue circled her navel, and the tightness ramped up a notch. Anticipation made her squirm, but he put a lid on that quick, clamping down on her hips to force her into blissful submission. Her limited ability to move jacked up the intensity of every sensation until she was clawing at the bedspread and silently begging him to make her come.

But no, Hades was indeed a master of torture, and he took his time scooting lower, his tongue trailing along her abdomen and skimming her mound. She jerked upward, her body instinctively following his mouth as he kissed the crease of her leg.

"You okay?" His voice was a deep, sexy growl that sent stabs of pleasure shooting through every nerve ending.

"Uh-huh," was all she could manage.

He chuckled as he spread her legs and settled between them. The brush of his hair against the sensitive skin of her inner thighs made her hiss in pleasure, and then that soft, prickly Mohawk shifted, finding her center. She moaned as Hades bobbed his head up and down between her legs.

"Oh...my," she breathed. "How...naughty."

He nodded, sending a silky caress over her sex. "There is no part of me that can't bring you pleasure," he purred, the vibration adding to the amazing sensations that cascaded over her in an erotic wave.

His hands slid up and down her legs, circling her ankles and tickling her calves as he brushed his hair over her sex in slow, decadent sweeps. Tension built, a writhing knot of need that grew hotter with every erotic bob of his head. She needed more, and he knew because his head came up and his tongue came out and her eyes went wide when she realized what he was about to do.

"Yes, please," she whispered.

With a raw, erotic curse, he spread her with his thumbs and dipped his head. His mouth met her core, engulfing her in heat as his hot breath fanned the flames. She cried out at the first tentative touch of his tongue. The tip flicked whisper-light over her oh-so-ready knot of nerves before he used the flat of his tongue to lick all of her at once, from core to clit.

She fell back with a strangled moan and drove her fingers through his silky hair to hold him there, to keep him doing exactly what he was doing so perfectly. He lapped at her, starting with long, lazy licks before changing up and swirling his tongue between her folds. But when he pushed his tongue inside her and curled it firmly as he pulled back, she bucked so hard he had to pin her with his hands on her thighs so he could do it again.

Relentlessly, he drove his tongue inside her and licked his way back out, over and over, until the steam building up inside her exploded. The orgasm he'd given her in the shower had been amazing, but this...this made her not only see stars, but join them. The supernova of ecstasy sent her hurtling into the heavens—where she'd never felt like this.

The pleasure rolled over her in great waves, and just when she thought it was over, Hades did something with his fingers and tongue that sent her spiraling out of control again. She heard a distant shout...his name. She'd screamed his name...

Somewhere deep inside her it occurred to her that someone might have heard, but as Hades brought her back to Earth with a series of gentle, slow licks, the danger they faced slipped away until all that was left was the big male prowling back up her body, his lips glistening, his eyes smoldering with the promise that there was more to come.

* * * *

Hades had never in his entire life been this turned on. As an angel, he'd had a couple of sex partners, but he'd been overeager and underexperienced. The encounters had been nice, but all these years later, he could barely remember them.

As a fallen angel, he hadn't had much opportunity to get down and dirty, but when he had, he'd taken advantage of it. The rare times when Azagoth allowed him out of Sheoul-gra, he'd hit every succubus he could find, visited every demon pleasure palace he could get to in his allotted time.

He'd learned a few things, for sure, but one thing he'd never learned was to care. To take the time to enjoy a female with not only his body, but his mind and soul. Maybe because he'd always known he couldn't get attached to anyone, so he'd kept his distance, used jokes and a carefree attitude to breeze through a one-hour stand.

But Cat changed all that. She'd wormed her way into his heart like a dire leech, and all he could do was hope she'd drain him.

Bracing himself on his fists, he looked down at her as she lay panting, her face flushed, her lips parted to reveal just a hint of pearly teeth and tiny, pointed fangs. As the tip of his cock prodded her wet opening, she gasped and rolled her hips, inviting him in.

"I've never done this before," she said. There was no shyness, no self-consciousness, just a plain and simple fact that left him speechless for a second.

"But...Zhubaal," he finally blurted.

She shook her head, making her hair shift in shiny red waves on the pale yellow bedspread. "Nothing happened."

Oh, great, so he'd been a jealous jackass for nothing. It was probably a good thing he hadn't given in to his desire to rip Zhubaal's head off and shove it up his ass every time he saw him, too.

Hades looked into her gorgeous, guileless eyes, loving that she was trusting him to be her first. Pride swelled, but close on its heels was shame. This might be the only time they had, and to take the gift of her virginity, knowing they might never again—

"Knock it off." She dug her nails into his shoulder, the little pricks of pain snapping him out of his train of thought. "I can see your mind working, and I know what you're thinking. I'm capable of making my own decisions, and even if we can't be together again, I want to always have this, same as you."

Ah, damn, she was a gift. This was going to be worth anything Azagoth put him through as punishment. Anything.

Reaching between them, he gripped his cock to guide it inside her, but once again, she clawed him. "Wait. I want to..." She trailed off, a burst of pink blooming in her cheeks. "I want to taste you."

At those words, his cock damned near humiliated him. It jerked in his hand, all, *yes, please, and do it now.*

"Okay," he said, proud of how he didn't sound completely strangled with lust, "but only for a second. You've got me way too worked up."

Her cocky grin made him regret agreeing to this as he climbed up her body and kneeled next to her head. He barely had time to push his unruly erection down when she lifted her mouth to it and flicked her tongue over the bead of pre-come at the tip. He hissed at the contact, hissed louder when she did it again.

And then the crazy little angel swallowed his cock from the head to the base and sucked like she'd been born to do this. A sound somewhere between a shout and a bark escaped him as she slid her mouth upward and swirled her tongue around the crown. Holy hell, she was no tentative kitten lapping at a bowl of milk. This was a she-tiger with an appetite for man, and—

He pulled back and squeezed his cock so hard he lost his sight for a heartbeat. A hot climax pulsed in his balls and his shaft, and there was no way he was blowing down her throat. He needed to be skin-on-skin with her, body to body, sex to sex.

For the first orgasm, anyway.

"Not nice," he scolded, but she just gave him a wide-eyed doe look he might have bought if he hadn't just experienced the rabid carnivore she really was.

"I thought I was being *very* nice." She batted her eyes, still playing innocent, which only made his cock throb harder.

Time to teach her a lesson.

In a quick motion, he flipped her onto her belly and dove between her legs again, lifting her hips for prime access as he stabbed his tongue into her dripping sex. She cried out in surprise and pleasure as he licked her, this time not even trying to be gentle. He growled against her core, nibbling and feasting as he ground his cock against the mattress to keep the bastard happy.

Then, just as her cries and breaths signaled that she was on the edge, he rolled her again. Her legs flopped open, spreading that beautiful pink flesh wide for him. He wanted to lick her some more, but the foreplay had set him on fire, and the bed-humping had fanned the flames.

Time to burn.

He positioned himself between her thighs and pushed against her opening. She arched, giving him even more access, and his head slid into her warmth.

"Tight," he groaned. "Ah, damn, you're tight." Her eyes caught his, held them as he pushed in a little more. Like many angels, she didn't seem to have a barrier, but the invasion still couldn't be comfortable. "Does it hurt?"

"No," she breathed. "It just feels...right."

She couldn't have said anything better. Throwing back his head, he thrust deep. At her cry, he panicked, but the expression on her face wasn't pain. It was bliss. She was so ready, so eager, and he was so damned lucky.

He pulled nearly free of her body and slid back in, keeping an eye on her, gauging her reactions in case he hurt or frightened her, but she was gloriously free of inhibition, fear, or discomfort.

"More," she begged. "Don't hold back. I want it *all*."

It was the same strength of character she'd exhibited in the Inner Sanctum, the drive to get what she wanted at all costs, and this time, he was going to give it to her.

Dropping to his elbows, he kissed her as he pumped between her legs, his thrusts growing faster and harder as his climax began to tingle at the base of his spine. The wet slap of their bodies grew more furious as she clung to him, wrapping her legs around his waist with more strength than he'd imagined she had in her entire body.

She met him thrust for thrust, both with her hips and her

tongue. He heard the bed banging against the wall and sliding across the floor with the fury of their joining, and shit, he was close, so close that when she came, all he could do was hold on for the ride.

Her sex rippled along his shaft, wringing the climax from him in long bursts that bordered on agony. Sweet, sweet agony. He couldn't think, couldn't see as he came once, then twice, the second sending his entire body into spasms of ecstasy. He filled her, but she filled him, too, with emotion he'd never known.

And as he collapsed on top of her, his skin coated in sweat, his lungs struggling to pull in enough air, he wondered if he should tell her how he felt about her. Would she believe he was capable of love? He hadn't thought so, but what else could explain his inability to stop thinking about her? What else could explain his willingness to disobey Azagoth? Would it be fair to tell her he'd fallen hard for her?

They had, after all, only known each other for a short time. Worse, Azagoth might kill him.

And then, as if just thinking about the male was a curse, the door slammed open. The Grim Reaper burst inside, the whites of his eyes swallowed by inky black, swirly pools. Massive, leathery wings brushed the ceiling, but it was the set of ebony horns sprouting from his forehead and curling over the top of his skull, that filled Hades with dread. Azagoth only took out his horns when he was pissed.

Yep, Hades was dead. And this time, he had a feeling the "mostly" part wouldn't apply.

Chapter Nineteen

This was a nightmare.

Terror winged its way through Cat as Azagoth strode into her little apartment, black horns jutting from the top of his skull. Lilliana had once said that when the horns came out, so did his temper.

Which was bad, considering that he did most of his killing while being perfectly calm. She didn't even want to *try* to imagine what he'd do while seriously pissed off.

She and Hades leaped off the bed, and while she scrambled for a robe, he very coolly pulled on his pants. Azagoth had the decency to avoid looking at her, but his eyes burned holes through Hades. Who, for his part, showed no emotion at all, although he did keep himself between her and Azagoth. It was sweet of him to want to protect her, but she had a feeling he was in far more danger than she was.

"Azagoth." Hades held his hands up in a placatory gesture, but Azagoth kept moving toward them in a slow, predatory gait. "This isn't—"

"Isn't what it looks like?" Azagoth's words, sounding as if they'd been dredged in smoke, were a dare, and Cat hoped Hades didn't take it.

"No," Hades said, standing his ground and looking completely unruffled. "It's exactly what it looks like. But it isn't Cat's fault. *I* came to *her*."

Tugging her robe closed, Cat stepped next to Hades. "Please,

Azagoth," she begged, and she'd go to her knees if she had to, "don't punish him. He saved my life."

Azagoth halted a few feet away, clenching and unclenching his fists at his sides. Claws at the tips of his fingers shredded his flesh, and blood began to drip from his hands. "And you felt grateful enough to sleep with him?"

"Of course not. This started before he saved me." Cat immediately realized her mistake when Hades groaned and Azagoth growled. Quickly, she added, "It was all my fault. He kept telling me he couldn't, and I kept...seducing him."

"You expect me to believe that?"

"It's the truth," she said, "so, yes."

Azagoth turned to Hades, and was it her imagination or had his horns receded a little? "And what have you got to say?"

"She's telling the truth. But..."

"But what?"

"But I could have resisted more. I chose not to." He took her hand. "I want her."

"I see." Azagoth scrubbed his palm over his face, leaving behind smears of blood like evil war paint. "Lilliana has made me soft," he muttered. He dropped his hand and studied each of them in turn before focusing his laser gaze on Hades. "Will you fight for her?"

Hades growled. "I would fight Revenant himself for her."

Azagoth's upper lip peeled back to reveal a set of huge fangs. "Would you fight me?"

"I'd rather not, but if forced to, yes."

The expression on Azagoth's face became stony, sending a chill down her spine. "Will you beg?"

Beg? What a strange question. But it seemed to get a rise out of Hades, because he stiffened. "I...have never...begged."

"I know."

Hades dropped to the floor so fast and hard his kneecaps cracked on the stone tile. "Please, Azagoth," he began, his gaze downcast, his hand clasped against his thighs. "I've served you well, but if you want me to do better, I will. If you want to torture me every day for the rest of my life, I'll gladly submit. All I ask is that you allow me to see Cat between sessions." He lifted his head, and she had to stifle a cry at the liquid filling his eyes. "I am sorry about your son. His death must sit on your heart like a bruise, and if I could heal it, I would. I can only keep trying to make it up to you, but without Cat, I don't know how long I can survive to do that. Please, my lord, let me find the same happiness that you've found with Lilliana." His voice cracked with emotion. "*Please.*"

Cat lost it. Truly, hopelessly, lost it. Sobbing, she sank down next to Hades and wrapped herself around him, needing to comfort him as much as she needed comfort. Her heart ached and her throat closed, and her skin tingled with the sense of goodness that radiated from Hades. Right now, he wasn't a fallen angel who ruled a demon purgatory. Right now he was a male, in pain and vulnerable, whose intentions were truly pure.

"Yeah, yeah," Azagoth muttered. "Fine. Get up. You have my blessing. That wasn't so hard, was it?"

Cat nearly burst with happiness as Hades blinked up at Azagoth. "Holy shit, so that's all I had to do was beg for your forgiveness?"

"Yep."

"So I could have done that centuries ago?"

"Yep." Azagoth's voice took on a haunted quality that struck Cat right in the heart. "All I ever wanted from you…after enough pain, of course…was an apology for taking my son's life."

Cat's eyes watered anew as Hades swallowed hard. "I am truly sorry, Azagoth."

And that fast, Azagoth's appearance returned to normal, the blood gone, his eyes glinting like gems. "I know."

Then, in a move that left Cat speechless, he offered a hand to Hades. Clasping Cat's hand first, Hades reached out with the other and allowed Azagoth to bring them to their feet. The two males locked gazes for just an instant, but in that brief, intense moment, something passed between them. Something she could only describe as mutual respect, and by the time Azagoth stepped back, she knew that this was the beginning of a brand new relationship between the two.

Hades tugged Cat close. "You know, I'm glad I didn't beg sooner, because if I had, I wouldn't have Cat."

"Yeah, well," Azagoth said wryly, "you *did* have Cat, and let me tell you, everyone in Sheoul-gra knows it."

A hot blush spread over Cat's face. Now she knew how Azagoth had learned about them. As the blush worked its way down her body, Hades planted a kiss on the top of her head, and the blush turned instantly to fierce, uncontrollable desire.

"I think," she said, "that everyone is going to know it again."

Azagoth cringed. "I'm out of here." He paused. "Before I go, do either of you know why my Seth statue is fucking itself?"

Cat nearly choked on her own saliva, and Hades held his hands up in denial. "No idea what you're talking about."

"Really." Azagoth's dubious expression said he wasn't buying it. "So you have absolutely no idea who glued Seth's penis to his ass?"

"Nope." Hades slid his hand to Cat's butt and gave her a playful pinch. "Didn't you say you were leaving?"

Muttering obscenities, Azagoth hotfooted it out of the apartment, and Cat turned to Hades with a sly smile. "You are very naughty."

Hades's eyes glittered as he trailed a finger along her cleavage. "You think?"

"I know." She went up on her toes and brushed her lips over his. "What do you say? Should we show everyone why they need to invest in earplugs?"

Hades tore open her robe and tugged her to him. "Earplugs? Baby, we're gonna need to soundproof this room after what I'm going to do to you."

"And what," she said, as she cupped his swelling erection, "would that be?"

"Everything."

"Promise?"

He reached around and slid his fingers between her cheeks as he lowered his mouth to hers. "Promise."

As it turned out, Hades kept his promise. And as it also turned out, everyone knew it.

* * * *

"Hello, Cataclysm."

Cat yelped in surprise as she whirled around to face the newcomer who had flashed into the courtyard in front of Azagoth's manor. She'd just been on her way to the Unfallen dorms to help Lilliana set up a new training program after spending an entire day in bed with Hades, and if she hurried, she could get back in time to join him in the shower.

"Reaver," she breathed. He stood there next to the fountain, his angelic glow radiating around him. "It's good to see you again. Azagoth is—"

"I'm not here for Azagoth." His deep voice rumbled through every cell in her body. "I'm here for you."

Her heart skipped a beat. Then another. And another, until it felt as if the organ was nothing but a shriveled husk in her chest. What if he was here to finally punish her for her stupidity in helping Gethel conspire against him?

"Me?" she croaked. "Why?"

"Because your actions in preventing the escape of millions of evil souls has earned you a reward." He smiled, his blue eyes sparkling. "I'm here to give you your wings back."

She sucked in a harsh breath as relief and joy filled her with such happiness that her body vibrated. He wasn't here to destroy her! But...why not?

"I don't mean to sound ungrateful, but...surely you understand what I did to you and your family. You know my history with Gethel, yes?"

Dark shadows flashed in his eyes, and she instantly regretted bringing up the evil bitch who had tried to start the apocalypse. "I am very well aware of your role in Gethel's machinations. But I also know you didn't realize the depths of her depravity until it was too late." The shadows disappeared. "She's paying for what she did, and you've paid the price as well."

"I'm not sure I have." She looked down at her bare feet as if her fresh blue nail polish would help her out. "I haven't apologized to you, either. I'm so sorry, Reaver. I didn't know what Gethel was planning, but I knew it wasn't good. I tried to go to Raphael, and he swore he'd look into it, but—"

"He didn't."

She shook her head miserably. "No."

"That's because he was tangled up in a million different plots to overthrow Heaven and screw me over," Reaver said. "I've always thought your sentence was too harsh, but once I learned that it was Raphael who sentenced you, it made sense. He wanted you out of Heaven because you knew too much."

"But I didn't know anything," she protested.

"I know. But he couldn't take any chances. Forcing your name on you was unnecessarily cruel, but not exactly a shock. He was, as one of my Seminus demon friends would say, a major dickmunch." He smirked. "Raphael's gotta be hating life right now."

No doubt. Thanks to Reaver and his brother Revenant, Raphael was sharing a ten by ten cage with Satan, Lucifer, and Gethel for the next thousand years. Wasn't long enough, in Cat's opinion.

A rabbit scampered across the courtyard. It might have been one that Reaver had brought to repopulate what had once been a dead realm. "So anyway," Reaver said after it disappeared under a bush, "you're forgiven. Come home, Cat. You'll even get your name back."

Once again, joy engulfed her, as if she'd been swallowed by the sun. The fact that Heaven wanted her back was all she'd wanted when she'd first arrived here, scared and lonely and full of regret. But now...now she was happy. Happier than she'd ever been in Heaven.

"Thank you, Reaver," she said. "But I'm afraid I'll have to turn down your offer."

One blond eyebrow shot up, but given that she'd just refused to get her wings and halo back, she thought he'd have been more surprised. "It's Hades, isn't it?"

Now she was the one who was surprised. "Ah...how did you know?"

"It makes sense." He cocked his head and looked at her with an intensity that made her feel positively naked. "Are you sure you want to stay here as an Unfallen? Your powers are muted, you're nearly as fragile as a human—"

"I'm sure. I don't need powers down here, and with people

like Hades, Azagoth, Zhubaal, and Lilliana around me, I don't need to worry about my safety."

He nodded. "Cool. But know that if you change your mind, the offer will remain open as long as you don't do anything to betray Heaven or Earth. And you do understand that you could accept my offer and still be able to travel in the human and heavenly realms while living and working here in Sheoul-gra, yes?"

"I understand. But Hades resides in the Inner Sanctum, and as a fully haloed angel it would be far too dangerous for me to live there with him." She laid her hand on his forearm reassuringly but pulled it back before his Heavenly goodness burned her skin to ash. "Being Unfallen puts me at a serious disadvantage everywhere but here. Here, it's actually more protection than if I were an angel. I'm okay with it, Reaver. Really. Not everyone has to have badass superpowers to be something special."

"Can I at least give you the ability to choose your own name? Or give Nova back to you? It's a beautiful name."

A lump formed in her throat. That was the first time anyone had spoken her Heavenly name in months. It brought back memories, so many of them, both good and bad. But it was her past, not her future.

"Nah," she said. "I'm happy with who I am now. Raphael tried to shame me when he gave me my fallen angel name, but I won't let him do that anymore. I'll keep it to remind me to make wise choices."

"Then so be it." He pulled her into a brief embrace. "Be happy, Cataclysm."

Then he was gone, and she was holding empty air.

Chapter Twenty

One month after moving in with Hades, their new "crypt" was finally finished.

Azagoth had completely removed all restrictions on Hades, and they now had a decent house that matched the ancient Greek style of the rest of Sheoul-gra. Unfortunately, Hades had been so busy meting out punishment to the demons who had participated in the uprising that he hadn't had much time to enjoy it.

She'd taken today off from her new job working with the Unfallen, and she was going to make Hades do the same. They needed some quality time together, and she had the most amazing picnic planned.

He was at the Rot, as usual, which, besides their home, was the only place she was allowed to go in the Inner Sanctum. He'd taken her once to Cloud Cuckoo Land so she could thank the demons who had loaned her and Hades their home, but he'd made it clear that it was far too dangerous to do it again.

She finished dressing in a cute violet and black plaid skirt and a black tank top and gave the little wooden dog on Hades's desk a stroke along its back and tail, laughing when it snapped at her. It was a silly little ritual she'd developed every time she left the house. Hades had promised to make her a tiny cat to match, but he'd see if he could enchant it to purr instead of bite.

Rubbing her belly in a futile attempt to quell the anxious flutters, she stepped into the portal and arrived at the Rot a heartbeat later. She hated this place, couldn't help but think of the spider room every time she was there.

Malonius was at the entrance, and he gave her directions to some sort of classroom in the prison's upper tower where Hades was supposed to be dealing with a group of unruly incubi. She could only imagine what kind of punishments would be doled out to sex demons.

She climbed the narrow, winding stone staircase and found Hades sitting on a stage before a horrified audience. As she entered through the door behind the stage, Hades spoke, reading from a book in his hands.

"Fill me with your filthy pee stick." He paused for dramatic effect. "And lick my lush, melon-like boobies."

She tripped over her own feet. Pee stick? Boobies? What the hell?

"Come on, boy," Hades drawled, his voice pitched high as he read from what was clearly a woman's point-of-view. "My old pussy needs some young meat."

Cat cleared her voice to announce her presence, although, really, it was more like choking. Hades looked over his shoulder, his face split in a wide grin.

"Baby! Hey, it's good to see you." He waggled his brows as he gave her outfit a once-over. "It's especially good to see you in that."

She looked out at the roomful of demons, all human in appearance, as they sat in their too-small chairs, their eyes wild, their faces pale. Clearly, they were miserable.

"What *are* you doing?"

Hades held up the book. "I'm reading bad porn to a captive audience."

"Bad porn? *Bad?* That's a compliment. Whatever it is you're reading is horrifying. Whoever wrote it should be roasted slowly over a bed of coals."

Hades's grin widened. "I like the way you think." He waggled his brows. "Wanna play with my pee stick?"

She did, but not until he stopped calling it a pee stick. "Is that an actual offer or are you just having fun saying 'pee stick'?"

"Tell you what," he said, bounding to his feet. "What do you say we head back to my place, and I'll whip us up a nice pot of mac and cheese—the good kind in the blue box—and you can tell me what you like to call dicks."

"Does this mean we're done?" someone called out from the audience. "Please?"

Hades snorted. "Stay put. I'll get a sub in here." He glanced at his watch. "You only have twenty days and three hours left of listening to atrocious porn, and then you can go back to being the perverts you are." He waved, and they groaned. "See ya."

"That was kind of cruel," Cat said as they headed toward the portal that would take them to the house.

"But funny." He threw his arm around her and planted a kiss on the top of her head. "So? What's up? Are you breaking me out of prison for something good?"

"Yup." They entered the portal, but instead of passing her hand over the symbol that would take them to his place, she took them to Azagoth's realm. As they stepped out into the receiving room off the kitchen, she explained. "We're having a picnic."

He scowled. "Here?"

"Hardly." Taking his hand, she led him through the mansion and outside to the portal that could whisk them to the human realm. Azagoth had released his restrictions on Hades's travel, but so far, Hades hadn't taken advantage of his newfound freedom. It was past time he did.

He kept silent until they arrived at a sunlit meadow surrounded by mountains and looking out over a vast, azure lake. A bald eagle cast a shadow on the water as it flew overhead in search of a meal, and somewhere in the forest, a coyote yipped.

"Crater Lake." He inhaled the fragrant air, a bouquet of pine and summer wildflowers. "It looks just like the picture."

She'd done a lot of scouting to find the exact location where the photo had been taken, and Reaver had escorted her to keep her out of danger. Heck, Reaver had even arranged for her parents to meet her here a couple of days ago. They'd been sorry for the way they'd treated her, although her father had still been a little cool. But then, he'd always been a bit stuffy.

They'd been horrified by the thought of their daughter hooking up with the Jailor of Souls, had tried to make her reconsider going back to Heaven, and when she refused, they'd promised an open line of communication. Even her brothers and sisters had agreed to contact her. It was far more than she ever would have hoped for.

"Come on." Squeezing Hades's hand, she led him to the bottle of wine and basket of fried chicken, potato salad, and fruit she'd laid out on a red and white checkered blanket. Thanks to Reaver and a little invisibility spell, animals had left everything alone.

Hades sank down on the blanket, extending one leg and propping up the other to rest one arm casually across his knee. He looked absolutely edible like that, more at ease than she'd ever seen him.

"I've never been on a picnic before," he said as he peeked into the basket.

"I know. You told me once." Kneeling next to him, she poured two glasses of red wine and handed one to him. "My coworkers and I used to do it all the time in Heaven. Everything is so beautiful that it makes you want to be out in nature, enjoying every minute of it."

His gaze dropped, and even his blue hair managed to look sad. "Do you miss it?" he asked quietly, as if worried about her answer. "You gave up so much to be with me."

"No," she said fiercely, reaching over to tip his chin up so she could look him directly in the eyes. "I would have given up far more if I'd gone."

"I love you, Cat," he whispered. "I don't know what I did to deserve you, but I hope you know that I'd do it all over again to be with you. Thousands of years of loneliness was worth every second you've been in my life."

Something caught in her chest. Tears stung her eyes. That was the first time he'd told her he loved her.

"I love you, too," she rasped. "I can't believe I ever thought that Sheoul-gra couldn't be my home. You were right. Home is where the people who want you are."

"Mmm." He looked at her from over the rim of his glass, his gaze heating, focusing. Holding her in place.

Very slowly, he set down the glass and shifted so he was on his hands and knees, prowling toward her like a tiger with prey in its sights. Excitement shot through her. Electric, shivery excitement.

"Do you want me?" He pushed her backward, lowering his body over hers.

"Yes," she hissed as he scraped his fangs over her jugular. "Oh, yes."

One hand slid beneath her skirt and found her wet and ready. "Then take me home."

With so much love she thought she might burst, she very happily welcomed him home.

Z

Acknowledgments

First, I want to thank my amazing readers. You are the most enthusiastic, supportive readers out there, and I love bringing this world to you.

I also want to send out huge, heartfelt thanks to Kimberly Guidroz, Pamela Jamison, and Liz Berry for all of their hard work. You ladies are absolutely incredible!

Chapter One

Inside Sheoul, the demon realm sometimes called Hell, evil was everywhere.

It dripped off the sides of the sheer rock walls in streaks of black acid that ate into the stone with a hiss. It wafted through the humid air on tendrils of mist that reeked of sulfur and decaying flesh. And, as Vex watched, it oozed like toothpaste from out of a fissure in midair that only people like her could see.

Her purple-tipped black hair, already short and spiky, stood even more on end as the thing squeezing out of the fissure, a dead demon's soul, popped free of whatever realm and mystical enclosure it had been inside. The toothpastey glob took a transparent, vaguely humanoid shape, but its glowing crimson eyes were sharp and clear. A malevolent wave of rage and hate rolled off the soul, and Vex backed away, even though escape was impossible for her.

She was what her parents had called a *daemani*, a demon soul magnet, a person to whom souls stuck like glue. According to them, most *daemanis* couldn't prevent it from happening, and that was a serious pain in the ass. If a demon died near Vex, not even the Grim Reaper's personal *daemanis*, creatures called *griminions,* had a chance to collect the soul before it got sucked into her and stored as a glyph on her skin.

The demon shrieked, a sound only she or another soul-sensitive person could hear, as it struggled to keep from being sucked into the prison of her body. In a futile attempt to avoid the inevitable, she fled, her booted feet nimbly negotiating the rock shard-strewn ground that was all too common in this part of Sheoul.

But no matter how fast she ran, every time she looked over her shoulder, the distance between her and the soul had decreased. Closer. Closer. Oh, shit—

A fireball of pain exploded against her lower spine, knocking her off her feet and sending her tumbling down a ravine infested with thick, thorny vines that tore at her exposed flesh and nearly ripped her knapsack off her back. But it was the misery of the soul settling in that left tears streaming down her face.

Agony, like a million hellfire ants crawling beneath her skin, wracked her as she scrambled to her feet and clawed her way back to the trail. The demon inside her tore at her mind, shrieking at a maddeningly high pitch that made her gut twist.

"Female." The deep, serrated voice startled her, and it must have startled her newest hitchhiking soul too, because the demon spirit stopped freaking out, giving her a chance to catch her breath.

Palming one of the blades hidden in her boot, she shoved to her feet and stared up at the massive armored demon. He had to be at least eight feet tall, with horns poking up through the matte black helmet. Mahogany skin stretched tight on the only exposed parts of his body, his long, clawed hands and his craggy face. She grimaced in oral hygiene horror as his cracked lips peeled back from crooked and rotten—but sharp—teeth and five-inch tusks.

"Who are you?" The symbol etched into the shoulder piece of his armor marked him as a servant of the necromancer she'd come to see, but someone had been trying to kill her for months, and until she knew who they were and why they wanted her dead, she had to be extra careful.

"I am Othog," he growled. "You are here to see the great and horrible Frank?"

The word Frank supposedly meant something really scary in some obscure demon language, but Vex had to struggle to keep a straight face.

"Yes," she said, concealing the blade in her palm. She'd already picked a vulnerable chink in his armor to slide the blade through if the guy pulled any shit. "I'm here to see the...Frank."

He made a sweeping gesture with his arm, and his armor creaked like nails on a chalkboard. "This way."

Demons weren't the most trustworthy folk, so she kept her weapon ready as she followed him down a well-worn path she swore hadn't been there before. Bony hands punched through the vegetation, grabbing at them, and random puddles of what she could only assume was steaming blood formed and dissipated as they trudged along the trail. After what seemed like hours but was probably only a few minutes, they reached a passageway that led deep into the side of a mountain. Pulsing veins ran along the dark walls, as if the mountain itself was alive. Maybe it was. Sheoul was weird and dangerous, which was why she'd chosen to live in the human world.

Not that humans weren't also weird and dangerous, but as a supernatural being she had little to worry about from weakling mortals.

A few dozen yards ahead, an orange glow emanated from an opening in the mountain, and as they got closer, the air went from humid and hot to humid and searing. At the end of the passage, around a corner framed by fang-shaped pillars as tall as a skyscraper, she stopped dead, her jaw falling open.

A massive chamber had been built as a hive-like structure, with holes carved into the sheer walls where bizarre, insect-like demons skittered between them. What she assumed were hollowed-out tunnels crisscrossed the space overhead, running like connective tissue from wall to wall.

"The great and horrible Frank is there." Othog gestured to a dude who could have been her escort's twin, except that Frank was taller. And bigger. And his horns were caked with blood and bits of dried flesh.

Charming. She *really* did not like demons.

Squaring her shoulders, she strode across the hard-packed floor, kicking aside old bones and skulls that littered the area. Frank stood near a bubbling vat the size of a wine barrel, his hands moving through the sickly greenish-brown vapor that rose from the boiling liquid.

"Excuse me, sir," she said politely. Demons like him expected arrogant displays of alpha bullshit, so she always looked for ways to throw them off or make them underestimate her. "I'm here to see you."

He turned to her, his lips stretching into a grotesque grin. "An *emim*," he said, his enormous tusks making his words sound like drunken slurs. "I haven't seen one of your kind in centuries."

How he knew she was an *emim*, the offspring of two fallen angels, she had no idea. Didn't really matter, she supposed. "Yes, I'm quite special," she said dryly. "Now, if we could just get down to business."

"You have something to offer me."

"Souls," she said. "I have four...no, five...souls to sell. One is at least a Tier Four on the Ufelskala and worth more than the other four combined—"

He hissed. "Shut up, *soul scavenger*." His beady eyes shifted to the nearest demon besides Othog, a wrinkly, fat creature with what looked like metal spikes sticking out of its leathery face. Frank lowered his voice. "Do not speak of such things."

"First of all," she said, keeping her voice low, but she couldn't hide her irritation at having been called a soul scavenger. "The politically correct term for what I am is *daemani*. Second, I have souls to unload, and no one is buying anymore. I'm willing to give them to you at a fifty percent discount. Half a million each for the four weakest. Three million for all of them. That's a hell of a deal, if you'll excuse the pun." The dude didn't crack a smile at all. Tough crowd. "I was told you might need them."

"Oh, I need them." His snout-like nose wrinkled. "But not enough to risk my own soul."

Argh! This was so frustrating. Not just frustrating, but terrifying. The demons inside her fought constantly, were in a never-ending battle to see who could try to possess her. Fortunately, none of the souls were very strong or evil...except the one that had attacked her a few minutes ago.

That one needed to go, and fast. "What is going on? Why is everyone suddenly so afraid to deal in souls?"

The demon reached into the bubbling brew and plucked out what looked like a finger. Demons were so disgusting. And he'd had the nerve to insult *her*. For the millionth time, she thanked her parents for raising her in the human realm.

"Because those who buy and sell souls are being slaughtered," he said as he popped the finger into his mouth.

Well, that explained why half of the people who usually bought from her were missing and the other half refused to see her. "By who?"

"Unclear." A piece of...gah...a fingernail...hung out of the corner of his mouth. "There are rumors that Satan wants all souls for himself, but that doesn't make sense, not when he's never taken issue with the soul market before."

Othog, cleared his throat. "Some say Satan was destroyed by Archangels who are now ruling Sheoul."

"Bullshit," Frank said. The piece of finger was still there, jiggling as his scaly lips moved. "Angels couldn't mount that kind of attack on Satan. Not inside Sheoul, and not without us hearing about it."

"Then what's your theory?" she asked. There had been rumors floating around for months about a possible new ruler in Sheoul, but she hadn't believed any of them. After all, who could overthrow Satan?

Frank's forked tongue snaked out to catch the little bit of fingernail, and she swallowed bile, trying desperately not to gag. "I've heard whispers that someone named Revenant is sitting on the throne. I know nothing about him, but if my sources are correct, he's a traitor who betrayed Satan."

No demon was powerful enough to wrest control from Satan. Which meant this Revenant person could only be one thing. "Is he a fallen angel?"

Frank picked his teeth with one long claw. "Some say he's a Shadow Angel."

She whistled under her breath. A Shadow Angel, according to legend, was the most powerful class of fallen angel in existence. Only Satan, and maybe Lucifer, were more powerful. Although she'd heard that Lucifer had been destroyed by one of the Four Horsemen of the Apocalypse.

Which was ludicrous. The Four Horsemen were myths, and Lucifer probably was as well. Heck, the only reason she believed in Satan was that her parents were once angels, and if they said he existed, then he probably did.

"Look, I guess it really doesn't matter what he is or if he even exists. I need to sell these souls." Actually, she just needed to release them. The problem was that they couldn't be released without another, equally powerful soul magnet around, otherwise they just got sucked back into her. "Give me a name. Any name."

"There is only one." Frank bared his never-seen-a-toothbrush teeth, and his voice went low and ominous. "And his name…is Azagoth."

She had a feeling she was supposed to be surprised or in awe or something. "Who the hell is Azagoth?"

Frank gestured to his crony without answering her question. "He will take you to the entrance to Azagoth's realm."

Realm? The guy had his own *realm*? "Wait." She shrugged away from Othog. "I want to know who this guy is."

"He is someone I would not want to face."

Great. If the most powerful necromancer in the Ghul region of Sheoul didn't want to face this Azagoth person, she didn't want to, either. But she was desperate, both for money and to rid herself of her newest passenger on the soul train, so she allowed Othog to escort her to a Harrowgate that took them to a circle of stones deep in the Russian wilderness.

"A drop of blood in the center should grant you access." Othog disappeared into the forest, practically melting into the foliage, before she could ask any questions.

Okay, well, she had to get this done. She jabbed the tip of her finger with one of her blades and stepped close to the circle. But just as she was about to cross the stone line, the hair on the back of her neck stood up, and even before she heard a voice, she knew she wasn't alone.

"*Emim*. Let me kill her."

In a single, smooth motion, she drew twin blades from the sheathes at her hip and spun around to face the newcomers. Two big dudes in black hooded robes stood there, their ageless, remarkably handsome faces telling her little except that they probably got a lot of ass.

They had swords at their backs, but something told her these two were more than lethal without the blades. She was an expert fighter, but the power she sensed coming from the hooded dudes left her in the dust.

Under her skin, the demon souls writhed, agitated by the presence of the newcomers.

"Who are you?"

The rude assholes didn't answer, but when their magnificent feathered wings flared, she knew. Angels. So. Much. Shit.

The angel on the left, the one who had spoken, lunged at her, but she was ready. She dropped and rolled, kicking out her foot to catch him in the knee.

"Leave her!" Right Angel's voice rang out, and a split second later, heat exploded near her head and she was thrown to the dirt. For a moment, she thought she was dead. But then she was yanked to her feet by a vicious hand around the back of her neck.

"What the hell?" Left Angel peeled himself off the ground, his robes smoking, his eyes burning with anger as he glared at Right Angel from under the hood. "Why did you protect her?"

"Because she's carrying souls." Right Angel squeezed her neck, stopping her from stomping on his foot. "If you kill her, they escape. We need to take her to Azagoth."

"Oh, bloody hell," she snapped. "That's what I was trying to do when you bastards attacked me for no fucking reason."

"Why are you going to see him?" Right Angel shoved her into the center of the stone circle, his hand still clamped around her neck. "Did he summon you?"

"Did he *summon* me? Why would he summon me? I don't even know who this Azagoth idiot is."

Left Angel gaped at her like she was a complete moron. "He's the Keeper of Souls, you vile demon dimwit. You're going to see the Grim Reaper."

Chapter Two

Being the Grim Reaper's second-in-command wasn't the worst job in the world, but as Zhubaal listened to the bloodcurdling screams coming from the room at the end of the shadowy hallway, he was reminded that it wasn't the best job in the world, either.

However, it *was* a necessary one if he ever hoped to find his beloved Laura, whose soul had once been trapped here in Sheoulgra, the Alcatraz of demon, fallen angel, and evil human souls. She'd been here for decades until, thirty years ago, she was paroled—reborn—her soul ensconced in a new body. Zhubaal had been searching for her new identity ever since, but so far he hadn't had any luck tracking her down.

He would, though. The oaths that bound them to each other were unbreakable. Pure. And he was tenacious as shit.

He *would* find her.

"Damn." Razr, a fallen angel who Azagoth had recently appointed to act as Zhubaal's own second-in-command, came up next to Z and stared at their boss's office door. "Who's in there with him?"

Z cast a sideways glance at the guy who, as usual, wore plain brown monk-like robes and flip-flops. Why he dressed like that, Zhubaal had no idea. Razr refused to talk about it no matter how drunk Z got him. "Some Orphmage who has incredibly bad judgment and thought he could blackmail the Grim Reaper."

"Shit." Razr rubbed his tattooed, bald head. "You're gonna make me clean up the mess, aren't you?"

Grinning, Zhubaal clapped him on the back. "Quit whining. This should be the last one today—" He broke off as a sharp, tingly sensation washed over him in a wave that was almost...sexual.

Not that he knew what a sexual wave felt like. Not really.

Sure, he experienced desire like every normal fallen angel, but lonely orgasms weren't exactly anything to get excited about.

And this particular wave definitely didn't mean an orgasm was impending. It meant that someone had activated the portal connecting Sheoul-gra to one of several portals in the earthly realm.

A visitor was inbound, and the intense residual electric current pulsing through his veins meant the newcomer wasn't your average lowlife demon begging for an audience with the person in charge of reincarnating souls. Which also meant whoever was about to show up was probably an egomaniacal douchebag.

Razr felt it too, and he barked out a laugh. "Bet you wish you were the one getting to clean Orphmage bits off Azagoth's walls now, huh?"

No, but only barely. He wasn't in the mood to deal with some arrogant demon or holy-rolling angel who reminded him of who he used to be. Not when he'd just learned his latest lead on Laura's reincarnated identity had fallen through.

Shooting Razr the finger, Zhubaal exited the building and took the stone steps down to the courtyard two at a time. The fountain in the center sprayed a fine mist over his bare arms as he hurried past it to the portal platform that sat like a miniature helicopter landing pad twenty yards away.

A column of white light struck from out of the featureless gray sky above, and when it cleared, two angels he recognized stood inside the stone circle on the portal pad. He had no idea who the weapons-heavy female with the short black hair with them was, but she was as pissed as a wet cat being held by its scruff.

The angel, who Z knew only by the code name Jim Bob, had his hand wrapped around the back of her neck, forcing her to walk on the tiptoes of her thigh-high boots as they stepped off the platform. Every time she reached for one of the weapons stashed around her body in various holsters, he swatted her hand away as if she were no more bothersome than a gnat.

Jim Bob shoved her forward. "We found this... creature...

attempting to break through the portal."

The female's violet eyes burned with fury. She was pretty, in a dangerous sort of way, which only made her prettier. Oh, she wasn't Zhubaal's type; he'd always gone for females with less makeup, fewer weapons, and more clothes. But that didn't mean he couldn't appreciate a smoking hot female who looked like she could chew him up and swallow too.

As if you know what that would be like.

"I wasn't trying to break through." She lashed out with her foot and kicked Jim Bob in the shin, but he didn't even flinch. Then again, he was twice her size and built like a tank. "I was trying to activate the portal. You know, like a normal person. You feathered morons interrupted."

Jim Bob yanked her off her feet and held her at arm's length, like one might do with a sewer rat. "She's *emim*." He sneered, baring his teeth. "I can practically smell the wrongness of her."

"Gee, asshole," she growled, still doing her best to kick him, "why don't you tell us how you really feel about my kind."

The other angel, a raven-haired pretty-boy code named Ricky Bobby, snorted. "Your kind should be destroyed. Fallen angels are traitorous scum who weren't meant to breed. They and their *emim* offspring deserve to be slaughtered."

What a tool. If Zhubaal were anywhere but here, he'd lob a ball of acid fire at Ricky Bobby's haloed head. "You know I'm a fallen angel, right?" He gestured to himself. "I mean, I'm standing right here."

Jim Bob and Ricky Bobby stared, completely unmoved. Holier-than-thou pricks. Literally holier, since they were actual Heavenly angels and Z was one of those traitorous scum who wasn't meant to breed.

He sighed, tired of dealing with two angels who couldn't be *too* angelic if they were associating with the Grim Reaper. "Release the female. I'll take it from here. Razr is inside. He'll show you to Azagoth's office." He reconsidered that, thinking that Azagoth's office wouldn't be presentable for a while. "Or the library."

Jim Bob opened his fist and dropped the female to the ground. "I can find Azagoth on my own."

"You know the rules, Jim Bob," Z said as the female leaped to her feet and glared at the two angels. "Outsider dickbags can't roam around without an escort."

Jim Bob's eyes flashed pure white, twin bolts of divine lightning, and Zhubaal wondered if the guy was actually capable of bypassing Azagoth's power-dampening spell and delivering a damaging strike. He didn't know Jim Bob's true identity or what kind of angel he was, but one thing was certain; the angel was powerful. Even here in Sheoul-gra, where everyone but Azagoth was limited in the use of their inherent supernatural abilities, Jim Bob exuded danger. And arrogance.

He was definitely high up on the angelic food chain.

The asshole.

"Don't even think about it, angel." Zhubaal's fallen angel wings erupted from his back as he summoned one of the few powers Azagoth allowed, a dark shield of evil energy capable of temporarily disrupting any Heavenly energy that struck it. "I have more power here than you do."

A slow smile spread across Jim Bob's face. "Do you really think so?"

"Want to test me?"

For a long moment, Z was sure the guy was going to attack. But even as the air between them crackled, Jim Bob's eyes went back to normal. "One day. But today I don't have time to kick your ass. I will see Azagoth *now*."

With that, he strode toward the building, extending his massive white wings in a dismissive fuck-you gesture. The chickenshit. Ricky Bobby went with him, giving off his own powerful vibe and a rude flap of dove gray wings. He'd only been here with Jim Bob twice, and he hadn't spoken a word until today. Zhubaal hoped he'd go back to dickish silence for future visits.

"Those guys are major assholes," the female muttered.

Zhubaal tucked away his leathery wings, still hating how naked they felt without Heavenly feathers even after all these years. He'd eventually sprout feathers, assuming he survived a few centuries, but they'd likely be ugly, malformed, twisted by evil.

"Angels generally are." Zhubaal turned to her, amused to find her glaring at the angels' backs while fingering the hilt of a blade at her leather-clad hip as if fantasizing about plunging it into their skulls. He'd like to see that. She'd die, of course, but hey, at least Z had Razr around to clean up the mess.

Still, it would be a shame to see her slaughtered. Not many *emim* made their way down here to seek an audience with Azagoth, especially not ones who looked like she did.

He let his gaze drop from her rounded hips to her slender thighs, where her ripped black leggings disappeared into purple-laced midnight boots with stiletto heels. How the hell did she fight in those things?

He dragged his gaze back up, admiring her flat, bare midriff and the leather top that was little more than a bra covering ample breasts. *Barely* covering ample breasts. Her short black hair, dyed purple at the spiky tips, teased the shell of her ears, and damn it all, his mouth watered with the desire to take the lobes between his teeth and make her purr.

And what the hell? He never fantasized about females like this. His focus had been on no one but Laura since before he fell, and even the one foray into experimentation he'd taken with Cat last year had been more about seeing if he was still functional than anything.

Or maybe he'd just been lonely. A hundred years without so much as a kiss was a long freaking time.

"You like what you see?" She sauntered toward him with slow, deliberate steps. Somehow, her spiked heels didn't wobble on the uneven ground no matter how hard her hips popped with each step. "Do you?"

Why, yes. Yes, he did like what he saw. But she hadn't chosen such a sexy outfit for Z's benefit and he knew it. "You're wasting your time with me, and if you're planning to seduce Azagoth, you should know he has a mate. And Lilliana does *not* share."

She stopped a couple of feet away, her fingers still fondling the blade. Which shouldn't be erotic but somehow was. "I'm not here for that."

No doubt seducing Azagoth wasn't her primary goal, but he knew her kind, knew her racy clothes were tools she'd use if she needed to. And something about Azagoth got all the females—and males, for that matter—worked up. Once she laid eyes on him, she'd try to seduce him. They all did.

"What's your name? And what is your business with Azagoth?"

Stepping closer, he lowered his voice and looked down at her from his extra foot of height. "And keep in mind that I'm his gatekeeper. You *will* tell me or you won't get off this platform."

She coyly fingered the plunging neckline of her top and batted her jewel-toned eyes. "I'm Vex, and I have a proposition for your boss."

"I'm Zhubaal, and I need a little more than that." He narrowed his eyes, refusing to be charmed or seduced. But damn, she really did have nice breasts. "What kind of proposition?"

For a long moment she stared up at him, her ruby lips pressed together in a stubborn line of silence. Just as he was about to send her back to whatever realm she'd come from, she gave up the seductress BS and held out her right arm.

"See these glyphs?" She traced the outline of one of five squiggly black circles with the tip of one amethyst-painted fingernail. "Touch one."

"If this is a trick—"

"How stupid do you think I am?" she snapped. "If Azagoth is really the Grim Reaper, he's one of the most powerful beings in the universe. Do you honestly think I'm here to piss him off by screwing with one of his *griminions*?"

Well, that was insulting. "I'm not a *griminion*," he ground out. "*Griminions* are ugly little freaks who collect souls when a demon or evil human dies. I'm just your standard everyday *minion*."

She rolled her eyes. "I know. I was being funny. You're the *Grim* Reaper's minion. *Griminion*." She nudged him with her arm. "Come on. Touch me."

Anxious to be rid of this obnoxious female, he gripped her wrist and pressed his fingers against two—or maybe three—of the circles.

He had no idea how many of the things he touched because the moment his skin came into contact with them, the powerful burn of sheer evil shot through him and knocked the breath from his lungs. Holy hell, what were those glyphs? Malevolence seared his skin and forced superheated blood to flow like lava through his veins as he released her and stumbled backward, his head spinning.

"They're souls," Vex said, her voice cutting through his agony. "That's what you're feeling. They attached themselves to me, and I think Azagoth might want to take them off my hands."

The overwhelming evil drained rapidly away now that he was no longer touching the glyphs, but another sensation remained, one that once again took away his breath and left him shaken.

Familiarity. Comfort. Love.

Was it...possible? He knew the warmth of this, the desperate need to hold onto it, but the sensation was fading with every spastic beat of his heart.

Laura.

His fingers cramped, and he looked down to see that he was clutching his chest as if he could dig through his ribs to his racing heart.

He licked his dry lips and tried to summon enough moisture in his mouth to speak. He was afraid to hope, afraid to ask the question that sat on the tip of his parched tongue. But he had to. This was why he'd willingly fallen from grace all those decades ago. The reason he'd begged the Archangel Uriel to slice off his coveted maroon wings, coveted not so much for the color as for what they represented.

The best of the best.

Now he lived among the worst of the worst.

"Do you know who the souls belonged to?" he asked, deliberately spacing out his words so he didn't run his tongue like a kid hopped up on Halloween candy. "When they were in physical form, I mean."

She shook her head. "They don't speak to me." Pained shadows flickered in Vex's eyes, and he wondered what the souls were doing to her. He'd barely touched them and they'd given him a body migraine, but they were melded into her flesh. "Not with words."

He didn't need words. He stared at Vex's arm, at the thin, swirly lines that marked her skin, and he knew.

One of the souls in Vex's body belonged to his beloved. One of the souls was Laura.

Chapter Three

Vex stared at Zhubaal, but only because *he* was staring at *her*. Staring like she'd suddenly sprouted a halo.

But during the stare-off, she discovered that the blond, dark-eyed fallen angel was outrageously hot. Absolutely delicious in black jeans, combat boots, and a navy T-shirt that clung to a hard, muscular body. If she'd met him anyplace other than the Grim Reaper's freaking realm, she'd be testing the sexual promise that wrapped around him like a second skin.

But as it was, he not only seemed uninterested, he seemed shocked, or maybe horrified, by her.

"What's your deal?" she finally snapped. "What is it humans say? Take a picture, it'll last longer?"

"The souls," he said roughly. "You claim they speak to you, but not with words."

"That's not exactly what I said, but that's the gist." The souls vibrated, as if reminding her why she was here. They were probably as anxious to be free of her as she was of them. "Now, do I get to see the Grim Reaper or not?"

And if so, how could she work this to her advantage? She needed to sell these souls, but meeting the Grim Reaper was also a once-in-a-lifetime chance she couldn't let slip by. She was tired of being treated like a scavenger. Collecting souls paid well, but in the demon world, she was considered as loathsome as humans considered drug dealers. Working with the Grim Reaper would give her legitimacy as well as protection from the people who were destroying the underworld soul trade.

Zhubaal hesitated, but after a moment he jerked his head in a "follow me" motion and started toward one of the big buildings at the edge of what appeared to an ancient Greek city. She held back for a few heartbeats to get a good look at how well those jeans fit. *Niiice.*

"How do they communicate with you?" he called back to her. "The souls, I mean."

She caught up to him, her heels clacking on the cobblestones. "Um, they don't. I sense them. Like, I can feel how evil they are." She held up her arm. "Four of these feel like Tier Ones and Twos on the Ufelskala. But the other one...the newest one..." She shuddered. "The evil is as strong as anything I've ever felt."

It was stronger even than the soul that had possessed her years ago, that had sent her on a rampage through regions of Sheoul where she was no longer welcome. The nightmares from those two weeks of hell left her exhausted and emotionally drained far too often, but it was nothing compared to the guilt that ate at her every day.

She had to get rid of this soul and fast. She couldn't go through that again. She wouldn't. She'd kill herself before she allowed another evil being to use her body for slaughter and mayhem.

Zhubaal stopped so suddenly she whacked her shoulder against his arm. It was like running into a wall. A hard, tall, do-me-against-it wall.

"Do the souls interact?" he asked. "Can the strong ones torment the weaker ones?"

What an odd question. "Yes. Why? How is this relevant to my meeting with Azagoth?"

"Everything is relevant when it comes to Azagoth." He started walking again, taking her past a perfectly trimmed hedgerow separating the mansion's grounds from the other buildings, a sparkling fountain, and several Greek statues and seemingly random pillars that didn't support anything.

This was *not* what she'd expected to see in a realm run by the Grim Reaper.

Zhubaal led her up a stone staircase that ran the entire width of the building. "How is it that you collect the souls?"

"It's hard to explain." As they approached the giant doors, they swung open. "I'm a sort of magnet. They call people like me *daemani*, but if your boss deals in souls, he'll probably know that. If there's a nonhuman, supernatural soul in the area, it will find me."

"How? *Griminions* appear within seconds of a demon's death."

"They're too late if I'm the one who killed the demon or a demon dies near me." She made a habit out of not killing demons if she didn't have to, but shit happened because demons were assholes, and a lot of them deserved to die. "Once I visited a friend at Underworld General, and in the hour I was there, two demon souls got sucked inside me. Two! Those doctors must be terrible if they can't keep anyone alive. But now, if I need some fast cash, I take a stroll through the hospital." Well, not anymore. Not since the soul market crashed.

He gave her a judgey sideways glance. "I would keep that to yourself. Azagoth considers all souls to be his. If he knows you intentionally stole them out from under him, you'll pay with your own soul."

Azagoth was a greedy bastard, wasn't he? She'd keep that opinion to herself, too.

Zhubaal led her inside the building. She squinted in the torch-lit darkness, and holy freak show, they'd walked into a nightmare museum of statues. *This* was what she'd expected to see in a realm run by the Grim Reaper.

In a room that was seemingly endless, rows of life-sized stone figures of demons of all species were on display, all in various states of agony. Skulls and weapons lined the walls, some of the weapons buried *in* the skulls. Vex had been inside some seriously creepy and haunting places, many filled with bloody horrors she couldn't even describe. But something about this room was more disturbing than a room full of blatant gore.

Maybe the creep-factor came from the feeling that she was being watched.

"These are living statues." Zhubaal's boots thundered as he strode through the cavernous room. "Sometimes Azagoth doesn't kill his enemies."

Horror slithered down her spine as what Zhubaal said sank in. She gave a wide berth to an eyeless Silas demon that seemed to be reaching for her, its face twisted in misery.

"How long have they been like this?" Her voice sounded small in this place, and she didn't know if it was a trick of the space or if she really sounded like she wanted to be anywhere but here.

Zhubaal high-fived an elf-like Neethul statue as they walked past, and she wondered how aware the demons were of the world around them. "Some are new, within the last few decades, but most are hundreds, if not thousands of years old."

They'd been trapped for *thousands of years*?

The souls on her arm began to tingle as if frightened, growing into a violent vibration that became more intense the farther inside they went. The super evil soul, which she would now dub SuperEvil, began to claw at her. The souls always got antsy when she was near another soul magnet, but this seemed more like fear than the usual eagerness to get out of her body, even though the next host could enslave it, eat it, use it for spells...souls were all-purpose items that used to net a fortune.

She did the whole Lamaze thing through the psychic assault, but when Zhubaal narrowed his eyes, she stopped breathing like she was giving birth and smiled as if nothing was wrong. Once he turned away, she went back to Lamaze...just more quietly.

They finally exited the statue room, and just as they turned down a long, dimly lit hallway, the douche-bro angels brushed past them on their way out, barely sparing a scornful glance at them. Steps behind, a bald guy in a shapeless brown monk robe followed, presumably the angels' escort.

A dark-haired male in black slacks and a button-down shirt the color of dried blood emerged from a doorway at the end of the hall. The souls inside her freaked the hell out, vibrating so hard she thought her skin might come right off her body. They wanted her to run, to get away from here, and frankly, it was tempting.

Breathe. Don't let them see you as anything less than someone in perfect control.

"Z," the guy said, his deep voice as intensely captivating as his emerald eyes. This was Azagoth. No doubt about it. "I'm heading to the Inner Sanctum. You're in charge until I get back." He scowled, and his head whipped around to her so fast it was a blur. "Who are you?"

The souls screamed. They screamed so loud that for the first time, she heard them. Actually heard them and felt their fear. Not that she could blame them. Azagoth was terrifying, made all the more worse by his beauty. He was tall, dark, handsome, and he exuded danger that left her cold inside. Not even Tier Five demons could match this kind of soul-sucking cold.

"I'm Vex." Somehow she managed to not sound like a cornered mouse.

He turned back to Zhubaal as if he hadn't spoken to her at all. "I'll see her when I return."

Zhubaal's hand snapped out to catch Azagoth's arm as he started past him. "But my Lord—"

Azagoth turned his gaze on her once again, and her blood froze. "When. I. Return."

No! Run away! Escape! The souls shrieked, clawed, tore at her mind, even as Azagoth strode away. And it was then that she realized that this was the first time it had ever happened.

The souls didn't want out. They wanted to stay in.

* * * *

Dammit. Z hadn't been able to talk to Azagoth about his suspicion regarding Vex and the souls she carried. One soul in particular.

Oh, he could have tried, but he knew Azagoth, and the guy had been on the edge of an explosion. About what, Z had no idea. All he knew was that you didn't want to get caught in one of the Grim Reaper's concussive blasts. When that guy detonated, he went nuclear.

"What now?" Vex asked, and he wasn't surprised to hear the slightest tremor in her voice. But her violet eyes were hard, the eyes of a warrior, and if Azagoth frightened her, it didn't show. Impressive, especially for an *emim*, most of whom wielded very few of the abilities their more powerful fallen angel parents possessed. "I can't leave. One of the souls inside me is dangerous."

He lowered his voice as a resident Unfallen walked past on his way to the kitchens. "Dangerous how?"

"If a soul is powerful enough, *and* evil enough, it can possess me." Vex spoke with a flippant wave of her hand that didn't match up with the way her fingers trembled. "It's not a pleasant experience.

Weaker souls generally team up to keep more sinister ones at bay, but this one is crazy strong. Its malevolence is…I dunno, pure, I guess. I don't know how long I can last against it."

A chill crawled up Z's spine at the thought that Laura was trapped inside Vex with a malevolent demon. He'd met a handful of *daemani* in his life, but he'd never asked them questions about their abilities, let alone if the souls they packed around hung out together.

"What do you mean, pure?" He started back through the statue room to leave the building, and he got a kick at how she walked so fast he had to pick up his pace to keep up.

"The souls all have different...vibes. I can get a general sense of how old they are and how many lives they've lived." She grimaced at the statue of a genocidal Darquethoth scumbag Azagoth had impaled before encasing him in stone to suffer death pangs for all eternity. "Each life seems to mellow them out, for lack of a better word. But those who spend a long time living a single life...they tend to be really fucking strong. I'd bet that whoever I picked up today is either ancient or infected with great evil, and they definitely have a thirst for pain and death." She cast him a brief, impish smile. "And sex. So it's not all bad. But this soul is very, very angry."

He wondered if Laura's second life had "mellowed" her, although he couldn't see how. As an angel, she'd been the epitome of serenity, preferring to listen rather than talk, to negotiate for peace rather than fight. Those were the very qualities that had gotten her banished from their angelic warrior Order and led to her fall from Heaven.

Holy shit, after all these years of looking, was it really possible that he was this close to finally seeing his betrothed again? Did she know he was close? Or was she too busy trying to escape the evil soul inside Vex?

He slowed while the doors swung open. "Can the angry soul harm the others?"

Please say no.

"Yes." She practically ran outside, and he swore she breathed a sigh of relief when the doors closed behind them. "I can feel their pain even now."

The Ipsylum warrior in him rose up in eagerness to destroy whoever was hurting Laura, followed by frustration that there was no enemy to fight. "Can you stop it from happening?"

She paused on a step to look at him like he was crazy. "Um, no. Why? Don't tell me a big, bad fallen angel is worried about some poor little demon souls being bullied."

He couldn't care less about any souls but one. Laura had been so kind and gentle before her fall from grace, and even after, as a fallen angel, she hadn't changed much. But, as Azagoth had pointed out, she'd been killed before her soul could become too corrupted by evil. She'd also been Unfallen, an angel who had lost her wings but hadn't entered Hell in order to complete her fall and allow darkness to flood her soul. She'd been decent, even until the end, and it made him sick to think that she could, right now, be suffering in ways he couldn't even comprehend.

He ignored Vex's ridiculous question and walked her around the hedgerow. "This way."

"Where are we going? You didn't answer me about what we're doing now."

They turned down a cobblestone path that bisected a vast, grassy lawn that used to be nothing but scorched wasteland before Azagoth's mate, Lilliana, worked some kind of voodoo on his shriveled, blackened, Grinchy heart.

"Now," he said, "you get to check in to Sheoul-gra's finest luxury hotel."

One black brow arched. "Sheoul-gra's finest what?"

He gestured ahead, toward the buildings that spread out like wings behind Azagoth's great mansion, all laid out in replica of ancient Athens. "The one with the gargoyle pillars and the skull carved above the entry. I call it Motel 666."

"Clever. And just begging to be the site of a massacre." She rubbed her arm absently, and he wondered which of the glyphs belonged to Laura. She was *so* close, and it killed him to not be able to touch her. "So you're serious? You have a hotel?"

"They're more like what humans call dormitories."

"Dormitories?" A breeze ruffled her spiky locks as she glanced around. "For who?"

"I'll show you." He led her to the back of the building, which opened up into a courtyard where several dozen people sparred with various weapons under the barked instruction of fallen angels.

"Unfallen and Memitim."

She frowned. "Unfallen are fallen angels who haven't entered Sheoul, right? They can still be redeemed. But what's a Memitim?"

Lilliana waved from across the courtyard where she was talking to three of their newest Unfallen arrivals. Ever since Azagoth turned Sheoul-gra into a sanctuary for Unfallen looking for a chance to redeem themselves and earn their way back into Heaven, they'd seen a steady stream of new faces.

"They're all Azagoth's children," he said. "They're a special class of earthbound angel born to protect certain humans and earn their wings."

"Unfallen and Memitim," she mused. "Two sides of the same coin. One group was born with everything to gain, and the other was born with everything to lose."

His head whipped around to her. That was something Laura would have said. She always looked for the commonalities in people rather than the differences. It was another of the traits that had led to her being shunned by their Ipsylum Order. The thought irritated the twin scars where his luxurious wings that marked him as an elite warrior class had been sliced off. It had taken two years after his fall to grow his fallen angel wings which, while studier and more resistant to fire than his old wings, were inferior and uglier in every other way.

"What *is* your deal?" Vex rounded on him, one of those lethal heels grinding on the stone path. "Why do you keep staring at me?" She batted her eyes. "It's because I'm so hot, isn't it?"

He wanted to say it was because Laura was inside her somewhere, but the truth was that Vex *was* easy to stare at. Everything about her was the opposite of Laura. Tall, blonde, willowy, and conservative compared to short, dark, curvy, and dangerously sexy.

But was this the real Vex, or did the souls influence her? "I'm not staring," he lied. "I'm trying to figure you out. Do the souls affect your personality, even if they aren't trying to possess you?"

She laughed at a young Memitim who tripped over his own sword while practicing with it. "Sometimes." She turned to him, her big violet eyes still sparkling with amusement. "Like, once I killed this Alu demon asshole, and his soul got sucked into me. Do you know what they eat? Rotting flesh. Seriously. The more rotten the better. Until I was able to get rid of him, my mouth would water every time I drove past a dead animal on the side of the road." She stuck out her tongue and made a face that was so Laura-like that a wave of longing crashed over him. "So gross. And another time, I absorbed the soul of an incubus. I didn't realize it at the time, but damn, I was horny. For like, a month. Couldn't get enough, you know?"

No, he didn't know. But now he was picturing her trying to get enough, and it made him uncomfortably warm. And a little hard.

"So the souls inside you now could be influencing you?" Earlier, she'd mentioned the evil soul wanted things. Like sex.

His cock twitched, and he bit his tongue, welcoming the pain. Anything to keep from having thoughts he shouldn't be having. Laura might be influencing Vex, but it didn't matter. Vex was *not* Laura.

She shrugged. "The weaker ones might be having some minor effect, but when there's more than one, they tend to spend so much time fighting each other that they don't mess with me." She held up her hand. "Fingers crossed that SuperEvil holds to that."

Just in case, he was going to make sure Vex had a constant babysitter.

He took her to an unoccupied Motel 666 room on the second floor and sent a passing Memitim to fetch a guard. The space was small, with only the most basic of furniture, but this room had recently been vacated by an Unfallen who had given into the seduction of Sheoul, and he'd left a nice flat-screen TV behind.

She tossed her backpack to the cot. "This is it, huh? No pool? No coffee maker? No continental breakfast? I'm going to destroy you on Yelp." She jammed her fists on her hips in faux outrage, and his gaze automatically fell to the marks on her arm. "What *is* it? Why do you keep looking at them?"

He supposed it wouldn't hurt to explain why he kept staring at her and the glyphs. She was probably starting to think he was some sort of obsessive creeper.

"Because one of them is familiar," he said, his heart thumping excitedly at the reason for the familiarity. "It was something I felt when I touched you."

She donned a wicked grin that probably got her anything she wanted from males. "Was that 'something' horny? Because if you want to touch me again, I'm okay with that." Her tone was as flirty as her smile as she dragged her fingernail over the glyphs on her arm. "So are at least two of the souls."

"No," he ground out. "That 'something' wasn't horny."

"You sure?" The sultry gleam in her eyes nearly made him groan. "Do you want to touch me again to see?"

Yes. Hell, yes. He'd kill to experience that feeling again, was desperate to connect with Laura in any way he could. And what if she could feel him, too? If he caressed Vex's smooth, tan skin, would Laura know it was his touch?

Without thinking, he reached for her, but before he made contact, Suman, a burly Memitim with more muscles than brains, jogged into the room like there was a fire.

"I was told I was needed," he said stiffly, a soldier through and through.

It was probably good that he'd shown up, because as much as Zhubaal wanted to feel Laura, he wasn't sure he wanted to experience the loss of the connection with her again.

"Thank you, Suman," Z said, snapping himself into job mode. "I need you to watch Vex for a while. I'll send someone to relieve you soon." He turned back to Vex. "There's a communal bathroom down the hall, and I'll have food sent over. Stay put." As an afterthought, he added, "And be good."

Somehow, he wasn't surprised to hear her laughter all the way out of the building, and damn if it didn't make him smile, too.

Chapter Four

Vex was going crazy. How could anyone stand being trapped in such a tiny room? She needed space. Freedom to move.

It wasn't that she wanted to escape from Sheoul-gra. She wanted to explore it. She'd just had to figure out how to get past the babysitter. First, she'd attempted to leap out of one of the glassless windows, but apparently, some sort of invisible barrier allowed for airflow but not for solid objects to pass through.

Plan B proved to be a better idea because, as it turned out, her new guard, Vane, was one of the Unfallen who lived here, and he was extremely vulnerable to seduction.

All it had taken was a little flirty chatting while she nibbled from the bowl of fruit a perky redhead named Cat had brought her. The horny bastard had been practically drooling by the time she licked juice from the second strawberry off her upper lip.

Now, as she teased him toward the bed, she pretended to untie her leggings. The moment his eager gaze focused on her hands, she kicked upward and flipped into the air, catching him under the jaw with her boot hard enough to knock him the hell out.

He hit the floor with a satisfying thud. She did feel a little bad, though. He was going to have one monster of a headache when he woke up.

After that, it was an easy walk down to the grounds, which, like everything else, was much less...well, hellish...than she'd originally expected. Surely there was more here than pristine white buildings, lush grass and palm-like trees, and a well-kept cobblestone path that led to a sparkling pond. The landscape went on and on in all directions, and she wondered about boundaries. Were there any? Or was this realm as endless as its blue-gray, featureless sky?

A dove flew overhead, startling her and once again blowing away expectations. It wouldn't have surprised her to see a raven or a vulture, or even an eviscerаptor hunting for a spiny hellrat. But a dove?

She wandered down to the pond edge and propped herself against a tree trunk. The peacefulness was surreal here, in a place everyone associated with pain, death, and horror. Even the souls, who had been buzzing like bees under her skin, had settled down. Really, the Grim Reaper should be ashamed of himself. He wasn't so scary, was he? Maybe his reputation was all based on a big act, while in reality he was a big wuss. She'd encountered demons like that, who were all tough talk and very little action.

The Azagoth you met was no inferior being, and you know it.

Well, she could hope. Yes, she needed him to be willing to buy the souls inside her, but she'd also like to get out of this situation alive and with a monetary agreement that would secure her future, so if she had to fantasize that he was a big wuss, then that's what she'd do.

Heck, this entire realm was probably full of big wusses. The distant sounds of the Memitim and Unfallen in their training, mostly shouts, thuds, and screams of pain, didn't do much to back up her wishful thinking. And neither did the sound of angry, thudding footsteps coming up the trail behind her. She was busted.

And she knew without looking that it was Zhubaal.

Deep beneath Vex's breast, SuperEvil's buzz turned into a purr of delight, desire, and wickedness.

But, to be fair, when she turned around and saw Zhubaal standing there, his muscular arms folded across his broad chest, she experienced the same damned feelings, and she definitely couldn't blame her lust on any one of the souls inside her.

Except her own.

* * * *

Zhubaal glared at Vex as she stood next to the pond that, not long ago, had been filled with bubbling blood and aquatic demons and beasts, all a reflection of the evil that had consumed Azagoth. Now, thanks to his happiness with Lilliana, the pond was as clear as the crystal waters off Corfu in the Ionian Sea, its glassy surface catching the shapely reflection of Vex's perfect ass. She might not be what he'd always considered to be his "type," but he found himself admiring her more than he should, especially since Laura was basically right there with them.

Harnessing his frustration and guilt to use against Vex, he barked, "What the hell were you thinking?"

Her half-hearted, dismissive shrug didn't help his mood. "I wanted to look around. I was tired of being cooped up in that little room with nothing to do except watch the History Channel, horror movies, or reruns of *Gilligan's Island*." She looked at him as if he was at fault for the programming choices. "That's all that's on TV. Gore fests, history I don't care about, and a goofy old comedy. What's up with that? And how do you have TV down here, anyway?"

His beloved's soul was at stake here and she was worried about TV? "Who the hell cares? I could have lost her." The very thought made his chest constrict. "Don't leave your room again, or I swear, I'll chain you in it."

"Ooh, promise?"

"Yes." And he'd enjoy doing it. He could picture himself holding her against the wall as he snapped the cuffs around her slender wrists, and his groin tightened. So…yeah, he'd enjoy it. Too much.

Snorting, Vex kicked at a stick that was half-buried in the pebbles surrounding the pond. "I'm surprised you don't have a dungeon."

"We do. Several, including the ones Hades runs in the Inner Sanctum."

"Cool," she said. "Dungeons are...wait. Hades? He's real?"

Z nodded, because Hades was real, all right. A real dick.

"Huh." She jammed her fists on her hips and glanced around the landscape. "I'm learning all kinds of new shit today." Cocking her head, she studied him. "You said you could have lost her. Lost who?"

Damn. This chick could change a subject faster than an angel could flap his wings. "No one," he ground out. "And you could have *asked* Vane to show you around instead of knocking him out. You aren't a prisoner." Well, technically, she was, since he wouldn't allow her to leave until she released Laura's spirit. Small details.

"Oh. Well, how was I supposed to know?" She bent to pick a daisy growing at the water's edge, which allowed him a stellar view of her leather-wrapped backside until he forced himself to avert his gaze. "You told me to stay put."

"And look how well that worked," he muttered.

She straightened, her nose buried in the flower. "Is Azagoth back?"

"Nope."

She frowned, nose still in the daisy, and he couldn't help but admire the juxtaposition of this heavily armed warrior woman taking pleasure in a delicate flower. "When?"

"He'll be back when he's back." Azagoth rarely gave timeframes for anything, which was especially strange because he was usually an annoyingly structured person.

"That's very helpful," she said so brightly that he almost missed the sarcasm. "Where did he go? I heard him say he was going to…what was that place you just mentioned? The Inner Sanctum? What's that?"

He didn't see any point in lying or denying her information, and besides, he didn't have anything better to do. Razr was monitoring the portal, Lilliana was managing the Unfallen, and Z had made sure the kitchens, laundry, and groundskeepers were all on track. The rest of the day was his.

"The Inner Sanctum is where the souls go after Azagoth gets done with them," he said. "Some call it Purgatory, some call it a prison, but it's really just a big holding tank."

"I wondered where all the souls were." Curiosity glinted in Vex's remarkable eyes. Laura's interest had been easily piqued, as well, and he wondered if she was listening. "So, what's it like inside the Inner Sanctum? Is it...hell? The kind humans preach about? Or is it like this?" She made an expansive gesture with her hand. "Because this isn't very terrifying."

"You didn't see Sheoul-gra back before Azagoth found a mate." He watched her slender fingers tuck the daisy behind her ear, and he was once again struck by the stark contrast of the fragile daisy against her tough exterior. It fascinated him and left him conflicted because he couldn't figure out if he was attracted to *her*...or if he was attracted to her because Laura was in there somewhere. "But the Inner Sanctum is still mostly the stuff of nightmares."

"Mostly?"

He scooped a smooth round stone off the ground and skipped it across the pond, enjoying the tiny thrill it brought. He hadn't skipped stones since his youth, when Ipsylum drill sergeants took trainees to lakes in the human realm so they could learn aquatic combat techniques where the water was denser and colder than in Heaven. He and his friends—and Laura—would have rock-skipping contests during their breaks.

She'd always won.

"There are different levels, or rings, where the demons go, depending on how inherently evil they are," he said as the tiny ripples in the water died down. "They match up with the *Ufelskala* tiers you mentioned. Level one isn't much different than life here, really." According to Azagoth, Laura had been assigned to the first level after she'd been slaughtered, but she'd been reborn before Z had a chance to find her there. "The other levels get progressively more violent and miserable."

"Ah." She nodded as if she'd come to a great realization. "So that's why."

"That's why what?"

She smiled, and he cursed how easily she stirred his blood. It was wrong to be aroused by Vex when Laura was so close. And when he couldn't do anything about it anyway. His virginity belonged to Laura and always had.

"Why you aren't a total evil asshole," she said. "I mean, you might be an asshole, I kind of think you are, but you aren't *eeeevil.* Not super evil, the way fallen angels usually are. You know what's inside the Inner Sanctum, so you're trying to stay...I dunno, decent, I guess. That way, when you meet whatever horrible end you're destined to suffer, you don't get assigned to a lower level."

Whatever horrible end he was destined to suffer? He'd bet her horrible end came before his. But otherwise, what she'd said was true. He did struggle to keep evil from darkening his soul, something that was far easier now that Azagoth and his realm weren't steeped in hatred and malevolence.

Zhubaal had suffered like everything else in Sheoul-gra while the Grim Reaper's soul grew more and more sinister and corrupt. But now that much of the darkness had been lifted, and knowing what life was like in the Inner Sanctum, Zhubaal had sworn to never let himself sink too deeply into evil temptations. The Inner Sanctum's first level was absolutely his goal.

They had beer there.

"So...you have a girlfriend?"

Once again, the change of topic gave him whiplash, but he managed to shake his head.

She picked up a rock and skipped it like he had, except her stone went farther. "Then who is the 'her' you mentioned when you were yelling at me?"

"I wasn't yelling." He looked around for another rock. He couldn't let her win. "And it's complicated."

"Hmm. Complicated, you say." She tapped her finger on her chin, and he could practically hear the wheels turning in her head as she tried to figure out what "complicated" meant. He wished her luck with that. He couldn't untangle it himself.

"So this person...are you in love with her? Is she emotionally unavailable? Or involved with someone else?" Vex sucked in a sharp breath. "Ooh, that's it, isn't it? Being involved with someone else would be really complicated. So who is she? Azagoth's mate?" She clapped her hands, delighted by the gossipy speculation. "It is!"

"It's not Lilliana, and don't even think that." He found a stone of adequate shape and size and dug it out of the ground with his fingers. "Azagoth is dangerously territorial. Once a dude leered at her for too long, and then he made this slurping noise at her..." He shook his head, still amazed by the male's stupidity and Azagoth's swift and brutal reaction.

Vex bounced on her toes like a child listening to an exciting bedtime story. "Did he kill the dude?"

"No," Z said, "but he won't be looking at Lilliana again. He won't be looking at *anyone* again."

"Azagoth seems really dreamy," she sighed, and wasn't she a bloodthirsty little thing. So opposite of Laura, but he had to admit that he found that attractive in a female. Cruelty, no, but there was nothing wrong with a little eye-for-an-eye. Or an eye for a leer. "I mean, scary, too. But dreamy."

The twinge in his gut wasn't jealousy that she was drooling over Azagoth. It wasn't. Fuck that. "You and I have a very different idea of what constitutes dreamy."

"Yeah?" She folded her arms beneath her breasts, pushing them up even more, and damn her for drawing his eyes to her bold curves. "What's your idea?"

Hmm...should he go for brutal honesty or opt for tact? "The opposite of you." Brutal honesty.

She grinned, all ruby lips and perfect white teeth. "So...hideous? And scrawny. And lacking intelligence." She swept her hand through her short violet-tipped black hair. "And blonde."

Well, she had one of those right. Laura had been as blonde as he was, but her silky mane had flowed like molten gold all the way to her waist. He'd often imagined threading his fingers through it while they made love. And when he was feeling really *randy*, as they used to say, he'd fantasized about wrapping her braid around his fist and taking her roughly, propelling her to climax after climax until they fell, exhausted, onto their marriage mattress. Not that he would ever have told her that. Laura would have been shocked. Maybe even repulsed.

Vex tweaked his nose. "Dillyoon."

He froze, as stunned by the fact that she'd just *tweaked his fucking nose* as he was by what she'd said. His mind flashed back to Laura and how she'd teased him in an identical way so long ago. "How do you know that word?"

"Dunno." She shrugged. "Just one of those things you hear, I guess. Why? What's a dillyoon?"

Azagoth, where are you? Zhubaal needed to get Laura's soul out of Vex. *Now.* Laura had to be influencing Vex's behavior, and he didn't know how much more of it he could take.

"It's a type of butterfly faerie that exists only in one small region in Heaven," he said, watching her carefully for more signs that Laura was...what? Trying to communicate with him? Was that even possible? "Its wings are white lace, and its body is luminescent emerald. They get off on teasing angels." Laura had found them to be both adorable and annoying. He'd come down on the side of annoying.

"I met a faerie once." Vex wrinkled her nose. "They're mean."

"You've met the demonic version," he said. "Not the Heavenly one."

This time, her grin was sinister, and his body hardened, dammit. Had to be Laura. Had to be. There was no way his taste in females had changed this drastically. His dreams had always involved his lovely, virginal Laura, not leather-clad, half-naked, seductive teases.

"The demonic versions do not like flyswatters." Vex gave him a playful wink, and suddenly, it was like being in Heaven with Laura, taking a walk through the Iridescent Forest in between combat training sessions.

He moved nearer, studying her closely, as if he looked hard enough he'd see his beloved in Vex's eyes. "Is one of the spirits affecting you? Right now, I mean."

She paused, lifting her face to his until they were only inches away. "I don't know. I think...maybe. I feel more comfortable with you than I should. Isn't that odd?"

He watched her full lips as she talked, but he barely heard what she'd said. His focus narrowed on her mouth, until only one thing was on his mind.

"Shh," he murmured. "Kiss me."

"Excuse me?"

He didn't give her a chance to be outraged. He lowered his head and captured her mouth. Instant heat sizzled through him, catching him off guard. He'd only kissed one female since his fall from Heaven, and while the kiss had been arousing, it hadn't been remarkable. It had happened during a moment of weakness, when he'd nearly given up on finding Laura, and Cat had been there, needing him as much as he needed...something. But yeah, not remarkable.

This was *beyond* remarkable. It was familiar, and he could almost believe it was calling to his soul.

His body tightened as desire warmed his blood and brought an erotic, pulsing ache to his groin. Without thinking, he tugged the female against him, loving the press of her breasts into his chest. A delicate moan broke from her throat as she wrapped her leg around his thigh and rubbed her sex against the hard ridge of his cock.

"Laura," he whispered, and before her name had even faded from the air, he cringed with both guilt over kissing Vex and anger that he was letting himself get way too distracted. He was forgetting decades of discipline training that had afforded him endless endurance, patience, and even control over his bodily functions.

Pulling away, Vex scowled up at him, her eyes sparking violet fire. "Who the hell is Laura? An ex, I'm guessing?" She sucked in a sharp breath, her anger replaced by curiosity. "Ooh, is Laura also known as Ms. Complicated?"

He scrubbed his hand over his face. "You could say that." Inhaling deeply, he willed his pulse to idle out and his breathing to stop sounding as if he'd run a marathon.

"Do I remind you of her?"

For some reason, that amused him. "You are nothing like her. But you feel like her. And I haven't felt her in a long time."

She grimaced and backed away. "Ew. So you're perving all over me because my skin is as luxuriously smooth as hers or some shit? Where is she? Why haven't you seen her in a long time?"

"She was lost to me nearly a hundred years ago," he said. "She was reborn, but now...I think she's dead again."

"So she died twice? Talk about shitty luck." She narrowed her eyes at him. "Did you kill her one of those times?"

"No, and your skin isn't what I feel." Well, he had felt Vex's skin, and damned if it wasn't luxuriously smooth like she'd said. "It's what's inside you, Vex. Some of the things you're saying, the way you just kissed me." He closed his eyes, trying to hold on to the feelings the kiss had awakened, but all that did was make his pulse race again. "I think one of the souls you're carrying around is Laura."

"Oh." Out of the blue, she cupped his cock through his pants, and he somehow managed to not moan in ecstasy. "And here I thought I was the one giving you this impressive hard-on."

"It was you," he said, and for some reason, that irritated him. His brain might have been blowing circuits over Laura, but the rest of his body had been all about Vex. He stepped back, and it pissed him off that he did it reluctantly.

"Was this Laura person a succubus?"

He nearly laughed. "Hardly." At least, not in her first life. He had no idea what species she'd been during the second. "Why?"

Vex's voice went low and throaty, which made him even harder. "Because you make me wet."

"*What?*" he croaked.

Vex idly trailed her fingers through her cleavage, and his mouth was suddenly parched. "From the moment I got here, I've wanted to jump your bones. Maybe that's your girl talking."

He swallowed. Hard. "She wouldn't. Not through you. Not like that."

"You sure about that? Because right now, all I want is to drop to my knees and take you in my mouth." Before he could search his brain for a response, she went down to her knees in front of him, gripped his hips, and pressed her lips to the bulge in his jeans. The feel of her hot breath through the fabric and the bruising grip of her fingers digging into his ass cheeks froze him in place, his body completely shutting down his brain.

This is wrong.

She kissed lower on his shaft and then began to nibble her way up, following the slight curve of his cock behind the fly of his pants. Her head bobbed as she went, giving him the most erotic view he'd ever seen, and they weren't even doing anything. Not really.

If some male was kissing Laura between her legs through her pants, would they also not be doing anything?

Oh, hell, no. Raw, possessive anger expanded in his chest, and he stepped back with a hiss. Laura would never allow that to happen.

The Laura you knew wouldn't, but in her second life, she could have been a whore in Satan's harem.

Or a succubus.

"No!" he broke away, the lust so thick in his voice he nearly choked on it. "I told you. She wouldn't do this through you. She's not like you."

"No shit." Vex shoved to her feet, anger putting red splotches in her cheeks. "I'm alive and she's not."

Her words hit him like a blow, because as much as he hated to admit it, she was right. Yes, he was ninety-nine-point-nine percent sure he'd found Laura, but it wasn't as if they could be together. She would be sent to the Inner Sanctum, and even if Azagoth allowed Zhubaal to transfer to Hades's employ so he could be with her, she could be reincarnated at any moment, and he'd be in this same position all over again. Yes, he was thrilled to have found Laura, but this situation was less than ideal.

"I—" He broke off as a sharp buzz vibrated in his head.

Vex cocked her head at him, curiosity overriding anger once again. "Zhubaal? What is it?"

"It's Azagoth. He's back." And just in the nick of time.

Chapter Five

Vex wasn't sure what she expected to find inside Azagoth's office, but a relatively normal place of business wasn't it. The room was dark, decorated in blacks, grays, and mahogany, with a massive fireplace against one wall, the flames inside shooting six feet and more into the air. His monstrous claw-footed desk took up at least a fifth of the room, and as big as the desk was, the male sitting behind it made it seem small.

The souls inside her shrieked, throwing themselves against the barriers of her mind so forcefully that it felt like someone was taking a baseball bat to her skull. She furtively wiped away a bead of blood that dripped from her nose and cursed the marks on her arm that burned like fresh brands in Azagoth's presence.

But then, Zhubaal's rejection and insult burned nearly as badly.

She's not like you. She wouldn't drop to her knees to give a perfect stranger a blowjob.

Okay, he hadn't said that second part out loud, but the subtext had been as blatant as a triclops's third eye. And dammit, she could hardly believe she'd come on to him like that. Oh, she was unashamedly bold when it came to the opposite sex, but she'd never been *that* bold. The stupid souls inside her were playing some serious games with her sex drive and willpower. And thanks to this Laura person, Vex felt like she knew Zhubaal, which only ramped up her arousal and made his sexual pull even stronger.

"My Lord," Zhubaal said, and God, even his voice turned her on. It seemed like the more time she spent with him, the more time she *wanted* to spend with him. "Vex is a *daemani* with five souls on board." He glanced over at Vex's arm. "I believe one of them is Laura."

Vex watched from where she'd remained near the entrance as Azagoth's gaze cut sharply to hers, his emerald eyes glinting in the firelight. His expression was stony, forbidding, and she wondered if he ever smiled. Then she decided she didn't want to know what amused him, because if he was a typical evil maniac with godlike powers, he enjoyed pain, suffering, and death.

His gaze intensified, and she suddenly felt exposed. Vulnerable. The souls inside her shrieked louder.

He gave her a "come here" gesture with his finger. "Hello, Vex."

Trying desperately to ignore the pounding in her head, she strode all the way in, determined not to show an ounce of fear. Zhubaal remained where he was, and despite the fact that she was annoyed at him, she felt better that he stayed.

She also felt better when she caught him admiring her ass while she walked. Laura could suck it.

Clearing her throat, she stopped in front of Azagoth's desk. "Mr. Reaper."

"You can call me Azagoth." Leaning forward in his seat, he folded his hands together on his desktop. "When did you discover that you were a *daemani*?"

She had no idea why that was important, and she'd made a rule about not answering personal questions posed by massively powerful demons, but Azagoth didn't seem like the type who appreciated being dodged. So he was going to get a very personal answer.

"The day I started my period," she said, amused by the way his brow arched. Only a millimeter, but still. Zhubaal's exasperated groan was even funnier. "When I was thirteen."

Her parents had taken her to an underworld festival that day, even though she'd practically been doubled over with cramps. *Toughen up, sweetheart*, her mom had said. *If you can't handle that kind of pain, what are you going to do when some Aegis slayer runs you through with a blade?*

No Aegi had ever stabbed Vex, but at the festival, a Nightlash demon had been gutted right in front of her. She'd watched in horror as his soul rose from his dead body and got sucked inside her. No one else had seen, but when she told her parents what had happened, they'd taken her immediately to a friend of theirs, a fallen angel who was also a *daemani*. With Malice's guidance, Vex had built a business out of her ability, and she'd done well until now. Now she needed Azagoth's help to get back on her feet.

"Can you repel them?" he asked. "Or expel them without a conduit or another *daemani*?"

"No to all of it." She didn't like admitting to her weaknesses, but she suspected Azagoth would know if she was lying, and he was the last person she'd want catching her in a fib.

"And why, exactly, are you here?"

She took a deep, bracing breath. This was it, the moment that could save her livelihood...and her life. "I'm here to make you an offer."

"What kind of offer?"

"Put me on your payroll," she said firmly, "and I'll bring you souls." Man, if she could pull this off, she'd be the most infamous *emim* ever. Her parents would be so proud.

Azagoth's slow smile was so chilly she nearly shivered, and there went her dreams of infamy. "I already have people who bring me souls, and I don't have to pay them."

"Your *griminions* are only summoned when a demon dies," she pointed out. "I can bring you rogue souls that roam loose or that escape from their enclosures."

"And why should I care about them?"

"Aren't you in the *business* of souls?" She stepped closer, pressing her point home to take a position of strength. *Thank you, Daddy, for the lessons in negotiation.* She might have detested her father's lectures even more than her mother's combat training, but as a lawyer at a demon-run law firm, he'd known what he was talking about. So had her mother. "You were given an *entire realm* in order to house the spirits of those without physical bodies. It's your *job*."

His smirk said he didn't acknowledge her position of strength. And he might even be entertained by it. What a dick. "And how long did it take you to collect those five souls?"

"A couple of months," she said. "But that's only because I wasn't actively looking for them. I figure on average I can collect one rogue soul every sixteen hours."

The smirk got smirkier. "A single *griminion* can bring me a hundred in a day."

"Well, good for them," she said, her confidence flagging as she reached for the only ace she had. "But can they see rips in the fabric between dimensions? Can they capture the souls that squeeze through those rips?" She held out her arm, the glyphs glowing on her skin. "Because that's how I collected most of these."

Azagoth rose smoothly to his feet. "You can see the fissures in the walls of Sheoul-gra's Inner Sanctum?"

"Ah...I...guess?" She'd taken a stab in the dark with the dimensions thing. She hadn't known where the souls came from. "Not only can I see them, but I can sense where a rip is going to open." Usually they opened miles from where she was, and now that the market for souls had dried up, she'd gotten into the habit of going in the opposite direction to avoid picking up an evil hijacker. But sometimes, like yesterday, they popped open right in front of her.

Zhubaal eyed her speculatively. "I assume you usually sell the souls." He clenched his jaw, and she could only assume that he'd just realized that his precious Laura could have been sold to a slaver or soul-eater. "So why are you here instead of hashing out a deal in some skeezy necromancer's lair?"

"I *was* in some skeezy necromancer's lair. He told me to come to Azagoth." Zhubaal got that judgey look on his face again, and she huffed. "The market vanished almost overnight. Buyers and sellers are either dying or disappearing. The few buyers who are still around refuse to see me or anyone else hawking souls."

Other *daemani* were talking about forming a union and demanding answers. From whom, Vex had no idea. And given that someone was killing *daemani*, gathering together in a group didn't seem like the best plan ever.

Azagoth passed his hand through the flames in the fireplace, but they didn't burn him. In fact, the flames parted, as if terrified to so much as warm his skin. "So what you're saying is that you're so desperate to get rid of those souls that you are willing to risk your own soul by coming to me. Is that about right?"

Something about the cool, calm way he spoke made her internal alarms go off, and she got the sudden feeling she was walking into a trap. Her father would have told her to stay calm. Her mother would have told her to get ready for a fight.

Her mother hadn't possessed an ounce of self-preservation instinct.

"Yes," she said, going with her father's line of thinking, "but without the desperate part. I'm not desperate." She was *so* desperate. "And I'd rather not risk my soul. Zhubaal told me about the Inner Sanctum. No, thank you." She bounced on her toes and crossed her fingers behind her back in a ridiculous superstitious human gesture. "So we have a deal?"

Azagoth smiled, and a chill went down her spine. "The deal is this. You are going to hunt for souls, but I'm not going to pay you."

Before she knew it, she had a blade in her palm and was starting toward him. *Oh, hi, Mom.* "What the hell? What kind of bullshit is that?"

Zhubaal's hand clamped down on her shoulder, and he yanked her backward, disarming her so quickly she stared at her empty hand in disbelief.

Azagoth didn't miss a beat, and it was a little insulting that he didn't think she was enough of a threat to even waste an angry tone of voice on. "You need someone to dump the souls on, and there are very few people left who are willing to risk the King of Hell's wrath." Her expression must have been one of surprise, because he snorted. "What, you think I don't have my finger on the pulse of the underworld? You think I don't know that *daemani* are being hunted at the command of the king himself?" He laughed, but she certainly didn't find this to be funny in the least. "Foolish girl. I don't need you as much as you need me."

Son. Of. A. Bitch.

"I have to eat, you know." She snatched the dagger from Zhubaal and jerked out of his grip. Which was nothing like the way he'd gripped her earlier, his hands pressed firmly against her hip and the small of her back. "Selling souls is how I make a living."

Well, it used to be, back when buying and selling was a thriving market. She'd made a lot of money, but she'd lost it all when the underworld and human stock markets crashed during the recent near-apocalypse. Everything was gone now. Even her Audi and her two-million-dollar condo in sunny Florida were going to be repossessed soon.

Maybe she should have gone to college like her parents wanted instead of pursuing a career in trading souls. But come on, it was easy money, and she'd earned far more than she'd ever have made with any college career. They'd understood, but they hadn't liked it.

Azagoth folded his hands behind his back and faced her squarely. "If you want to be paid, then I expect daily results. I don't want five souls every three months, and I'm not going to pay per soul. You can move into one of the town residences if you need a place to stay. You will bring at least one escapee per day, and your salary will be no more than Zhubaal's."

She glanced over at Zhubaal, who shrugged apologetically. "Look at the bright side," he said. "You'll be too busy to need money, anyway."

Shit. She was trapped, and there was no way out of it. Azagoth might be a penny-pinching miser, but he was going to keep her safe. Plus, she got to brag to everyone that she worked with the Grim Reaper.

"Fine," she muttered. "It's a deal. Can we get these souls out of me now?"

Azagoth turned to Zhubaal. "Leave us."

Zhubaal went taut, his gaze shifting between Vex and Azagoth. "No, my Lord, I think I'll stay."

The temperature in the room dropped so fast she saw Azagoth's breath in the air when he spoke next. "I didn't give you a choice."

Baring his fangs, Zhubaal put himself between her and Azagoth. "I have been searching for Laura for nearly a hundred years," he said, his voice walking a fine line between respect and defiance, "and now that I've finally found her, I won't let anything happen to her."

Vex peeked around Zhubaal's shoulder and instantly wished she hadn't. Azagoth was pissed. She'd never seen eyes of flame before, and she never wanted to again. Holy crap, Zhubaal had some serious stones.

"Vex." If Azagoth's eyes were the fire, his voice was the black smoke. "Wait outside my office."

No. He'll kill Zhubaal!

Vex shook her head, trying to rid it of Laura's influence. And those thoughts *had* to be Laura's, because Vex didn't give a shit about the guy. Sure, he had some major appeal; he was hot as hell, probably knew his way around a bedroom, and he had giant balls...both real and figuratively. She knew because she'd gotten in a good fondle earlier by the pond, before he'd freaked out because she wasn't his stupid Laura.

She's not like you.

Right. Laura would probably stay and defend her adoring Zhubaal.

So Vex left him on his own.

* * * *

Zhubaal had probably made his last mistake, but right now he couldn't care less. Every instinct inside him demanded that he protect Laura, and if he had to give up his soul to do it, he would. She'd looked so desperate standing there, just as Azagoth had said.

That was Vex. Not Laura.

Damn it, he hated that the lines kept blurring with Vex, but it wouldn't be that way for much longer. Azagoth would free Laura and separate the two.

Zhubaal just might not be alive to see it.

"What the fuck was that?" Azagoth rounded on Zhubaal the moment Vex was out of the room. His eyes were pure flame, hot enough to scorch Z's face. "You have never disobeyed an order."

The fact that Z wasn't already dead was a good sign. "I never had reason not to."

"You still don't," he growled. "What the fuck did you think I was going to do to Laura?"

Anger over decades of Azagoth's vague answers and flat-out refusals to answer questions boiled over, and Z lost his shit. His wings sprouted, his fangs punched down, and he drew every ounce of power Azagoth allowed into his body.

"I don't know what you're going to do," Zhubaal snarled. "Maybe send Laura to the Inner Sanctum before I can see her? Or maybe reincarnate her so I have to go through another thirty years of hell looking for her?"

The flames in Azagoth's eyes snuffed out as he held up his

hand, genuine confusion in his expression. "Why would you think I'd do that?"

"You tell me. Why did you keep Laura from me all this time? Why didn't you tell me anything about her identity? I could have found her. Saved her before she was killed and ended up as a welt on Vex's body."

Azagoth shook his head. "I didn't know anything about her."

Z gaped at him in disbelief. "How could you not know? You're the Grim Reaper. Souls are your *job*," he said, echoing Vex from just a moment ago.

"I authorize a specific number of souls from each level to be reincarnated every day, but after the individuals are chosen, they enter the Infernal Abyss to be cast into a waiting fetus. Who—and what—they are born as is out of my hands or realm of knowledge."

Son of a bitch. "You couldn't have told me this earlier?"

"Would this information have helped you locate Laura?"

"No, but—"

"Then drop it." Azagoth's tone was deceptively mild, which meant he was reaching the end of civility. Which, Z could admit, had gone on much longer than he'd expected.

"At least tell me why you wanted me to leave the room while you extracted the souls from Vex."

Azagoth tapped a glass pad on the wall behind his desk, and a panel slid back, revealing a well-stocked bar, the newest upgrade to his office. "Because you don't need to see what I'm going to do to her." He poured vodka in two glasses and brought one to Z.

Baffled, he took the glass. "I'm not squeamish."

And he wasn't. He'd done things as an angel that had made his buddies puke for hours afterward, and he'd done worse as a fallen angel. But even as the words fell from his mouth, he doubted them. Vex shouldn't matter to him, but he didn't want to see her hurt. She'd brought Laura to him, and that had, at the very least, earned her his eternal gratitude.

"I know." Azagoth downed the liquor, and as he lowered the glass, shadows darkened his eyes. "But there are some things loved ones should never see."

It took a moment to let Azagoth's words sink in, and when they did, Zhubaal was glad he had the alcohol.

Holy crap. Azagoth was protecting him. Zhubaal had seen Laura's remains, her chest cavity laid open and her heart removed. The nightmares still haunted him, and Azagoth knew it, thanks to his love of throwing massive annual celebrations for Sheoul-gra's residents who had survived since the last party. At the most recent event, Zhubaal had had one too many of Azagoth's signature cocktails, a Bloody Reaper, and he'd blubbered all about his bad dreams. The next day, Azagoth hadn't said a word about it.

But he *had* poured Z another Bloody Reaper, because apparently, Z had looked like he'd needed "a little hair of the hellhound."

"I still want to be there when you free the souls," Zhubaal said. "If it were Lilliana, wouldn't you want to be there?"

"Fuck, yeah," Azagoth said. "And no one could tell me no. But it would be a mistake." He clapped his hand on Z's shoulder. "Trust me, Z. You don't want to see it, and I can't have you interrupting. There's a powerful soul inside Vex that could put up a fight, and I'm going to need all my focus to draw it out."

Z got that. During battle, even the most minor distraction could be deadly. Azagoth wouldn't be in any danger, but Vex could be. And if Azagoth had to destroy the evil soul inside Vex, the other souls could get caught in friendly fire. It wouldn't be the first time Zhubaal had seen it happen.

"Fine," Z agreed reluctantly. "I'll send in Vex. But I'll be right outside the door."

He didn't wait for Azagoth's response. He put down his glass and stepped into the hallway where Vex was waiting, lounging back against a pillar, one foot propped against the stone behind her.

"Took you long enough." She popped away from the wall. "Is he ready?"

He gestured to the door. "Go on in."

She started to go, but paused after a couple of steps. "You're not coming in, are you?"

The way she said it, her voice an impossible mix of hope and disappointment, made his gut twinge. He liked her. She might drive him insane, but there was something about her that made him want to learn more about her. He wished he could blame his desire on any influence Laura might be having on her, but it wasn't true. It was

Vex's spiky hair he wanted to touch. It was Vex's lips he wanted to kiss. It was Vex's body he wanted beneath him.

"No," he croaked.

"'Kay." Abruptly, she spun around and kissed him. She tasted like rainwater and flowers, reminding him of the pond and how good she'd felt against him. Just as abruptly, she bounced back with a cheeky smile. "Wish me luck."

With that, she disappeared into Azagoth's office while Zhubaal stood there, his excitement to see Laura tempered by his worry for Vex.

Chapter Six

Vex had no idea why she'd just kissed Zhubaal as if they were a real couple and she was seeking a good luck kiss before a job interview.

Wish me luck!

Ugh. She was an idiot. An idiot who was about to reunite him with the love of his life. And, apparently, afterlife.

Mentally cursing herself, she strode across the floor to where Azagoth was waiting expectantly by the fire. He watched her approach, and the closer she got, the more the room closed in on her. It had seemed so big before, but now it felt like a bathroom stall at McDonald's.

"I'm not sure how this will go," he said. "But we'll try the easy way first."

Oh, yes, she was all for the easy way. She'd gone through this a bazillion times, and everyone had a different method—most were quick and painless. But then, the souls she was selling always wanted to be freed, probably because they didn't know they were going to be captured by someone else. This current batch of souls knew, and they were already starting to claw at her mind.

Azagoth stepped up to her, stopping mere inches away. She expected him to start chanting like the warlocks, mages, and sorcerers she usually dealt with. Or that maybe he'd mix a potion or slice her palm and make her stand inside a protective circle while she bled on the symbols. Instead, he simply placed his hand on her forehead.

The souls went ballistic. Pain shot through her, a searing, mind-bending agony that felt like someone was pulling her spinal cord out of the top of her head.

"Stop," she gasped. "They don't want out."

"Of course they don't." He stepped back and the pain melted away, leaving behind a faint headache and wobbly knees. But the souls, stunned as far as she could tell, had quieted down to almost total silence. "Inside you, they feel safe. But they can sense me, and they know what I am. They know where they are because all but one have been here before." Shadows seemed to writhe in his eyes, and for a split second, she swore she saw a demonic face looking at her from behind his handsome one. "They know I judge harshly, they know Hades is waiting for them, and they know I'm going to send them to him."

Usually when demons said they were going to send you to Hades, they were being all blowhardy. But Azagoth sold it and made it fresh. Really fresh. She was about to pee in her favorite leather pants.

"Okay, I get why they're resisting, but you're the Grim Reaper." Did she really have to point this out? "You deal in souls. Shouldn't you, of all people, be able to suck some souls out of someone?"

"Yes." He looked troubled, which could only be bad. Really, really bad. "I should be able to extract the weaker ones without even trying."

"Then what's going on?"

Crimson glints flashed in his eyes, burning like angry embers, and she wondered if the flamethrower eyes would come next. She took a step back, just in case. "The powerful soul is holding them back. *They* want out."

"What?" She looked down at the marks on her arm as if the newest glyph could provide answers, but it wasn't any different than the others. It hadn't grown horns or teeth or formed demonic symbols. "The thing inside me is so bad that they'd rather deal with *you*?"

"I'm not sure if that's a compliment or not," he said dryly. "But in any case, the evil inside you is ancient. Perhaps as old as I am. It's going to take more than my command for her to leave your body."

Her? "I knew it!"

"Knew what?"

"That the super evil soul was female. Females claw more than males." Males were more about the blunt force trauma.

"I see." Azagoth clearly didn't care. He raked her with his gaze. "Now, take off your clothes."

"If this is some kind of bullshit ploy to get me to have sex with you—"

"I have a mate." His eyes glowed orange now, as if they were sucking the colors out of the fire, and the blood in her veins froze. And at the same time, a stab of envy pierced her because Azagoth's mate was lucky to have a male who was so fiercely faithful.

"Okay then," she said brightly, because awkward.

It took only a minute to strip down, and then she stood there, shivering even though she wasn't cold, as she waited for whatever he was going to do. She'd never been shy or self-conscious about her body, but there was something unsettling about being naked in front of someone who could probably see all the way to her soul.

As he moved toward her, he unbuttoned his shirt. "This is going to hurt." For the first time, there was a touch of sympathy in his voice. Which couldn't be a good thing. But neither could the fact that he'd just tossed his shirt onto the desk and was reaching for his belt.

What was he doing? "Will it hurt bad?"

"That depends." He stopped a foot away and peeled off his pants.

He was a commando guy, and holy shit, he was beautiful. It made her want to see Zhubaal like that, to see the six-pack she'd felt under his shirt and the erection she'd caressed with her lips. But this wasn't Zhubaal, so she snapped her gaze up to his face and locked it there.

"Depends on what?" she croaked in a humiliatingly rough voice.

"On whether you think agony is bad."

She nodded. "I do."

He laughed.

And then he punched his hand through her rib cage. Searing, ripping agony exploded through her entire body. The souls screeched and tore at her from the inside. The pain became all-consuming, the smell of blood made her gag, and she swore Azagoth's hand was wrapped around her spine.

She screamed as he yanked a bloody, squirming mass from her and threw it to the floor. Through her haze of pain, she managed a gasp of surprise. The thing writhing a few feet away was one of the demons that had been inside her, but it was in solid form. She'd never seen them as anything but ghostly wisps. Most of the time she couldn't even make out their species.

But the thing moaning on the floor was a female Umber demon nearly twice her size.

A two-foot tall creature in a brown hooded robe skittered into the room from out of nowhere, snatched up the bloody demon, and chained it to the wall. A *griminion*, she thought, and then she was immersed again in pain as Azagoth smashed his fist inside her body.

Twice more she went through the agony, but on the fourth try, she thought she was going to die. The room spun and turned into swirls of red and black and gray, and sharp, sharp teeth. She thought the teeth belonged to Azagoth, but he didn't look like a big, horned, dragon-demon. Right?

Delirious. She was delirious, wracked with fever and broken bones.

"*Fuck...hold on...fuuuuck!*"

Was that Azagoth's voice? She could barely hear, could only feel pain.

At some point, she realized she was lying on her back, and she thought her eyes were open, but everything was dark. No, there was a face... handsome... smiling... Zhubaal?

It didn't feel real, more like a memory. And as the darkness took her, all she could think was that if she had to die, dying with Zhubaal might not be that bad.

* * * *

Zhubaal was used to hearing sounds of agony coming from inside Azagoth's office. He'd learned to tune it out. But this was different. He felt Vex's raw, heart-wrenching screams all the way to his marrow. Azagoth had told him to stay out, but every cell in his body demanded that he do something besides stand in a dark hallway while his female was suffering.

Except Vex wasn't his female. Laura was.

She screamed again, and after what seemed like hours but was probably a couple of minutes, he hit his limit.

Heart racing in a panicked, spastic rhythm, he threw open the door. Instantly, the door ripped out of his hand and tore off its hinges, caught up in a whirlwind of evil spinning around the office like a tornado, with Azagoth and Vex at the center. The air pressure increased a hundredfold, becoming a crushing entity that sucked the air from Z's lungs and turned his eardrums into throbbing instruments of pain.

"Azagoth," he croaked, trying to see through the wall of malevolent wind. Long, skeletal hands reached for him and demonic faces snarled at him as they flew by the doorway, only to be stretched into more streams of spinning evil. "Azagoth, *stop*!"

Azagoth, morphed into a demon twice his usual size with massive horns jutting out of his dragon-like head, stood over Vex's unconscious, naked body. His gore-coated fist clenched the throat of a male Bedim demon whose dark skin had paled with terror. Azagoth's great head swiveled around to Zhubaal. He bared his teeth and snarled, but the wind died down.

Zhubaal had seen him like this before, his inner demon released by anger or contact with pure evil. Usually it was wise to leave him alone and let him come down by himself. Even Lilliana would sometimes back out of a room if he'd taken his demon out to play.

Zhubaal wasn't backing out.

In a blur of motion, Azagoth hurled the demon to the floor where two waiting *griminions* shackled him and dragged him over to where two females, a gray-skinned Umber and a big-eyed Daeva, stood against the wall.

He stared, desperate for clues, any sense that one of those demons was Laura. Would she recognize him? Would she remember that before she was a demon, she'd been an angel?

A moan pulled his gaze back to Azagoth and Vex. His heart shot into his throat now that he could see her clearly, her body lying limp in a pool of blood. Her sternum had been torn open, ribs and mangled flesh spilling out of her chest cavity.

Memories of finding Laura's body flashed through his mind, and he broke out in a cold sweat. Her killers had left her on the floor of the shitty apartment she'd rented in Poland where, as an Unfallen, she'd tried to fit in with humans and avoid fallen angels who would try to drag her into Sheoul.

They'd killed her instead. He'd hunted them for decades, and when he'd caught them, he'd gone full-bore eye-for-an-eye on the bastards. But he couldn't forget finding Laura lying in a dried pool of blood, her chest laid open like Vex's.

Even though he knew Vex's injury was of more a psychic nature than a physical one, and even though it was already stitching itself together, all he could see was Laura lying there.

He ran toward her as Azagoth shifted into his normal form, sans clothes and splashed in blood.

"She'll be fine." Azagoth stepped away from her, leaving bloody footprints on the stone floor. He was careful to avoid stepping on his favorite Slogthu-crafted rug, though. "She's stronger than I expected."

Z dropped to his knees next to Vex, more shaken than he'd like and unsure why Azagoth would have expected anything other than strength from her. "And the souls?"

Azagoth jerked his head toward the demons. "I was only able to extract three." His voice lowered to a deadly rumble. "The bitch inside Vex is holding onto the weaker soul and I can't do anything about it. She's taunting me."

"What the hell are you talking about?" Zhubaal took Vex's hand the way he'd done with Laura. It was cold. Not two-days-dead cold, but still, too cold. "Why can't you get them out?"

"I can," he growled, anger at his failure putting an edge on his words, "but doing so will probably kill Vex."

"*No.*" He leaped to his feet, rounding on Azagoth as if the male was going to start ripping the two remaining souls from Vex right now. "No," he said, more calmly. Why was he getting so worked up about this, anyway? "We'll find another way." He swallowed dryly and looked between the demons chained to the wall and Vex. "Where is Laura?"

"She's inside Vex."

Well, that explained why he'd been acting like a possessive idiot when it came to Vex. Closing his eyes, Zhubaal let out a nasty curse. "She's still in there with the fucking evil spirit."

A troubled look darkened Azagoth's already black expression.

"Take Vex to her room until I decide what to do. And don't leave her alone. The other souls had a restraining effect on the malevolent spirit. With little to hold it back, it could have a powerful influence on her. It could even possess her if she isn't strong enough to resist."

Cursing again, he gathered Vex's limp body in his arms and headed for the door. At the threshold he paused. "What kind of demon is this powerful soul, by the way?"

Azagoth, still naked, strode over to the bar and poured a whiskey. "When she lived in the demon realm, she was a succubus."

Z looked down at Vex, her beautiful face surprisingly peaceful in sleep, and he groaned. She'd mentioned that she thought one of the souls was a sex demon, and it turned out that she was right. Bad enough to be stuck with an attractive female, but one who could be possessed by a succubus? Throw Laura into the mix, and he was in for an impossible exercise in self-control.

Chapter Seven

Vex groaned as light pierced the barely open slits of her eyelids. Where was she? She blinked, and gradually, the blur in her vision cleared. She was in her Motel 666 room, lying on the bed with nothing covering her but a blanket. Zhubaal was sitting in the wooden chair across from her bed, his face buried in a book.

He peeked at her from over the top of the book. "Hey."

"Hey." God, she sounded like she'd swallowed a frog. "What happened?" All she could remember was pain like she'd never felt before. It was as if someone had been ripping organs from her body. She could still hear the screams, but she didn't know if they belonged to her or to the spirits as they'd been wrenched from her body.

"Azagoth removed three of the souls. You passed out, so I brought you here and cleaned you up. Lilliana and I have been taking turns staying with you since." Zhubaal twisted around and took a cup from the table beside him.

He held it out to her, and she sat up, wincing at the dull ache in her chest. Azagoth had the power of a locomotive behind his punches, didn't he?

Gingerly, she wrapped the blanket around her and took the drink from him. The greasy yellow liquid looked like chicken broth but smelled of sweet herbs. Something told her it was going to be *nasty*. But then, demonic potions were rarely made of tequila and margarita mix or milk and cocoa.

"I'm afraid to ask," she said as she eyed some floating mystery blobs, "but what is it?"

He hesitated, as if choosing his words carefully, which probably meant there was scary shit in the drink he didn't want to go into detail about. "It's a potion exorcists use to weaken souls when they've possessed someone."

"But I'm not possessed." Not yet, anyway.

"No, but Azagoth thinks it'll help prevent it from happening. Or at least make it easier for you to fight." He stretched his long legs out and crossed them at his ankles. He'd changed clothes since the last time she'd seen him, outfitted in combat boots, black military pants, and a form-fitting T-shirt. It was a good look for him, as if he was meant to be a warrior. "I consulted with a shaman physician at Underworld General to make sure it would be safe for *emim*."

Surprised winged through her at that. "Why? If it killed me, wouldn't all your problems be solved? The two remaining souls would be released." Actually, her spirit would as well. Not cool. The Inner Sanctum didn't sound all that great, and she had no desire to be reborn as an imp or a troll or some crap.

Some emotion she couldn't name softened the harsh planes of his face, but not his voice, which held the powerful tone of someone speaking an oath. "I did it because you brought Laura back to me. What you endured in Azagoth's office makes you worthy of that, at least." He gestured to the cup. "Drink it. If you don't, and the soul possesses you, death might be the next option."

Yeah...no. She glanced at the cup of hot liquid. "You're sure this will help?"

He shrugged. "Can't hurt."

"How reassuring," she said flatly. Bracing herself with a deep breath, she gulped the entire contents of the cup, and holy damn, she had to force that shit to stay down. She couldn't decide which was worse—the slimy texture, the chewy globs, or the flavor, an unholy mix of liver, rancid fat, and cinnamon with a dollop of honey.

"How long have I been out?" she rasped when she finally stopped gagging and swallowing bile.

"Twenty-one hours."

"Wow." She breathed deeply, enjoying the sensation of quiet inside her. She could still feel the two souls, but with three others gone, there was less buzzing in her body. "I feel so much better. I mean, I'm tired, but the cacophony of souls is gone."

"Can you feel the two that are left?"

As if in answer, an oil slick of evil spread across the surface of her own soul, and with it came a wave of sexual need so powerful she nearly groaned. Closing her eyes, she inhaled slowly, concentrating on forcing the soul back into its corner. Gradually, it retreated, but it left behind the throbbing ache of arousal.

She popped open her eyes. "Nope. Don't feel a thing." Except the driving need to get him into bed. "The mincemeat tea must be helping." She stood, pulling the blanket with her. "So what now?"

He sat forward, bracing his forearms on his spread knees. "Now we figure out how to get those souls out of you."

"Why couldn't Azagoth do it?" She put aside the cup and hoped she didn't have to drink any more of the nasty stuff.

"He could, but not without killing you."

"Oh. Well, I approve of his reluctance to kill me." She bent over to gather a spare set of clothes from her pack, and the blanket fell open in the back, exposing her to the cool air and Zhubaal's eyes. She could feel his gaze on her skin, hot and hungry. But it wasn't for her, was it? She'd bet her favorite blade that Laura was one of the two souls inside her. Turning back to him, she dropped the blanket. She'd never been modest and besides, if he cleaned her up after Azagoth's gore-fest of an exorcism, he'd seen her naked already. "What about Laura?"

Hastily, he glanced away, his gaze plummeting to the woven rug beneath her feet. How could anyone who'd spent any time at all in Sheoul be so embarrassed by nudity?

"She, ah...she's still inside you."

Bingo. She pulled on a pair of silky black underwear and her favorite pleated black and blue plaid miniskirt, and Zhubaal still didn't look up. There was something very sweet and respectful about that, something she had never, ever expected to find in a fallen angel. Usually they were horndogs who'd perfected leering.

Laura, you suck.

She cleared her throat of her bitterness. It was stupid to be jealous when Zhubaal was clearly dedicated to someone else. Even if that someone else was basically a ghost.

"So, let's say Azagoth gets her out," she mused. "You can't be together anyway because she's kind of dead, right?"

"Not...exactly." His gaze flickered over to her and back to the floor when he saw she still hadn't put on her shirt. "In the Inner Sanctum and some parts of Sheoul-gra, souls are solid."

Yeah, she'd figured that last part out when the first soul Azagoth ripped out of her went from a transparent wisp to a big, ugly Umber demon.

"How long have you been searching for her?" She shrugged into a silky blue, sleeveless top that hung almost to the skirt's hem and would conceal her dagger sheathes once she was armed. As she reached next to Zhubaal for her boots, her arm brushed his leg, and she bit back a needy groan at the sexual current that sizzled through her. She shot him a furtive glance as she sank down on the mattress, but if he felt anything at all, it didn't show.

"I've been looking for her since she was kicked out of Heaven nearly a century ago." He was still lounging like he belonged in her bedroom, and dammit, why did she have to like it? "She was killed soon after and reborn thirty years ago, but I don't know what species."

"Wow, so she could have been born something gross, like a Cruentus." She shoved her foot into a boot. "What would you have done if you found her and she was something horrible?"

He crossed his thick arms over his chest, and her mouth watered at the way his muscles flexed under his tan skin. "She wouldn't be."

Saint Laura strikes again. "Oh, and you just know that." There was no way he could miss the sarcasm, and sure enough, he smirked.

"Yep."

She zipped up her boot. "I know angels have a reputation for being faithful, but aren't you taking it a bit far? What kind of angel were you, anyway?"

"I was an Ipsylum."

"A what?" She tugged on the second boot.

"Ipsylum." His gaze dropped to her boot, and she zipped it up slowly, teasingly, loving how his eyes tracked her hand. He might not be hers, but she could do her best to make him regret that. "They're a specialized class of warrior angels."

"Bullshit."

His gaze snapped up. "Bullshit?"

"Yeah. Bullshit." After her parents died at the hands of angels, she'd learned everything she could about them. "I studied all the classes of angels, and Ipsylum isn't one of them." She ticked off her fingers. "There are Cherubim, Dominions, Principalities, Thrones, Seraphim, Archangels—"

"Whatever sources you got your information from are wrong. Over thousands of years, humans gradually learned of several Orders of angels, but they don't know all of them. Didn't your parents tell you about angels?"

She shook her head as she reached for the pile of weapons lying on top of the clothes someone had brought from Azagoth's office. "They answered my questions, but they didn't offer information. I think they were ashamed by whatever it was that got them booted, you know?"

Vex strapped a tiny, thin blade to the inside of her thigh, getting a kick out of Zhubaal's furtive glances as her skirt hiked high. When she finished, she tucked her leg beneath her and sat back against the hard pillow. It wasn't as if she had anywhere else to be, so she might as well get comfortable. Besides, she liked talking to Zhubaal. He was probably only humoring her because she was Laura's genie bottle, but it had been such a long time since she'd talked to anyone on a personal level that this was kind of...refreshing.

"I think that's why we lived in the human realm instead of in Sheoul, and why my parents pretended to be human. Partly because they were ashamed." She closed her eyes at the memory of her parents telling her how much danger they were in in the human realm, hated by both fallen angels who believed they should be serving Sheoul's interests, and angels, who were just assholes. "And partly to protect me from the paranormal world."

And it had worked until she hit puberty and sucked in her first soul. When her parents sought answers, it had put them on the radar for a lot of enemies. Eventually, the enemies had caught up with them, and they'd been killed. She hadn't even been close enough to catch their souls before *griminions* had, and worse, she'd never been able to take revenge.

Her parents' killers had been angels, powerful and far beyond her reach.

"So," she said, changing the subject before she got all sappy or started crying or some shit. "What do Ipsylum do? You said they're warriors?"

He nodded. "Highly trained, very powerful. In some ways, they're more powerful than Archangels. If angels are Heaven's army, then Ipsylum are the army's special ops team."

"Huh." She idly ran her fingers down the stiletto heel of one boot to test the sharp edge of the spikes that could punch through metal, bone, and flesh during a fight. Her mother's design. "What does Heaven need with a special ops team?"

Zhubaal came to his feet in a graceful surge and moved to the glassless window next to her bed. A breeze ruffled his hair as he looked out over the courtyard.

"Heaven needs specialized soldiers to assassinate powerful demons, spy in areas of Sheoul where not even Archangels can go, rescue human or angel hostages from demons...shit like that." He clenched his hands at his sides, and she wondered if he regretted his choice to leave his angelic life.

"That's awesome." Why couldn't she have been born an angel instead of an *emim* with useless powers like attracting souls like flypaper or being able to walk in stiletto heels on any surface without ever loosing her balance? Sure, she had killer reflexes and was stronger than your average human or demon, but still, in a world where angels could fly and demons could shapeshift or become invisible or manipulate the weather, she had to stretch to be considered even average. "If I were an angel, I'd want to be one of those."

He snorted. "Somehow, I'm not surprised."

"Why?"

Frowning, he glanced down at her arm and the remaining two glyphs. "Because you're the polar opposite of Laura."

"What does she have to do with it?"

"Laura was also an Ipsylum."

"No," she blurted, seriously thrown by that. The way he'd spoken of this Laura person made her sound like a milquetoast. "Really?"

"Really." There was a tap at the door, and he answered it,

thanking whoever was on the other side for a plate piled with sandwiches and fruit. He brought it over to her and placed it on the mattress beside her. "Eat. I have a feeling we're going on a little trip soon."

"A trip?" She perked up. She loved to travel. She just never had anyone to travel with. "To where?"

"To see a wizard in Los Angeles."

"I like L.A. Not so much wizards." Vex poked at one of the sandwiches. Looked like some sort of lunchmeat and cheese on wheat, but she'd seen what passed as meat in Sheoul. "I wanted to be an actress when I was growing up. My mom said I couldn't because I wasn't human, but my dad said that half the people in Hollywood are demons anyway, so I shouldn't give up." She plucked a grape off the plate. The fruit looked safe enough.

"So why did you give up?"

"Who says I did?" She tossed the grape into the air and caught it between her teeth.

"Well," Zhubaal drawled, "I don't see Channing Tatum down here making deals with Azagoth to sell souls to make money."

Smartass. She popped the grape and chewed, buying some time while she decided whether or not she should fuck with him.

Yeah, she should.

"I haven't hit it big yet." She plucked another grape from the plate and grinned. "But I'm finding that the porn industry is a great place to start. Maybe you've seen me in something recently?"

She couldn't tell if his expression was one of judgment, disgust, or curiosity. "Ah, no."

"You're missing out," she purred. "I have an idea. Why don't you bend over, and I'll pull that stick out of your ass." She winked. "We can make it fun. With a little lube—"

"We aren't starring in one of your pornos."

He seemed more than a little irritated, which cracked her up. "What's the matter? Are you lacking an adventurous spirit?" When he didn't answer, and in fact, looked a little flustered, she took advantage, coming smoothly to her feet to face him. "Are you Mr. Missionary Only?" She moved toward him, noting how his eyes shot wide, his nostrils flared, and his breaths came faster the closer she got. "Or are you into some kind of secret kink?"

He stood his ground, tensing and widening his stance, as if he expected a battle. "You are out of line."

"Why?"

"Because I'm not...available."

She halted in front of him and reached out to drag one finger playfully down his chest. "Oh, come on. You can't tell me you've been celibate for nearly a century." His only reaction was a twitch in his cheek, but it was enough. "Seriously? You haven't been with anyone since Laura died?"

"I swore an oath to her."

Holy shit. "But she died. Twice."

"Our oaths weren't meant to be broken by death," he said gravely.

What the hell? "So you're trying to tell me that even though she was reincarnated, you expected her to somehow remember an oath she took in a past life? Do you really believe that while she was alive the second time, she was celibate, as well?"

"Yes."

She laughed. Like, full-on belly laugh. Zhubaal was either naive or delusional. Maybe both. Poor, poor male.

"Some part of her would know," he insisted, irritation making his words fall like stones. "She might not remember me or our oath, but I'm sure she would have felt that she needed to wait for the right person. Had she not died, I'd have found her, and I would have been that right person." He glanced at the two remaining glyphs on Vex's arm. "Turns out, she found me."

Seriously delusional. "You think she somehow knew I'd end up in Sheoul-gra, so she hitched a ride here with me, just to see you?"

"Stranger things have happened."

That much was true. But God, he looked so sure, and yet, so sad. Vex, who had never been in love, who had never loved anyone except her parents, felt her heart break a little for him. Zhubaal might be delusional, but he felt deeply, and he was hurting.

Vex didn't have a lot of experience comforting people, but in this, she knew she could help. More importantly, she wanted to help. Zhubaal had taken care of her and kept her safe even though he didn't have to, and it was time to pay him back.

Reaching up, she cupped his cheek, following him when he tried to turn away from her touch. "Do you want to feel her?"

"What?"

Heart pounding, she stepped into him until her breasts were pressing into the hard planes of his chest. "Use me. Feel her." She lifted her face to his. "Kiss me."

He scowled down at her, wariness flickering in his eyes. "Why would you do this?"

"Because you and Azagoth are helping me." *And because I really want to kiss you.* Yes, she wanted to help, but she wasn't completely selfless. She wanted to feel his body, his mouth, against hers. "Let me return the favor."

For a long moment, he hesitated, his gaze locked on hers. Then, slowly, he dipped his head and captured her mouth with tentative pressure. The kiss was light, unsure, but she felt the sizzle all the way to her soul.

He wants Laura.

Of course he does. That's what this was about. Laura.

His tongue flicked across her lips, and she opened for him, inviting him into a deeper connection. Their tongues met, tangling together as he hauled her hard against him. Everything in her body lit up like fireworks, as if this was meant to be.

It's Laura. She must have sensed him, because all of a sudden, Vex's heart was beating in a spastic rhythm that didn't make sense. And then, as her heart beat even faster, practically throwing itself against her rib cage as if it wanted to break out and get to him, the reality hit her.

Her heart was beating for *him.*

A vague sense of love and need and loyalty wrapped around her like a warm blanket. It felt so foreign, yet so good and right. She'd never experienced anything like this, and her first thought was that her life had been so empty.

But this wonderful sensation didn't belong to her, did it? It belonged to the spirit inside her who she was beginning to hate. Zhubaal's precious Laura didn't even have a physical form, and yet she commanded fierce devotion from him.

Panic welled up, and she tore away, stunned to realize tears stung her eyes. "I'm sorry," she rasped. "I can't do this."

But then she looked at him, at the blazing heat in his eyes, at the barely-controlled way he was breathing, and in an instant, they were tangled in each other's arms again.

Zhubaal backed her up, putting her spine against the wall and his erection against her belly. He kissed her hard as he rocked his hips into her, the ridge of his fly rubbing her through the fabric of her skirt. The friction was delicious, but it wasn't enough. It wouldn't be enough until they were naked.

She lifted one leg and hooked it around his thigh, moaning at the way his erection caressed her aching sex. His hand slid between them to cup her breast under her shirt, and she loved the way her skin tingled under his touch, little pops of ecstasy that made her gasp, especially when he pinched her nipple between his fingers.

"Oh...my," she moaned, arching against him.

"Is she in there?" he breathed against her ear.

"She?" Vex was so lust-punched that it took a heartbeat before she realized what he was asking. " Laura?" She rotated her hips, increasing the pressure between them, and that lovely, bone-melting wave of love washed over her again. "Yes. And she wants you. She wants you so badly."

He shuddered against her, trembling even harder when she dropped both hands to his incredibly firm ass and squeezed before sliding her fingers between his legs from behind to tease his balls.

"It's been so long," he murmured between desperate kisses against her throat. "So long since I've felt you against me."

"Too long," she agreed, not even knowing what she was saying or why she was saying it. But it felt right.

Which was wrong.

She frowned. There was actually something very wrong about all of this. The mincemeat tea must be working, because she couldn't feel the evil soul inside her...which meant she shouldn't be able to feel the lesser soul, either. But somehow, love and affection for this male filled her.

Had the evil soul lessened its grip on Laura's spirit?

"Zhubaal," she gasped. "We have to find Azagoth. Now."

His head snapped up, and if she hadn't felt the need for urgency, she'd have stripped him naked right then and there. His lips, kiss-swollen and glistening, beckoned to her, and she couldn't help but imagine them forging an erotic path down her body. And his eyes, God, his eyes, they were pools of the kind of lust a male reserved only for his lover. How she knew that, since she'd never been on the receiving end of that kind of intensity, she had no idea. All she knew was that in this single moment, he was her world.

And she was his.

Except she wasn't. *Laura* was his, and Vex was merely borrowing her emotions.

"Let's go," she pleaded. "Please. Hurry." *Before I decide to keep Laura's soul so I can experience this feeling every day.* "I think he can exorcise Laura now."

There was a split second of hesitation that made no sense, but then he took her hand and dragged her out of her room and down to the common area.

As they started across the courtyard toward Azagoth's palace, a *griminion* scurried past them, its little chittering noises muffled by its hood. Deep inside her, the evil spirit stirred, probably sensing the *griminion's* ability to collect souls. Shit. SuperEvil was going to grab Laura and hold her hostage again, and although a small part of Vex wanted to hold on to Laura as long as possible, it wasn't fair to Zhubaal or herself. What she was feeling for him right now wasn't real. It was on loan from Laura.

With a cry of frustration and sorrow, she jerked away from Zhubaal and summoned every ounce of willpower she had to expel the souls inside her, knowing the *griminion* would gather them up.

And miracle of miracles, she must have caught SuperEvil by surprise, because the other spirit broke loose and shot out of her body in a cloudy wisp. Instantly, the *griminion* wheeled around and captured the spirit with one bony hand. It shrieked as it struggled against the *griminion's* hold, but Vex knew from experience, from witnessing hundreds of *griminions* capture souls, that the spirit—presumably Laura—didn't have a shot of escaping.

Inside her, SuperEvil tore around, punching and biting and clawing, letting loose a psychic volley of anger and pain that nearly drove Vex to her knees. She swayed unsteadily, but Zhubaal caught her around the waist and braced her against his big body.

"There." She pointed at the *griminion* and the wildly flailing soul. "It's Laura. I don't know why she's not materializing as solid. You said in Sheoul-gra they have physical bodies."

"Yeah." He stared at the spirit, which had taken a vague humanoid shape. "But only in Azagoth's office and the Inner Sanctum." Still holding her against him, Zhubaal looked down at her. "You okay?"

Caught off guard by his concern, she nodded dumbly, and he released her, but only after making sure she wouldn't do a face plant. Cautiously, almost hesitantly, he moved to the spirit and reached out to it with a trembling hand.

Vex held her breath as his fingers passed through the cloud-like shadow. His shoulders fell, and she knew.

"It's not her," he choked out. "It's not Laura."

His devastation hit her like a seismic landslide. The concussive blast of anguish struck her in an almost physical blow, knocking her back a step.

But even as she recovered from his pain, a sick sensation bubbled up in her belly. "Laura must be the evil soul inside me."

"That's not possible." He sent the *griminion* away and turned to her. The devastation she'd felt from him showed in his face, and her chest hollowed out. "No matter what species of demon she was reborn as, she couldn't have been so corrupted. Not Laura."

Not Laura. He was so blind when it came to that stupid female, and Vex sighed. "I know you want to believe the best of her, but I'm telling you, the spirit inside me has to be her. I can still feel her affection for you." She lifted her gaze to his and fell right into those gorgeous eyes as if she'd always known them. "There's only one soul left inside me, Zhubaal. Evil or not, it's her."

"No," he ground out. "She would never—" He sucked in a sharp breath, and his eyes shot wide. "Oh...oh, damn."

"What?" The way he was looking at her freaked her the fuck out. "What is going on with you?"

"There's not one soul inside you," he said. "There are two."

She jammed one hand on her hip and held out her arm, which clearly bore only one soul-glyph. "I think I'd know if there was more than one—"

Abruptly he was in front of her, his hands gripping her shoulders, his gaze drilling into her with so much intensity she couldn't look away if she wanted to.

"There are two souls inside you, Vex. The evil one...and yours."

With no warning, he kissed her. Captured her mouth in an erotic assault that brought tears to her eyes and joy to her heart. Her soul sang, like a violin that had finally found its bow. When he lifted his head and gazed into her eyes, she knew the truth before he even said it.

"It's you, Vex," he said hoarsely, and her breath left in a rush. "You're Laura."

Chapter Eight

Holy fucking shit.

Zhubaal couldn't believe it. After all this time and after all the false leads, he was looking at Laura. And he'd found her inside a flirty, brash, foul-mouthed *emim* who wasn't anything like the angel he'd pledged eternal faithfulness to. Not that he was going to complain. She could have been something far worse.

I've found her!

He dragged a ragged breath into his lungs and tried to let it all sink in. *Laura.* His heart thumped excitedly in his chest, but she didn't seem as thrilled. If anything, she seemed stunned, her body taut, her amethyst eyes glazed over.

"I know this must be a shock." The words fell out in a crazy rush. "And I know it sounds insane—"

"No, it doesn't." Shaking her head, she stepped away from him, and as much as he wanted to grab her, to hold onto her so she never left him again, he let her have her space. She hadn't had decades to prepare for this moment the way he had. But now that the moment was here, he realized that nothing could have prepared him for it. "I can feel it," she rasped. "God, I can feel *you.*" She swallowed. "It's freaking me out."

On impulse, he reached for her. "Laura—"

Wheeling out of his reach, she hissed. Actually *hissed* at him. "I'm Vex, not Laura." She jabbed an angry finger at him. "Let's get that straight right now. I don't know you, and you don't know me, and I don't care what kind of stupid damned oath Laura swore to you. *My* lips did not speak the words."

Ice filled his chest cavity. He'd fantasized about this meeting, and while he'd considered the possibility that she wouldn't remember, in no imagined scenario had he thought she might reject who she was.

Fool. Did you think she'd give up her entire life to run into your arms? He broke out in a cold sweat as a horrifying possibility popped into his head.

"Do you have a mate?" he blurted. "A lover?" Because he'd have to kill the guy.

She folded her arms across her chest and glared. "Do you really think I'd offer to pull a stick out of your ass if I had a boyfriend?"

"Well, since I don't have a stick up my ass, I figured the offer wasn't genuine."

She shrugged. "I'll try anything once."

He had a feeling she was messing with him, and it left him off balance. He was used to Vex's unpredictable behavior and odd sense of humor, but now that he knew it was coming from Laura, it was throwing him.

Except she's not Laura.

But she was in there somewhere. Vex had admitted it when she said she had feelings for him.

"Look," he said, still reeling from all of this, "let's go to my place and talk. I have sweet mead. You used to like it."

"*I* don't know what the fuck you're talking about," she said crisply. "And Laura was a dolt. That shit is nasty."

Son of a bitch. His dreams of being reunited with Laura had not gone like this.

"Z!" Razr jogged toward them, and Zhubaal hated that he was relieved to have something other than this awkward situation to focus on. "I summoned that contractor you asked for. He said he can get the human cable channels you want. He said HBO comes in fuzzy, but—"

"Hey," he said, clapping Razr on the back to shut him up before Vex figured out that Z'd asked for more channels after she complained. "Thanks. Tell him it's all good. And will you take

Laura—ah, Vex, to my quarters and stay with her? I need to talk to Azagoth."

Razr agreed, but Z didn't give Vex a chance to respond or argue. There was too much to say, and they both needed time for this to sink in. Especially Vex. He'd been searching for Laura for nearly a century, but obviously, she hadn't even known she was lost.

He should have expected that, should have expected how much it would hurt to find her and yet, somehow, to have lost her.

A knot of emotions tangled up inside him as he jogged to Azagoth's office. This should have been the best day of his life, but instead of being ecstatic, he was confused as hell, hurt, and angry.

It wasn't supposed to be like this. She was supposed to have remembered the oath, even if only on some subconscious level.

When he reached his boss's office, he threw open the door and strode into the center of the room. "You could have warned me."

"And you could have knocked." Azagoth sighed and looked up from the ledger he'd been writing in with a quill. "Warned you about what?"

"You know what," Z growled. "You could have told me that Vex is Laura."

Very slowly, Azagoth put down the pen and pegged him with a hard stare. "I told you Laura was inside Vex."

She's inside Vex. Okay, yeah, he'd said that. But it wasn't the same thing. "You said she was inside Vex. You didn't say she *was* Vex."

"Because she's *not* Vex. Vex is Vex. She *used* to be Laura."

"Dammit, Azagoth, you know what I mean." Z clenched his fists at his sides to keep from punching something that would get him turned into one of Azagoth's living statues. "You could have told me from the beginning so I didn't get blindsided, but you didn't, even though you knew."

"I *suspected*. I sensed that Vex's soul originated in Heaven. But it wasn't until I reached inside and touched it that I knew her soul was that of an Ipsylum, and there are very few of you."

"Why didn't you tell me, dammit? She was out for hours. Surely you could have found time to give me a, 'Hey, FYI, Vex and Laura are the same person.' I could have broken it to her without sounding insane and freaking her out."

Azagoth rose to his feet. "Does she have any memory of you?"

The question was like a blow to the heart. "No. Do you think it'll come back to her?" He tried not to hope, but he couldn't help but hold his breath as Azagoth walked around the desk and pulled a lever on the wall.

"I don't know," he said, as the wall panel slid back to reveal the cross-section of a tunnel. *Griminions* came from the right side of the tunnel, escorting souls through the portal on the left, but only after Azagoth had viewed each one. "Some people are gifted with soul-memory, some can access past-life memories through rituals or dreams, but others will never remember." He nodded approval as each soul passed, sending *griminions* through the tunnel in a steady stream.

Great. "So that's it? I'll always be a stranger to her?"

Azagoth looked at Z from over his shoulder and the soul parade halted. "Vex might never remember you, but her soul will." If Azagoth thought that was comforting, he was crazier than a ghastbat in the sunlight. "You're lucky she found her way here when she did. Jim Bob and Ricky Bobby saved her from one of Revenant's assassins."

Z's gut clenched. If the angels hadn't been there, he could have lost her. Again. And now he owed those two bastards. "She didn't say anything about that."

"She didn't know. They interrupted before the attack."

Damn. He'd forgotten that she would be in danger the moment she stepped outside of Sheoul-gra. "Can't you call Revenant or something?"

Azagoth snorted. "One does not simply *summon* the King of Hell." Z wondered if he'd be so la-de-da if it was Lilliana who was walking in the shadow of an executioner's ax.

"But you can contact him, right?"

Azagoth inclined his head. "I have ways."

"But you won't."

"I already have. He could be here by the time you get back from Los Angeles."

Of course. They still had to rid Vex of the evil soul that remained inside her. The thought that some vile demon had attached itself to her made him sick, and on the heels of that was anger and a desire to protect her at all costs.

"When do we leave?"

Azagoth produced a business card from out of his shirt pocket and flicked it into the air. Z caught it between two fingers.

"The address is on the card." Azagoth turned back to the soul tunnel, effectively dismissing him. "You leave now."

Chapter Nine

The journey to Beverly Hills via Harrowgates only took mere moments. Z would like to have flashed here, but his ability to travel in the blink of an eye was limited to places he already knew. Gates were almost as good though, invisible to humans and peppered all over the human and demon realms.

This particular gate opened up in a small, wooded park, and the moment Z and Vex stepped out, the bright sunshine nearly blinded him. How long had it been since he'd been anywhere but Sheoul?

Too long.

He generally avoided the human realm, not because he hated humans, but because they always reminded him of life before he lost his wings. He'd been free then. Well, as free as a warrior bound to his angelic Order and job could be, anyway. He'd gotten little time off, and he'd spent what free time he'd had with Laura. After he lost his wings and started working for Azagoth, he'd had just as little free time, and what he had was spent searching for Laura.

He glanced at her as they walked from the park toward the mansion where the demon they were going to see lived. She'd barely said two words to him since he'd picked her up from Razr and headed out. And didn't it just figure that now that Vex was finally behaving like Laura, he wanted Vex back. This sullen silence didn't suit her and only made the clack of her heels on the asphalt path more stark.

"Are you okay?" he asked as he guided her to a sidewalk that wound its way up a steep hill.

Vex sidestepped to avoid a low-hanging tree branch just off the path. "I don't know. This is a lot to take in." She glanced over at him. "You said Laura was Ipsylum. I'm still finding that hard to believe."

"She...*you*, didn't do well as a warrior. You didn't have the temperament for it."

She huffed. "Stop saying that. It wasn't me."

"Yes," he ground out, "it was. It was you before you were born as Vex. You were an angelic warrior, but not a very good one."

"All right," she said, her eyes flashing. "I'll play for now. I was Laura. So was the fact that I sucked as a warrior the reason I lost my wings?"

"Sort of," he said, ignoring her snippy tone. "You weren't built for violence. You were kind of like a lion who should have been a gazelle."

Vex frowned as they climbed a set of steps. "So how does a gentle gazelle get kicked out of Heaven?"

First, she'd been kicked out of the Ipsylum Order. But being an Ipsylum was more than just a job...it was truly a class of angel, and as much as Laura tried, she couldn't suppress instinct. And her instinct after being banished from not just her job but her family as well, was to rebel.

"She tried to fight the establishment," he said. "That rarely goes well." Not when the establishment consisted of a bunch of douchebag Archangels, Dominions, and Thrones who wanted to control everything. Z had to admit that as much as he'd loved Heaven, there was much more freedom in the human and demon realms.

Assuming one hadn't pledged loyalty to anyone. Like Azagoth.

It wasn't that Azagoth was a bad boss. Far from it. He was demanding but fair, cruel to enemies, but loyal to those he cared about. And the dude held a grudge. Hell, he'd only recently let Hades off the hook for something that had happened thousands of years ago. Azagoth's realm was his main priority, second only to Lilliana, and if your needs didn't square with that, too bad. If they did, he was happy to let you have whatever you wanted.

"So what happened to me?" She eyeballed him, a little more interested and less hostile now. "And how old was I?"

"We had just celebrated our fortieth name days when you were kicked out of the Ipsylum Order and joined a rebel group of angels who have been working to shift the balance of power in Heaven for thousands of years." He'd begged her to not get involved, but she'd been sure she could operate within the rebel faction without being caught.

"Now *that* sounds like me," she said with an impish grin that was pure Vex without a trace of Laura. "But why did she do it?"

"Archangels are in charge right now, but that hasn't always been the case," he said, watching a white delivery truck turn up the drive to the mansion. The sign on the side said, "Devilish Delights," and if the malevolent vibe coming off it was any indication, whatever was in that truck was bad news and not delightful at all. "Thrones used to rule the roost, with Dominions always struggling to gain more power and more control over everyone's lives, angel and human. But during the great Angel Rebellion, when Satan was ultimately cast out, Archangels took the opportunity to frame Thrones and Dominions as the bad guys, and they took over. Now there's a unified faction of angels of all Orders who want to overthrow the Archangels."

Vex rubbed her arm absently, and he wondered if the evil soul inside her was stirring. He'd given her another dose of suppressant before they left, but Azagoth had warned them that each dose was less effective than the one before it. "What does all of that have to do with Ipsylum?"

"I told you that Ipsylum are Heaven's special forces, but they're also Archangels' swords. When the other warrior angels are battling evil around the human realm, Ipsylum are battling evil within the angel ranks. So when an Ipsylum goes rogue, the Archangels act fast and with no mercy. You were caught plotting with the rebels before a year went by. Frankly, I'm surprised all you lost was your wings."

She frowned. "Were you...were we still together?"

He swallowed hard as the memories assaulted him. "Even as I held you in my arms after your wings were severed, you told me you loved me." Angels had dragged him away from her, but he'd fought so hard they'd had to chain him and bind his wings. It had taken years to find her again, but he'd been too late. She was dead, and he spent decades hunting the bastards who had killed her.

"It must have been hard for you."

It had been devastating. "Hard enough for me to lose my wings and family over it."

A warm breeze mussed her hair, creating spiky peaks he wanted to smooth with his palm. So very different from Laura's long blonde tresses, and he wasn't so sure it was a bad thing. "You really loved me...ah, her."

Okay, yeah, it was time to revert back to the *her, she*, and *you* part of the story. "She was my world," he said softly. Now he had to figure out how to fit Vex into that world.

But what if she didn't fit? The very thought put a knot in the pit of his gut.

"What was she like?"

He smiled. "She was beautiful," he said, but that didn't take away anything from Vex, who was stunning in a different way. Hell, he couldn't keep his eyes off the narrow strip of exposed flesh between the top of her boots and the hem of her skirt. Every time a breeze ruffled the pleats, he caught a glimpse of her fine, toned ass and silk underwear. "She had blonde hair and blue eyes, rare among Ipsylum. And she had the most amazing wings." All Ipsylum had the same deep burgundy wings, but hers had been tipped with silver, as if they'd been dipped in glitter. "We were born in the same year, so we grew up together."

They'd done everything together, from learning to fight to learning to fly. Thankfully she'd been better at flying than fighting, because more than once her agility and speed in the air had saved her life when her pathetic battle skills failed.

He stopped at the gated entrance to a massive mansion. To humans, this was the residence of Rowan Arch, a rich, influential Hollywood producer. But to demons, this was the lair of a powerful fallen angel who, while in the human realm, was capable of commanding human and demon spirits to do his bidding. But his true gift was his ability to drain power from souls to strengthen his own abilities. Azagoth hoped he could weaken the soul inside Vex enough for him to remove it.

"How do we get inside?"

"Rowan installed his own Harrowgate."

She whistled low and long. "He must be a serious badass with a shit-ton of money or human sacrifices or something. They don't give out private Harrowgates to just anyone."

No, they didn't. He looked around until he saw the telltale shimmer of a gate against the backdrop of the stone perimeter wall. "There."

The gate dropped them directly inside Rowan's manor. At least, he assumed he was inside the manor. They'd materialized in a huge, cold room more suited to a slaughterhouse than a rich dude's McMansion. Meat hooks hung from the ceiling, bloodstains darkened the concrete, and at least a dozen demons and humans waited for an audience with Rowan behind an iron fence on both sides of the room.

Azagoth had assured Zhubaal that he and Vex wouldn't have to wait, and he hoped his boss was right. He didn't want to be here any longer than he had to.

Ramreel demons armed with crossbows and swords stood watch near the double doors on the far side of the gymnasium-sized room, and two pasty-skinned, eyeless Silas demons roamed around, their creepy presence keeping the other waiting demons in line.

Vex leaned over and said quietly, "Whatever you do, don't kill anyone."

"Why not?"

Her gaze shot around the room, and he got the impression she was logging every weapon, cataloguing every individual, preparing for the worst. He could almost believe that she'd retained their Ipsylum training, except that Laura had never been this observant or prepared.

"Because the souls will jump inside me before Azagoth's *griminions* can get here."

Ah, good point.

"Also," she added, "if the bitchface inside me possesses my body...kill me."

He turned his head so fast his neck cracked. "What?"

Stopping in the middle of the room, she grabbed his arm and yanked him close. "I can't go through it again. If Azagoth can't exorcise the demon, kill me." She squeezed his biceps, digging her nails into his skin. "Don't make me beg. If you love Laura as much as you say you do, you won't want her to do the things this demon will force her to do. Please."

Please don't let them kill me.

He closed his eyes, once again hearing the words Laura had spoken to him while they'd waited for the Archangels' judgment the day she lost her wings. He hadn't let her die then, and he wouldn't now.

Opening his eyes, he pinned her with a hard stare. "Azagoth won't fail," he swore.

"If he does—"

"He won't."

She opened her mouth to argue more, he was sure, but snapped it shut as a Ramreel approached them, his armor clanking as loudly as his hoofed feet.

"Mr. Arch will see you now." He focused his small eyes on Vex, and Z bristled. "Female. I would extract payment...from you."

"Payment?" Vex produced a blade from who-knew-where and held it casually at her hip. Damn, she was fast. Laura would have cut herself. And she wouldn't be standing there, shifting her weight into an attack stance and readying for a fight. Z held back, prepared to obliterate this asshole now that he had his powers in the human realm but wanting to see how Vex handled it first. "What kind of payment? And for what?"

"For allowing you through the Harrowgate," he said, his gray lips turning up in a grotesque sneer. "There was a sign at the entrance."

"Yeah, well, we missed the sign," Z said, "so back the fuck off."

"I will have payment." The Ramreel, a good two feet taller than Zhubaal, swung his massive head back around to Vex and stomped his hoof on the floor. "You will only scream for a minute."

Z had always prided himself on his self-control, but both pride and self-control got tossed out the window when Laura was threatened. Vex had warned him not to kill anyone, but he welcomed the rush of power that funneled to his fingertips, ready to burst from him in a searing stream of hellfire.

His leathery wings flared high as he stepped between the Ramreel and Vex, his fingers flexing with the desire to destroy.

"Touch her," he said, his voice scraping gravel, "and I will rend you limb from limb and then fuck your dying corpse as you bleed out."

The Ramreel's hand tightened on the giant mace he carried, and

Z wondered if the sheep-brained idiot was stupid enough to take a swing. Just as Z prepared to take a pre-emptive strike, the demon shrugged and lumbered off.

"Wow," Vex breathed.

Zhubaal nodded. "Yeah, powerful stuff, huh?"

"Well, it's quite the visual." She flipped the blade between her fingers before sliding it into her boot. "I mean, I'm assuming you won't take the time to strip him before you draw and quarter him, which means that to fuck his dying body, you'll have to take off his bloody pants. That'll be really awkward, you know?" He stared at her, almost unable to believe this was truly Laura. "What? I'm just saying that to make a threat effective, you've got to think it through."

"It was off the cuff," he said, exasperated.

"Clearly."

He ground his teeth. Vex's new name suited her. Just as he was about to tell her that, the double doors at the other end of the room opened, and a human in a tuxedo beckoned them inside.

"You ready?"

There was a fierceness in her gaze that he couldn't help but admire, so he was taken aback when she shook her head. "I don't know."

"What do you mean you don't know?" he asked, incredulous. "This might be your only chance to get rid of the demon you're carrying around inside you."

"And it'll also make me beholden to Azagoth for the rest of my life."

"But you'll be alive," he pointed out. "He'll protect you from Revenant's forces."

The look she gave him, one of sadness and maybe a touch of revulsion, made his heart sink. "But what is life if you're bound to someone all the way to your soul?" she asked quietly.

He stiffened. "You mean like we are to each other?"

"Exactly." She rubbed her arms as if cold, but it was about a thousand degrees in the room. "I can feel you, Zhubaal. I feel so much love for you, but it's not mine. It's hers. It's Laura's. So you can understand why I can't enter into a contract like Azagoth's so lightly." She met his gaze with a steely one of her own. "Not when I wish I could break the one with you."

Chapter Ten

The devastation in Zhubaal's expression tore Vex apart. He didn't deserve what she'd said, but it was the truth. She was still reeling from everything that had happened in the last couple of days, and she suspected she'd still be reeling tomorrow. And the next day. And the next week, month, year...

I was an angel who pledged my eternal, everlasting love to the male standing beside me.

No, *Laura* had done that. Vex wasn't that stupid.

"Are you coming, or not?" The elderly tuxedo guy managed to look bored and annoyed at the same time as he stood in the doorway.

Zhubaal's expression was cold when he turned to her, and her stomach lurched. She'd hurt him deeply enough for him to shut down, and she wondered if Laura had ever done the same thing. Somehow, she doubted it.

"Well?" he asked, his voice as chilly as his gaze. "Would you rather work for Azagoth or take your chances with the demon inside you and Revenant's forces?"

Obviously, she had to choose Azagoth. She just didn't like it, and she wanted to at least feel as if she had some control in the matter.

She started toward Tux, relieved when she heard Zhubaal's heavy footsteps behind her.

The chamber they entered was nothing like Vex would have expected. This guy was some sort of super wizard or something, so she figured his lair would look like a movie cliché...the way most sorcerers' lairs really looked.

But Rowan had money and taste, and the room they entered could have been a museum of demonic art and artifacts. Haunting paintings by noted demon and even angelic artists lined the walls, and the shelves were practically sagging under the weight of stone statuettes, clay masks from various demon tribes, and carvings made from bones. Even the floor rugs had been woven in various styles and from various materials depending on the maker's species and culture.

If the chamber wasn't what Vex expected, Rowan was exactly what she'd expect from a fallen angel. Tall, dark, and handsome. Sure, his hair was platinum blond and his eyes were pale blue, but damn, the darkness emanating from him was intoxicating. It definitely made SuperEvil stir, sending a warm buzz to the tip of every nerve ending.

When she looked over at Z, she could tell he felt Rowan's power as well. His eyes gleamed with bloodlust and his hand had fallen to the sword at his side, as if he was ready to do battle.

She shivered in forbidden delight. A battle between two fallen angels would be something to see.

"You're turned on." Zhubaal's voice, low and so close to her ear she nearly jumped, went through her like a purr.

"Does that disgust you?"

"No." For some reason, he sounded mad, like he wanted to be disgusted but wasn't.

"Hello." Rowan, dressed in a black sweater and khakis, moved toward them so smoothly he glided. "I have been waiting for you."

"For what, ten minutes?" Z asked.

Rowan blinked before giving Zhubaal a wary once-over. "Yes." He smiled, flashing fangs. "Azagoth sent word that you are in need of this." He held up a vial of black liquid.

"And that is?" she asked.

"It will force the soul inside you to the surface, where Azagoth will be able to exorcise it without killing you."

Zhubaal paced around the room, hand still on the hilt of his sword as he studied the decor. "Why is this potion necessary?"

Rowan's smile made SuperEvil vibrate with desire, and Vex

clenched her teeth, concentrating on keeping the demon down. "Because Vex has the soul of an angel but the body of a lesser being. That allows some of the oldest, most evil demons to access an incredibly powerful soul and cement themselves to those who are mistakenly called, "living."

"Mistakenly?" She snorted. "I'm quite alive, thank you."

He laughed. "Ours are borrowed bodies, subject to decay and death. Souls are our true forms, solid in Heaven and in Sheoul-gra. But the Dark Lord will one day rule the demon and human realms, where all souls will be solid, eternal, and subject to great suffering."

SuperEvil felt such pleasure at his words that Vex nearly gasped at the flood of orgasmic sensation at her core. Somehow she managed to offer a sarcastic smile. "Gee, yes, that sounds great. Now, how does the potion work?"

"You will drink it, but only in Azagoth's presence." He handed it to her, and she was surprised that it was hot enough to be uncomfortable in her hand. "The demon inside you will react according to the species it identifies with, and you will have no way to control it. Azagoth will be your only hope of stopping it."

Zhubaal cursed under his breath. "The demon is a succubus."

Rowan laughed. "Then Azagoth can have some fun while he's...taking her."

A growl erupted, a sound Vex could only describe as something being dragged against its will from the pits of hell, and suddenly Zhubaal was in the other fallen angel's face, the tip of his sword jammed into Rowan's throat.

"You will not speak that way about her." Black veins rose to the surface of Zhubaal's skin as his anger brought out the *fallen* part of the angel in him.

SuperEvil began to vibrate violently under her skin as her excitement level rose. A hum blasted Vex's eardrums, growing so loud she could no longer hear either Zhubaal or Rowan, who seemed to be in a fang-ridden snarl-fest.

It was so hot.

No! It wasn't hot. It was dangerous and violent and...oh, God, heat flushed her body and flowed in electric currents to her breasts and pelvis. Desire overwhelmed her, and she ripped off her top before she knew what was happening.

Stop! But she couldn't. The soul was taking over, wrestling control away from her while using the furious energy created by the two fallen angels to do it.

"Stop," she gasped, but the males didn't seem to hear. Zhubaal had Rowan up against the wall now, and there was blood on the floor and on Rowan's face and all she wanted to do was tear off the rest of her clothes and put her naked body between them.

We'll fuck them both. SuperEvil's voice clanged in her ears. *We'll hurt them, make them like it, and when it's done, one will kill the other.*

Vex tried to scream, tried to warn Zhubaal. But she was drowning in a pool of oily malevolence, unable to surface, and all she could do was scream inside her head as SuperEvil held her under and set its sights on Zhubaal.

Chapter Eleven

The smell of blood and danger hung heavy in the air, electrifying it, giving Zhubaal a power punch of adrenaline that jacked him into battle mode. Rowan hissed through bloody fangs, a happy result of Zhubaal's right hook.

Oh, this had only been a scuffle so far, two alpha males testing each other, but Zhubaal knew where he stood. Rowan was strong, a fallen angel with the kind of power that would make even very evil demons piss themselves.

But Z was stronger, and Rowan knew it.

"You care far too much for the female," Rowan gritted out. "It will be your downfall."

That was probably true, but it didn't mean Z wanted to hear it. Especially not from some sleazeball who promised fools fame and fortune if they gave up their firstborns or their mothers or whatever it was Rowan asked for in return.

"And you care too much about running your mouth," Zhubaal said. "That will be *your* downfall." He pressed upward with his blade, puncturing the delicate skin just under the bastard's chin. The fresh stream of blood made his cock hard and his balls throb...no, wait.

He frowned, confused by the powerful sexual need coursing through him. Rowan seemed as perplexed, and they both gasped when a sexual wave crashed into them in an almost physical blow that knocked the air from his lungs. What the—

Fuck.

He wheeled around, and his mouth dropped open. Vex was

sauntering toward them, naked except for her thigh-high boots, her hands cupping her full breasts as her thumbs flicked across the nipples. Holy shit, it was the most erotic yet inappropriately timed thing he'd ever seen.

"Your blood," she purred. "I want to bathe in it while I fuck you."

His entire body jerked in shock. *Oh…shit.* The succubus had possessed Vex. He'd failed to protect her, and now she was paying for it.

Panic made his breath burn in his throat. "Vex, listen to me."

"She can't hear you." Succubus Vex cocked her head. "But how sweet...I can feel her love for you. She'll be pissed when she finds out your cock was inside me and that *I* gave you the best fuck of your life." She slid her hand between her legs, and next to him Rowan made a sound of lusty approval.

Very calmly, and without even looking, Z shoved his sword through the male's belly. It wouldn't kill him, but it should take the edge off his libido. And if that didn't do it, castration would.

Rowan shouted in agony and stumbled backward, his feet slipping in his own blood. The doors burst open and his army of Ramreels and Silas demons poured inside, weapons ready.

Time to go. He darted toward Vex, but she spun away, grabbing a dagger from her pile of clothes in a fluid sweep.

"Vex!"

In a graceful surge, she danced between several of the demons, slashing and stabbing, somehow avoiding their blows. Three fell, holding their guts as they spilled out of their bellies.

Son of a bitch, she was good. She'd eviscerated two of those guys with the heels of her boots.

A Silas swung at Vex with a studded club while her back was turned. Z flashed in, catching the bastard by the wrist before the blow landed. With a quick twist, he snapped the demon's arm and flung him into a gang of guards running toward them.

"Gotta go, Vex!" They had to escape this clusterfuck before one of the dying demons croaked and got sucked into her. He snatched the potion from off the floor where she'd dropped it before seizing her around the waist as he flashed them out of there.

At least, flashing out of there was the plan. It didn't happen.

Instead, momentum launched them into the wall.

"Shit!" He cursed as his shoulder wrenched hard in the collision. "The place is warded!" He should have known. Rowan would have to be an idiot to not ward his lair from unauthorized entrance and exit.

Vex wrenched around and punched him in the jaw. His head snapped back, but he held onto her as he bulldozed through the guards, sending them scattering with a blast of searing energy that shot out of him in a three-hundred-and-sixty-degree shockwave.

"Release me!" the Vex-thing screamed, clawing and biting as he half-dragged, half-carried her to the exit.

He ignored her, blasting two more demons with enough juice to blow them apart and throw bone shrapnel into the poor bastards who had been waiting to see Rowan. Vex hurled herself away from him, but in a stroke of luck, she slammed into the door, shoving it open and giving him a chance to catch her before the spirits of the demons he'd just killed got drawn into her.

Swinging her into his arms, he flashed out of there, but as he did, he caught a glimpse of Rowan out of the corner of his eye and felt the bite of a lightning strike against his hip. His yelp of pain disappeared behind them as they materialized on the landing pad inside Sheoul-gra, his status as a resident allowing him to bypass the ward that kept everyone else from flashing in or out.

Razr was there almost instantly, sprinting across the courtyard. He shouted at a nearby Memitim, who darted toward Azagoth's palace.

"Don't touch her." Still struggling to hold onto her, Zhubaal snapped his wings around her, shielding her from all eyes but his.

Azagoth flashed in, his eyes swallowed entirely by inky blackness. "The potion," he rumbled. "She needs to drink it."

Z couldn't do much with his arms wrapped around Vex, so he flipped the vial into the air with his fingers. Azagoth caught it, popped the stopper, and forced the contents into her mouth. He snapped her jaw shut and stepped back, somehow keeping her from opening her mouth to spit out the potion even from a distance.

"Swallow," he growled, and Vex snarled and thrashed, but obeyed. Azagoth's black marble eyes rolled up to meet Z's gaze. "Hold her steady and put away your wings."

Neither was easy to do, but he stashed his wings and held her tight, her body pressed against his. Still, she was freakishly strong and squirmy, and there was no way he could do this by himself.

But there was also no way he was allowing Razr—or anyone—to touch her. She rocked her head back, smashing her skull into his nose. Pain shattered his face, and she did it again, layering the agony with another skillful blow. And another.

Son of a...*fuck*! A stab of red-hot fire went through his foot and up his leg. *She stabbed me in the foot with the heel of her fucking boot.* The thought barely had time to form before her other boot came at him. He kicked his leg back and she stomped the ground hard, missing his boot by a hair.

"Azagoth," he hissed. "Hurry!"

"Hold her still," Azagoth roared.

On impulse, he bared his fangs and bit into her throat. He'd used his fallen angel fangs in battle before, and he supposed this counted as a fight. But this was different. Always before, the taste of his enemy's blood enraged him, fueling the violence and his strength. But Vex's blood energized him. Aroused him. He knew that, for many fallen angels, feeding wasn't a necessity, but its application for pleasure was well known. By everyone but Zhubaal.

Until now.

As Vex's silky blood flowed over his tongue, he felt her relax. It was subtle, a mere drop of one shoulder and the tiniest shift of her head to allow him more access, but it was enough to give Azagoth the break he needed.

His fist punched through her chest. She screamed, and if Z's mouth hadn't been locked on her throat, he'd have screamed, too. Now he knew why Azagoth had wanted him to wait in the hall last time. Seeing her agony, *feeling* her agony, tore him to shreds. Laura had been killed this way. Vex had suffered through it in Azagoth's office and now, again, while Z was letting it happen.

Seething hatred for the one hurting her rose up, and although it made no sense, he wanted to kill Azagoth for this. His wings shot out from his back as if they had minds of their own and his fangs pulsed as desire to kill the thing causing Vex's pain consumed him.

Azagoth roared, and all around them the air went still. The trees closest to them exploded as if they'd been struck by lightning, and the water in the courtyard fountain blasted upward.

Rearing back, Azagoth ripped a cloudy, shapeless mass from Vex's chest. As if the realm was breathing a sigh of relief, everything returned to normal, and Azagoth flashed away with the succubus's spirit.

Vex collapsed against him, and he scooped her into his arms. Very gently, he wrapped his wings around her, shielding her from the view of the Memitim and Unfallen who had gathered to watch the show.

He glanced over at Razr. "I'm taking her to my quarters. See that someone brings some food. Maybe some broth."

Razr bowed and took off as Z headed toward the mansion. He could have flashed to his quarters, but he didn't want to give up even a second of holding Vex like this.

Moaning, she wrapped one arm around his shoulder to help support herself.

"Is it over?" she whispered. "Did I shame myself?"

A chill sliced through Z. She'd asked the same question after her wings had been severed. She'd laid in his arms, bleeding and quaking, worried that, in her haze of pain and fear, she'd sobbed or pleaded for a deal or begged for mercy.

"No," he said hoarsely, just as he had all those years ago. But this time he didn't have to lie. "You didn't."

She smiled weakly up at him. "I'm naked."

Laughing, he pulled his wings tighter around her as they mounted the steps. "I noticed."

"Did you like it?" She rested her head against his neck, and the intimacy of it made his heart lurch.

"Except for the gaping hole in your chest."

"What?" She struggled to look down at herself but he caught her chin with his thumb and lifted her face to his.

"I'm kidding." Tenderly, because she was probably sore all over, he pressed a lingering kiss into her hair. He loved how her spiky locks tickled his lips. "Well, you did have a gaping hole, but it's healed."

"Good." She yawned. "Make love to me."

He missed a step, stumbled, and flashed them to his quarters before they did a face plant. Standing in the middle of his palatial living room, he stared down at her. "What?"

"We've waited a long time, don't you think?"

Holy shit, was she serious? His dick believed her, and if he didn't put her down in the next couple of seconds, she'd know it. "A hundred and forty years." And two months, three weeks, and six days, counting from the year they were born, of course.

She gave him an impish grin. "I was thinking a couple of days."

Folding away his wings, he laughed again. Before Vex came into his life, how long had it been since he'd laughed?

Over a hundred years, probably.

"Come on," he said, holding her tighter as he strode down the hall to one of the five bedrooms. Azagoth wouldn't earn any accolades for providing lavish living wages, but he was generous with the perks. "You need to rest and finish healing."

She tried to hide another yawn behind her hand. "Do not."

"Do." He took her straight to the shower, where, fully clothed, he held her under the hot, cleansing spray. She didn't seem to mind, merely settled her head against his chest as the blood and the day's events flowed down the drain.

After drying her, he took her to his bed, leaving a trail of water from his soaked clothes behind. The king-sized four-poster took up only a small part of the master bedroom, most of which was a waste of space. The reading nook was cozy, he supposed, but he rarely had the time to use it. Until now, all of his free time had been spent looking for Laura. The hot tub, built seamlessly into the polished white marble floor and fed by hot springs from Sheoul, filled another nook, but again, it went mostly unused.

"Nice place." She winced as she burrowed under the covers, reaffirming his conviction that she needed to finish healing. "Do you know what kinds of things we could do in that hot tub?" As he drew the comforter up to cover her shoulders, she winked. "I can snorkel."

His cock twitched as his wet pants got really fucking tight. "Maybe later," he croaked. "I'm going to change clothes and get you some ice water—"

Her fingers closed around his wrist. "Stay," she said softly. "Please. Lay down with me."

There was no reason for his reluctance, but he hesitated anyway.

Only a couple of hours ago she'd wished she had never exchanged vows of loyalty with him, and now she wanted him to stay with her when she was exhausted, in pain, and vulnerable.

We're both vulnerable. And really fucked up.

Vex loved him with Laura's love. He loved Laura, but how much of Vex was Laura?

He wondered if Underworld General Hospital had mental health specialists on staff, because they both might need an appointment.

Vex squeezed his wrist, prompting an answer. "Yeah. I'll stay." He looked down at his dripping clothes. "I have to change first."

"Just take off your clothes. We can be naked together."

His heart gave an excited thump, which was followed by an immediate breakout of a cold sweat. What if he couldn't control himself? Oh, he wasn't going to attack her, but he wasn't sure he could resist her, either. She might have been kidding about them waiting for a long time, but he hadn't been joking at all.

"Oh, criminy," she mumbled. Her heavy lids closed, and her voice began to fade as she spoke. "Have you always been this uptight?"

"No," he said as he shed his clothes, doing his best to keep turned so she couldn't see his trembling fingers. Or his erection. "I used to be worse."

That wasn't a joke, either.

His heart was pounding as he climbed under the covers with her. He'd never been naked with a female before, and his body was telling him all about it. His skin was so hypersensitive he could feel every individual thread in the eighteen-hundred-thread count sheets. His lungs were pushing air in and out like he needed oxygen to run a marathon. And his cock was as hard as the marble hot tub he never used.

Although Vex didn't open her eyes again and her breathing settled instantly into a deep, easy pattern, she slid her hand across the mattress to find his. His heart sang.

His Laura was home.

Chapter Twelve

Vex would really like it if the next time she woke up she wasn't in a strange place, in a strange bed. At least this time she woke up alone in her body. There were no parasitic souls inside her. Just...peace.

Smiling, she rolled over.

And bumped into a warm body.

Startled, she opened her lids and found herself looking into the most gorgeous eyes she'd ever seen. "Zhubaal," she whispered.

He shifted, propping himself up on one elbow. "Hey." He reached out and brushed a knuckle over her cheek with so much tenderness she nearly wept. "How are you feeling?"

"My chest hurts a little, but otherwise, good." Her smile faltered. "But I don't remember anything after—" She broke off, horrified as the memories filtered back into her brain. "Oh, God, the succubus possessed me."

"It's okay. It wasn't for long."

"Did I...did I hurt anyone?"

"Only scumbags." He snorted. "And damn, woman, I'd want you on my battlefield any day."

His compliment gave her warm fuzzies. "Bet you never said that to Laura."

"No," he said, and the troubled expression on his face made her regret her words. He still loved Laura, and Vex definitely was not her. Well, technically she was, but not in any way it mattered.

"So," she said as she tentatively trailed her finger over the back of his hand. "Where do we go from here?"

"You," he said, "are going to soak in the hot tub. It'll be good for your aching muscles. I'm going to get us breakfast."

She glanced over at the tub that could easily hold Zhubaal and ten girlfriends, and a twinge of jealousy tweaked her. Actually, no, it was a giant wave of jealousy, and it crashed over her like a tsunami.

Before she could stop herself, she blurted, "How many females have you had in that thing?"

He jerked, taken aback. "None."

Oh, right. That crazy vow of loyalty. Still, she blinked, amazed that he hadn't taken advantage of all the delights to be had in a steaming pool with bubbling jets. "You have some seriously amazing willpower," she mused. "Because I'd make daily use of that sucker."

A shadow passed over his expression, and damn it, she just realized what she'd said. He'd been faithful to Laura all this time, and in this weird, twisted reality he lived in, she was Laura, and she *hadn't* been faithful.

Way to jam a dagger straight into his heart.

"Hey," she said, reaching for him. "I didn't mean it."

He shrugged off her touch, and in the shadowy light from a lamp in the reading nook, she saw his expression turn savage. "How many males have you been with?"

No, this wasn't uncomfortable at all. "Zhubaal, I don't think—"

"How. Many."

Annoyed at his tone and the question, she sat up, not caring that the sheet fell away to expose her breasts. "That," she said firmly, "is none of your business. My life before I met you was my own. It's still my own. It was your choice to be celibate for all this time, and it was my choice to enjoy myself. I like sex, and I'm not ashamed of it. If you can't deal with that, it's your problem, not mine. Now," she said, whipping the sheet away to reveal her entire naked body, "do you want to make up for lost time?"

As expected, she'd just taken the edge off his anger. His eyes shot wide, going even wider as she spread her legs, just a little, to reveal a hint of her arousal. She was wet already, had been since she got to Sheoul-gra, and now she knew why. Oh, yes, she loved sex, but she'd never been drawn to any male as quickly and as feverishly as she had been to Zhubaal. Her healthy sex drive combined with the already established familiarity thanks to her past-life history, had made her want to have him inside her almost from the second she saw him.

She couldn't stand it anymore. Spreading her legs wide, she beckoned to him with one hand while sliding the other down her stomach. She watched him as her fingers found her cleft, loving how his nostrils flared and the veins in his neck stood out with every hard swallow.

"I'm waiting," she said in a teasing, singsong tone as she rubbed her hand back and forth over her smooth mound.

The blatant hunger in his expression fed her own, and she reached for him, intent on pulling him down on top of her, but to her shock, he reared back and scrambled off the bed. He stood next to it, his eyes wild, his chest heaving. Alarm rang through her, and she sat up.

"Zhubaal, what's wrong?"

Jamming his hand frantically through his hair, he shook his head. "This isn't how it was supposed to be."

"How what's not supposed to be?" Before the question was even out of her mouth, she knew. "This is about Laura."

He nodded. "I know you don't want to hear that—"

"It's okay," she said softly, surprising herself. Laura had proven to be a big pain in the ass, but she had been a huge part of Zhubaal's life, and Vex needed to accept it.

And he had to accept that she wasn't Laura.

No, she didn't know where this relationship was headed, but she did know she wanted to explore it. How could she not? She'd never felt as though anything was missing in her life, but the emotions he'd awakened in her couldn't be contained. They had a connection she couldn't deny, a connection that had been missing with every sexual partner she'd ever had.

Maybe that was why she'd never gotten serious with anyone. There'd never been even the most minimal connection. Maybe the stupid vow *had* affected her in this life. Because no matter how great the guy was, she'd never been able to make a relationship last for more than a couple of weeks. Even then, she'd only hung in for the sex. Emotions had never come into play.

"It's not okay." He scrubbed his hand over his face. "We were cheated out of everything we wanted. Our first time wasn't supposed to be like this."

She rolled her eyes. "Let me guess. You and Laura probably planned to make love for the first time on marshmallow clouds cradled by rainbows while listening to harp music." His defiant glare said she was pretty close to being on target. "We don't have clouds or rainbows here, but we have a big bed, all the right parts, and I take an herb that prevents pregnancy, so why don't you tell me what's really going on?" His nervous swallow made something in her brain click, and without thinking, she blurted, "Zhubaal...are you...a virgin?"

Cheeks bright with embarrassment, he averted his gaze and nodded. "She wanted to wait until we were wed."

This isn't how it was supposed to be.

Of course it wasn't. He'd expected his first time to be with someone inexperienced. Probably shy. And here Vex was, ready to get raunchy and do things that would probably have given Saint Laura the vapors.

Well, there was plenty of time to be naughty. Right now, Zhubaal needed a gentler touch. And she wanted his first time to be special. She couldn't be Laura, but she could at least give him that.

She'd be *honored* to give him that.

Slowly, so he wouldn't feel trapped, she wrapped herself in the blanket at the foot of the bed and scooted over so she was on her knees on the mattress in front of him. They were equal height like this, allowing her to look him directly in the eyes.

"Now," she said softly, "tell me how it was supposed to be." Holding the blanket closed with one hand, she cupped his cheek with the other. He stiffened, but at least he didn't pull away. She leaned in, until she was a mere inch from his lips. "I assume you planned to start by kissing?"

He hesitated, and her gut dropped. She wanted this more than she'd ever wanted anything. Her first time had been a drunken fumble-fest with Brad Fisher, captain of the high school football team, in the backseat of his car, and she'd never really taken it slow with anyone. She wasn't one for cuddling or being romantic, and she'd always been more about the goal than the journey to get there.

But for the first time, the journey *was* the goal.

"Yes," he finally said, closing the distance between their mouths. His kiss was unsure at first, so delicate that his lips could have been butterfly wings. But as she melted into him, he deepened the kiss, his tongue sweeping along the seam of her lips. Like a total pro, he slid his hand around to her neck, caressing her skin, kneading her into putty.

"And then?" she murmured against his mouth.

He nipped her bottom lip, the pinch of pain shooting straight to her core and making her moan. "And then I'd strip her."

Pulling back, he peeled her fingers from the blanket. It fell away, pooling around her knees. His gaze raked her, and she held her breath. What did he think of her? Did her body match up to Laura's? Shit. She wasn't used to being self-conscious, but then, she wasn't used to being reincarnated, either.

"You're so beautiful," he said, his voice as thick with need as his cock, which jutted upward in a graceful arc that made her mouth water.

"Now what?" *Please say you want me to take you in my mouth.*

"Kiss me again." Somehow, that was even better, and her heart fluttered with happiness. He stepped into her until his knees hit the mattress and his erection pressed into her belly, her breasts into his chest. "Like you mean it."

She slanted her mouth over his. "I mean it," she whispered, wrapping her arms around his shoulders.

He kissed back, hard, his tongue pushing past her lips and teeth to thrust against hers. One arm came around her back to brace her as he lifted her up and laid them both down on the bed so he was half-on, half-off of her, one big leg tucked between hers. All the while, he kissed her senseless, never breaking contact. But as he gripped her hip to tug them closer together, he raised his head and looked down at her, his gaze glowing with need.

"I want to explore you," he said, and she grinned, desire spiraling wildly through her. Now he was talking.

Still, she didn't want to come across as too forward...not yet, anyway. She'd definitely introduce him to her adventurous, uninhibited side, but later.

She slid her hand over the firm muscles in his back to the even firmer muscles in his ass and gave him a playful squeeze. "Explore all you want."

Beneath his skin, he quivered. God, she loved his reactions to her. Loved how he closed his eyes and inhaled deeply, as if grounding himself in this moment before dropping his mouth to her throat. He nuzzled her, kissing and licking, as he cupped her breast in one hand.

She arched into his touch, telling him without words that he didn't need to treat her like a fragile piece of crystal. He got the hint, caressing her breast with more pressure, flicking and pinching her nipple with his fingers as he kissed a hot path from her neck to collar bone. His hips rolled slowly, rubbing his erection against her hip, mimicking what she wanted him to do between her legs.

Her sex throbbed at the thought, and she bit back a growl of frustration. Then he sucked her breast into his mouth, and she sighed with pleasure. Gently, he swirled his tongue around her swollen nipple as he shifted to cup both breasts, massaging and stroking.

"That's so good," she moaned, and he smiled against her skin.

He worked his way lower, kissing as he went. But as his lips found the hollow of her belly, he slowed, as if he wasn't sure how she'd react if he kept going. To help him along, she shifted and spread her legs so he was forced to settle between them.

Taking her cue, he dragged his tongue down until he reached the top of her cleft. His hands trembled as he wrapped them around her thighs and pulled her open for his hungry gaze. The tips of his fangs peeked out from his parted lips, and she suddenly wanted him to bite her. She'd slept with a guy with fangs once, but she hadn't allowed him to penetrate her with them.

Zhubaal could use his any way he wanted to.

He licked his lips, his eyes feasting on her waiting flesh. "I'm not sure..."

"Yes," she said quickly. "You're sure. You can do it. *Please* do it." God, his tongue was *made* to do it.

His smoldering gaze snapped up to hers. "Oh, I plan to." He flicked his tongue over a fang, and her breath left her in a rush. "I'm just not sure she would have let me."

Laura was a fucking fool. "I'll let you do anything you want," she murmured, and then she lost her voice as he lowered his mouth to her core and his warm breath bathed her in shivery sensation.

His tongue slipped out to taste her so delicately she barely felt it. It was so sweet the way he was exploring so gently, but she wasn't made of eggshells. Still, this was his first time, and he needed to find his way.

He kissed her lightly, maddeningly lightly. His lips feathered over her, nibbling but not tasting. He scooted down so he could adjust his hands to lift her hips, spreading her wider as her legs fell open. When his lips touched her again, it was with another delicate kiss before he tilted his head and drew his tongue up the crease between her sex and her thigh.

So close, and yet...she whimpered at his diabolical torture.

He explored her relentlessly, licking and kissing her inner thighs and the outer-most regions of her sex, teased her so well that when his tongue finally clipped her clit, she cried out and startled him.

"Are you okay?"

"No," she breathed, shoving his head back down. "You stopped. Not okay."

He chuckled against her, his lips tickling her before he opened his mouth over her core and licked her with the flat of his tongue. She cried out again as the tip flicked over her hypersensitive knot of nerves.

"You taste like ambrosia," he whispered against her core. "I *love* this."

Not nearly as much as she did.

Bolder now, he lapped at her with increasing enthusiasm, varying his speed and the pattern of his tongue, and she came off the bed when he plunged it deep inside and swirled it while she squirmed and thrashed.

"Tell me what you want." His voice was a guttural, resonant growl that shivered through all her feminine parts.

"Just keep doing what you're doing." She spoke between halting, panting breaths. "But stroke yourself while you're doing it. I want to see how you jerk off," she breathed, "so I can do it for you later."

His head popped up, his half-lidded eyes blinking. For a heartbeat she thought she'd crossed some sort of *Laura wouldn't do this* line that would snap him out of what they were doing. But an eager rumble rose up in his throat as he palmed his cock and dropped his head between her legs again.

Oh...*yes.* She couldn't really see him stroking himself, but she loved imagining his hand wrapped around that thick erection, the fat, plum head pumping in and out of his fist. His tongue lashed at her, dipping inside her and circling her clit, but when he latched on and sucked, she couldn't take it anymore.

She shouted in ecstasy, the climax ripping her apart over and over. He might not be experienced, but he had one hell of an erotic instinct.

Which he proved by licking her gently, bringing her down slowly until she was too sensitive to handle it. He pressed his lips against her in a final, lingering kiss, and when he lifted his head, the hunger in his eyes nearly undid her again.

A soft growl rattled the air as he prowled his way up her body, his gaze locked on hers, the tips of his fangs visible between his glistening lips.

"That was amazing," she said hoarsely.

"I don't know what I'm doing." He paused to lap at her breast. "But I like learning. I like listening to how your breathing changes depending on what I'm doing with my tongue. I could do that for hours."

Oh, jackpot.

"I'd let you do that for hours." She reached between them and found his cock. As her fingers closed around it, he moaned. Smiling, she guided him to her entrance. But just as the blunt tip touched her heated flesh, he locked up, his body trembling.

"Zhubaal?" She stroked his neck, and he let out a little purr that rumbled all her erogenous zones. "What is it?"

He looked down at her. "I'm savoring this." He pushed his hips forward, just enough for the head of his cock to dip inside her, and he moaned. "Also, I don't want to embarrass myself." His sex-swollen lips tipped up in a self-deprecating smile, and then his head fell back as he lowered himself between her legs.

When he was fully inside her, their bodies connected, a strange, incredible energy seemed to form a circuit between them. Her brain shorted out, flashing not images, but emotions that they had once shared. Together. And that was when she knew. Knew that this was a moment over a hundred years in the making. Whatever minor doubts she'd had were gone. Vex had never believed in soul mates, but as her soul touched Zhubaal's, she knew the truth.

They belonged together.

Chapter Thirteen

Perfection. There wasn't another word that could so adequately describe the feeling of being joined with Vex this way. Watching him with half-lidded eyes, she undulated beneath him, her soft, panting breaths matching his. He could still taste her on his tongue, could feel her hot core clenching around him, and he let himself drown in the moment he'd begun to doubt would ever happen.

It had been *so* worth the wait.

He had no experience at this, but his body knew what to do even if his mind didn't. Very slowly, he pumped his hips, hissing as her silken sheath rippled and contracted, squeezing his length with every leisurely thrust.

"You feel...incredible." Dropping to his elbows, he took her nipple between his lips and teased it with his tongue. She made the sexiest sounds when he did that, and she made an even sexier one, a breathy groan, when he scraped a fang over the plump swell of her breast.

Arching, she took him deep and clawed his back with her nails. Ah...damn, that was good. The pain and pleasure combined to make everything more intense as he moved against her, savoring every sensation. He wanted to spend forever like this, but after a hundred and forty years of celibacy, this felt too good. He knew he wouldn't last long.

He dropped his mouth to hers and kissed her with renewed urgency. A sound broke from her, needy and passionate, as she wedged one hand between their writhing bodies and cupped his sac.

Her fingers were magic, rolling his balls between them, pinching the taut skin.

Perspiration bloomed on his forehead and his blood pounded through his veins as he picked up the pace, his body taking over as his thoughts scattered.

"You're mine," he rasped. "Finally, you're mine."

"Zhubaal...Z...yes, oh, yes..." She arched, pressing her breasts against him and crushing his hips between her powerful thighs. "Now," she gasped. "I want to see you come."

Her words, her use of his casual nickname, all of it triggered a primal response, obliterating his ability to think. All he could do was feel as he lunged into her, pumping and churning, powerless to control his body as the orgasm crashed over him in a violent, euphoric tidal wave. His body bucked, reaching for another peak. It struck him before the first one died down, and when the third hit him, he was sure they'd been transported to Heaven again.

Oh, yeah, this was way better than the sad, single orgasms he had by himself.

Beneath him, Vex went full noodle, her legs falling to the sides, her arms splayed out on the mattress. "I don't think I can move," she breathed.

He collapsed beside her, his chest heaving, his skin damp with sweat. Damn, that had been beyond his expectations, which was saying something, since he'd been fantasizing about his first time since the day he'd popped his first erection.

"Well." Shifting so she was facing him, Vex twined their fingers together, and for some reason, that struck him as more intimate than anything they'd just done. Maybe because sex, even if considered an expression of love, still became about strict biology at some point in the act. Holding hands was about affection. Had she finally accepted the inevitability of their relationship? "Was it all you imagined?"

Closing his eyes, he brought her hand up to his mouth and pressed his lips to her knuckles. "It was more. Way more."

"So, what now? In your losing your virginity scenario, what happened next?"

Next? He'd never gotten past this part. Before Laura lost her wings, they'd been wed in his fantasies, but after that...

"Marry me," he blurted.

"What?" Vex blinked. "Whoa." She sat up, releasing him. "Slow down there, Slick."

Frowning, he propped himself on one elbow. "What's the matter? It's what we always wanted—" He cut himself off, realizing his mistake even as frost formed in her eyes.

"We?"

He winced. "I know, you don't remember." It was probably a good thing since Laura had wanted a big, frilly celebration, the thought of which had given him hives. Still did. "We have time to figure it out." He reached out and trailed his fingers along the seam of her legs where they were pressed together, remembering how they'd gripped him as he'd thrust inside her. Her inner thigh was wet with the evidence of their lovemaking, and his cock stirred again, eager to make another mess. No wonder people were so obsessed with sex.

It was awesome.

"You could move in with me," he said, because hey, he hadn't just humiliated himself enough by proposing before they'd even caught their breath.

"I might have to," she muttered, shifting so he had access to anything he wanted. He loved that about her, how freely she gave him her body and how unself-conscious she was. "Everything I have in the human world is being repossessed thanks to the soul market crash."

"Well, it's good that you won't be doing that kind of work anymore." He leaned over and kissed her thigh, tasting them both on her skin. "It's dangerous."

"It is," she hedged, nudging his head toward her core. Oh, yeah. "But that was my choice, and I don't regret it. I had to make a living, and it was either that or porn." He jerked his head up to stare at her. She grinned, but he wasn't amused. "What? Why are you making that judgey face again?"

He sat up, his desire dulled by the topic of Vex with other males. "There are things that are hard for me to accept," he said roughly. "I'm used to the Laura who wouldn't pull petals off a flower because it would damage them. To hear you talk about capturing souls and selling them, or starring in skin flicks...it's...hard to grasp."

She ran her hand through her sex-mussed hair, leaving even

more spikes and grooves. "You said you didn't care about the porn. Was it okay because you didn't know my soul was also Laura's? But now that you know we're the same..."

"You didn't do any porn. I know you were teasing. My point is that Laura wouldn't have even teased. The subject would have been...unseemly...to her."

Vex barked out a laugh. "Oh, my God, Laura was a freaking prude. How could you stand her?"

Abruptly, anger replaced the last echoes of arousal, and he swung out of bed. "You don't know her. And you aren't even trying."

She sighed. "That's because you want me to be her, and as much as you wish I was, I'm not."

That wasn't true. Not really. But it would be nice if she would at least make an attempt to recall some of their life together. Or not make fun of it. "Don't you remember any of it?"

"Nothing." She hurled the word at him like a rock, and sure enough, it struck its mark and left a bruise.

"There are people we can see." His voice was clipped, his frustration evident as he yanked open his armoire and tossed a robe to the bed for her. "Demon psychics who could help you remember—"

"No." She swung her legs over the side of the bed and shoved to her feet. "Don't you get it? How many times do I have to say it? I'm not Laura. And I don't want to be Laura. I only know this life, the one given to me by parents who weren't perfect, but who I loved. Denying my life would be denying them. I like my life, Zhubaal."

"You like it?" Was she serious? She used to be an angel. An elite angel. Even if she wasn't very good at it. "You like being the generic offspring of two fallen angels? You like having so few abilities and little power?"

"You're one to talk." She snatched up the robe with an angry sweep of her hand. "Do you like being a fallen angel? Are you proud of the things you've done in the name of evil?"

He swiped a pair of sweat shorts from his drawer. "I did it for you."

"Oh, fuck off," she snapped, clutching the robe to her chest.

"You do *not* get to lay the blame for all of this on me. You did it for yourself. Maybe you sucked at being an Ipsylum and were looking for an excuse to get out of it. Or maybe you weren't happy with yourself and used Laura's fall from grace to avoid facing that fact. I don't know. But what I do know is that you need to understand that my name is Vex, not Laura. And I've done a lot of things Laura would probably never have done, and I'm not sorry. I told you I like my life, but apparently Laura didn't like hers."

"She loved her life," he shot back, but even as he said it, the words rang hollow, and Vex called him on it.

"Really?" she taunted him. "Because if Saint Laura was so happy, why was she so eager to give up being an angel? If she was so content, why didn't she marry you when she had the chance?"

He ground his teeth, vexed—literally—by the argument and the fact that he felt like he was losing it. "Ipsylum can't marry until they pass their fiftieth birthday. We had ten years to go when she was kicked out of the Order."

Sighing, she shook her head. "Look, maybe we should just relax for a while. Feel like a dip in the hot tub?" She tossed the robe on the bed once more before walking across the room and dipping a toe into the steaming water. "We can play *Hot Tub Time Machine*."

"Is that a sex game?" The thought that she might have played it with another male was enough to flip his jealousy switch again.

Laughing, she splashed at the water with her foot. "It's a movie. Something you might know if you had decent cable down here." She beckoned to him, making her breasts bounce hypnotically. "Come on. You can go first. If you could go back in time in your bubbling time machine, where would you go?"

"That's easy," he said with a shrug. "I'd go back a hundred years and stop you from losing your wings."

She'd started to get into the pool, but froze with one foot on the top step. "Excuse me?"

Her tone, so shocked and defiant, pissed him off. He'd understood why she'd resisted her past, but damn it, why was she so determined to completely deny who she used to be and who they were to each other?

"If I could go back in time, we wouldn't be in the situation we're in," he pointed out. "We'd be who we're supposed to be."

"You bastard," she whispered. "You *bastard*!" She wheeled around, her face mottled with fury. "You still don't get it, do you? You still think your precious Laura is perfect. But I have news for you, asshole. You might have made love to Laura, but it wasn't Laura who made love—no, I take that back. It wasn't Laura who *fucked* you. It was me. It wasn't Laura who has been living in the human and demon realms for the last thirty years, who grew up with parents she loved in a life that was happy. You want to erase all that? You want to erase *me*?"

"I don't want to erase you," he shouted. "I want you to...fuck, I don't know. I just can't understand how you didn't know about me. On some level, you should have felt that there was something missing in your life. That all those guys trying to get in your pants weren't the right ones." Bottled up anger rose like steam from the hot tub as he clenched his fists at his sides to keep himself from shaking sense into her. "I waited all this time for you. I *sacrificed my wings* for you. And what did you do? You bopped around your happy little life, fucking God only knows how many males, while I spent every waking moment of every day searching for you like a damned idiot!"

Tears shimmered in her eyes as she looked around, presumably for her clothes, but they'd been left in a ball on Rowan's floor. "So that's who you want me to be? The innocent, sweet, shy girl you say I was?" She stormed over to the bed and snatched up the robe again. "Because I can't be her. I can't be anything but me. I love you, but I won't change who I am for anyone." She tied the robe around her waist and spread her arms wide. "This is me. You either love me for who I am, or you find someone else to love. But either way, Laura is gone. And right now, so am I."

She slammed out of the room, leaving him alone with nothing but his memories and his misery.

Chapter Fourteen

Vex had been gone from Sheoul-gra for two days, and in that time, Zhubaal had done nothing but sit in his quarters and get drunk. Razr had come by twice, only to get empty alcohol bottles lobbed at his head. Lilliana had come by as well, but Z didn't let her in. Even Cat had tried to talk to him, but seeing how she was the only other female besides Laura/Vex he'd kissed...ever...he shut her down. He didn't need to be reminded of yet another romantic failure.

It wasn't until Azagoth sent word that Revenant was finally on his way that Zhubaal emerged from his quarters. On the bright side, his hangover was pretty mild.

Zhubaal approached the landing pad, surprised to find Lilliana already there. She didn't usually meet visitors, but hey, apparently he was clueless about females.

Light blasted the pad, and Revenant appeared, his massive wings extended as if he'd flown in. As the most powerful being in Sheoul, he could have flashed into Sheoul-gra, but he and Azagoth had worked out a deal of mutual respect, and as long as Azagoth toed the line, Revenant was willing to follow the rules and not squash them all like bugs.

Zhubaal liked that in a demigod.

Azagoth appeared next to Lilliana and greeted Revenant with a handshake. The King of Hell had changed his look since Z had seen him last. Sometimes he was bald, sometimes blond, but today his hair, waist-length and so black it hurt to look at, wasn't the change. Neither was the full suit of wicked-looking matte charcoal armor, the shoulders and elbows adorned with sharp spikes, all of which Z had seen before. But the black cape was new. It hung heavy, as if it were made of rubber, but only when he got closer did he realize that it definitely was not made of any common material.

Azagoth shook his head as he eyed the new addition to Revenant's wardrobe. "Capes are stupid. They're nothing but liabilities during a fight."

"Oh, hey," Lilliana said, elbowing her mate lightly in the ribs. "Don't say exactly what you're thinking or anything."

Revenant laughed. "He's an asshole, but he's right. Which is why this is no ordinary cape." He nodded at Z. "Grab it. I dare you."

Curious, but hoping he didn't get vaporized, Z reached for it, only to have it slip through his fingers as if it were nothing but air. But a moment later, his hand stung like he'd been bitten by a venomous fire imp.

"Damn," he breathed as he shook his hand out. "What the fuck is that?"

"It's made from the hide of a Darquethoth."

Lilliana winced. "Ew."

"Ah, don't shed a tear for him," Revenant said as he admired the cape. "He was a douchemonkey. He should have thought a little harder about betraying me." He turned around, and for a moment, he seemed to disappear from the neck to his boots. "Cool, huh? It repels magic and it's impenetrable by sharp objects and bullets. Everyone should have one."

"Aren't you immune to that stuff anyway?" Zhubaal asked.

He wagged his finger. "*Nearly* immune. A spear or bullet can impale me, but they won't kill me. It'll hurt like hell and piss me off, though." He glanced between the three of them. "So what am I here for? Azagoth said it was urgent. It better be, because I have a birthday party to go to."

"A birthday party?" Zhubaal wasn't quite sure he'd heard that right. The guy didn't seem like the cake and balloons type. "You go to birthday parties?"

"When it's for my niece and nephews, fuck yeah. There's always at least one brawl at Horsemen parties." He waggled his brows. "Good times."

"You'll have to tell me what they thought of my gift," Azagoth said, and his smirk was about as evil as it got.

"I'm afraid to ask." Lilliana sighed.

Zhubaal wasn't. "What did you send?"

Azagoth's green eyes sparkled with mischief. "I hired a clown. One of those summoned ones that wreaks havoc until you kill it." He shrugged. "I figured the least I could do would be to provide some entertainment."

"That's terrifying," Lilliana said, shooting her mate a glare.

Revenant laughed. "It's hilarious." He clapped Azagoth on the back. "Let's get this over with so I can get to the party and watch the show."

As Azagoth and Revenant flashed to what Z assumed would be Azagoth's office, he wondered why the hell he'd been required to greet Revenant. But when Lilliana gently laid her hand on his arm, he realized he'd been duped, and she was probably the architect of the dupery.

"Is everything okay?" she asked. "You've been locked away in your room, and Vex hasn't been back. We're all worried."

Worried? They were worried about him? No one but Laura had ever worried about him. Not even his parents. As pitiless and efficient warriors, Ipsylum took a survival-of-the-fittest approach to life, something he'd rejected as Laura fell further and further behind in their studies and training. Gradually, their brethren began to shun her. Z had stood by her side, helping where he could, cheating if he had to, all to keep her from being banished from their Order.

But when her own family cast her aside like an injured hell mare that couldn't keep up with the herd, he hadn't been able to protect her anymore. He'd fought like hell, fought until his bones were broken and his skin was blackened by holy fire, but Laura had been ripped away from him by the people they'd both trusted most.

"I'm fine," he lied. He wasn't even close to being fine. Every beat of his heart hurt, as if it didn't know why it was bothering to pump lifeblood through his dead body. He hadn't felt this way since Laura died, and in a way, this was even worse, because the female he loved was still alive. She just wasn't his.

"Zhubaal," Lilliana began as she steered him toward the courtyard fountain, "what happened between you and Vex?"

He'd just spent the last two days angry and drunk, convinced that their falling out was her fault, but right now, with a little clarity and more blood than alcohol in his veins, he'd freely admit that everything could be laid at his feet. Everything.

Humiliation made his skin shrink. "I screwed up," he said, despising himself more with each word. "I expected her to be something—some*one*—she's not. Then I rejected the person she is."

Lilliana reached out to run her fingers through the water as they walked past the fountain. "When I first came here, I did the same thing to Azagoth. I expected him to be a monster."

"I remember." He gave her the side-eye. "But he *was* a monster."

"He was," she agreed. "And in a lot of ways, he still is. But my point is that I knew what I was getting into, and I rejected him anyway because I didn't give him a chance." She stopped and turned to face him. "Did you give Vex any chance at all?"

He felt sick to his stomach, because no, he hadn't. He'd judged her based on memories colored by blind love and guilt. A lot of guilt. He'd always blamed himself for not being able to protect her from being banished, losing her wings, or getting slaughtered.

And then, once he found her again, he'd insisted that Vex wasn't the real her. That somehow, if he could just break through the outer Vex he'd find the inner Laura. He'd wanted her to be that sweet angel he'd loved, because if he could get her back, he could make amends and banish the guilt he'd been harboring for nearly a century. So in a way, he'd wanted to erase Vex, just like she'd said.

He'd been a selfish piece of shit.

How could he not have thought about how crappy her existence had been as Laura? He'd been the one good thing in her life. Now there were a lot of good things in her life, and he wasn't one of them.

Son of a bitch.

Now he got it. Now he knew why Azagoth hadn't told him that Vex was Laura. Vex was *not* Laura. She was Vex, just as he'd said. But at the time Zhubaal wouldn't have accepted it. He'd had to learn that on his own, and he had, but not before royally fucking it up immediately after making love to her for the first time.

"Zhubaal?" Lilliana prompted. "Did you give her a chance?"

"No," he croaked. "You know I didn't."

She reached into her jeans' pocket and pulled out a scrap of paper. "Before she left, we got her personal information. For employment purposes, of course." She winked. "She's even got a Facebook profile. Says she's single. You should probably go beg her forgiveness and then get her to change her status to *in a relationship*."

Z's heart gave a great, happy thump. "Thank you, Lilliana," he said. "I'm glad Azagoth found you."

Now he had to go find *his* mate. He just hoped he wasn't too late.

* * * *

The moment after Azagoth closed his office door, he poured Rev and himself a stiff whiskey, an expensive label given to him by Revenant's Horseman niece, Limos, and got down to business.

"The barriers that keep demon souls inside Sheoul-gra are failing," he said, handing a highball glass to the Shadow Angel, "and it's your fault."

"My fault?" He put the glass to his lips and watched Azagoth from over the rim. "Have I been killing so many of my enemies that you don't have room for them?" Revenant asked that question with a straight face and a deadpan voice, but Azagoth knew him well enough to know he was being sarcastic.

"No," Azagoth said, just as reasonably. "But nice job with that. You've sent me some real bastards to deal with."

"Thank you."

Ignoring Revenant's insincerity that only echoed Azagoth's own, he explained. "The problem," he began, "is that your policy of reincarnating only souls of lesser evil means that the Inner Sanctum is filling with highly malevolent demons, more than we've ever had to house at once. It's causing an instability in the containment system itself, and it's creating weak spots in the barriers. Demons who are in the right place at the right time, or who are evil and powerful enough to exploit the structural failures, are escaping." He was also taking a huge hit in business. Before Revenant's mandate, Azagoth had taken bribes of money, gifts, or favors in order to reincarnate high-level evil demons.

Even Heaven had taken notice of the instability in the Inner

Sanctum, hence the visit from Jim Bob and Ricky Bobby. Oh, his Heavenly spies had come on other business as well, but Jim Bob had made it abundantly clear that the Archangels were starting to get their halos in a twist.

Revenant gazed into the fire, the flickering light casting shadows on his stern face. "You're going to have to find a way to shore up the barriers."

"Why? Why the fuck are you doing this?" Azagoth slammed his glass down on his desk and strode over to him. "Look, buddy, you're new to this, but I've been handling souls for thousands of years. I keep the Inner Sanctum and Sheoul balanced. That's always been the cornerstone of our Creator's vision. Balance. The human realm is a balance of good and evil, but it's weighted toward good. Sheoul is the exact opposite, weighted more heavily toward evil. If you mess with that, the results could be disastrous."

"Thank you for the lecture about the fine balance between good and evil," Revenant drawled. "It's not as if I run Hell or anything." He knocked back the rest of his drink, never taking his gaze off Azagoth. "You understand why I want only the lesser evil souls reincarnated and the more malevolent ones kept imprisoned, yes?"

"Actually, I'm not clear on that," Azagoth said bitterly. This was his turf, and he didn't appreciate being left out of the loop. "I've assumed it's because you're an angel, not a fallen angel, and you still have connections to Heaven. Or, you know, decency."

"Decency?" Revenant snorted. "Those Heavenly bastards can suck my dick. I don't care about them. What I care about is the fact that Satan's prison will only hold for a thousand years." He appeared to consider that. "Well, nine-hundred and ninety-nine now. It's a prophecy that can't be averted. When that evil hellratfuck bastard finally breaks free, it's foretold that Armageddon will begin."

"And you don't want him to have an army of evil at his fingertips." Revenant was smarter than Azagoth had given him credit for.

"Exactly. I might be the Grand Poobah of Hell, but that doesn't mean I want evil to win the ultimate battle of all battles."

It was sound thinking, but there was going to be a different kind of Armageddon happening if the Inner Sanctum's walls fell and billions of demon souls spilled out into Sheoul and the human realm.

"Bottom line," Azagoth said. "I can get mages and builders to reinforce the barriers, but there's only so much they can do. We need a release valve."

"Fine." Revenant waved his hand dismissively. "Reincarnate more Tier three, four, and five demons, but not in the same numbers Satan allowed. Cut by two-thirds."

Azagoth winced. He'd have preferred to cut only by a third, a half at the most, but he wasn't going to complain. This would go a long way toward easing the explosive pressure of evil in the Inner Sanctum, for a little while, at least.

"I have another matter." Azagoth spoke over the sound of a shriek coming from inside the closed soul tunnel. He hadn't opened it yet this morning, and the *griminions* and their wards were getting restless. Idiots. Where most of them were going was far, far worse than where they were now. "I need your goons to lay off one of my employees. She's a *daemani*, and she's collecting souls who escape through the rifts in the barrier." He glanced expectantly at Rev. "I assume you're behind the collapse of the soul market."

"Of course."

Figured. And it made sense. High-ranking Orphmages and Charnel Apostles had formed a coalition against Revenant, and their prime source of spell power was the life energy from souls. Rumor had it that they were devising a demon version of a nuclear weapon to use against Revenant, and the moment Revenant heard that, he'd crushed the infant insurgency in its cradle.

"So you'll make sure Vex is safe?"

Revenant inclined his head. "I'll get the word out."

Excellent. Now he just had to get Vex and Zhubaal back together. He hoped Lilliana made some headway already. He'd been rooting for the guy, had even done a little of his own investigating in an attempt to find Laura. But he believed in fate, and he didn't doubt that two souls who were meant for each other would always find their way back no matter how many lives it took to do it.

And speaking of souls, Azagoth launched into the final piece of business he wanted to discuss with Revenant. "Before you go, I do have one more little thing. A gift." Not out of the goodness of his heart, of course. Strings were definitely attached, and when the time came that he needed a favor, he'd yank those strings like a damned puppet master.

Revenant rubbed his hands together in glee. "I love presents. What is it?"

"The most recent escapee from the Inner Sanctum. I was going to punish her, but I thought she might be of some use to you. And if not, I'm sure you know someone who would salivate at the chance to make her existence hellish. A certain Horseman, maybe? All of them, since it's their birthdays? Or Harvester, perhaps?"

"I'm intrigued." Revenant's voice went low, dark, and pure predator.

Azagoth willed a section of his stone wall to slide open, revealing a female standing in a cage, her gaze defiant. Bold. Until she saw Revenant.

"Revenant," Azagoth said, "you might have already met my guest."

Revenant laughed, a deep, dark sound that made the female cower at the back of the cage. "This couldn't have happened on a more appropriate day." He moved toward her, slowly, a panther stalking a rabbit. "It's good to see you again, especially since your son killed you before I could do it. And he did it far quicker than I would have." With every step, she shook harder, until the cage's metal joints began to rattle. "But life and death is all about second chances, isn't it, Lilith?" His wings snapped up with a crack that shattered Azagoth's highball glass. "And don't worry. I'll be sure to tell the Horsemen their mother said happy birthday."

Chapter Fifteen

Vex was never getting on Facebook again. Happy people and their grammatically challenged memes annoyed the shit out of her.

She slammed her laptop shut and tucked it into her bag. Today was moving day. Azagoth had offered to send Memitim to help her move some of her belongings into her assigned quarters in Sheoulgra, and they'd have an easy time of it because she really didn't have much she wanted to take. As long as her apartment was far away from Zhubaal's quarters, she'd be happy.

Hades's mate, a chick named Cat, had come by yesterday with paperwork for her new apartment, which shocked the hell out of Vex. Azagoth really did run his realm like a mayor, and apparently, Cat helped keep track of who lived where.

Memitim and Unfallen stayed in the dorms, Azagoth, Zhubaal, Razr, and a handful of Azagoth's most trusted staff lived in his palace, and all other servants lived in apartments in other buildings. And now, thanks to Zhubaal, everyone got basic cable and two movie channels. Which was awesome, because she'd die if she couldn't watch *Game of Thrones*. Now if she could just get *The Walking Dead*, leaving the human realm might not be so bad.

But there was no way she was going to deal with Zhubaal to get it.

Her heart clenched. How could she miss him so much when she'd only known him for a few days? Yeah, yeah, there was the whole bitchface Laura thing and their eternal, fated soul-mate bullshit, but she wasn't buying it.

Oh, the fact that her soul knew his had no doubt hasted her feelings along, but when she saw him in her mind, she wasn't seeing old memories. She was seeing him skipping a rock across a pond. She was seeing him laugh, the way his eyes sparkled and the muscles in his cheeks twitched as he smiled. She was seeing him kissing his way up her body and sheathing himself inside her for the first time, his expression filled with wonder at the tender intimacy they shared.

That was who she missed. Not the Zhubaal from some winged fairy tale life he'd said they'd had in Heaven.

A knock at the door startled her. The Memitim were here already? But no, when she opened the door, there were no earthbound angels standing on her porch. There was, however, a fallen angel she didn't feel like talking to on her porch.

"Go away." She slammed the door in his jerk face and turned, only to smack into his broad chest. Yelping in surprise, she leaped back. "Zhubaal! What the hell?"

Damn it, she knew she should have warded the house. Then she wouldn't have to look at his handsome face as he stood there in well-worn jeans, a T-shirt that did nothing to hide hard-cut abs, and a black leather jacket that probably concealed an arsenal of weapons.

"Vex, we need to talk."

"Oh, it's Vex now? Not Laura?" She brushed past him to grab her bag. If he wasn't leaving, she would.

"Please, Vex." He caught her by the arm and pulled her around. "Listen to me. I love you—"

She yanked out of his grip. "You love *Laura*."

"I *did* love Laura." He jammed his hands into his jeans' pockets and fixed his gaze somewhere behind her. "I loved her more than my own life. She was my world and my reason to live." His gaze focused and shifted, catching hers. "But she's gone. I understand that. And it's okay because I have you."

She gaped. It had all sounded great until that last bit. "So I'm a consolation prize? You can't have Laura so you'll settle for me?"

"What? No! Never." He gripped her shoulders and bent so they were eye to eye. "I've fallen in love with you *because* you're Vex. Not because I thought you were Laura. She's in the past now. I don't want what she and I had. I want what you and I *can* have. We just need time and to get to know each other."

Vex couldn't believe what she was hearing. Or maybe she was afraid to believe what she was hearing. "You mean, if Laura was standing right beside me, and you had to choose—"

"I'd choose you." He released her to pace around, jamming his fingers through his hair over and over. "God, Vex, I think I was so desperate to find Laura because I felt guilty about everything that had happened to her. And when I found you, I thought that if I could just get you to remember, I could somehow fix the past. But I was an idiot. We were so young when we made those promises to each other, but we've both grown into the people we should be. I'm not the person I was back then, either. You're not Laura, and I'm glad."

Tears spilled from her eyes, running down her cheeks in a stream. "Really?"

"Touch my soul, Vex." Stopping in front of her, he took one of her hands and pressed it over his heart. "On my honor, it's you I want. Only you. I would *never* erase you." His heartbeat pounded into her palm as if it agreed.

On the verge of sobbing, she tried to lighten the mood. She'd never been good at the mushy stuff, anyway. "We have to have sex for me to touch your soul, you know."

"I know." His smile was pure, masculine hunger, and she was just as starved.

"Take us to your place," she purred. "We're going to play Hot Tub Sex Machine."

"I thought it was *Hot Tub Time Machine*," he said, adding a wry, "I have a better answer this time."

Laughing, because he couldn't possibly have a *worse* answer than last time, she dragged her finger down his abs to the fly of his jeans. "This is the porn version. If you're okay with that, of course."

Sure as shit, he was.

* * * *

Zhubaal couldn't believe his good fortune.

An hour ago, he'd been at rock bottom, lost, angry, and a little hungover. Now he was sprawled on a bench in his hot tub, watching with admiration as Vex stepped into the water, her curvy body naked and waiting for him to do naughty things to it.

He might not have a lot of experience, but he'd had a long fucking time to fantasize, so he figured there wouldn't be much of a learning curve. And even if there was, well, his Ipsylum instructors said he'd always been an enthusiastic student and a quick study.

He'd kissed her senseless and teased her before they'd stripped, and even now, as she moved toward him, her eyes were glazed with passion. Passion he'd put there. And now he understood that no matter how many lovers she'd bedded in the past, *he* was the one who had ripped off her panties with his teeth and whispered erotic things against the glistening flesh between her thighs. *He* was the one who had put her at the brink of orgasm when he tasted her breast with his fangs, drawing tiny twin droplets of blood that didn't come close to sating his hunger. And *he* would be the only one to do any of that ever again.

He took his straining erection in his fist and stroked, getting a kick out of that little catch in her breath as she watched him under the water. He pumped faster, adding a twist at the head, and she licked her lips. Oh, yeah, he could get used to having control over her like this, to rendering her speechless—

"I'm so going to suck on that."

He nearly choked on his own tongue. Damn, he loved how audacious, uninhibited, and unpredictable she was. It caught him off guard...and kept him from getting too cocky.

Planting one knee on either side of his hips, she wrapped her arms around his shoulders and sank down on his lap. Her folds cradled his shaft as she settled in and captured his mouth with hers.

There was nothing sweet and lingering about this kiss. No, this was raw and hot, punishing him for being a total ass while stoking the fire between them. She battled him with her tongue, nipped his lip and drew blood, rocked on his lap so his cock ground against her sex in the slippery water. He moaned as she raked his shoulders and neck with her nails and rubbed her breasts against his chest.

She was a master at balancing pain with pleasure, but he had a feeling she was letting the balance tip slightly in favor of pain this time. Not that he was going to complain—hell, he was going to beg her to do it harder.

Abruptly, she pulled back. "Wanna see how long I can hold my breath? Because I'm a champ." Grinning, she slid off his lap like a wet seal and spread his legs, going to her knees between them at the bottom of the tub, so deep that the water came up to her chin.

"Vex—"

She ducked her head under water and swallowed his cock in one glorious motion. Holy...*fuck, yeah.* He hissed in surprise and pleasure as she sucked him deep and lashed him with her tongue. This was the first time a female had put her mouth on him like that. The sensations were unbelievable, beyond anything he could possibly have imagined. Vex's lips and teeth were magic, working together to deliver more of her pleasure/pain punishment.

Harder.

As if she'd heard his mental plea, she nipped his crown and pinched his balls, and he shouted in ecstasy.

She soothed him with a pump of her fist and gentle suck before taking him deep again. Hot water swirled around him as her tongue swirled around the head of his cock, and okay, she'd been right about sex in a hot tub.

These things were made for it.

With a final lick across the tip of his dick, she popped her head out of the water, her grin as impish as when she'd went under. "If you liked that, move over to the top step."

He narrowed his eyes at her. "What are you doing?"

She pushed the button on the side of the tub and the jets roared to life as she nudged him with her foot. "Hot Tub Sex Machine, remember?"

Best. Answer. Ever.

He did as he was told, moving to the other side of the tub. Sitting on the top step, the hot water just covered his thighs and the foamy bubbles lapped at the sensitive spot at the base of his shaft. His cock jutted out of the water, and knowing Vex liked to watch, he took it in his hand while she positioned herself in front of him, bent over, hands braced on his spread thighs. His erection gave an excited jerk. What was she doing?

A teasing smile tipped up her mouth as she dropped her head and lifted her ass so one of the jets struck her between her legs. Closing her eyes, she moaned, and he damned near came before her lips even touched his throbbing erection.

Holy shit. Zhubaal had never seen anything so erotic in his life as Vex as she tongued the slit at the tip of his cock and pumped her hips, fucking the hot jet. Opening her mouth over his crown, she took him deep and sucked upward so hard his hips came out of the water. As he sank back down, she slid her hand under him so her palm cradled his balls and her fingers tickled the seam of his ass.

Second only to finding Vex, this was the greatest moment of his life. He drowned in bliss, captivated by the motion of her head in his lap and how every once in a while, she'd look up at him with the fucking sexiest expression on her face. She was loving this as much as he was, and the sounds she made...sweet hell.

Her mouth worked harder and her hips pumped faster as she rode the jet. He threaded his fingers through her hair, the wet strands sticking up in wild spikes. The style suited her, sassy and colorful, short and sexy.

But nothing was as sexy as the way her skin flushed and her cries of passion went deeper as she neared climax. On the verge himself, he wanted to push her over the edge. Shifting, he angled himself so he had better reach and more range of movement. He slid his hands down her slippery body to her ass and lower, letting his fingers spread her wide and totally open to the powerful jet stream.

She cried out as she took the full force of the water. At the same time, ripples of pleasure cascaded through him, and he shouted as he came in a searing blast of heat. The sight of her swallowing his hot flow sent him into orbit again, but he wasn't done. Even as he came down from his second orgasm, he lifted her away from him, spun her around, and bent her over the side of the hot tub.

"Oh, my," she breathed as he shoved her forward and off her feet so she didn't have any purchase, leaving her vulnerable to whatever he wanted to do to her. They'd made love before, in bed, going slowly, but deep down he'd sensed that racier, frenetic sex was more her style, and frankly, he was pretty sure it was his, as well.

She gasped as he spread her wide with his thumbs and speared her with his tongue. He ate at her wet sex like he was starving, licking and sucking until she was whimpering with need. "Please...Z..."

Her moan was the most powerful aphrodisiac ever, and he gave her one more lingering thrust of his tongue deep inside her before replacing it with his cock in one powerful stroke.

She fit him like a glove, tight and warm, her satin walls contracting around him in waves from the base of his cock to the tip.

"Fuck," he breathed, holding himself rock-steady for a moment, afraid he'd blow if he moved.

He gripped her hips tight to keep her motionless, but it wasn't long before she started to squirm. Feeling a little sadistic, he waited a few more heartbeats, forcing her to wriggle more as her body sought what it needed.

When her needy curse echoed through the room, he couldn't take it anymore as his sexual instincts that demanded he satisfy his female screamed to the surface.

He pounded into her, the pace growing more frenzied with every passing second as she lay beneath him, utterly helpless against his every whim and every change in tempo. The sound of skin slapping skin joined the rhythmic splashing of the waves they were creating against the side of the pool. This was incredible...so fucking amazing...

Pressure built in his shaft, until it felt like his balls were boiling and his blood was steaming. His wings shot up and out as he threw back his head and roared as he came in a blinding blackout of ecstasy.

Vaguely, he felt her clench around him, milking him with her orgasm. The room spun as he bucked against her, riding the climax that seemed to go on forever. He filled her with his stream, his body jerking as his cock grew sensitive and his muscles turned to liquid.

Unable to support his own weight any longer, he collapsed on top of her, catching his upper body with his wings. Holy shit. He wasn't going to be able to walk for a week. Maybe they could just stay here and alternate between the bed and the hot tub. Maybe the shower, too. The things they could do with soap and the detachable shower head...

Vex stroked the long edge of one wing, and a freakishly potent sizzle of lust shot straight to his groin. "Are these sensitive?"

"They never were before," he mumbled against her slender shoulder. "I guess they get that way during sex."

She pressed her lips against the leathery skin, and he shivered with unexpected pleasure. "Well," she said between panting breaths, "if they are in any way sexual, we're gonna use 'em somehow."

It should have been impossible for him to get hard again, but...nope. Now his head was full of fantasies involving Vex and the tips and arches of his wings.

Gently, he lifted off her and drew her into his arms as he settled down in the hot tub with her seated next to him, her legs draped across his lap as she snuggled against his chest.

"Thank you." She pressed a lingering kiss to his neck.

Closing his eyes, he idly caressed her leg. "For what?"

"For accepting me for me."

He couldn't believe he almost hadn't. He'd been so damned stuck in a vow and the past that he couldn't see what was in front of him. Vex was magnificent, and he'd nearly thrown her away.

"The first time we made love," he rasped, "I was with Laura. This time, I was with you, Vex. I gave my virginity to Laura like I promised I would, but everything else, for the rest of eternity, belongs to you."

All this time, he'd been looking for an angel, but what he'd found was his soul.

And even better, he'd found its mate as well.

* * * *

Also from 1001 Dark Nights and Larissa Ione, discover Razr.

Sign up for the 1001 Dark Nights Newsletter
and be entered to win a Tiffany Key necklace.

There's a contest every month!

Go to www.1001DarkNights.com to subscribe!

As a bonus, all subscribers will receive a free
1001 Dark Nights story
The First Night
by Lexi Blake & M.J. Rose

Turn the page for a full list of the
1001 Dark Nights fabulous novellas...

Discover 1001 Dark Nights Collection Four

ROCK CHICK REAWAKENING by Kristen Ashley
A Rock Chick Novella

ADORING INK by Carrie Ann Ryan
A Montgomery Ink Novella

SWEET RIVALRY by K. Bromberg

SHADE'S LADY by Joanna Wylde
A Reapers MC Novella

RAZR by Larissa Ione
A Demonica Underworld Novella

ARRANGED by Lexi Blake
A Masters and Mercenaries Novella

TANGLED by Rebecca Zanetti
A Dark Protectors Novella

HOLD ME by J. Kenner
A Stark Ever After Novella

SOMEHOW, SOME WAY by Jennifer Probst
A Billionaire Builders Novella

TOO CLOSE TO CALL by Tessa Bailey
A Romancing the Clarksons Novella

HUNTED by Elisabeth Naughton
An Eternal Guardians Novella

EYES ON YOU by Laura Kaye
A Blasphemy Novella

BLADE by Alexandra Ivy/Laura Wright
A Bayou Heat Novella

DRAGON BURN by Donna Grant
A Dark Kings Novella

TRIPPED OUT by Lorelei James
A Blacktop Cowboys® Novella

STUD FINDER by Lauren Blakely

MIDNIGHT UNLEASHED by Lara Adrian
A Midnight Breed Novella

HALLOW BE THE HAUNT
A Krewe of Hunters Novella by Heather Graham

DIRTY FILTHY FIX by Laurelin Paige

THE BED MATE by Kendall Ryan
A Room Mate Novella

NIGHT GAMES by CD Reiss
A Games Novella

NO RESERVATIONS by Kristen Proby
A Fusion Novella

DAWN OF SURRENDER by Liliana Hart
A MacKenzie Family Novella

Go to www.1001 DarkNights.com for more information.

Discover 1001 Dark Nights Collection One

FOREVER WICKED by Shayla Black
CRIMSON TWILIGHT by Heather Graham
CAPTURED IN SURRENDER by Liliana Hart
SILENT BITE: A SCANGUARDS WEDDING by Tina Folsom
DUNGEON GAMES by Lexi Blake
AZAGOTH by Larissa Ione
NEED YOU NOW by Lisa Renee Jones
SHOW ME, BABY by Cherise Sinclair
ROPED IN by Lorelei James
TEMPTED BY MIDNIGHT by Lara Adrian
THE FLAME by Christopher Rice
CARESS OF DARKNESS by Julie Kenner

Also from 1001 Dark Nights

TAME ME by J. Kenner

Go to www.1001 DarkNights.com for more information.

Discover 1001 Dark Nights Collection Two

WICKED WOLF by Carrie Ann Ryan
WHEN IRISH EYES ARE HAUNTING by Heather Graham
EASY WITH YOU by Kristen Proby
MASTER OF FREEDOM by Cherise Sinclair
CARESS OF PLEASURE by Julie Kenner
ADORED by Lexi Blake
HADES by Larissa Ione
RAVAGED by Elisabeth Naughton
DREAM OF YOU by Jennifer L. Armentrout
STRIPPED DOWN by Lorelei James
RAGE/KILLIAN by Alexandra Ivy/Laura Wright
DRAGON KING by Donna Grant
PURE WICKED by Shayla Black
HARD AS STEEL by Laura Kaye
STROKE OF MIDNIGHT by Lara Adrian
ALL HALLOWS EVE by Heather Graham
KISS THE FLAME by Christopher Rice
DARING HER LOVE by Melissa Foster
TEASED by Rebecca Zanetti
THE PROMISE OF SURRENDER by Liliana Hart

Also from 1001 Dark Nights

THE SURRENDER GATE By Christopher Rice
SERVICING THE TARGET By Cherise Sinclair

Go to www.1001 DarkNights.com for more information.

Discover 1001 Dark Nights Collection Three

HIDDEN INK by Carrie Ann Ryan
BLOOD ON THE BAYOU by Heather Graham
SEARCHING FOR MINE by Jennifer Probst
DANCE OF DESIRE by Christopher Rice
ROUGH RHYTHM by Tessa Bailey
DEVOTED by Lexi Blake
Z by Larissa Ione
FALLING UNDER YOU by Laurelin Paige
EASY FOR KEEPS by Kristen Proby
UNCHAINED by Elisabeth Naughton
HARD TO SERVE by Laura Kaye
DRAGON FEVER by Donna Grant
KAYDEN/SIMON by Alexandra Ivy/Laura Wright
STRUNG UP by Lorelei James
MIDNIGHT UNTAMED by Lara Adrian
TRICKED by Rebecca Zanetti
DIRTY WICKED by Shayla Black
THE ONLY ONE by Lauren Blakely
SWEET SURRENDER by Liliana Hart

Go to www.1001 DarkNights.com for more information.

About Larissa Ione

Air Force veteran Larissa Ione traded in a career as a meteorologist to pursue her passion of writing. She has since published dozens of books, hit several bestseller lists, including the New York Times and USA Today, and has been nominated for a RITA award. She now spends her days in pajamas with her computer, strong coffee, and fictional worlds. She believes in celebrating everything, and would never be caught without a bottle of Champagne chilling in the fridge…just in case. After a dozen moves all over the country with her now-retired U.S. Coast Guard spouse, she is now settled in Wisconsin with her husband, her teenage son, a rescue cat named Vegas, and her very own hellhound, a King Shepherd named Hexe.

For more information about Larissa, visit www.larissaione.com.

Discover More Larissa Ione

Razr: A Demonica Novella
Coming April 11, 2017

New York Times bestselling author Larissa Ione returns to the Demonica Underworld...

A fallen angel with a secret.

An otherworldly elf with an insatiable hunger she doesn't understand.

A cursed gem.

Meet mortal enemies Razr and Jedda...and the priceless diamond that threatens to destroy them both even as it bonds them together with sizzling passion.

Welcome back to the Demonica Underworld, where enemies find love...if they're strong enough to survive.

On behalf of 1001 Dark Nights,

Liz Berry and M.J. Rose would like to thank ~

Steve Berry
Doug Scofield
Kim Guidroz
Jillian Stein
InkSlinger PR
Dan Slater
Asha Hossain
Chris Graham
Pamela Jamison
Jessica Johns
Dylan Stockton
Richard Blake
BookTrib After Dark
The Dinner Party Show
and Simon Lipskar